Graham's Gang

Graham's Chronicles II

Jeff Hawksworth

Graham's Gang
Graham's Chronicles II

Paperback Edition First Publishing in Great Britain
in 2013 by aSys Publishing

eBook Edition First Publishing in Great Britain
in 2013 by aSys Publishing

Second Edition Published in Great Britain
in 2014 by aSys Publishing

Cover Artwork by Teresa O'Neill Photography

ISBN: 978-0-9930718-4-3
aSys Publishing
http://www.asys-publishing.co.uk

Contents

Prologue...1
Chapter 1...7
Chapter 2..18
Chapter 3..22
Chapter 4..26
Chapter 5..38
Chapter 6..56
Chapter 7..70
Chapter 8..89
Chapter 9...103
Chapter 10..117
Chapter 11..148
Chapter 12..157
Chapter 13..162
Chapter 14..175
Chapter 15..189
Chapter 16..203
Chapter 17..218
Chapter 18..233
Chapter 19..252
Chapter 20..257
Chapter 21..295
Chapter 22..319
Chapter 23..327
Chapter 24..351
Chapter 25..373
Author's Note...375
About the Author......................................377

Disclaimer

This is a work of fiction. Names, characters, businesses, places, events and incidents are either the products of the author's imagination or used in a fictitious manner. Any resemblance to actual persons, living or dead, or actual events is purely coincidental.

Acknowledgments

My thanks to the many people who have continued to help me and I apologise to any I fail to mention.

Once again, I would particularly like to thank Jan Painter, Joan Wilson, Jim Simmons, Lin and Steve Lockwood, Mick Cooling, Sue Outland and Aline Lepkin Daly for their encouragement and patience with the early drafts. Also Linda Skingsley whose proof-reading was superb, again.

Whilst I have used some licence in describing the premises, there is a Sardaar restaurant on the Narborough Road, it is vegetarian and the food is delicious.

Once more, I offer my thanks to Nicola Mackin of AS Publishing, who formatted and published all three books.

Above all, my special thanks belong to my long-suffering wife Pam whose unending support and encouragement helped to ensure that this dream came true.

FINALLY, MY WARMEST THANKS TO YOU, BECAUSE YOU'RE READING THIS.

Prologue

Grant Haddon's father, Clive, was a self-made man. A genius with people management and he knew how to market ideas which included the franchising of a nationwide chain of seafood restaurants, still the primary source of the family's great wealth. It is said that it takes one generation to create wealth, one to hang on to it and one to lose it. Grant fitted his role as second in line perfectly.

Great wealth is rarely created in thirty five hour weeks; more likely eighty and without a family life or holidays. When the endeavour demands that sort of commitment from husband *and* wife an only child often grows into a slightly different sort of person. One whose life is short on affection but very pampered, with an hedonistic lifestyle and pathological self-interest. So it was with Grant. At six foot three, with an athletic build, a gentle yet pervasive voice and a shock of prematurely grey, no, silver hair, he fitted the image of an urbane, sophisticated member of the local elite. Like his parents, he had only one child, Christine, more usually known as Chrissy.

An effective management structure ensured that his father's business empire would continue but Grant had little interest in the day to day affairs. Not that he wasn't ambitious, quite the contrary. He enjoyed his wealth and used it to forge a course through life that included all the trappings; a private jet, a sixty foot motor cruiser moored at Marathon, in the Florida Keys, a number of vacation homes and a prodigious sexual appetite which until recently he had satisfied with any and every willing female he came across. But then along came politics.

In a sense, his political ambitions crept up on him, beginning in the year he was recruited by the chamber of commerce and

Governor to help persuade a Taiwanese company to site their new assembly plant in the state. In fact on the three hundred acres of scrub owned by another of his companies, though the authorities weren't aware of that at the time. The competition had been fierce and since it was all out of the State, the Governor saw this as his only opportunity. He worked closely with Grant though they both knew they were the outsiders.

That was until the Taiwanese chief executive stayed at the mansion to enjoy Grant's brand of hospitality, and his wife.

April was an international model when Grant had met and woo'd her but after their marriage it was clear that she was no more than arm candy. She could be wilful and at times spiteful but what she couldn't do was sustain an intelligent conversation. He sometimes wondered why he'd chosen her but then recalled her charm in those earlier days when her face was known globally and international stars welcomed her to their parties. The sex had been good but having a child by caesarean section devalued her. The work and invitations dried up quickly though their relationship took a little longer to founder.

He'd been discreet to begin with but the further they drifted apart the less he cared. In time she'd become a drunkard, distanced from Grant by her unwillingness to share him with so many other women, and occasionally, the infections they sent him home with. That state of affairs may not have been happy but it was, for the most part, expedient, even to the extent of having the lawn man trim more than the lawn edges, leaving April with some post coital comfort and a heart-shaped thicket of pubic hair. They slept in separate rooms and since Grant was out most days and April was drunk by four in the afternoon, they rarely spoke, unless special occasions like the Taiwanese visit demanded it.

The dynamics of their relationship changed again that night. Grant and his guest had spent the day golfing and returned to the mansion for an evening meal. She was drunk, as usual, but stoically sat through the meal until the men retired to the terrace for brandies and cigars. Moments later Grant returned and succinctly set out his requirements and the consequences of her refusal. He also set out a row of photographs that depicted one of her encounters with the lawn man, adding that a court, particularly one of the local ones, with whom he had such good relations, would take a dim view of a drunk and adulterous wife and be sure to grant him a divorce, without being generous in awarding a settlement.

It was a polished and perfectly timed ambush that he had rehearsed thoroughly. The alcohol and pictures of her in such shocking positions left her defenceless. Within minutes she had written a note he dictated and went upstairs to get ready, as instructed. The note was left on their guest's pillow and read by a man whose sensibilities had been dulled enough by alcohol to liberate him from the scruples one would normally expect of a guest, notwithstanding his admiration of the American female figure, particularly April's. He responded to the invitation with alacrity and whilst the act was over quickly the damage was permanent. April's descent into outright alcoholism began the next day but in the early hours of that first morning she spent a long time scrubbing herself under a hot shower and sobbing.

Their guest was due to leave the next morning and discovered a slight chill in the atmosphere. Grant managed to strike the perfect balance of a caring host who suspected yet couldn't really believe that his guest might have cuckolded him.

The Taiwanese executive was polite but quietly aghast at what he had done and the damage he might have caused to his career, marriage and public standing. He couldn't be sure whether his host knew about his aberration, which he reflected with some chagrin, was an uninspiring 'quickie' in any event, but he was terribly ashamed.

When the time came to part Grant grasped his guest's hand with both of his and locked eyes, "Sir, I want you to understand that I love this state and the people in it. I hope that you will come to share that view if you haven't already. I trust you will see that investing here would be the right thing to do."

He did.

Grant's taste for publicity and public standing began with the public approbation and esteem that resulted from that episode and he followed a logical progression into local politics. The combination of support from his team of lackeys, local dignitaries and the republicans began to give substance to his aims and now, at last, the senate was a credible target. There were drawbacks of course and perhaps the greatest was a return to marital fidelity. His political advisor was adamant and graphic. If his dick stayed out of his trousers he would stay out of the senate. It would be a long haul since the next election was over five years away.

Grant's self-interest had found new boundaries since the Taiwanese visit and was accompanied by a callous indifference that was nurtured by his political team. In spite of warnings he continued to see one of his longer standing lovers, though it wasn't enough and he was left wanting.

By a sickening coincidence, his daughter was twelve years old and beautiful. In the last year so much had changed in their relationship yet he felt no regrets or guilt for what he had done or for the fear and loathing he had engendered.

Chrissy used to be an attractive girl, with the light honey tan, flawless complexion and great bulk of wavy auburn hair so typical of American girls. Even by US standards she led a privileged life, in a sixteen bed roomed mansion set in forty acres of ground in Chapel Hill, west of Raleigh, Georgia. Full-time staff were on hand to feed, chauffeur and care for Chrissy and her two horses, just as a team of visiting specialists took care of the grounds, swimming pool and tennis coaching.

At school she had excelled at sports and worked hard at achieving the maximum from her academic abilities. The phrase 'Could try harder' was never used in her reports, until she learned too much too soon.

Twelve year old girls should join giggling huddles to discuss boys with that early adolescent mix of scorn and interest that would succumb to the frisson of exchanging notes and sneaking kisses.

They should not know how to masturbate a tumescent male member or clean up the resultant mess.

They should not know what it is to be fondled by a grown up.

They should not be having sex.

They should not need to be on the pill.

They should not know what it is to have an abortion.

Above all, they should not come by all this knowledge at the hands of their father.

She was still only twelve years old and looked more like a trailer kid, with matted hair and at times, an unpleasant body odour. It didn't stop him.

The abortion had been expensive, entailing a discreet flight up to a clinic in Canada and the expense of a new horse, though Chrissy hadn't shown much gratitude for that. For her part, the horror of the operation persuaded her to take the pill as directed, even though her father took it to be a tacit acceptance of his needs.

Today had been less difficult than usual because the maths teacher stayed at home with a dental abscess instead of carrying on at her about a lack of interest and dumb insolence. With luck, her father would still be in town and she could grab a sandwich before seeking the sanctuary of her bedroom. There were no locks on the bedroom doors but a week earlier she had managed to fit a bolt to the inside of hers. Grant was furious but she had involved a member of staff who had purchased the bolt for her and had thought to mention it to Grant, saying how well he understood a teenagers' need for privacy. To have torn it off the door would have raised too many questions.

Head down and feeling certain of making it to her bedroom, with the tray bearing a sandwich, yoghurt and glass of soda, she gave a small startled scream when her father stepped out of his study and barred her way. The glass of soda toppled over and shed its contents on to the polished wooden floor.

"Leave it, Mary will clean it up, I need a word." He extended an arm to direct her into his study.

"No, I'll clean it up."

This time his voice carried a little more force, "No, it's OK, I said leave it. Just step in for a moment please."

"But Daddy, I'm hungry, please, can I eat my sandwich. Please." The last word was uttered in a pleading note but she knew the signs, knew that he would prevail. He placed a hand on her shoulder and spoke quietly, come on hon', I won't keep you long, just a couple things we need to attend to."

"Pleeease Daddy, I'm hungry and I'm tired. Please Daddy, I don't want to."

Her pleas continued as he pushed her into the study. A book-lined room with plush dark green carpeting, a large mahogany desk and two small leather sofas that bridled a heavy mahogany coffee table. The room contained odours, of leather, books and polish with a sense of masculinity she had always found comforting as a child. But not anymore. These days it was a place she sought to avoid. Today, as she was eased into the room and heard the lock turned she noticed that one of the sofas had been turned around to face the desk. "Please Daddy, I need to go to the bathroom."

"Later." He took the plate from her and told her to sit on the sofa. When he returned, he was already undoing his trouser belt, his mouth slightly open and a sheen of sweat on his face. She rolled onto her side and curled up defensively, "Please Daddy, I don't want to."

He no longer spoke but joined her on the sofa, spooning and pawing. It was then that she saw the laptop on the desk. It had been turned towards the sofa and a red light indicated that it was recording everything; her pleas, torment, tears, shame and rape. Eventually, as he made his dreadful trespass, she could do no more than stare at the camera with hatred, as though condemning it for its complicity.

Chapter 1

Leicester 12th April 2005

Jimmy waited behind the dustbin until just after 7.00am before timidly knocking on his best friend's door.

He had found the sheltered spot behind the dustbin around midnight and crawled into the plastic sack that had been pushed into the handle of the lid, awaiting use. It protected him from the gentle wind but it was still so cold and so very lonely. He wouldn't have dreamt of disturbing his friend in the middle of the night, but he did spend the time imagining the welcome he'd receive the next morning. Warm thoughts to hold onto as he lay by the bin and shivered through the small hours. Time passed slowly and sudden noises startled him; perhaps a cat investigating another bin or an urban fox scavenging. A distant cat fight seemed particularly savage and prompted him to wonder what other animals might be abroad that night. He knew that he wouldn't see any dogs unless they were runaways, since most would be curled up in a warm kitchen somewhere. Just as Sally used to be. She was the best dog anyone could ever have.

Once again, like so many other times in the last year, in the quiet of night when he was alone, his memories brought a gagging grief with them and he curled up tightly in defence, blocking further linked thoughts that were darker still.

Eventually other noises woke him from a doze. The whine of a milk float, sharing the silence with the chinking of milk bottles and gates being opened and closed. A toilet flushing, the faint burring

ring of an alarm clock and an indistinct but urgent call for some-one to rise.

Then he saw someone walk by on their way to work and decided that Graham and Nancy should be up and about. After struggling to his feet he gathered the sack around him and shuffled down the side of the house to the front door, as fast as the sack would allow.

They weren't up, but Nancy had been drifting in and out of a doze for over an hour, relishing the security and warmth of the quilt. She hated the ritual of showering and dressing on cold morn-ings when her muscles and joints shared her reluctance to start the day. The door had been left ajar after Graham's last visit to the loo and Nancy snapped awake, unsure whether the timid tapping was real or part of her waking dream.

There it was again, a gentle tapping for a few seconds. She strug-gled into her dressing gown and descended the stairs with a stiff-legged gait, stretching muscles that had been in slumber for seven hours. A glance at her wristwatch confirmed her suspicion that it was early; at a quarter to six, very early, but she was too foggy to consider any possibility of a threat and opened the front door with careless disregard. She squinted her eyes and peered out and then dropped her gaze until it lighted upon the small shivering form that clutched a large polythene sack to its chest.

"Hello Aunty Nancy"

"Jimmy! What on earth are you doing here, and at this time of the morning." Her eyes widened as the truth struck her, "Oh my God, you've been out all night haven't you? Come in, quickly, you must be absolutely frozen."

It was as though the sight of Nancy triggered a nervous release and the shivering became extreme, rendering speech nigh impossi-ble. The small boy leapt up over the doorstep in sack-race fashion and clutched Nancy's dressing gown tightly, his head on one side and pressed against her stomach. Easing him to one side she shut the door and allowed the comforting to continue for a short while before taking him by the shoulders and easing him back to gain eye contact. "Hmm, OK, questions later, let's get something warm around you *and* inside you. We'll get you out of this for a start."

She helped him out of the sack and led him into the kitchen, to sit at the kitchen table next to the heating radiator. After putting the kettle on Nancy ran upstairs and roused her partner, Graham, before snatching his dressing gown off the back of the door and returning to the kitchen.

A few minutes later Graham stumbled into the kitchen looking faintly ridiculous in a ski jacket over his striped pyjamas. As ever though, the observers' eyes would be drawn to the cleft on the right-hand side of his forehead and dissected by a thin white line that extended down over his cheek and jaw. Closer examination would detect faint traces of the stitches but they were fading quickly. As soon as his gaze fell upon the child his confused expression changed to one of warmth and pleasure, "Hullo maytee, this is a surprise."

Nancy was sitting opposite Jimmy and both clasped a mug of tea. She cut in, "This little rascal has run away again and has been out all night, he's still shivering, look."

Graham sat down next to the boy and asked, "What do you 'av to do to get a cup of tea 'round here?"

Two brown eyes looked up at him with a grateful eloquence.

Nancy pushed herself up from the table and looked upwards in mock despair, "Oh struth, I should have known better than to expect a sensible conversation this early."

Moments later a steaming mug was placed in front of Graham who murmured his appreciation and savoured a few cautious sips. A minute or two passed and Nancy's heart melted as she noted the boy's posture and actions mirrored Graham's, exactly.

In that moment they looked like a model family sharing an early rise, rather than a couple only recently established in a relationship that was forged out of tragedy, who were being visited by a disturbed runaway from a care home whose life had been devastated when he witnessed the violent death of his mother at the hands of his father.

This cast of three had an astonishing amount in common, sharing a secret history of life's dramas that few would believe.

GRAHAM PARSONS was 46 years old when he witnessed an attack on a small boy by his mother's partner that caused fatal injuries. The attacker fled and Graham was cradling the dying child in his arms when he experienced an out-of-body experience that could only have been the sharing of a passage from this life. Shortly after he suffered serious head injuries when he confronted and was attacked by the child's assailant.

His recovery from the subsequent coma was complicated by flashbacks and terrible headaches, but as he became more active he began to 'see' or otherwise sense images of children suffering abuse. Both he and his wife were frightened by his 'dreams' to such an extent that they began to question his sanity.

Until that dreadful day in February the previous year, when he waited for a bus outside a small terraced house in Leicester and suffered a 'mind's eye view' through the eyes of the child who sat under a work surface weeping quietly, terrified to make any sound, as his mother lay on the floor before him, being kicked to death by his father. Moments later his father inflicted fatal injuries on the boy's closest friend, Sally, the fiercely loyal dog who had bitten the man out of fearful distress at what was happening.

Graham's whole existence changed from that day on, in ways that Ann, his wife of twenty two years couldn't understand or deal with. She could only suspect insanity, something she was terrified of and wholly unable to cope with. She left him in the September of that year.

After many more telepathic experiences he began to accept his special sense, until last December when his attempt to save a dying baby nearly cost him his life and left him with the additional facial scar.

* * *

JAMES EVERARD, or JIMMY as he preferred to be called, was a severely damaged child whose behaviour had caused a number of foster parents to concede defeat. He still took every opportunity to run away from the care home and on one such excursion had been hit by a car, sustaining a broken femur. In the hospital he had refused to communicate with anyone until an odd-looking man, also a patient, sat by his bed and started talking to him. He explained that he had a 'funny head' that could sometimes see and feel things children do when they are very frightened and bad things that are happening to them. He went on to describe what it was like in the kitchen when Jimmy's Dad did such bad things to his Mum. Everything he said was true, as though they had been sitting side by side. But then Jimmy listened fearfully to this stranger describe the terrible fear he had known, the crying—so quietly though, in case his father heard and came after him, into his small refuge under the work surface.

Most adults would have screamed for security to remove the man by that point but like most six year olds, his acceptance of such a strange tale was total. He listened as the man spoke about Sally and the bad thing that had happened to her. Graham described her perfectly and Jimmy was finally prompted to speak, saying that she was a great dog and that he'd taught her to beg for tit bits.

Many visits by Graham followed, often accompanied by Nancy, who Jimmy thought was smashing. For no particular reason, Jimmy began and continued to call her *Aunty* Nancy. When it was time for Jimmy to be discharged Graham and Nancy promised to stay in touch and to take him out for day trips. It was a beacon of light in a darkened young life.

* * *

NANCY GARRETT had suffered the unthinkable. The loss of her seven year old son, killed by her partner. Her contact with Graham began out of her concern for his welfare, in the knowledge that his injuries had also been inflicted by her partner and left him with stroke-like disabilities. Her initial visits were timid but a friendship blossomed. Then, one fateful day, after he had accepted the reality of his gift, she persuaded him to re-live the experience of cradling her dying son. Her acceptance of his telepathy was total and their friendship evolved through the shared experiences of what most would think of as bizarre. After Ann walked out of his life their friendship gradually grew into something much more. Whilst she still retained her council house in the street named Nutmeg, she hoped and prayed that her move into his house would be permanent.

* * *

"OK, geniush, shtart by telling us 'ow you knew where we lived and 'ow you got here." Graham's speech had continued to improve but the impediment caused by his head injuries would never clear completely.

Jimmy had stopped shivering though he was unaware of it. His attention was focused on Nancy as she busied herself in the kitchen. The smell of toast made him realise how famished he was. He was so emboldened by feelings of accomplishment and well-being that he offered an explanation without the usual sense of caution. "When we were in hospital you told me where you caught the bus in Leicester, outside our old house and your address was on the letters you sent me."

"Sooo to begin wiv, you ran away from the home?"

Jimmy looked down at the table and after a few moments nodded slightly.

"I can unnerstand 'ow you knew the way to your old house, but how did you get there?"

Jimmy kept his head down, "Don't know. Just walked."

"Sho when how did you get here?"

"Same bus as you. The driver said it was the last one and I shouldn't be allowed out at that time of night."

"How did you pay your fare?"

"Didn't." The following silence continued until Jimmy felt compelled to elaborate, "I told the driver that some bigger boys had taken my money off me and he said that he wasn't going to see any kid my age left out at that time of night." He glanced up at Nancy who was waiting at the cooker for a pan of water to boil for the poached eggs and with the hint of a guilty grin added, "He told me to tell my mum off for letting me out so late." The irony was not lost on Nancy who had been watching. She turned around to tend the pan of water and hide her reaction.

Nothing more needed to be said, though Nancy and Graham would have felt better for hearing an angry tirade from the child; for the dreadful absence of any contact by them, apart from a weekly letter to the care home. No visits, none of the promised outings and none of the very special support or relationships this child needed. Instead of having someone to cuddle up to on those bad, bad nights, he lay in solitude and re-lived the morning his mother was kicked to death, just a metre away from his refuge. And then the terrible head injuries to the best friend he'd ever had, a black mongrel named Sally. His nightmare still found him at night, taking him back to the kitchen and time telescoped to more horror as Sally made it to her young master still yelping in agony. There she shakily made it onto his lap and he gathered her into his small arms, rocking to and fro, weeping. His mother had crawled partway across the floor and raised an arm towards the sink before collapsing back. He had started to move out of his hiding place under the work surface but quickly retreated in fear of his father's return and what he might find if he did reach his Mum. The neighbour had peered through the kitchen window some time later and called the Police who attended the scene an hour after the father had left. The tableau was still in place with the boy holding his dead pet and rocking to and fro.

He had no-one to cuddle on those nightmare nights or in the morning when he struggled out of his wet pyjamas and pulled the sodden sheets off the bed. Instead the other kids doled out a quota of unfeeling cruelty as children so often do.

He was well behaved at the home but unwilling, or unable, to communicate normally. As one carer aptly said, 'a grey little character'. One thing he excelled at was running away, which he did, often.

Jimmy couldn't understand how Graham and Nancy could keep writing to him yet fail to keep their promises of visits and excursions. They had tried to explain why procedures had to be followed but even they were at a loss to understand the weight of bureaucracy.

Naively, they now realised, they contacted the care home to make arrangements to take Jimmy out for the day. The person they spoke to was startled by the notion of releasing one of their charges to strangers, so much so that to begin with she thought it was a prank. Eventually, the truth in varying forms dawned on everyone and procedures came into place.

Graham and Nancy completed the application form for fostering children, in as full a form for a day trip as for providing a long term foster home. The Social Services contacted them and in due course they received a visit by a social worker who inspected the house and spoke to them about the regulations and the need to consider their plans carefully. Confronted with Graham's facial devastation, the stitch marks and scar were still livid then, she also mentioned their need to run Police checks. Graham drew her attention to the list of referees which included a Detective Sergeant and a Child Protection Officer, continually pointing out that they only planned to take an individual child out on day trips but the interviewer doggedly continued, adding brightly at one point that they may decide to take more children on. Graham started to correct her but sank back into a polite silence, realising how difficult it would have been to explain why Jimmy was so special.

They were also required to attend a preparation course where they sat through a well-meaning but largely inappropriate agenda. The process was the same for everyone, and an acceptance would be for all or nothing.

Further meetings with the social worker were deemed necessary and references were taken up before she prepared her report, recommending their approval as foster parents. Three months had passed by and they were told to expect a further wait of at least four weeks before the report would be considered by an independent panel.

Until approved as full foster parents they were not allowed near Jimmy, not even for an hours' visit. Meanwhile, a six year olds' light of hope faded away. Graham could only begin to imagine the desperation that drove Jimmy to run away from the home again and track them down.

Breakfast was over and Jimmy had readily agreed to help with the washing up while Graham went back upstairs for a shave and shower. By the time he returned to the kitchen Nancy was enjoying another cup of tea and watching Jimmy draw on the notepaper they had found in the drawer.

Time passed and Nancy called in to say that she would be late getting to her cleaning jobs. Thankfully, it was one of the days Graham didn't attend work. His job as car park and trolley attendant at a local superstore was for just three days a week, Thursday to Saturday.

It was time. "Nanshy, could we boys have a glass of coke please. We've got shome sherious talking to do and I'd rather not do it without a coke in front of me." Jimmy's head remained hunched down over the paper and his concentration on the task in hand had increased. A glass was set down by his arm but he showed no reaction.

"Maytee, would you be kind enough to look at this for me pleashe." He reached over to the nearby kitchen surface and dragged a large red transfer file across and dropped it onto the table. The thump it made bore evidence of its volume and served to startle Jimmy into looking up.

Tapping the side of his nose with his forefinger he continued, "Now, you won't undershtand very much of this but," he leant down until his head was next to Jimmy's and said in a lighter, but surprised tone, "Neither do I! The people in charge of everything must think you are very, very important. More important than the queen even. I reckon I could take her out for tea without sho much bother." He opened the file and quickly summarised the different letters and forms in terms a six year old might understand. "Then they sent someone to see us and made sure that if we put you up for the night the bed was nice and soft. And they didn't just ask us a lot of questions. They've been in touch with lots of other people to shee if *they* think we're good enough to take you out. Excushe me." He picked his glass up and took a fortifying gulp. Jimmy did likewise.

"All thish has taken three months. That'sh a quarter of the way to next Christmas! Which I might add will be spent here with us,—if you wanted to." Several nods indicated that an arm and leg would willingly be traded for such an opportunity. Graham reached behind and removed a wall calendar from a hook. A full year planner was printed on the reverse and Graham pointed at January. "That'sh when we first met in hospital, shortly after Christmas." He started to cross each day off, announcing the move from one month to the next until he reached the 12th of April. "That'sh today and all those days have passed by." He dragged the pen over the spent period. "They've said we should know within a month, which is there." As he drew a heavily-marked square around the 15th of May a sense of anger and frustration swept over him, prompting him to say something foolish, though if it helped Jimmy get through even part of the next month he would argue that it was worth it. "If you haven't heard by then, catch another bus here on this day." As he drew a triangle around the 23rd May he received a sharp kick of censure on his ankle. He continued, "I would like you to take thish pen and calendar back with you so that you can crosh each day off when you go to bed." He felt the boy tense and allowed a moments' pause by reaching forward for another mouthful of coke. Jimmy followed suit.

Graham spoke quietly, "I'm shorry maytee, but if we didn't take you back they would say that we were not good enough to see you at all and then we would never get to Skegnesh." He paused to allow time for things to sink in. "Would you like me to see if Aunty Sarah could drive you back, we'll come with you."

There was the slightest nod and Nancy left the table to telephone the care home and Sarah Whiting.

Jimmy slowly leant against Graham and began to cry. Graham wrapped him in his arms, and thought of the trauma this child had lived through,—and his eyes filled too.

Ironically, Sarah was a Social Services Child Protection officer who had witnessed Graham's gift first-hand and was part of the very small group who knew of it. She had met Jimmy whilst visiting Graham in hospital and had helped, via contacts, to fast track certain elements of the approval process. Her natural affinity with children ensured that Jimmy came to call her Aunty too. Since Graham and Nancy didn't own a car Nancy had telephoned Sarah to beg a ride back to the home.

"Oh, that poor child, done a runner again has he?" She listened as Nancy described the details and gasped as she learned of his night spent in a plastic sack. "Of course I'll come, and we'll treat him to a burger and milkshake on the way."

Chapter 2

The journey back from the care home began in silence. Somehow they all felt they were failing a child who was so desperately in need of friends and support, and much more. Of course, his case was so special because in Graham, Jimmy had someone who had *shared* his trauma. The youngster would not have been able to articulate the special value of Graham's friendship but then no-one would have believed him anyway.

Eventually Sarah spoke, "How are your headaches?"

Graham was sitting in the front passenger seat and turned towards her, "You mean am I shtill getting 'hits'?"

"Well, yes I suppose I do."

Graham's passage of discovery through the previous year had involved a number of people other than the victims and perpetrators, and whilst he wanted things kept secret some incidents necessitated the use of professionals who each journeyed through the stages of utter disbelief, denial, startled acknowledgement and ultimately, from experience, total belief. They included the brusque but soft-centred Doctor Donald Williams, his friend Sarah Whiting and a Detective Sergeant Adam Harding, known at the station, out of earshot, as 'Breadbin' in acknowledgement of his shape and the local chain of baker's shops who shared the same name.

Though it had no name they formed a group to work with Graham and both Sarah and Harding had used Graham's gift to discover and deal with some dreadful cases of abuse. Oddly enough, Doctor Williams was the only member of the group who had not witnessed one of Graham's episodes yet he had been the first to accept Graham's gift following the rescue of Sam, a young boy who was being beaten and burned by his mother's partner. Williams had treated the boy after Graham had got him back to his natural father though it was only because he knew the father quite well that he allowed himself to be persuaded not to involve the authorities. Instead he had insisted on interviewing Graham.

In the meeting that followed, against all reason, the Doctor believed Graham's tale, or at least couldn't dismiss it and subsequently met with his friend Sarah to share his tale. As a Child Protection Officer she thought he'd been extremely stupid for not involving the authorities in the matter of child abuse. But that was before she met Graham.

In due course therefore and in different ways all of the group members came to believe in Graham's gift and to love or admire his understated manner, often in the face of dreadful knowledge.

On the previous Boxing Day Graham had acted to save the life of a baby girl and in so doing confronted the father who was entrenched in a three day binge on crack cocaine. Believing Graham to be a figure out of his drug-induced imagination, bent on stealing his stash, the man inflicted life-threatening knife injuries. With emergency care both Graham and the baby, Esther, survived. The child's mother had suffered a drug-induced cardiac arrest and was found that night submerged in the bath. Her father, Esther's grandfather, was a multi-millionaire named Harvey Calder whose impassioned plea for information persuaded Graham to share his secret with him also.

All were sworn to secrecy out of respect for Graham's fear of publicity and of becoming a specimen for study.

The recovery from the attack required more than the simple growth of tissue. The horror and shock of such violence was exaggerated by Graham's mind's eye which still carried the image of a baby just hours away from death by malnutrition. Now, some four months after the event, Nancy would still leap up and change channels on the television when an appeal for the starving appeared, with images of stupefied children with huge eyes. Graham would gasp and look away.

Meanwhile the group had decided to give him space and wait for him to decide whether or not to continue using his extra sense.

Science acknowledges that it knows relatively little about the brain but subjects such as Extra Sensory Perception, (ESP), and Telepathy are accepted as entirely possible, simply awaiting discovery. August bodies such as Edinburgh University have been studying the subject for years.

Graham had never tried to assess or explain what had happened to him. He knew *when* it happened and guessed that it had something to do with the dying child but the why's and how's were beyond him and for that matter would have confounded modern day scientists. He had simply come to accept it, as an additional sense, but the choice of whether or not to continue wasn't his to make. The segment of his brain that had been activated nearly two years earlier still functioned, though since Christmas he had avoided contact with children or situations where he might pick up signals. The pain and shock had long gone but so had his confidence. It would have been so easy to retreat to his home and stay there in quiet isolation and he tried to for the first two months, but Nancy would have none of it.

Last Christmas they had decided to share their lives only hours before they were sharing a ride in the back of a speeding ambulance and she would be damned if 'a mere stabbing' was going to get in the way of that.

Her determination served them both well. Graham returned to work at the beginning of March and they committed themselves to regular outings to cinemas, parks and shops. One of the key inducements was their ongoing application to the fostering authority so that Graham could honour his promise to Jimmy, of visits and days out, including the day in Skegness they'd discussed so often.

The single *benefit* to have come out of the episode was that whilst in hospital he was given the opportunity of working with a truly gifted speech therapist who had changed his stroke-like speech impediment beyond measure. After four months work his speech was almost normal, though he still had difficulty with his S's.

Sadly, his left arm was still weaker than the right and when tired his gait would become a slight shamble.

* * *

"Yesh, they are shtill there." He added with a wry smile, "But I've been trying to avoid them."

Sarah paused as she negotiated a right-hand turn then nodded, "Yes I suppose I can understand that, but it's good to see you back at work."

"I shtill get hits from things like the trolleys and some of them are bad, but I haven't felt able to take any action."

"We've all been thinking of you and everyone sends their best wishes. We could meet up and chat about things if you would like to. It might help to share."

Graham stared out of the windscreen in thoughtful silence until they pulled up outside the house. In the back seat Nancy remained still, sensing that something else needed to be said.

Graham continued to gaze ahead but sighed and said, "That would be a good idea, we should meet up shoon." He paused for a moment and added, "After thish morning I realise I can't ignore things anymore."

Sarah declined the offer of a cup of tea, citing the need to catch up with the days' appointments, but she promised to contact the group and organise a meeting. As they got out of the car she called out, "Oh hang on." She recovered a huge handbag from the rear seat and reached into the cluttered maw. Seemingly against all odds she immediately retrieved a vellum envelope addressed to Graham and handed it to him. "I was asked to wait until I thought it appropriate before handing this to you. Do let me know what it says." She gave them a big grin and blew them a kiss.

As she drove away she glanced in the mirror and watched them link arms and walk towards their house. She could only guess at the torment Graham must have suffered at times, yet couldn't help feeling a certain frisson when she thought of what might lie ahead.

Chapter 3

He was not a hero. How could he be? With a cleft in his forehead, now overlapped with the scar from a knife attack, weakened limbs and slurred speech he was more like a cripple. Last year, in just a few months he had been frightened on many occasions and sustained injuries twice. The sheer violence of the last attack didn't begin to affect him until a week or two after he left hospital.

Until then he had been buoyed by his survival and support from their friends, but at home, in the silence of their bedroom, dreams would take him back to that doorstep where he would see a flash the light reflected off the knife blade as it completed its arc of searing pain.

More troubling was the recurring dream that had also started on his return from hospital. Tenuous and unclear, it was as though he was in a darkened room, lying in wait for something to happen, something that was deeply unpleasant. Each time he felt a mix of fear and confusion yet there was no escape. He knew, instinctively, that there was nothing he could do to avoid the threat. The tiniest sound seemed amplified and time dragged, denying him proper rest for most of the night, yet nothing happened. He woke exhausted from each one with a memory of unending fear and no idea of the cause.

In all other respects his life had been enriched by Nancy. Last Christmas he discovered how much he loved her and they set up home at his house shortly after; which is to say that he asked her to move into his house while he was in hospital. Even now he could recall how much he looked forward to going home, to Nancy. When he did manage to get out of hospital she had transformed the house yet with a delicate touch. It was still very much his house, but the 'Ann' had been removed and the 'Nancy' had established a presence with pictures and knick-knacks. His former wife had set up home with another man and was now keen to divorce, demanding title to their life savings and leaving Graham with the house.

Ironically, the difficulties they had experienced in seeking approval by the fostering authorities had been quite bonding since they shared an equal desire to spend time with Jimmy.

His return to work signalled another step forward and their lives began to fill with the comfort of little rituals and practices. On Fridays Nancy would meet Graham at the end of his shift and they would do the weeks' shopping at the store to secure his staff discount. On Saturdays they would catch a bus into Leicester where they would amble around the shops and have a cappuccino at his favourite coffee bar. Provided something reasonable was showing, they would often go to the cinema on Wednesday afternoons when discounted rates applied.

The unhappy combination of disabilities arising from his head injuries rendered him incapable of going back to his clerical job at Leicester College but by happy chance he found himself in the right place and time to secure employment at the local superstore, gathering trolleys in from the car park and generally keeping the area tidy. It was little more than minimum wage but the exercise and fresh air were good for him. He shared the shift with an amiable sort named Colin and he had come to cherish the friendship and support of the general staff. One or two of his adventures had given him star status within the store and all new employees would be introduced to him, presumably as part of sharing the stories.

Formerly, he had often received 'hits' of varying strength from the shopping trolleys he gathered in the car park or sometimes he would see and feel things by being close enough to a child. Since returning to work he had taken to wearing thick gloves and avoided getting too close to people. In spite of those measures he had still received occasional hits though he had managed to close his mind to them, often by literally running in the opposite direction.

After waving Sarah off they went into the house without a word. Nancy had made a cup of coffee and they sat at the table regarding the expensive-looking envelope.

"Do you want me to open it?"

He shook his head and picked it up. "No thanksh, I need to." He opened the envelope and withdrew a sheet of expensive vellum laid paper crisply folded. The text was neat but written in a bold hand, with a fountain pen.

* * *

Dear Mr Parsons,

Since I asked Mrs Whiting to withhold this letter until you were well enough to be reminded of your experience on Boxing Day I trust that you are, in fact, well on the road to recovery.

I believe you know the circumstances surrounding our family tragedy and whilst there is little we could have done about my daughter's drug addiction we were shocked to discover that we had a granddaughter, Esther. I am pleased to advise that she is making excellent progress, as you will see from the enclosed photograph. Apparently she suffered some kidney damage, which they tell us is manageable, though it was a miracle that in her weakened state she didn't pick up an infection. Had she done so her chances of survival would have been slight.

But on the subject of miracles, I must consider you. I wanted you to have this photograph as evidence of the gift you have given us and whilst I will honour my promise to keep your secret I cannot stop thinking about it. I am not an emotional sort of person but I am moved when I think about your special ability and since Mrs Whiting told me that you had employed it before I can only imagine what it must have meant to others.

The truth is that I cannot find the words to adequately thank you for what you did for us.

When we spoke in hospital you mentioned that, with me, only five people know about this. If those people ever meet or act as a group I would be honoured, no I would <u>beg</u> to be included. Please believe me when I say that I would do anything I could to help you.

As I said before, I shall always be in your debt.

Yours faithfully,
Harvey Calder

P.S. We managed to get a copy of Esther's birth certificate and celebrated her first birthday on the 11ᵗʰ February.

* * *

"She's a pretty little thing." They were sitting opposite each other at the kitchen table and Nancy exchanged the photograph for the letter Graham had finished reading. He looked at a picture of a young child sitting in a high chair, staring at a cake with a single burning candle with wide eyes. The flame was reflected in her eyes and her open-mouthed grin mirrored the excitement of her clapping hands. She was a pretty one year old with short blonde hair, and a complexion that defied anyone to believe she had been at death's door with malnutrition only six weeks beforehand. There was nothing left to say. Nancy reached across and gave his hand a squeeze.

It had become a day of reconciliation, he accepted that. Jimmy's visit and this letter were enough to make him realise that he had no choice. Somehow he had been given a gift which wasn't his to hide. He cast back to the previous autumn and remembered the terrible scalds on Kirsty Randle's back, that would have become fatal if he hadn't known where she lay. It was solely thanks to his extra sense that Adrian Tunstall would no longer be sodomised by his father and business partner. There were so many others too. His gift belonged to those kids, not him.

Chapter 4

Two days later Nancy watched Graham tying up his boots before leaving for work. After wrestling into his ski jacket and gloves he walked up to her and exchanged a kiss. "Shee you later." As he turned to go he grinned and waved his enclosed hands, palm outward, "Today the glovesh are off!" The play on words was not lost on Nancy and in any other circumstances she would have chuckled but this flippancy was unwelcome.

"Graham, you listen to me. I don't want to hear about any daft stunts or heroics. Take care of yourself, please, for me if not for yourself." He returned and hugged her, "Promish."

* * *

Mary Stretton didn't feel the same way about Thursday mornings, in that they were still two long days away from the weekend. She had taught ages seven through nine for the last twenty seven years and whilst she disliked teaching *per se*, her experience allowed her to plot an easy course through what was left of her career. Ironically, she also disliked children, though she would never have admitted to that strength of feeling, arguing instead that she merely found some of their more irritating ways irksome.

In the early years she had enjoyed the freedoms of enlightened times when strict rules were made and when necessary enforced with the cane. She controlled her classes with a strict but fair precision where each child knew what was expected, when and how. Each day would begin with prayers and end with ten minutes of chanting the times tables. It was simply a matter of control.

Though quite portly, she delivered her tuition in a high-pitched voice which rose to a shriek when angered. All of her flock would at some time or other have their senses assaulted at close quarters, by an unpleasant mix of high decibels and rank halitosis. She had an unruly mop of wavy brown hair, now flecked with grey and her fashion sense belonged in the fifties with an almost belligerent disregard for anything that might please the eye.

One control strategy she had been rather proud of she named *DARE*. 'Divide and rule entirely.' It enabled the operator to control classes of almost any size and could be applied in so many ways, but there were two key components.

The first involved constant reference to the group of children who worked hard and achieved results. This served to reward the workers and ensured that most of the class aspired to join them.

Second; isolate the idle and low achievers. The injustice of having to spend an unequal amount of time trying to get these kids to work only served to ensure that the rest of the class, average and up, would suffer. The rest of the class should know that this sector was to be avoided at all costs.

Other areas of isolation and segregation would include the feeble at sports, or perhaps the scruffy or smelly ones. In fact any child who was in any way defective deserved the treatment. It was a win, win strategy that controlled a large number, as many as forty five in the early years, and perversely enjoyed the support of the class. Each student would enjoy the comfort of having someone to look down on at some point. After all, any group must have runt.

Of course, many practices had been consigned to the old days, before politicians played patsy with the educational system, turning it from one of the World's best to one of abject mediocrity. They even established the inspectorate *Ofsted* to enforce a system more committed to educational targets and tick lists than the established and proven teaching regimes that allowed teachers to simply get on with the job. Nowadays punishment was at best benign and she could detail many examples of contemporary student power that bordered on anarchic. Worse still, she had been afflicted with the 'Teachers Assistant' for two afternoons a week whose judgement and loyalty would always be in question as long as she spent time in other classes, especially with the newbie teachers just out of college. That said, the current one seemed to have succumbed to Mary's ways and now knew better than to offer an opinion but caution was still called for; though at what cost! Whenever the assistant was in class the pupils' behaviour deteriorated, as though they'd been let off the leash and discipline needed to be re-established every time. It was easily done, particularly if one or two children had isolated themselves by their behaviour. They would be 'cut out' of the pack and savaged as soon as she had them to herself again.

Timothy Dexter was a perfect candidate for such isolation and came to represent a little light relief if called for. His hair was spiked in matted disarray and his clothes were becoming greyer by the week. He was a skinny little wretch with buck teeth and the constitution of a wet tissue. By now she could reduce him to a blubbering jelly by simply sneaking up in from behind and shouting "Boo" in his ear. The rest of the classroom would laugh at the spectacle.

Thus, by tacit appointment Timothy had become the classes' kicking boy.

Mary thanked God she only had five years to go before retirement. The unwelcome mix of Ofsted, semi-skilled amateurs and changing curriculums all meant added work. Before, thanks to many years of experience, preparation for classes had been minimal. Now the goalposts were constantly on the move and worse still, measured.

Nevertheless, more often than not she was the first out of the car park each afternoon. She'd served her time.

* * *

In spite of his willingness to accept hits the morning passed by quietly. Thursdays were often quiet and time dragged for want of work to do. Lunch in the canteen followed the usual routine of soup and a sandwich enjoyed with the banter from the shop staff. None of them knew about his gift but his efforts to get help for an abused child, left in a car last summer were part of the store's lore and one of the reasons for his popularity.

Linda joined him for lunch and they chatted about things in general. She was on the enquiry desk the day he enquired about the job vacancy and had shared his delight at getting the job. They had been firm friends ever since.

The first 'hit' occurred when he least expected it and in a most unusual context. He had been asked to go into the store and help move some pallets when he saw a youngish boy, perhaps ten or eleven making small jumps in the cereals section in an attempt to reach the Shreddies. Graham pulled a packet off the shelf and with a smile handed it to the boy, "There you go." He was rewarded with a big smile and thank you but as the packet changed hands an emotion of such strength hit Graham that he stepped back in shock. He felt incredible. Not just a sense of well-being, free of anxieties, it was an emotional clear blue sky when the world is *good*; when every sense was on a high. His heart felt full to bursting.

The moment of contact was fleeting and the background to such joy was unexplored, but he did notice the boy's buoyant delivery of the carton to a trolley being held by a couple.

He would never know that Dan worked as a legal executive and had been married to Amy for eleven years before he drank too much at the office Christmas party and succumbed to the sexual advances made by one of the junior clerks. Wives and partners had not been invited and it was always a mystery how he had even managed to complete the act but he had in such a drunken state. His remorse kicked in almost immediately, in inverse proportion to his flagging erection. He had never been unfaithful and was beside himself with guilt until a friend and colleague pointed out that it was an aberration, unlikely to ever happen again and news of it should never be shared. Sadly the gonorrhoea he'd contracted *was* shared and the marriage ended. Their seven year old son, David was devastated.

Two years later Dan had become a committed bachelor. Amy was the love of his life and two attempts at new relationships had ended disastrously. On their weekends together David would pass on news from home and both were troubled when Amy formed a relationship with another man. Thankfully, it only lasted long enough for Amy to discover the man's drug dependency.

It was time for reason and forgiveness. Though Graham didn't know it, he'd experienced the joy a nine year old boy felt for the reconciliation that had taken place two days earlier, when his dad moved back into their home.

The remainder of the day passed without incident but when his shift ended Graham was still in high spirits and decided to walk the two miles or so home rather than catch the bus. Spring was his favourite season, when the grass was a vibrant green and the spring flowers filled the roadside verges. His favourite flower was the King Alfred daffodil which seemed to herald a new spring with its bold, bright statement of colour in early March. The rush hour traffic that hustled by went unnoticed as he strode out. All in all, he thought, it's a good day to be alive.

They had taken to enjoy a glass of wine together before dinner, chatting about their days while Nancy cooked. His happy story called for a second glass and a hug before they settled down in front of the television with their meals on trays.

Later, when they lay curled together in bed and their heart rates settled, they sank into that special post-coital sense of ease. Graham murmured, "I'm very happy you know." Nancy shifted slightly, "I should hope so, 'specially now you've got me." He gave a small chuckle and rolled over on to his side smiling, "Too true. Night, night, God bless." They were both asleep within minutes.

Friday and Saturday passed without any extreme experiences. He would often pick up threads of mild and often unthinking cruelty, where for example a parent had ridiculed a child's work or inflicted punishments deemed too harsh by the child. He knew that most children suffered such things to some degree and would survive them. The behaviour he was concerned about, and fearful of, was the cruelty that either injured a child or marked them in some permanent way, be it physical or mental. His association with Sarah Whiting made him realise how much of it occurred in a supposedly civilised society. Her dedication to child welfare was, by her own admission, only just strong enough to cope with the knowledge that so many cases of abuse went undiscovered.

She telephoned them on Saturday evening to advise that the next meeting of the group would be on the evening of Tuesday the twenty fourth at her house, where she would provide something to eat. When asked for details of anything they didn't like they declared themselves willing to try anything except Witchetty grubs. The telephone was on 'hands free' and Nancy called out just in time to stop Sarah from cutting the connection. "Sarah, that letter, the one you gave to Graham, some of it concerns the group. Hold on a moment." She dashed back to the kitchen and returned with Harvey Calder's letter. It was read out in full and they all agreed that his inclusion in the group had merit, but Sarah thought that before inviting him to attend the others should have an opportunity to veto the idea if they wished and suggested that the final decision should wait until the meeting. Someone could contact the 'applicant' then.

Half an hour later, by prior arrangement, two great friends appeared on the doorstep laden with fragrant wrapped parcels. As Graham opened his front door the aromatic mix of fish, chips and vinegar wafted over him and he ushered Tony and Sam Pearce in with a sweep of his arm. "Sam, how on earth can your Dad keep up with your wardrobe when you're growing at that rate?"

Tony rolled his eyes upward and said, "Tell me about it! We spent a very unhappy hour discussing designer labels on trainers last week and I still refuse to pay eighty quid for a pair of fancy plimsoles."

Sam stopped and turned to his father, "Da-ad, they are *not* plimsoles and *I* am not the geek you're trying to make me into!"

Graham interrupted, "And *I* am famished. Let'sh eat and argue at the shame time." They all grinned as Nancy appeared, received hugs from the visitors and announced that the plates were in the oven warming and the table was set.

Sam was nearly eight years old going on sixteen and whilst capable of giving his dad a hard time all the grown-ups present remembered the vicious bruising and rash of cigarette burns his mother's partner had inflicted just over a year ago. Sam was then a quiet, frightened child, whose abuser had threatened him into a lonely isolation, terrified of telling anyone for fear of retaliation. On balance, it was good to see some spirit, particularly for Graham whose actions helped the boy's natural father to secure custody.

The banter continued into the meal. Tony was in the middle of explaining how good the fish from their favourite fish and chip shop was and that Sam had chosen the *un*healthy, plebby option of sausage in batter. In response Sam made a feature out of unwrapping the large aromatic specimen covered in light crispy batter. Tony stopped mid-sentence and regarded the delicious spectacle whilst his son looked up with an air of condescension. There followed a short period of negotiation resulting in a slice of sausage being exchanged for a wedge of battered fish and an admission that the sausage was pretty good, no *very* good after all.

The meal continued with the constant chatter of easy company, each vying for an opportunity to add a comment or story. Banana and ice cream followed the main course before coffees appeared for the adults and Sam's glass was replenished with his favourite, cherryade. Graham announced that it was time to get down to some serious business and began to set the monopoly board out as Tony added, "Ah, we would like to propose an amendment to the rules."

Graham turned to Nancy with a look of mock horror, "They can't do that, it's not proper. Rule amendmentsh have to be shubmitted in writing to an approval board not lessh than ten days before hostilities commence sho that they may be refused in good time."

Tony glanced at his son with a look that said 'watch and learn'. "In that case we would like to propose *two* rule amendments. First; that future rule amendments may be proposed without having to give notice. Could we have a show of hands please?" Father and son raised their hands immediately and looked across the table with relish. Graham followed their line of sight to find that Nancy had raised her hand too. "Oooo, you Judas."

Tony continued, "I believe that is carried which brings us to our original proposal, the rule amendment. Rather than choose and gather your colour streets we propose that you *must* buy whatever you land on. Sam tells me that a friend introduced him to that idea and it produces some interesting results."

"Nonshense, what happened to the idea of a strategy. Thish is becaushe I got Mayfair and Park Lane last time and wiped you all off the board."

Nancy cut in as though he hadn't said anything, "I think that is a really interesting idea."

"Hah! Ish there no end to this woman'sh treachery!"

Nancy looked at him with a small smile, "Let's find out. All those in favour raise your hands"

It became a totally different game, where each player ended up with a mish mash of properties. Houses could not be put on streets until all those bearing the same colour had been acquired and so the horse trading began. Bids were made and blocked by counter bids. Forced sales, arising from fines or spells in jail were exploited savagely until finally, Nancy carried the day by bankrupting anyone who landed on her green collection, graced with hotels. The banter had continued throughout and they were all exhausted when Graham started to pack the game away. With 'hostilities' over Nancy made hot chocolates for everyone and they adjourned to the easy chairs in the lounge. Odd tit bits of gossip were exchanged but for the most part they enjoyed their drinks in a companionable silence that witnessed Sam's descent into slumber. Nancy had rescued his mug as he rolled to one side and fifteen minutes later helped him into his coat. She snatched the chance to give him a hug and peck on the cheek as Tony moved forward to accept his charge and made their way to the car.

They both stood at the front door to wave father and son off, though the street lighting didn't permit a view of the occupants of the cars darkened interior. As it drew away from the curb they saw a small white hand appear at the window waving and Graham heard a tiny whimper at his side. He reached around and held her tightly, murmuring gentle shushes as Nancy placed her head in the crook of his shoulder. She wept gently and said, "My Chris would have been nine now." There was nothing more to say.

That night, in bed, they held each other and chatted about future plans, in particular the day excursions they might try when the authorities eventually allowed them to take Jimmy out. Neither voiced a wish to end the day thus and both knew a need to close each day with a positive, though it had been just as important for Nancy to save a niche in her heart for the son who had been killed and to visit there when prompted.

* * *

He felt so tired yet was so afraid to sleep. Still sensitive to every sound he recognized tiny details of his location, though it remained a room in total darkness. The smell of the pillow, the soft yet lumpy nature of the mattress, a faint drizzle of rain pattering across the window, a distant purr of traffic and faint murmuring from the television downstairs. He felt so lonely and afraid yet dare not move or make a sound. So tired, his own shallow breaths marking time like a macabre metronome. So it dragged on through the night until eventually, and with some gratitude, he roused to the demands of his middle-aged prostate with a pressing need to visit the toilet. Relieved, he crept back into bed and took comfort from the sound of Nancy's gentle snoring, enough comfort to sink into proper slumber.

* * *

The following morning he thought about discussing his dream with Nancy but decided against it. Whilst Nancy would always be prepared to discuss his experiences, unlike his ex-wife, he decided that the content was still too vague to share. Above all, he didn't believe that a life was at risk.

He ambled through to the kitchen, opening curtains as he went. It was Sunday, that much was evident from the Sunday paper spread across the table underneath a mug of tea and Nancy's hunched form, clad in her cuddly blue dressing gown. He poured himself a mug of tea and sat down beside her reading the half of newsprint available to him. He knew she hated that, just as she knew he was being mischievous. With a sigh she burrowed underneath the paper and withdrew the colour supplement, slapping it against his chest with a, "Go, shoo!" Graham did as he was told and sat in his usual chair opposite. The following twenty minutes passed silently, save for the audible gulps of tea and rustling of pages but since he was first to finish he decided to begin making suggestions of what to do on such a fine Sunday morning.

"How about finding a musheum to vishit?"

"No."

"How about catching a bush over to Loughborough and having a trip on a Shteam train?"

"No."

"Alright, what about the Shpace centre?"

A sigh, "No."

"I know let'sh go up to Bradgate park for a walk and bacon butty."

Nancy finally looked up from the paper but remained hunched low, "I know, let's leave Nancy alone for a while so she can finish the paper. In fact, how about going upstairs and having a shower you smelly man."

He straightened his back indignantly, "I do not shm . . . "

"Whatever."

"I shall go and enhance an already pleashant natural odour but you haven't indicated a choice."

"Walk and butty, now go!"

Bradgate Park is an 840 acre country park situated seven miles north west of Leicester that was the birthplace of Lady Jane Grey, the woman who would later lose her head over King Henry the Eighth. Now it is a public area criss-crossed with delightful walks that could include a moderate pull up to the high spot, marked by a ruin named 'Old John' and spectacular views. A herd of deer and visitor centre add to the experience but Graham and Nancy were particularly taken with the dogs.

Lots of people were out, with dogs of all sizes, colours, temperaments and breeds. It was fun to identify which owner belonged to each dog and whilst many were clear matches there were some surprises. Most memorable was the huge man, built like a tank and looking like an agricultural worker who swept a scruffy little cairn terrier off the ground when confronted with two Dobermans who might have thought it was a rat. Graham certainly did, and said as much disparagingly. Thanks to the many outcrops and copses the park didn't feel crowded but by noon they had done enough walking and rewarded their efforts with a hot chocolate and bacon butty at one of the cafes in Newton Linford, the pretty village adjoining the park. On such a beautiful day it was a great 'feel good' thing to do.

It was over their lunch that Graham voiced a connection that might have explained their interest in the dogs, having never shared any previously. "Jimmy wouldn't feel sho lonely if he shtill had his dog."

Nancy pursed her lips, "Hm, Sally? He could never have one at the home though."

"No, I know. But maybe if we had one they could play together on the days we took him out."

"Blimey, do you know what you're suggesting. A dog's one hell of a commitment. You can't drag it out of the cupboard and dust it down for the occasional visitor you know."

"Well yesh I do know as a matter of fact, 'cosh we alwaysh had a dog when I was a boy. Always the shame breed, a Welsh Border collie."

"We didn't have a dog. My father would never allow it."

"But if he had, what breed would you have chosen?"

Nancy took a few moments before replying, "Well, I've always liked Boxers, they always look happy and eager to please."

Graham grunted, "That'sh becaushe they are very shtupid though very pleashant village idiotsh. Colliesh are the intellectualsh of the dog world."

"You mean the collies that spend their days running around after sheep."

He chuckled at her response to his criticism of her choice. "I could tell you shtories about our dogs that would amaze you."

She put her head to one side slightly and paused thoughtfully before saying, "So tell, please. I know very little of your background beyond the recent history I actually witnessed and we've never really discussed your childhood before,

Graham shrugged, "Not a lot to tell really. We lived in a terraced house in Earl Shilton. I was an only child though I can never remember feeling put out by that. I had lotsh of friends and we were alwaysh in and out of each other's houses. Either that or we'd be off over the fields playing soldiersh or cowboysh and Indiansh. Then a shtick would be a machine gun or a tomahawk and a few balesh of shtraw a fort, until the farmer caught ush. He ushed to go nutsh. Mum and dad worked at one of the local hosiery mills, though I can't think of the name now. She was a machine operator and he wass the maintenance man, more a Jack of all tradesh really."

He went on to chronicle an average childhood and adolescence in the late sixties and early seventies, when it was such a good time to be young. When jobs were for life and cares were few. Not particularly well off but happy. Holidays were on a shoestring, but they enjoyed one a year without fail, usually in a rented caravan on the east coast and each one a storehouse of memories. His story continued through their lunch and closed while they were waiting for the bus back into Leicester.

"So that's my life history, now tell me yoursh."

Nancy gave a quick shake of her head, "Nah, there's nothing of interest in there. The only thing of importance was a bad thing, which was Mum dying of cancer when I was ten. I've already told you. Dad died over ten years ago and my sister lives in Australia. I haven't heard from her in years; we've never had much to do with each other. All I *will* say is that there were times when we had no money and I remember being hungry. I certainly don't remember any holidays."

"There musht be more. What did your Dad do?"

"He worked in the building trade, a bricklayer. Work came in fits and starts. It was feast or famine. We didn't get on though. I left home and lived with my Aunty Kit when I got the job in a hosiery mill over the other side of town."

"You're being a bit niggardly with the details."

"No I'm not, it's just not interesting that's all, trust me and anyway, here's the bus."

Chapter 5

Detective Sergeant Adam Harding's old Ford Sierra was like him, dishevelled. Not that Graham or Nancy would have complained. They were grateful of his offer of a lift to Sarah's house and he entertained them with a summary of recent criminal activities, from the benign to violent and the cunning to comic. He then asked, "So, what news about your vetting, for visits with that lad, um what's his name?"

"Jimmy. He got tired of waiting and ran away again. Shpent the whole night in a plashtic sack by our dustbin and joined ush for breakfasht."

"Hmm, that's the sort of dogged undertaking I've come to expect from you. I trust that *unlike* you he survived the adventure unharmed."

"Yesh, we delivered him back to the home shafe and shound, and very unhappy."

"They're being a bit slow aren't they? I assume you've spoken to Sarah about it, but why not have another pitch tonight, see if she can push things a little harder."

Nancy spoke up from the back seat, "I spoke to her last week and she promised that she was still on the case. I don't think there's anything else we can do."

Harding flicked a hand towards Graham, "D'Artagnan here might take it into his head to help with the next escape bid!"

"Tell me about it. When they were having breakfast together Graham gave the poor kid a calendar and marked the date we should be given the all clear but then went on to mark another date in case there was a delay. That was the day they agreed for another escape. Can you believe it."

"Yes, in the short time I've known your partner it's exactly what I would expect."

"Next thing we'll know he'll be sitting in one of your interview rooms again."

Harding half chuckled, "And no doubt conning a taxi ride home in a patrol car,—again."

"Exshcuse me, may I be included in thish conversation about me?"

"Be quiet, you're the felon."

Shortly after driving through Narborough on the Coventry Road Harding took a left on to a hard stone driveway, passing between two ancient and deeply grooved oak posts that must have supported a gate at some point. It was quite a long track but the verges and hedgerow were neatly kept. Parking was clearly defined in an area outside of the farmyard and a path to the back door ran alongside the farmhouse, well clear of the working part of the yard. From the smells, it was clear that livestock was kept though there was no evidence of a milking parlour. A small gate that was set in the wall just across from the back door, marking the route from the house to the yard suddenly burst open and an overweight border collie barrelled through towards them. It's madly wagging tale promised a friendly welcome and it moved along the row accepting pats and strokes from each guest. Sarah had seen them pass by the window and hurried to the back door to meet them. "Chocks, leave our guests alone, I know where you've been even if they don't" Chocks accepted the instruction pragmatically and made her way back through the gate.

"Hello you lot! You found us then. Welcome to Glebe Farm, come on in." The last instruction was called out over her shoulder and accompanied with a 'follow me wave' as she strode back into the house. Entrance was through a small glazed porch where a row of shoes and boots lined one side. Nancy led by removing her shoes and placing them in line. Harding followed Graham's example and took a moment to regard the hole in his sock and the exposed big toe. He gave a shrug and followed the others, just in time to hear Sarah exclaim, "Goodness, you didn't need to take your shoes off. Only family have to do that, because of the mud, and other stuff." Her eyes passed over all six stocking feet but when she saw Harding's she became even more flustered. She beckoned them in to a large warm kitchen where an old oak table took precedence. A row of cupboards ran along the length of one wall opposite a large inglenook fireplace that contained a huge AGA stove, obviously the source of the cosy warmth and mouth-watering smells. The table was set for five and Sarah picked up a bottle of wine from its centre and passed it to Harding with a corkscrew. "Would you do the honours please Adam, Doc isn't here yet so we can get a head start."

Harding obliged while Sarah returned to the stove and tended a steaming pan. The pop of the cork sounded too loud in the temporary silence but once the glasses had been charged and distributed Sarah raised hers in a toast. "Welcome Graham, it is so good to see you here." "Here, here." said Harding, followed by Nancy, "And another here." It was a daft moment that was acknowledged with a burst of laughter. Any awkwardness was forgotten and everyone began chattering at once. Sarah excused herself and returned with their shoes, "Here put these on, this is a farmhouse kitchen and that's a tile floor, which strikes cold." She leant towards Harding with a hint of a smile, "And I do so like a man who's prepared to make a statement."

A few minutes later they heard a knock at the door and a voice, "Hello, anyone in?" A chorus of 'No's' responded and Doctor Donald Williams stepped into the kitchen to be met by four beaming faces. He looked pointedly at the wine bottle and asked, "Is that still the first?" Graham looked at his watch just as pointedly and replied, "Yesh, but I hope you've brought a note."

"Falling this far behind with the wine is punishment enough for being the last thank you." He held his hand up, "Don't worry, I'll pour my own." After glancing at his watch he grumbled, "I'm not even late dammit."

Sarah gestured with her glass, "Don't worry there's plenty more and Stan is driving you all home. I shall bring the drivers back in the morning."

There was a chorus of declinatures with Donald and Adam promising that it wouldn't be necessary. Sarah answered with an authoritative "It will be." She reached across to a wine rack and presented Williams with another bottle, "Here Don, open this one please."

The coq au vin and crispy roast potatoes cooked in goose fat and dressed with sea salt were accompanied by spring cabbage from the garden. Periods of chatter were intermittent, separated by silences as each savoured the wonderful flavours. But above all, the gentle warm ambience of the surroundings made it such a perfect place to renew their companionship.

Halfway through the meal two broad and extremely tall men came in from the yard. Both looked tired and after shedding their overalls and being introduced moved to the sink and scrubbed their hands and arms. They responded to questions about the farm until they had finished washing then made their apologies, retrieved two plates laden with sandwiches, cheese and crisps out of the fridge and made their way out of the kitchen. Moments later they heard the murmur from a television. Sarah quickly advised that the men had eaten their hot meal at lunchtime.

The wine continued to flow freely and by the time Sarah offered them a slice of lemon meringue pie most of the group had become quite garrulous. There had been an unspoken agreement to avoid the evening's agenda until after the food but Sarah pointed out that time and sobriety were fast disappearing.

The Doctor opened the meeting. "Graham, I'm delighted to see you back in the frame. We've been quite worried you know."

Sarah followed, "Every single case you were involved with has concluded well, at least as far as the children are concerned. Sadly, some of the perpetrators are still at liberty but at least the children are safe."

Williams moaned, "It's ironic really, I was the first one of this group to discover you and your gift yet I'm the only one who hasn't witnessed it. One day perhaps." He looked at Graham, "How have things been, still getting signals?"

Graham explained that after his last injuries he had been frightened to start again and found that he could deaden his sensitivity, at least to some extent. He described what had happened two weeks earlier when Jimmy landed on their doorstep and the rationale for his change of heart, going on to describe his recent 'hits'. After a short pause he looked around the table and said, "You know, I feel a lot eashier about thingsh thish time."

Nancy clasped his hand and gave it a squeeze, "Well I don't. How long will it be before you get yourself injured again." She turned to the others, "We need to find ways of keeping him out of trouble."

Graham smiled at her and shook his head, "No what I meant wash I'm not afraid of my extra senshe. I shtill don't undershtand it but I'm not frightened by it anymore."

Harding took his opportunity, "Yes, but Nancy's comment does raise an issue I must draw everyone's attention to. Last year we were lucky to get the results we did but in future we need to understand what is required for the law to act. Solid, irrefutable evidence is a must but that can be negated if any of us does something daft, like trespassing on private property." They all paused for a moment to recall Graham's adventure that saved the life of an abused child after he had entered a garden without permission and ignored demands to leave. The dog attack that followed put him in hospital.

Sarah leapt to Graham's defence, "But Adam, if Graham hadn't acted the girl would have died."

The Detective nodded, "So we need to find an answer to that problem. When you have days out with Graham perhaps you should arrange a closer liaison with our Child Protection Officer, Pat Geary. You know each other quite well and she has a warrant card. Also, don't forget that eventually, and I'm amazed it hasn't happened already, the press are going to cotton on to things. I take it that we still want to keep this lot private."

Graham piped up, "Definitely!"

Harding delved into his pocket and produced a mobile telephone and charger. "Well this is a start. One of the best ways to stay safe and produce watertight cases is to *communicate*. This is an old 'phone I haven't used for a long time but I've had a 'pay as you go, chip put in and I stored the numbers for all of us in the memory. I've also stored Pat Geary's number in there." He turned to Graham, "You may not recall meeting her but she was at the scene when you were playing at dog's dinners. She knows nothing about your sense or this group, but there may be a situation where you have to involve her."

Graham accepted the gift with thanks and was relieved to be given the instruction manual also. Everyone else noted the mobile's number for storage on their own telephones.

"So" said Sarah, "Where do we go from here? More outings?"

Harding raised his hand, "Before we do any more of those I think we should agree some working practices and it's a bit late to start that tonight, besides I think it would be a good idea for us all to give some thought to the matter."

Sarah looked a little crestfallen but saw that the proposal had received approval from everyone else. That settled she brightened and asked if there was any other business and groaned loudly when Graham said there was. He produced the letter she had passed on from Harvey Calder and asked them all to read it. That done, he asked the obvious question, "Do we let him join us or not?"

Harding expressed doubts, "This group will keep growing if we let it, until it becomes unmanageable. At what point do we lose control?" He looked at Graham, "What do you think. It's your secret more than ours."

Graham nodded an acknowledgement, "I can shee that, but thish man knowsh about me and shometimesh making shomeone one of us is the eashiest way to make sure he keeps the shecret."

"Or," interrupted the Doctor, "It means we make him privy to even more secrets."

"That'sh true. But will he treat thish that lightly? It wash his daughter who died. Whatever he did would be in memory of her."

Harding spoke slowly, as he gathered his thoughts, "There is another consideration and I can't think of any particular example offhand, but there is a great potential for things to go tits up around Graham, as we've already seen. Sometimes the only way out of a problem requires money and I understand that Mr Calder is a wealthy man. I'm not suggesting that we allow him to join so that we can exploit him but his letter makes clear just how much he wants to help."

Sarah's input was called for but she seemed on edge and keen to move on. "I'll go with the majority on this one, but he does appear to be genuine. Let's vote!"

They did so and Graham was charged with the task of inviting him to the next meeting. Williams had faltered but soon acquiesced and the decision was unanimous. Without pause, Sarah cut in, "Now! Is there any other business!" The Doctor smiled and looked around the table, "I dare anyone to try."

Sarah bristled slightly but continued, "Well as a matter of fact I do have another matter to raise. I have been pestering the foster agency for weeks now and as some of you know Graham and Nancy's application to act as foster parents was scheduled for the panel's meeting next month. A couple of days ago I called at the office and offered my body to the Executive Officer in exchange for a great favour. After some thought he agreed to the favour on condition I retracted my threat." She opened a table drawer and extracted a buff envelope before continuing, "As a result, your application was squeezed onto this month's agenda, for the panel who met today." Suddenly her eyes started to fill, "Oh bother, I'm being silly, here, congratulations!" She pushed the envelope across the table to Graham and Nancy who stared at it open-mouthed.

They didn't need to open it but Graham pushed it to Nancy before turning back to Sarah. "Thank you sho much. I can't wait to shee Jimmy'sh face." They all broke into applause and Sarah fetched a tray of flutes from the side before retrieving a bottle of champagne from the fridge. "I didn't know whether to start the evening with this news or wait until now. It seemed an especially nice way to close our reunion. Trouble was, as time wore on I became more and more fidgety! Oh Don, I'm all fingers and thumbs. Would you do the honours please?" She handed the bottle over and turned to Graham and Nancy, "You *must* see his face and as soon as possible. I have a dreadful week ahead but how about we go and see him on Sunday morning, I'll make the arrangements tomorrow and pick you two up around ten o clock."

Graham stepped forward and hugged her, "You've been shuch a good friend, thank you."

"My dear man, I wish I could do this sort of thing every day, instead of, . . . well, you know."

The Doctor filled the flutes with champagne and called for another toast, "Let us drink to Jimmy's grand days out."

* * *

He answered the telephone after just two rings, "Calder."

She paused, mentally checking the abrupt response, "Hello Mr Calder my name is Nancy, I'm Graham's partner. He's the one who . . . "

"Oh heck yes, I know who you are. How are you both?"

"Very well thank you. We got your letter last week."

"In that case things haven't been so good, and for some time, I'm sorry. I suppose Mrs Whiting told you that I'd asked her to hold on to the letter until Graham was fully recovered."

"Yes. He's here with me now, we have a hands free thing on the telephone." Graham cut in quickly, "Hello Mishter Calder."

"Please, call me Harvey and believe me, it's a pleasure to get a call from you." He left it at that, allowing Nancy space to carry on."

"In your letter you mentioned the group and that you thought we might meet up at times. Well we do, and last night we discussed your letter and, well if you wanted to meet up with us it would be OK."

There followed a silence, broken only by the gentle hissing caused by the hands-free facility and eventually the sound of the receiver at the other end being handled. "I can't tell you what this means to me. I felt so certain that you were acting as a group, a very special group and one I shall forever be indebted to."

Graham cut in again, "But itsh a very, very shecret group Mr. . . . , Harvey."

"Yes, I haven't told a soul about it, not even my wife. But by 'eck I'm looking forward to meeting you all. When is the next meeting?"

It was Nancy's turn, "We don't know yet, but probably some-time next month."

"Well, in the meantime may I meet with you two, on a purely social basis?" Nancy and Graham looked at each other and he gave a shrug that indicated 'why not'. She leaned slightly towards the telephone unit, "Well yes, if you would like to, what do you have in mind."

"Well we could meet in Leicester one day and have a bite to eat, or for that matter why don't you come here for lunch. Audrey has been desperate to meet you, though she only knows the official version of what happened. So far as she is concerned you are still a hero and she doesn't *need* to know the full story, but it would still give her an opportunity to thank you."

"Well, yes that would be fine, thank you."

They considered their diaries and agreed on Monday the second of May at noon. Harvey gave them his address and directions on how to get there before easing the call to a close. "There is so much we can talk about but let's wait until we meet up. Until then take care. Bye bye."

At the other end of the line both said their bye byes.

Graham pulled his A to Z out of the bookcase and checked the location of Harvey's house, "Blimey, I thought ash much. Hish place is one of the great big onesh opposite the golf club." Nancy looked over his shoulders but the street map didn't tell her much. She would take his word for it, "So, you'd better find a tie to wear."

He looked up, "Ha! And you'd better give your tiara a polish. I'll get you shome *Duraglit* tomorrow."

Nancy gave him a friendly shove and then frowned, "How do we get there, I don't think there'll be any buses and a taxi will cost the earth."

Graham had already considered the matter, "We shall catch the Oadby bush and get off at the race course, then walk across. No problem. 'Courshe we could alwaysh invite them over here. We could give the *Minton* dinner service an airing and open that '59 bottle of *Chateau La Tour.*

She gave him another shove, "You're getting nervous about this aren't you?"

"No, definitely not!"

"Well I bloody well am."

The following morning, as he set out to work, Graham glanced down at his baggy work trousers and the heavy work boots, necessary for the job; one for which he was paid so little. 'Yes' he thought, 'I'm bloody well nervous too!'

* * *

Friday the twenty ninth of April marked Graham's return to form. The sky had delivered a steady, penetrating drizzle all day and though his waterproof jacket protected him from the rain it was heavy and impervious. People had hurried to their cars, hunched and miserable, abandoning their trolleys where they had parked rather than returning them to the collection areas. It was Friday, one of the busiest days of the week and both Colin and Graham had spent the day quick-marching across the whole site. As Colin said, 'gathering in the strays.' As a result, their sweat *inside* the heavy jackets had made them as wet as they would have been without them.

It was four forty five, just fifteen minutes before the end of his shift when Graham leant against a brick pillar for a few moments to catch his breath. He had just shepherded a train of trolleys into the sheltered area next to the main entrance and watched the people pass by. Most looked weary, many show signs of irritation, and some were enraged by a slow-moving queue or oncoming shoppers unwilling to give way. Whatever the behaviour, they all looked depressed. No-one smiled or chatted to a neighbour and even the clothes were drab and damp. It occurred to Graham that climate might explain why the Russians seemed such a dour race and why they drank so much vodka.

Yet in the midst of that sea of despair, one young person stood out. Graham felt a squeeze of fear and knew something was wrong.

The boy looked normal enough. His hair stuck out and up in tousled disarray and his faded blue anorak hung on his thin frame, still wet though not very waterproof. He walked with his head down but looked up briefly when a trolley was pushed close enough to represent a threat. Graham noticed from the form of his upper lip and a glimpse of white that the front teeth stuck out. Without conscious thought he began to move across the flow of shoppers towards the boy who was carrying a small plastic bag. In those few moments Graham experienced a range of sensations unlike any of the others he had experienced. Later, he would identify them as a mix of despair, loneliness, and utter submission, but when he reached the child his feelings were so intense he was only able to take short, shallow breaths.

"Exshcuse me, may I have a word with you pleashe?" Even as he spoke Graham detected a tensing of muscles that heralded flight and quickly positioned himself in front of the boy guessing, correctly, that there wouldn't be an attempt to dash around a grown-up. "My name ish Graham and I collect the trolleys from the car park and take them to the door, but I have a bit of a dishability and today hash been awful." He pointed to a trolley shelter thirty yards away, "That is the very lasht lot for me to do today but I am so tired I'm afraid I'll crash into a car. Would you do me a very big favour pleashe and help me push them over there, it'll take just two minutesh." Such a request from a grown-up couldn't be refused and besides it was not in Timothy's nature.

His job, Graham explained, would be to hold on to the front trolley and arrest any sideways movement that might occur when they were pushed from behind. Since both hands were needed Graham took the plastic bag off Timothy and placed it on top of the rear trolley. A safe delivery was accomplished minutes later. Enough time for Graham to identify the large box of *paracetamol* and its significance.

Graham held out his hand as he addressed the boy, "Thank you very much indeed, I cannot tell you how much that helped. My name ish Graham, what's yours."

Timothy Dexter looked at the hand with some trepidation and murmured, "Timothy." This man seemed friendly enough but he was still a stranger even if it would be rude to refuse a grown-up. He began to extend his hand and nervously changed the movement, clasping both hands in front.

Graham gave a short nod and continued, "Good name that. Do you prefer to be called Tim or Timothy?" The response was a shrug of the shoulders and a shuffling of the feet. This sort of attention from a stranger was uncomfortable.

Graham went down on one knee and caught the boys' eye. He spoke softly, "Tim, do you believe in magic?" He raised a finger quickly, "No that'sh not the right word, but let's put it thish way, do you think that I might have been here today, in thish very spot at thish very moment, so that I could shtop you taking all those tablets?"

Tim's eyes widened in shock and he began to move. Graham reached forward a grabbed the boy's arm, gasping as the darkness came.

* * *

He moved to another place where he knew, truly knew, the despair of being bullied. Not just by peers, he saw a plump woman with a vicious twist to her mouth, could hear her high pitched shriek, knew fear and pain in many forms and knew helplessness. Tears, weeping, were part of a dreadful process. He knew that people thumped, tormented and shouted to produce the reaction, yet lost interest when their goal had been achieved. Crying was therefore, paradoxically, both an incentive and conclusion. There was no hope of relief. Finally, he felt an unutterable depth of despair when just that morning a very special whistle had been taken by two older children who made new threats, really frightening ones. Graham couldn't sense their ages, yet knew, as all schoolchildren do, that they were 'seniors', in the last year. They were so much bigger and much more frightening. Finally, he sensed that this child could take no more and had used some special money to make his purchase. It was the money he'd been saving for the last seven months, to spend on his holidays."

* * *

The 'hit' had chronicled so much suffering over such a long time yet took only seconds and Timothy witnessed only a momentary loss of focus in his captor's eyes. He was becoming scared and wanted to get away but was shocked by Graham's next words, "Tim, do you think it wash a cruel thing to do, taking that shpecial whistle? It was your Grandad's washn't it?" The boy's jaw dropped, he was quite unable to respond.

"You see, I think it wash a terrible thing to do, but how terrible do you think it would be for your Grandad to lose you? Would you want to hurt him that badly?" This time Graham waited for a response, knowing that the boy was desperately racking his brains for a rational explanation for what this man was saying. But he was also saying it so gently any sense of threat fell away. Finally, Graham broke the silence and called for a response with a "Hmm?"

Timothy moved his head in a small circular motion, unable or more likely unwilling to be any more definitive.

"Now I want to tell you some very confidential thingsh but firsht we have to go and see the lady at that deshk who will give you your money back for the tabletsh." He led Timothy to the help desk, still manned, thankfully, by his friend Linda who refunded the money immediately. The boy was still shaken by the turn of events and keenly aware that the man, who was holding on to the refunded cash, was resting a hand on his shoulder and directing him towards the cafeteria.

Since staff were not allowed to consume food or drink in the public cafeteria whilst on duty Graham slipped out of his jacket, ready to point out that his shift had ended. He purchased a mug of tea and Timothy selected a fizzy orange before being led to a two-seat table by the window. As soon as they were seated Graham spread the cancelled till receipt out in front of Timothy and counted out the cash, receiving a nod in acknowledgment of a full refund. The boy had to stand in order to stow the cash in a trouser pocket and for a brief moment he considered making a run for it. Graham caught the momentary signal and spoke softly, "Now Tim, please be seated, there'sh a good chap."

It was ironic that he wanted to keep his gift secret, out of a fear of discovery by the media and being treated like a circus freak, yet he felt so able to speak of it with children. For one thing they accepted it, without question, and in any event, if they spoke of it to grown-ups their tale would be laughed at and blamed on an over-active imagination. Timothy glanced around and saw that the cafeteria was almost full. He didn't feel quite as threatened but he was still worried by how this stranger knew so much. The whistle and the tablets, the kids at school *and* Miss.

"Now Timothy, I owe you an explanation, but because it'sh very special it'sh also a bit difficult to believe."

Graham pointed at the cleft in his forehead, "You see, I wash hurt very badly and I wash in a coma; that's a very long sleep. When I woke up I found I could see things, bad thingsh that sometimes happen to children. For example, I know, I can *see*, how much you are being bullied and how much it makesh you cry, yet I've never met you before." He smiled and added, "It really ish a short of magic. By the way who ish that fat lady with a screechy voice?"

Timothy did what any eight-year old would do when such a significant and feared authority was ridiculed. He hid his mouth behind a hand and giggled nervously. "That's Mrs Stretton."

"Hmm. She bulliesh you too doesn't she."

Timothy looked fearful of making such a disclosure, particularly about an authority, but finally he nodded, looked down and picked up his drink.

A new voice interrupted their meeting, "Where have you been, I've been waiting by the staff door for you."

Graham looked up at Nancy as she approached the table and opened his mouth in surprise before the situation dawned on him. "Oh blimey, it'sh Friday, shopping night."

As she drew close to the table she saw the slight figure sitting opposite her husband and grew concerned. There must have been a 'hit'. She reached across to the next table for a chair and sat down on the aisle side of theirs. She smiled at Tim and introduced herself, "My name is Nancy, what's yours?"

The boy was clearly affected by the appearance of another stranger, and looked at Graham, as if for confirmation, but a waitress passed by at that moment and laid all his fears to rest. "Ello Nancy, have you come to take him 'ome then. It'll be time to start work again if you don't get 'im out of 'ere soon!"

Nancy chuckled, "Well he's got time enough to buy me a cup of tea."

"Yeah, nice one, and we can both teach 'im to do 'is own washing up as well."

The exchange served to validate the man's credentials and Tim began to relax. Nancy engaged him in small talk while Graham went for the cup of tea. He returned with a small 'Kit Kat' bar for each of them and noted the immediate 'thank you' from Tim. He spent a few moments unwrapping his bar before lowering his head towards Tim, "You don't fanshy having a go at pershuading my wife to say thank you, do you?"

Tim looked up at Nancy, anticipating a reply and was confronted with her warm brown eyes, "Please tell his lordship that he's got off very lightly for leaving me outside for so long. He's going to get as many thank you's as I got sorry's."

Graham met the boys returning gaze and said, "Can you remember that lot?" A shake of the head. "Good, neither can I, thank heavensh!"

He allowed a short silence before addressing Nancy, "Tim has been having a bit, no, a *lot* of bother with bullies and wash just telling me about them. Sheems they just do it to upset him and get him crying." He caught Nancy's eye before adding, "And that includes 'Miss'. Jusht this morning they took his Grandad's whishtle which meant a great deal to him. You're really upshet by that aren't you Tim?"

The boy nodded but wouldn't make eye contact.

"We met outshide and I had one of my funny turns. I knew how bad thingsh were and how upset poor old Tim had become. He had jusht bought a very large box of paracetamol, for himshelf —and that upset *me* I can tell you." He reached across the table and placed his forefinger on the boy's wrist, "But that can be forgotten about now, can't it? A shecret."

This time a much more pronounced nod, but still without eye contact.

Graham pushed a little harder, knowing that he needed the child to share his experience. "The boys that took the whistle weren't in your class were they?"

This time he spoke, "No."

"Were they bigger boys?"

Another nod.

Nancy lowered her head next to Tim's and said gently, "Do you know them?"

His gaze was still locked onto his glass when he spoke, "No, but one of them is Linda Croft's brother. She's in my class."

Graham responded, "But they didn't *jusht* take your whishtle did they Tim. I know how much they frightened you. What elshe did they do?"

Tim wouldn't look up or speak, demonstrating his discomfort by wriggling in his seat.

"Come on maytee, surely you know we're friendsh."

Seconds passed before he could speak, "They said they were going to take me in for questioning and then they would do me in."

That was the threshold. Once he had told them about that threat the rest was easy. In fact his chronicle of physical and psychological abuse was all the more hideous for being delivered in an almost off-handed manner. It was as though he felt that he deserved to be treated so dreadfully.

Graham and Nancy listened attentively and occasionally she would stroke the boy's arm in support. Time slipped by and a new friendship was forged.

When he finished, they all shared a sense of relief. For Timothy it had been cathartic but his new friends had found it harrowing.

Nancy ruffled his hair and drew him into her arms. "Kiddo, you have just done a very brave thing and I'm very pleased to have met you. But what these people have been doing is wrong. Very wrong. Have you spoken to anyone else about it"

Tim shook his head immediately.

Graham sensed why. If 'Miss' was party to it all, who was there to turn to. He tapped the table with his finger, as if to call attention. "Tim, would you do us the honour of joining ush for a drink next Friday?"

Tim nodded, "Yes please."

"Good. I am not sure what we can do yet, but I do know a lady who is a bit of an expert in these thingsh. I am going to shpeak to her tomorrow and next Friday I can tell you what she thinks. How about that."

Tim looked up at Graham and with a smile nodded.

"There is jusht one thing. Promish me, faithfully, that you won't try and hurt yourself again."

Tim expression became solemn and he nodded, "I promise."

Nancy said, "Good. In that case I shall look forward to seeing you next Friday. You will probably see Graham driving his trolley trains but I shall try to get here a little earlier so you and I can get to the *Kit Kats* first." As she was speaking another puzzle sprang to mind, "Tim, how did you manage to buy those *Paracetamol*, you're too young?"

He dropped his head, though in truth, after his purchase had been blocked by one cashier he'd been quite pleased with himself for devising a solution. He explained, "I told Mickey Withers that my mum had a migraine and he got them for me. He's not very bright but he'll do anything for a bottle of cider and I had enough money for that too."

Nancy nodded her acknowledgement of his ingenuity and finished their meeting with, "I think you'd better be heading home now though, your mum and dad will be wondering where you are."

As Tim wriggled off his seat he murmured, "Just my Mum. Thank you for the drink and the *Kit Kat*." He gave them a wave and 'Bye' before trotting towards the main doors.

Nancy watched him go, giving and receiving a further wave as he ran past the window. "I wonder what the story is behind 'just my Mum'."

Graham shook his head, "I don't know, but there are plenty of single parent familiesh out there." He looked at Nancy before adding, "But I would never have believed that a seven year old could know such deshpair. How could someone that age be pushed so far that suicide was an option."

She knew that he had shared that despair when he *connected* with Tim and how badly it would have affected him. She would hear him crying in his sleep that night and would hold him but for now she squeezed his forearm and gave him an encouraging smile, "Come on, we need to do the shopping for tomorrow's outing."

Chapter 6

The following day was May the first, part of a public holiday which promised heavy traffic on the roads, particularly in view of the fine weather. Sarah had suggested avoiding crowded hotspots such as theme parks and towns by heading out towards Loughborough for a walk in the *Outwoods*, which at that time of year would carpeted with bluebells. After a picnic lunch she thought they might consider climbing the nearby *Beacon Hill*. Nancy said that after a mornings' walk and one of Sarah's picnics she'd prefer a descent.

Dew on the lawns sparkled in the morning sunshine and the clear blue sky was forecast to remain so. Just after nine Sarah drew up outside their house in a large and extremely dirty Peugeot estate and sounded the horn. All four tyres bore a collar of dried mud and the panels behind were graced with a fan of dried spray, though there was still just enough paint in sight to identify the light metallic green colour. As Graham and Nancy strode along their front path they saw the front passenger window descend to reveal Sarah chortling to herself. At the same time a circle of condensation blossomed in the rear window, backed by an arc of black and white fur, beating from side to side like a ragged windscreen wiper for the opposite window. The car had three rows of seats but the rear set had been folded down for the additional passenger.

Sarah called, "Good morning hikers, what a lovely day for it."

Graham and Nancy had been ready since eight and Sarah later told them that their exit from the house looked more like a military manoeuvre. As they strode up the garden path she'd half-expected to hear someone shouting 'Hut, hut, hut.' Mildly embarrassed by her observations Graham retorted by saying that as he left the house he thought they might be travelling in the muck spreader.

Sarah had organised the catering by offering to provide a main course with Graham and Nancy left in charge of the cakes, sweets and soft drinks. For appearances' sake they chucked in a few apples and a bottle of spring water but otherwise things were as un PC as a six year old could hope for. Nancy held up the cool box she had been carrying and with a nod of her head asked, "Do you want this in the back?"

"Good Lord no, put it on the back seat with mine, Chocks can burglarise most things."

Graham sidled into the front passenger seat and grinned, "Morning, and again, thanksh. We've being looking forward to this for sho long."

Sarah beamed back, her eyes bright, "So have I, believe me."

"Bringing Chocks was a good idea, no a *great* idea."

"Do you think so? I had a few doubts, what with the death of his dog and all that went with it."

Graham had no such doubts, "Having a dog to play with will probably be the highlight of hish day. Believe me." He buckled into the seat belt and glanced around. The seats had been swept but the carpet was still a mix of dried soil and straw plus, judging by the faint agricultural smell, a trace of more potent matter.

Sarah caught his visual audit and explained, "I thought I'd bring Stan's old tub rather than my little runabout. If it turn's cold we have enough space to eat in here and if Chocks rolls in anything I'd rather she travelled in this car. My colleagues moan if mine becomes a bit 'farmy'. Mind, that usually means that we use their car and I don't have to drive. Bonus really."

Graham thought that it would need to be arctic before he would eat in the vehicle, but said nothing. Once they were on the outer ring road Nancy leaned forward to escape Chock's welcoming licks and smelly breath. "Why did you call her that name?"

"Oh that was easy. We had her just before Christmas, four or five years ago, I'm not sure, but somehow we left her in the lounge alone and she managed to dig her way into the pile of presents under the tree. She located a very large box of chocolates, unwrapped it and ate the lot. Hence the name. Afterwards she was pretty sick but that didn't put her off. She's as good as gold with anything else, food or sweets, but no matter how much we've tried to correct her, we cannot shake Chock's belief that chocolates belong to her and I suspect there's some chocolate in your cool box. You wouldn't believe some of the tricks she's pulled or places she's broken into. Thankfully, she never goes upstairs so that's where we store our chocolate. I'm sure that's how she became so fat, at least originally, and we'd put her current excess down to yet more pilfering but we've just learned that she's in the family way. Not too many studs strut their stuff around us but we think the father is the collie from next door. I hope so, he's a gorgeous animal, with a wonderful temperament."

Nancy chuckled in appreciation of the tale but continued to lean forward, away from Chocks, who was holding herself in position by pressing her jaw down on to the seat edge, grinning and panting in delight. She couldn't help wondering what else the animal had been eating; it certainly wasn't *Cadbury's*.

Graham had been staring out of his window without focus and allowed a comfortable silence to continue for some minutes. He had slept badly and decided to voice his concern, "I'm very nervous."

Sarah glanced across and smiled, "And excited too, I would imagine."

"Hmm, but he's been through so much I don't know how he'll feel. Will he be comfortable with ush for a whole day or will he run away even."

Sarah allowed him silence to develop his thoughts.

"I want to help him," he paused, searching for the word until at last it came to him, *heal*. Whatever we do, I want it to be right."

Sarah patted his knee, "Graham, I have never been more certain of anything in my life, and who knows what you two will get up together in the future. Then, there's always,," She stopped and after a pause Graham prompted her, "What?"

"Oh, nothing, I'm planning too many Skegness days for you. I'm just going to enjoy watching and learning!" A moment later she looked at the interior mirror and announced, "Tripe."

Nancy realised she was being addressed and looked up at the eyes in the mirror, "Sorry?"

"Tripe. She loves it, but it gives her bad breath. Well actually, the by-product is normally emitted from both ends so we're lucky today. Another hour or so and you won't notice."

The reply came back with feeling, "I can't wait."

The care home was situated on the corner of two minor roads and surrounded by a low blue-brick wall which was topped by a municipal-looking metal rail fence. In all, making for a seven foot tall perimeter. A small tarmac play area lay alongside the building and two children were playing 'catch' with a tennis ball. The vehicle entrance was sealed with a heavy pair of metal gates held in the middle by a substantial chain and padlock but the pedestrian gate was next to it lacked such obvious security though it was certainly locked. A small box with a small grill and a button labelled 'Call' was fixed to the wall. Sarah pressed the button and after introducing themselves to the tinny voice that responded, heard the electronic lock click free of its housing. They all stepped inside and waited for the gate to swing shut before walking along the short concrete path towards a set of steps that ended at a large green, semi-glazed door. As they climbed the steps a shadow appeared behind the tinted glass panels and the door was swept open by a middle-aged blonde lady, who wore a broad smile, "Mr Parsons, Mrs Arnold? I am so delighted to see you here at last. Welcome! My name is Pat Ensor"

Graham's first impression was in fact, wholly accurate. He determined that whilst her blonde hair was fake, with dark roots clearly evident, everything else about her was genuine. With her broad grin and dimples she seemed just a micro-second shy of bursting into laughter and her dress code would have looked cool in *Disneyworld*. Her T shirt bore a picture of the *Disney* mascot with the logo 'I love Mickey!' and a bright pink baseball hat was tucked into the waistband of her light brown cord jeans. He couldn't help himself as his gaze continued downwards to the huge slippers that extended out from the bottom of her jeans. They were light grey but each had a pair of eyes and droopy ears. A dark grey nose on each toecap completed the hound dog image so well and so ridiculously that he burst out laughing. Reaching forward to grasp her extended hand he exclaimed, "Mrs Enshor, it is already a pleasure to meet you."

Still beaming, she ducked her head slightly in acknowledgement of his approval and invited him in along with Sarah and Nancy who shook hands in turn. They entered the large Victorian hall with a large dark oak staircase on the left and a passage heading down the right-hand side towards the back of the house. The floor was a mix of black, white and dark blue tiles that would have better suited a public works building, yet even here the warden had applied a light anarchical touch. The huge newel post at the bottom of the stairs had been given a light grey wig and plastic red nose. Pat followed their gaze and chuckled, "That's Dougall. I don't know whether you remember '*Magic Roundabout*' but he was the doggy character in it. His friends Brian the snail, Dillon the rabbit and Florence the girl are further up the stairs, oh and there's Zebedee." She waved a hand, "If you don't remember the programme I'm not going to try and explain him." Graham laughed, "I loved the character but I wouldn't like to try and explain the whole programme!"

She nodded her agreement, "We have a full set of videos so most kids leave here as *Magic Roundabout* devotees. She directed them towards a door at the end of a short passage to their left that bore a plaque with the word 'Office'. Sarah led the way and on reaching the doorway looked back at the warden who gestured for her to push the door open. Jimmy sat on a heavy oak dining chair that stood just inside the room against the wall and was high enough to allow him to swing his legs to and fro. Still pale, with straight fine brown hair that was cut quite short, he looked at them, smiling but without moving. He had obviously been told to sit there and wait for them but now, confronted with the miracle he had waited for, for so long, he could do nothing else. His satchel sat against his side with the strap crossing his torso to sit on the opposite shoulder. Someone had obviously searched the toy cupboard for the bright green plastic binoculars that also hung on a strap around his neck.

Finally, Graham recognised the calendar he had given him that Saturday morning, now tucked under his arm. It was a frozen moment in time until Graham murmured very quietly, "Hello maytee, we're here at last." It was enough. By the time Jimmy had wriggled off the chair and ran to him Graham had got down on his knees and opened his arms for a hug.

Moments later Jimmy took a step back and pulled the calendar from under his arm. "You can have this back now."

Graham turned it over to find that since his last escape to their house each day had been carefully scrubbed out. "No, you keep it by your bed, but look at all those daysh you haven't had to crossh off. Thanks to Mrs Whiting here, we managed to sort things out early."

Pat Ensor reached for the calendar, "I'll take care of this until you get back. Then we'll find some way of hanging it on the wall shall we?"

Jimmy nodded and turned back to Graham, "Are there any birds where we're going?"

"Too right there are and all sizes."

He held up his binoculars, "I've brought these to see them with."

"Good thinking." After struggling to his feet Graham added. "In that case we had better be on our way." He looked across at the warden whose smile still lit the place up. "Yes, have a lovely time. He'll be hungry in no time because he's been in that chair since he got up. A bomb wouldn't have moved him. I delivered a bowl of cereal but he didn't manage anything else."

Sarah smiled, "We have an enormous picnic, I should think he'll be bringing a doggy bag back to share with you."

Pat ruffled Jimmy's hair, "Did you hear that Jimmy, bring some back for me won't you?"

Her charge nodded but then looked up at her with a smile, "There won't be any left, you watch!"

"All right then, I'll settle for some crumbs; now off with you."

A seven o'clock curfew was agreed and the party left the premises. Graham was just behind Sarah and as the door was closed he spoke quietly over her shoulder, "If ever there wash a round peg in a round hole that wash it."

She glanced over her shoulder, "Couldn't agree more. She's smashing isn't she?"

Halfway to the gate Jimmy ran alongside Nancy and took her hand. "Hello Aunty Nancy."

She was charmed by the child's actions, correcting the omission of not greeting her in the home and squeezed his hand gently, "Hello you. I hope you're feeling fit, Mrs Whiting has found some big hills for us to climb."

They were approaching the car and as Sarah walked around to her door she called over her shoulder, "Just call me Sarah."

Jimmy hardly heard her as he caught sight of Chocks, dashing from one side of the luggage space to the other in her excitement. Eyes wide, barely able to contain himself he called out, "You've got a dog!"

Nancy answered, "Yes, She belongs to Sarah. Her name is Chocks, she is fat, smelly and has bad breath. Other than that I think she's lovely."

Her words went unheeded as a back door was opened and he was allowed to climb into the car. Chocks was trying to work her way over the back of the seat to meet the newcomer but her obesity and the headrests defeated the attempt. The black and white pennant of a tail was wagging so hard that the sweep had switched from an arc to circle. She grinned at Jimmy over the seat, switching her weight from one front leg to the other and trying to make contact with a mix of sniffs and licks. Jimmy had to admit, privately, that her breath was dreadful but it didn't matter. Once the grown-ups had belted themselves in he had to face front and be seated, allowing Nancy to secure his seat belt. Chocks 'locked on' to the seat back immediately behind Jimmy and continued to pant happily. As they pulled away from the curb he looked out of his window and thought about the day ahead. His heart felt as big as the clear blue sky.

The *Outwoods* is a mixed woodland of over a hundred and ten acres that lie just south west of Loughborough and half way down a long descent from the eastern escarpment of the Charnwood forest. The southern half consists of gentle green banks and easy walking but the northern half has a number of steep slopes and rocky outcrops that provide kids with a wonderful setting for adventure. There, one can stand at the stone wall perimeter and look across the rooftops of Loughborough two miles away, or continue on public footpaths all the way into town, though most walkers continue around the woodland in a large circle.

They parked in the car park on the south western edge of the woods and set off through the gentle upper slopes that were carpeted with an astonishing density of bluebells. The dappled sunlight that filtered through the canopy changed the uniform blue into a breathtaking variety of shades. Even Jimmy hauled on Chocks' lead enough to stop and wonder at the sight. Sarah, who was just behind him, ready to help out if Chocks decided to bolt, sanctioned his request to pick some for Mrs Ensor though they agreed to wait until the walk was over when some of the dog's water could be used to keep the harvest fresh. She suspected that it was an SSSI site with regulations about the picking of wild flowers but this was one parade she simply couldn't rain on.

Jimmy and Chocks headed off like a dog sleigh, occasionally disappearing around corners but always located by the boy's calls to slow down and his laughter when they were ignored. After they had covered half a kilometre she called Chocks who knew an executive command when she heard one and reversed direction to climb back up the slope with her new pal in tow. By the time they reached the grown-ups both were panting and it was clear that the initial excitement had worn off Chocks. Sarah removed the lead and the game became much more haphazard. They ran off down the path but this time Chocks would disappear into the undergrowth following a line of scent or imaginary prey until Jimmy's calls finally prevailed. He found that a combination of calling and running away worked best though once, when he was running down a slope she barrelled up behind him and tapped the back of his knee with her snout. He went down like a puppet without strings, and rolled down into a mass of dead leaves that lay at the bottom, laughing hysterically. He lay for a moment to gather his breath and Chocks took the opportunity to sweep in and lick his face. "Argh, Chocks, that stinks!"

Chocks, whose tail had never stopped wagging, accepted her new companion's cry in customary fashion and headed off for more smells. They continued down to far edge of the wood where Jimmy clambered up on to the smaller outcrops and leapt down onto ground below where beds of dry leaves and leaf mould cushioned his falls. The grown-ups who had finally caught up were invited to watch and applaud though all declined to join him.

They had followed at a more sedate pace, relishing the sound of Jimmy's laughter. Sarah voiced their thoughts, "Sometimes kids can come through truly dreadful times and yet still find joy. I cherish that ability but there must be times he goes back to the trauma. When I spoke to Pat Ensor last week she gave me a little more background info. Apparently he still refuses to mix with the other children and fostering was impossible. As you already know, he just kept running away. Tantrums and bed-wetting are commonplace, but then many of the kids there suffer those. Even so, I didn't know what to expect today."

Nancy nodded, "When you mention all those things, cropping up with just one child and then multiply that by the number she's responsible for it makes me even more impressed by that lady."

"It's still way shy of a true home with his biological mother," she paused in thought, "And father for that matter, if he hadn't been a murdering thug. That said, I'm learning new stuff today. I deal with this sort of thing all the time but I rarely get to actually experience this end of the equation."

"Yesh." Graham said with feeling, "Me too."

As they turned left to head back up the hill conversation fell away and they allowed the warm ambience of the day to hold sway. Every once in a while someone would call Jimmy's name and receive a cheerful response.

But as he climbed Graham's memories returned. Like a tidal flow, they wouldn't be denied, images and sounds he would have liked to forget flooded back.

When they reached the top of the path they found Jimmy seated at one of the picnic tables on the edge of the car park. His right arm was draped over Chocks who sat on the seat beside him, still panting with her tongue hanging out. Behind them, on the table, lay a small bunch of bluebells

"Well done that man! You've claimed a picnic table for us." Sarah continued in a low questioning tone, "Cho-ocks?" The great pink tongue completed a swift lap of her jaw before disappearing inside and with a dog-grin Chocks jumped down from the seat. She knew from her mistress's voice that she wasn't in too much trouble just as she knew that seats are for people and ground is for dogs. "Right, we'll let this old codger stay and hold the table while the rest of us get the picnic out of the car."

Graham adopted an aloof poise, "Call me an old codger if you wish, but I am quite happy to oblige you by shtaying here and watching you lot work. Now please hurry along, I'm hungry."

Sarah nudged Jimmy's shoulder, "Get him. If we hear any more of that he'll get what's in the dog bowl and Chocks'll have a real treat." Jimmy responded with a firm nod of agreement.

Sarah had prepared a perfect picnic of sandwiches and savoury pastries, accompanied with small individual salads and dipping sauces. Her home-made wholegrain bread with chunks of cheese scored best for the adults but crisps and samosas were Jimmy's first choices. He was quite content to let the grown-ups gossip, while he sneaked tit bits under the table to Chocks who had stationed herself out of sight. The arrangement worked well until he attempted to pass down a significant piece of best cheddar, an indulgence Sarah couldn't sanction. "Chocks scoffs anything she can get Jimmy, but not my cheese, it would be like pushing it down the garbage disposal. If you don't want any more put it back in the dish and I'll take it home for the lads. Better still, offer it to Graham, I'm sure you could train him to beg." Graham obliged by hanging his tongue out, panting and holding both hands up in front of his chest, removing any note of censure from the moment.

Nancy opened the cakes and biscuits, setting them down within easy reach of Jimmy and asked, "OK, you look ready to start again, what would you like to do next?"

The answer was easy, for he had only just become aware of the green binoculars, still around his neck and held them up. "We could see some birds."

"A done deal," said Graham who pointed across the road at the ground that continued rising. "When we go up to the top of that hill you should see shome big birds, called Buzzards."

Nancy had followed his gaze and anxiously asked, "Have we got to go up there?"

"Of course!" Sarah allowed a pause for effect before continuing, "You can get there by foot or by car."

Nancy's shoulders dropped in relief, "Wheels for me please."

Graham put a hand on Jimmy's shoulder, "Not for us! We shall climb all the way." He leant towards the boy who had obligingly put on a determined look, "Do you know what it's called?" Jimmy shook his head. "It'sh called Beacon Hill and while we are walking I will tell you why."

There are two car parks at Beacon Hill, one at the base on Breakback Road and the other at the top of the park on Beacon road. Not huge, but at eight hundred and two feet it is the second highest spot in Leicestershire. After dropping the males off at the bottom Sarah and Nancy drove up to the higher car park, promising to amble part of the way back down to meet up.

Graham soon became too winded to talk and was sweating furiously, but it didn't matter, since anything Jimmy said was addressed to Chocks, who was also showing signs of fatigue. Several times they stopped and the toy binoculars were pointed skyward, particularly when Graham pointed something out but no comment was made. The short breaks were welcome opportunities for Graham to catch his breath but eventually, after pointing out the promised buzzard, he noticed a mix of disappointment and concern pass over the boys face.

"What'sh the problem maytee?"

Jimmy tried them once more before replying. "I can't see anything."

Graham tried them and no matter how much he adjusted them, could only see a pale circular blur. Finally, he held them away from his face and saw immediately that one of the lenses were missing. As he handed them back he pointed the vacant aperture out, "There's a lens misshing I'm afraid. It musht have fallen out in the other woods."

The look of disappointment soon gave way to one of concern, how was he going to explain it to Mrs Ensor?

Graham offered some reassurance, "Don't worry, I'll explain to Mrs Ensor and I'm sure we can find another pair."

The comfort was accepted, at least in part, but when they neared the top and met the ladies it was the first thing he mentioned. Sarah and Nancy said they were sorry he had missed his bird watching but dismissed the loss in the same way that Graham had. It was enough to restore his spirits and the outing continued. A few minutes later they stood at the summit where a toposcope provided names for the surrounding landmarks, though some were lost in the heat haze.

They all found a seat and shared pop and biscuits. Chocks inserted herself under Jimmy's arm and gazed hungrily at the biscuits in his hand. He pretended not to notice until all but a mouthful remained and the dog shuffled slighty to remind him of her presence. It would have been her piece in any event.

By the time they got back to the car it was four thirty and the car park was emptying. Since their house was almost en route to the care home they agreed to stop off for a cup of tea. The air was cooling rapidly but the car's interior still held the daytime heat. As they drove away Jimmy wound his window down slightly and Chocks thrust her head alongside his to enjoy all the inbound scents. Without thinking he reached up and stroked the soft skin under her snout.

Tea was a straightforward refreshment stop until Graham nudged Jimmy, who was sitting at his side. "Right then maytee, I hope you've enjoyed yourself."

He was rewarded with a nod and "Yes thank you," and was suddenly moved beyond words. The boy's mother had obviously taught him the value of please and thank you but he had lost her. The simple thank you snatched at something inside and Graham paused for long enough to blink the moisture from his eyes. "Well that's good becaushe we've enjoyed it too. You're a likeable sort of chap as it happens and Nancy and I would like to invite you to shtay here next weekend, . . . if you would like to."

What might have appeared reticence was in fact closer to excited disbelief and after the moments delay he looked up at Graham and across to Nancy, "Yes please."

"Done deal then. Nancy will pick you up on Saturday morning and we'll drop you back on Sunday evening. We've done some planning because I work on Saturdaysh so Nancy will pick you up and take you into town for the day, then you can come back and shleep here.

They delivered him back to the home in good time though just as they reached the gate Jimmy called out, "Wait a second." He ran back to the car and used both hands to wrestle with the door handle. Once open he clambered in and knelt on the seat to give Chocks a hug. With the open-hearted wisdom of most dogs she obliged by allowing him to wrap his arms around her and rested her head on his shoulder.

Pat Ensor opened the door and spread her arms, "Welcome back explorers, hug please." Jimmy moved forward and offered up the green plastic binoculars, "I'm sorry Mrs Ensor but the binoculars got broken." None of his companions had realised how concerned he'd been by the calamity but if they had, all would have expected Pat to respond the way she did.

"Well thank heavens for that. They weren't much good anyway and now that they're out of the way we can look out for a better pair."

It had been a day without television, computer games, shops or gadgets and with the days' only anxiety laid to rest it had been just about perfect.

* * *

Sarah drew up outside Graham's house and twisted in her seat, "Well, I'm shattered, but what a lovely day!"

Graham took her by the arm and reached across until he was able to give her a hug and kiss, "Too right it has and all thanksh to you."

She wagged her finger at him, "Thanks, but I see it as a team effort. It wouldn't have happened without you two." He gave her a half-smile of acknowledgement but she saw caution in his eyes and sensed there was more. "Is there something else, something you want to talk about?"

He looked down at his lap and gave a sigh, "There is shomething we need to talk about but it has nothing to do with Jimmy or today. I don't want to spoil today so it can wait until after the holiday." He looked up at her then, "It's another cashe, a boy named Timothy."

Her heart skipped a beat. Any reluctance to discuss it on a bank holiday was lost to the overriding realisation that they were working together again, dealing with issues that meant so much to her. Issues she spent most of her waking hours trying to check, stop or more often only impede. "Oh my. Well you know I couldn't leave here now, without knowing the details. I think we'd better have another cup of tea don't you."

Chapter 7

The following morning Nancy rose early so that she could finish her cleaning jobs by mid-morning. They were both exhausted from the previous days' hike and the late night due in part to a mutual desire to re-visit the days' events as they lay in bed. Nancy's foremost thought as she threw teabags into mugs, was that she could have done without a visit to the Calder's house for lunch. A nice quiet day would have been preferable. She hadn't even met these people though she knew they were wealthy and would no doubt have little in common with her. There was a connection with Graham that would override any differences and she hoped that their interest in him would be enough to leave her under the socialising radar. She'd already suggested that he went alone but he wouldn't hear of it, arguing that as a key member of the group she would have to get to know Harvey anyway.

By the time she returned from work she had become irritable in her disinclination and snapped at Graham when he suggested they get a move on to catch the bus. He sensed her anxiety and kept quiet, knowing that it wouldn't help to discuss things.

They caught the bus into Leicester and hurried across to Charles Street for bus number thirty one, which would take them to within one and a half kilometres of the Calder house or would have if they had been there fifteen seconds earlier. The damned thing was still close enough to read the number on the rear panel. Thankfully, at that time of day they were running every eight minutes or so but they were already tight for time.

By the time they passed the Railway station it was clear they were going to be late and a shared anxiety broke the ice. Graham put things into perspective, "OK so we're late, there is nothing we can do but apologishe when we get there. Until then nothing we shay or do will change thingsh so let's be cool." Nancy couldn't argue with that logic and burst out laughing. She rested her head on his shoulder and voiced her concerns, "I can see me being left with his wife who is probably a keen golfer and a member of God knows how many Ladies Circles. I'm going to feel so *little*."

"No you're not, unlessh you allow yourshelf to be. Just go in there, high five them, kick your shoes off, flick a bogie at their hall mirror and ask where the Kahzi is. That'll hold their attention."

"Oh yeah, great and what do you plan on doing?"

He looked surprised by her question, "I'll be watching you, of courshe."

They got off the bus opposite the race course and began the long hasty hike up Stoughton Drive. Both sides of the road were graced with mature trees and huge houses served by in and out drives, until they reached the halfway point, slightly winded and were surprised to see a sign on the right for *Stamford hall* which also declared it to be part of Leicester University. It looked incongruous in the heart of such a wealthy area. They were just as surprised to find a bus stop on their side of the road which indicated the buses numbered eighty stopped there. Clearly, the route continued in the direction they were heading.

Nancy pulled at Graham's arm and asked, "So why didn't we catch the number eighty oh wise one?"

He shrugged, "I didn't know there *wash* a number eighty, or that it went up here."

"Oh for Christ's sake you were the one who checked the bus timetables."

"Ah there's the rub. Jusht because I was the one to make the effort it's all my fault."

Nancy looked up at him as her jaw dropped. She was speechless. After a few more yards she looked ahead, her mouth still open. They continued in silence until another bus stop came into view, and when Nancy spoke it was as much to herself as anyone else,

"I don't know whether to bang *your* head against that bus stop post or mine."

The road seemed to go on forever but at last they reached a three-way junction and turned right into Gartree Road, which had even grander houses though on the right hand side only, overlooking the rolling countryside that lay opposite. The only footpath was on the left hand side and the manicured grass frontages on the right were broken only by tarmac drives, usually two per house. In spite of her anxieties, Nancy was enthralled. A few minutes later they stood opposite their destination. Only one drive they noted, but it lay in the centre of the frontage which was defined by a four foot tall red brick wall that curved in to the entrance where a pair of heavy wrought iron gates lay open. The block-paved drive ventured into the property for about forty yards before dividing into a large circle around a shrubbery that was enclosed by the same brickwork as the one in front. Two cars were parked on the drive but Graham and Nancy paid them little heed. By then their scrutiny had found the house and they both gazed in awe of the huge property. On the right lay two double garages with what looked like living quarters above. To the left lay a huge white house. In the centre, above the front door, was an enormous window. The central building itself was more than they had even imagined, but it was contained within two gabled sections, each the size of Graham's house.

In spite of being late they could only stand and stare for a few moments before Graham voiced their thoughts.

"Shit."

Seconds later he squeezed her hand and they crossed the road with pulses racing. After what seemed an age they stood before the oak door and Graham pressed the brass door bell. Even that had a solid expensive feel to the button action and a tinkling bell sounded from inside the house. Nothing more was heard until the handle rattled slightly and the door was opened. No doubt influenced by the house, Harvey Calder seemed larger than Graham remembered from the single time they'd met, in hospital. But then so was his smile, "Hello, it's so nice to see you, please come in."

He was tall and well-built, with thinning brown hair and a clean-shaven slightly craggy look that was founded on a broad square jaw. His smile seemed to fill the width of his face and was mirrored in his brown eyes. Later, Graham would come to think of it as an honest, open face that belied the intellect and inner strength of the character behind it. As they grew to know him, it became clear how he was able to start a business from nothing and sell it for over eleven million pounds.

He was dressed in casual clothes that screamed quality and Nancy would have put money on the wristwatch being a Rolex. His voice was of medium depth with a distinct Yorkshire brogue that carried a strength and charm. He ushered them in and took their coats. As Nancy handed hers over she explained, "I'm sorry we're so late but we missed the bus connection and then we discovered that we could have picked a better route."

Harvey looked delighted to see them but glanced beyond and realised there was no car. He was startled, "Bloody Hell, I never thought, well, what I mean is I should have asked. It would have been easy to pop across and pick you up." He continued, demonstrating his inborn ability to smother embarrassing moments by addressing them head-on. "You just expect everyone to drive cars today which is extremely thoughtless, forgive me." There was also something in the way he said it that charmed Nancy, an almost blunt inflection yet with a mix of sincerity and simplicity.

Graham responded, "I should have made the effort years ago but, . . ."He finished his explanation with a shrug.

"Well you certainly won't need a bus to get home. Come and meet the wife." He ushered them in and led the way down the hall past a wide staircase that was carpeted in the same deep pile mint green carpet they were walking on and pushed at a door that opened onto a large farmhouse style kitchen. Their first sense was of wood; the floor and wall cupboards bore the honeyed lustre of solid oiled oak as did the refectory table and the eight chairs that nestled against it. Any further appraisal was interrupted by the appearance of the figure that straightened up in front of the oven, hands in bright green oven gloves which held a steaming ovenware dish. The smell was mouth-watering. The oven door was pushed to with a knee and the oven gloves dumped onto the light marble work surface as the lady made her way towards them. She was around the same height as Nancy but carried an extra stone or so. Ample without being fat. She was wearing a cream blouse and beige trousers though the neutrality of colour served to emphasize the wide brown leather belt with a large silver buckle; hallmarked, Nancy had no doubt. Her hair was white and beautifully cut to neck length, encompassing a round clear face that shone with pleasure as she spoke, "Hello, thank you for coming, I've been so looking forward to this." Like Harvey she had retained her Yorkshire accent and looked to him for introductions.

"Graham, Nancy, this is my wife Audrey." He sniffed loudly and added "Who still feeds me like a king." He scanned the kitchen before asking, "Where's madam?"

Audrey was shaking hands with the guests and nodded towards the doorway that was next to the one they had come through, "She nodded off on the settee. It'll do no harm to leave her." The last statement carried an inflection that was clearly an instruction aimed at Harvey who might otherwise have brought her in to show them. In pride of place on the end of the work surface stood a silver picture frame that held a picture of two children; one Nancy recognised from the photograph that had accompanied Harvey's letter to Graham. She asked Audrey for permission before picking the frame up and it was only then that she saw the division. There were two separate photographs in the frame, both of beautiful young girls and Nancy's mouth dropped at the realisation of who the other girl was. They looked similar but one was many years older and the picture had been taken on a beach. Her face alight with joy. It was mother and daughter. She looked at Audrey in shocked dread, "Oh I'm so sorry, this must be a private thing."

Audrey had healed, at least to some extent, but genuine, simple sympathy still cut through her defences. Her eyes welled up and she quickly wiped a tear away, "Don't be, if it hadn't been for you two we'd have lost, . . . everything."

Nancy's eyes shone with tears as she stood before Audrey, still holding the picture frame, unsure of what to do. Here was someone who like her, had lost a child but they had only just met and whilst Audrey seemed a nice person Nancy was still intimidated by the obvious wealth and scale of the surroundings.

Audrey thought for a moment before continuing, the tears still welling, "Harvey told me about your loss. We have a great deal in common." It was enough, for as she spoke they both moved to close the distance separating them, and hugged tightly.

Harvey patted Graham on the shoulder a said quietly, "Come on chum, let's get a beer out of the fridge and sit in the conservatory until the ladies have finished sorting lunch." He led the way through the kitchen and out of a pair of double doors, pausing en route to withdraw two dumpy bottles of beer from the fridge. Graham guessed the conservatory to be the same size as the ground floor of his house, furnished with heavily cushioned cane seating. A large hot tub had been installed at the other end which was clad in timber. The only plant was a tall aspidistra in the far corner next to a door that matched the cladding and which Graham guessed, correctly, led to a changing room. He wouldn't have guessed that it also led to a sauna, steam room, circular full body shower and small gymnasium.

Harvey gestured for him to take a seat and from there he could see a large a manicured lawn surrounded by borders full of colour and life. A medium height hedge marked the distant edge of the lawn but an ornamental gate in the centre suggested that there was more beyond. Nearer to the house brightly coloured outdoor toys lay scattered across the lawn and for want of anything else to say Graham ventured, "It won't be long until a Wendy house arrives."

Harvey chuckled, "Before Esther came along Audrey protected that lot against any threat. Now, if Esther mentioned a pony I wouldn't be surprised to wake up one morning and find one grazing out there. We have someone do the lawns and help out with the vegetable plot but she manages all the borders and the greenhouse."

Graham asked, "What do you do with your time? Sarah tells me that you sold your company."

"Well for the moment I'm being retained on a consultancy basis but that won't last for much longer. I've been a bit of a workaholic really so there aren't any hobbies to turn to and I don't fancy part-time work. One thing I can do is be a better grandparent than I was a parent, and that is something I'm prepared to give a lot of time to." He paused and chuckled, "Sarah seems to have been an excellent go- between. We met up for lunch, I don't know whether she told you." Graham shook his head. "She was very concerned for you and very protective. Wouldn't countenance any contact by me, but she did tell me about your original injury and contact with a dying child. In spite of our first-hand experience it's still a lot to take in you know."

Graham interrupted, "Did you know, Nancy was that child's mother?"

Harvey nodded, "Yes, that's why I thought is wise to leave the ladies together though I must add that Audrey still doesn't know about your er . . . special sense. The rest is no more than she could have gleaned from the newspapers, which includes the sanitised version of events you allowed out to the media."

"Thank you. I am terrified of the pressh getting hold of it and turning me into a circush freak."

"Have you ever thought of working with a research team, say from a university?"

"No." It came out a little sharper than intended and he smiled deprecatorily, "Shame difference really, there'sh big money tied up in research and shomeone would publish a piece sooner or later."

Harvey nodded thoughtfully, "Hmm, I remember that the US military were trying to develop telepathy during the Vietnam war. It seemed to fit with everything else that was going on at that time, flower power, free spirits and hallucinatory drugs. So far as I'm aware it fizzled out, though I'm beginning to see what you mean. I would hate to think of the military taking an interest in you."

Graham looked forward, his eyes unfocused as he considered the prospect. Harvey allowed his guest the silence for a few moments, until he returned to the present with, "You say that Sarah has told you all about me, could you be more explicit. She didn't tell me anything about you."

"Ah, then please forgive the imbalance. First of all I'll tell you what I know about your circumstances. I know where you work, where you used to work, about your injury and the theory that your contact with Nancy's son at the point of death left you with a telepathic ability to sense child abuse. She also told me that your marriage fell apart as a result of your experience, or at least the strangeness of it, I believe that your wife thought you were going mad." Graham nodded in confirmation. "That all led to last Christmas when you sensed Esther's near death state from neglect and suffered a knife attack when you tried to rescue her."

"Did she tell you about the other onesh?"

Harvey tilted his head in anticipation, "No."

Graham was not prepared to venture there, it would take too long and the ladies would be joining them soon, "It can wait until the group meetsh."

"In that case I shall redress the balance and give you some information about me. I was born in 1946 and spent the early part of my childhood learning to hold my own in a large family. We lived in Thorne which was a mining town, my father was a miner, and my childhood was a typical one for that time. Everyone was poor and nobody locked their doors it was such a close-knit community. I have five brothers and one sister. Eight of us packed into a two up two down terraced house with a great deal of make do and mend, yet we never *felt* poor. I remember one of my brothers, can't remember which one, saying that all our clothes had had someone else in them before us and got a thick ear for his observation. The mine closed down through flooding when I was about eight years old and Dad was transferred to the pit near Stainforth though we stayed where we were and he was bussed in. My brothers all followed dad into mining as soon as they could leave school but my sister and I made it into the grammar school. She became a nurse and is now a theatre sister at Jimmy's hospital in Leeds, St James I should say.

I left school with a handful of GCE's and became an apprentice to a local plumbing company and hated every minute. As soon as I got my ticket I was out of the door. That was in the late sixties and jobs were two a penny. I became a sales rep for a company in Chesterfield selling animal feeds and spent most of the time driving around Nottinghamshire and South Yorkshire in a Morris Minor. The farmers didn't take to me because of my age but I persevered and eventually won them over. Farmers are the same anywhere, damned difficult to get to know but if you prove yourself their trust is total. I still keep in touch with some of the families now. Audrey agreed to marry me in nineteen seventy two and within a few months my employer sold out to a much larger farm supply company. I was offered unemployment or a job in their new hardware and feed store. I chose the latter and in nineteen seventy three decided I could do better. Audrey's family hail mainly from around Chesterfield and an uncle had a small industrial unit he let us have for a peppercorn rent. Even so, it was a tough time and as things progressed, more by accident than design, we found ourselves specialising in DIY and craft hobbies. We were lucky and we grafted, it needs both in good measure, but a few years ago I sold the chain of stores for enough to see us out." He added with a wry smile, "If we're careful."

Graham glanced around as if assessing his surroundings, grinning broadly, "Shlumming it you mean?"

"Aye, I'm still a cautious Yorkshireman at heart."

In spite of the prejudice and trepidation he had felt on seeing the house Graham began to like Harvey and his simple honesty. Still grinning he glanced to his left and shrugged, "I'm not sure what category I belong in. Walking wounded I should think."

"That might be true. There can't be many folk with your distinguished features!"

"Ha, distinguishing you mean. I'd better not take up crime," He tapped the crease in his forehead, "I'd not lasht long in an identity parade with this."

Harvey expression became serious, "Do you suffer any after effects?"

"I really don't know. I still get headaches, shometimes terrible ones, but they only come after a hit." He waved his forefinger in a circle by his temple, "A 'hit' is the name we give to any of my special dreams. My ex decided I was either mad or epileptic and the doctors wanted to run a bunch of tests but that would entail telling them everything, otherwise it would be like teshting someone for loss of balance without knowing they'd had a leg off."

Harvey finished his beer and set it down on the floor. "Fair enough, but setting the trigger, or cause to one side, what if there is a physical flaw in there," He tapped the side of his head, "That might show up on a scan. I could arrange for a very discreet series of tests down in London. I'd be very happy to . . . "

Graham was shaking his head, "Thank you but I'd rather keep this thing under wrapsh."

Just then the ladies joined them, each was holding a wine glass filled with a clear fizzy liquid. Audrey answered her husbands' enquiring look, "Yes, it's only lunchtime and we're drinking gin and tonics. Strong ones." Audrey had followed Nancy into the conservatory and it took a few moments for Graham to notice the small figure clinging to her leg. The blonde curls were most evident but Esther buried her face in Audrey's trousers, shuffling along to keep pace and remain out of view. Harvey stood and walked into the kitchen while the ladies sat in two of the other chairs. Audrey set her glass down on a small table and gathered Esther up onto her lap. En route she risked a quick look at the stranger before snuggling into the comfort of her grandma's arms. "You are a silly," murmured Audrey as she stroked Esther's curls, "Nancy and Graham have come to say hello to you."

She was slim but obviously healthy, dressed in a pale green T shirt and blue dungarees, but Graham was smitten by the bright green canvas shoes that were rocking to and fro. Shoes in miniature, the epitome of everything that stood for infancy. His thoughts were broken by a tap on his shoulder by the beer bottle on offer from Harvey, "Here you go, not a lot in these things is there."

Lunch was delicious. A dressed rocket salad and warm focaccia bread accompanied the lasagne Audrey had removed from the oven when they arrived and the burgundy wine was a full, heavy red that was gentle on the tongue and at thirteen per cent proof, savage on the senses. Both sides had spent the morning worrying about the meeting but time slipped by unnoticed as the conversation rolled on without pause. Esther occupied the high chair at the end of the table between her grandparents and by the end of the main course had regained enough confidence to add her own two penny worth to the conversation. They finished with home-made vanilla ice cream after which Nancy helped Audrey clear the table while Harvey organised the coffee percolator.

Graham took the opportunity to slide across and get better acquainted with Esther by teaching her to put a bit of bread on the handle of a spoon and striking down on the bowl as hard as possible, to see how far the missile could travel. She caught on quickly and delightedly claimed a slice of bread from Graham which she tore into airworthy pieces. By the time coffee arrived the floor was littered. Nancy rolled her eyes, "Please excuse him."

Audrey grinned in delight as a piece of bread shot over her shoulder, "Nonsense, I think he's made a friend for life." Coffee was distributed and while Esther was occupied Audrey took the opportunity to talk about Claire. "Graham, I know that Harvey has already thanked you but I want to as well. I *need* to thank you and to make clear just what it means. Unless the nightmare happens in your family you can never know how devastating drug addiction is. When you see your child succumb a piece of you shrivels in horror and in time you realise that there is nothing you can do. I'm not sure I have words enough to describe the experience, but when we were told of her death we'd become so estranged we didn't know Esther existed. It was a terrible time, you see, but no matter how far apart we'd drifted, she was still our child and we grieved for her. At the same time we were frightened for Esther; she was so close to death."

Harvey reached across and took her hand. His gesture caught her by surprise and she caught her breath, unable to say more. He took over, "See, nowadays, if you're lucky, you have perhaps twelve or fourteen years to instil a sense of right from wrong, good and bad, do's and don'ts. After that your children go out into the world and face heaven knows what. As a parent you can only hope that the examples you set are enough, but it's only a hope. Drugs know no bounds, they blight the lives of people from all backgrounds and parents can't be there when temptation shows up. We lost a beautiful, loving child to drugs and realise there was little we could have done but when they told us that we had a granddaughter it felt like an act of divine mercy." Graham was startled to see a glaze of moisture on Harvey's eyes when he continued. "You were instrumental in granting us that gift and there is nothing I wouldn't do for you. That is my oath and I want you to remember it."

The silence that followed had an eerie quality until even Esther sensed something unusual and demanded to be freed from her seat.

It broke the spell and Audrey gathered the infant up, realising that a nappy change was called for too.

Their cups were empty and Harvey stood up, "Tea or coffee?"

Nancy looked up, "We should really be going now, you've had us for long enough."

Harvey would have none of it, "Nonsense, you can have another drink before you go. Now what's it to be."

His guests replied in unison, "Tea please."

Audrey returned to her seat and sat Esther on her lap while she laid the selection of toys she had carried through from the other room. By now Esther was perfectly comfortable with the visitors, particularly after being shown the missile trick and was delighted when Graham joined her on the xylophone. He was sitting at the opposite corner of the table and soon tired of stretching but Esther would have none of it. In no time she had engineered her transfer, with toys, to Graham's lap and play commenced.

Audrey and Harvey looked on in delight until Esther turned towards Graham and noticed the strange cleft in his forehead with an open unabashed gaze. With the open honesty of a child she reached up with a finger to trace and investigate the feature. Audrey called out, "No Esther" and began to reach forward for the child's arm but Graham held up his hand, "No, she's jusht being curious.

They have no inhibitions at this age, it's delightful. Anyway, I think my kidsh are entitled."

Nancy glanced quickly at Audrey who was looking faintly puzzled and pressed her foot firmly against Graham's, saying firmly, "Graham, do you realise the time. We must be going, now." She turned to Audrey and added, "We didn't intend to abuse your hospitality like this, it's gone four."

Audrey was forced to return to the moment and with feeling, replied. "Nonsense, we've *thoroughly* enjoyed it, all three of us. If you wouldn't mind I'd look forward to repeating it, soon."

Nancy smiled, "Thanks, I'd like that, and I know that Graham would too." She glanced across at him, still sitting opposite with Esther on his knee and looking flushed.

Harvey was privy to the hidden meaning in Graham's statement and decided to support Nancy's initiative, "Well if you're sure I'll call you a cab. I had planned to drive you back but I had a bit too much wine."

Nancy raised her hand, "No Harvey, please don't bother, we can catch the bus back, especially now that I know we can catch one just around the corner." She cast a meaningful glance at Graham who put both hands up in surrender, without a word.

Harvey had already dialled and moments later gave someone his request for a taxi. It was obviously someone he used regularly since he only gave them his name but Nancy winced as she considered the cost. She couldn't refuse to use the taxi now it was on its way though she decided to lessen the cost by being dropped in the city rather than go all the way across to Mapton.

Even then conversation continued in a relaxed fashion, albeit in a generalised way. After just a few minutes the doorbell rang and Harvey checked to make sure it was the cab. Coats were retrieved, hugs and handshakes exchanged and sloppy kisses were furnished by Esther, who remained on the doorstep with Audrey while Harvey walked to the car with them and opened the door for Nancy, bending as he did to tell the driver to put it on his account.

His smile and gaze was warm and genuine when he straightened, "Thank you so much for coming Nancy, we've enjoyed it."

Without thinking she stood on tip toe and gave him a peck on the cheek, "And so have we. Thanks."

Five minutes later, the two couples were over a mile apart and both were reviewing the event. The departure afforded them the freedom to express their true feelings and all four participants said what a lovely time they'd had. Esther meanwhile, had installed herself on Audrey's lap at the table and having found a spoon in a saucer was casting around for ammunition.

She handed her card through the partition window and watched the secretary read it then do a double take. "Mrs Tenson is expecting me."

"Yes Mrs Whiting, I saw your name in the diary," she didn't add, 'But it didn't say what you were!' "I'll let her know you're here." Sarah noted that her card was delivered to a room across the corridor rather than employ the telephone. Once there a full entrance was made rather than leaning through the doorway and the door was closed behind her. No doubt the Head Teacher was being given an opportunity to deliver the gossip. The immediate exit indicated that it was not to be.

Angela Tenson was forty eight years old and had been head of the school for a little over ten years, long enough to see her role change from a Head *teacher*, into a Chief Executive, answerable to the staff, parents, public and education authority for health and safety, employment law, budget control, curriculum-based statistics, public relations and finally, it seemed, the education of her charges. Years earlier, in happier times, she had been able to schedule some slots in each week to teach, but she no longer had time for such indulgences.

She dressed impeccably and still managed to squeeze into some size ten dresses and although her short dark hair had begun to show light flecks of grey, she still exuded the appearance and airs of a successful woman, comfortable with her role. Softly-spoken and amenable with her governors or with concerned parents, yet crisply authoritative when necessary. Like so many people she needed to be a master of many situations. With the visitor's card in her hand she strode out of her office to meet the Child Protection officer and wondered what was in store.

She opened the security door, another modern-day necessity, and stepped forward, extending her hand, "Mrs Whiting, I'm Angela Tenson, the Head, please come through."

Sarah declined the offer of tea or coffee and settled into, or rather onto the hard chair facing the Head's desk. They spent a few moments discussing generalities before Angela placed her elbows on the desk and clasped her hands. "You indicated in your telephone call that you wanted to discuss an issue with me, in your professional capacity, yet," she paused and glanced down to the open diary at her side, "You thought it best to keep this visit unofficial. Almost a contradiction in terms I think."

In that moment Sarah realised that she had made a mistake. This woman was a consummate professional unwilling to play at being 'off the record.' Anything important enough to involve a CPO should be official, there were no half-measures.

She bowed her head and collected her thoughts. Once again, she needed to create a believable version of events that didn't include mention of a battered middle-aged man who had telepathic connections with damaged children.

Graham and Nancy had looked to her for help. She was long past playing the devil's advocate and believed all that Graham told her. More tellingly, whilst she knew how sincere Graham was his natural diffidence could easily leave a horrible situation understated. If he spoke of cruelty or abuse, she knew now that every word was to be taken literally. The only times she had seen him become aggressive were when he discovered cruelty first-hand and even then he had more often than not become a victim of violence himself.

She had promised to do something, and now she was making a hash of it. After taking a deep breath she began again, remembering the name plaque on the door. "Ms Tenson, I am unable to make this official at this stage because my informant has insisted on anonymity. That said, the information I received was compellingly complete and detailed a *culture* of bullying in one of your classes, *including* verbal abuse from the form teacher, to such an extent that a victim was pushed to the point of suicide. I don't want to introduce too many specifics because to do so may compromise individuals who shouldn't be isolated by any actions you take, but I must tell you that the form teacher is a," she glanced down at her pad, "Mrs Stretton." She took another deep breath, "I am therefore asking you to initiate some form of remedial control, though I realise how difficult that may be."

"Do you. Do you really Mrs," she glanced down at the card on her desk, "Whiting. Because, let me be quite clear about this. You want me, *as* a professional to accuse another professional of gross misconduct, based on an anonymous tip-off. A professional who has taught children of the same age for over twenty years, and now teaches children of parents who were also taught by her, and who still regard her with awe. Since this is an *unofficial* meeting I am not obliged to furnish you with any information, particularly when you have slandered one of my teachers." Sarah tried to interrupt but was stayed by the Head's raised hand, palm outwards, "I use the word 'slander' deliberately, since your allegations seem to be based on hearsay, but the information I am prepared to impart is that I have never received a complaint about Mrs Stretton. Never. I am therefore unable to act on a second-hand complaint from someone who doesn't even trust me to be discreet."

"Ms Tenson, just because no-one has complained yet doesn't mean it isn't happening. I really do understand your position and your defence of a colleague but all I'm asking is that you perhaps monitor the situation."

"That suggests that we don't already manage ourselves adequately Mrs Whiting. I can assure you that all schools undergo more scrutiny now than they have ever done. I'm very sorry, but in the absence of anything specific, there is very little I can do."

It was clear that the meeting was over, Sarah's card was dropped into one of the desk drawers and the head looked at her expectantly. Sarah tried to contain her growing anger. She had been slapped down and made to feel like a playground tell-tale when she knew, without any doubt that a child had been driven to suicide and saved by incredible chance. She stood and dived into her attaché case for another card before leaning forward and dropping it on the desk. "Thank you for sparing me the time Ms Tenson, you should keep that one to hand rather than dump it out of sight, because if any child is driven to do anything dreadful I will come back in a *very* official capacity and you *will* have cause to regret acting the way you have."

"How dare you come in here and threat . . ." The heads words were cut off by the sight of Sarah heading out of the door which was then firmly closed.

Sadly, both *professionals* would regret the way they had handled things. Sarah had been driven by concern yet unable to prove anything. Angela was an executive officer trying to make sense of a system that changed almost monthly and was based on the enforcement of regulations rather than the encouragement of excellence.

In the silence that followed Sarah's departure she reviewed her handling of the situation and regretted the high-handed way she had treated her visitor. It just seemed such a weak allegation about a teacher who had always stayed off the radar, when the younger ones, just out of college, needed so much attention. Sadly, economics demanded that they employ a significant number of young and inexperienced staff since senior teachers were too far up the pay scales and salaries were easily the largest component of the budget.

Hardly a day went by without a meeting with at least one of the governors and her deputy, appointed just six months earlier, was proving to be very needy. He *had* to start making decisions himself without referring everything to her. All that and SATS, Ofsted, *and* parents who were becoming more belligerent by the day.

Of course there were occasions when she had heard some shouting as she passed Mary's classroom but there was never any question of unruly classes. Furthermore, she had never received a complaint *and* she had to respect over twenty years' service. It was thanks to Mary's management of her class that teaching assistants could be assigned to less experienced teachers.

She wondered how Sarah had come by the information. It was obviously acquired in the course of her work, probably in one of her home visits and if the source was a child in that peer group the tale would have suffered the embellishments of a seven year old. For that matter it could have been parents trying to deflect some of the official attention they were getting. But why keep it unofficial? What was she expected to do with that? *Unofficially* disrupt a class and wreck a career? Her irritation returned as she mentally cited examples of the harm caused by the media to all sorts of professional people by employing unsubstantiated slights and innuendos.

Even so, she sighed and cast out a mental apology to Sarah for the high-handed way she'd behaved, it could have handled it better.

Finally, she decided on a compromise and settled down to write a memorandum to all staff, emphasising the need to watch for and eradicate bullying. She could do no more.

Sarah agreed with the head on that one count only. It could have been handled better, by both of them. She should have provided specifics, perhaps even identifying Timothy. Head teachers should be professional enough to act without divulging the victim's name, but the bloody woman hadn't acted very professionally that morning. After only a little more thought in that vein she realised that in this case Timothy's name wouldn't need to be mentioned. If half of what Graham had told her was true the child was isolated from the pack anyway and everyone would know it was him. She decided to check the department's records to see if he or his family had been visited before but the problem of how to keep him out of things remained. Perhaps a meeting of the group was called for.

That Tuesday had started altogether better for Graham and Nancy. A plain brown envelope looked like any other bill until Nancy turned it over and saw their address written in green ink. Inside she found a piece of foolscap paper folded around another, smaller envelope. The paper bore a note, written in the same green ink;

* * *

Dear Graham and Nancy,

Jimmy refused to go to bed until he had written the enclosed letter. He was getting himself into such a state I gave in. We both look forward to seeing you on Saturday.

Best regards,
Pat Ensor.

The smaller envelope contained his letter.

Dear Graham and Aunty Nancy,

Thank you for the picnic and walking. The bluebells were pretty and Mrs Ensor likes them too. Next time I will pick some for you. Jumping off the rocks was great but Chox wouldn't do it. She always wags her tail and she pants a lot. I love Chox.
Can we have a picnic next Sunday please.

Love Jimmy

* * *

She passed it over to Graham who sat on the other side of the breakfast table 'limbering up' on his daily trio of Sudokos. "Last Shunday," he waved the letter in the air, "I was moved by how well-mannered Jimmy was. I reckon his mum did a great job while she was alive and now look at hish life. Like shomething out of a Dicken's novel."

"Speaking of Dickens, this cleaning maid has to get a move on to clean those solicitor's offices or it'll be the workhouse for both of us."

Chapter 8

"It was all very unpleasant I can tell you."

Graham pictured Timothy and recalled the promise made to him, "But Sarah, we can't leave it there. That kid was ready to kill himshelf."

"Goodness, I *know* that!" Sarah's voice rose automatically as she shared his concern, "But there is nothing more I can do short of telling everyone the truth, and what would that do, I ask you. Probably get me certified."

Graham realised how impotent yet concerned Sarah was feeling and lowered his voice, "I can see that. Ish there *anything* we can do?"

"Right now, the only thing I could think of was to call a meeting of the group and that isn't as daft as it sounds. Remember, we have a Doctor and a Detective who might be able to suggest another approach."

"True, and it would be better than doing nothing."

"My thoughts exactly. Meanwhile, we need you to meet him as planned on Friday to keep his spirits up. It's bound to help if he knows others care about him."

Sho when would it be possible to meet?"

"Ah, well I hope you don't mind but I've already spoken to the others and we are all OK for next Tuesday evening if that's good for you. That's a week today."

Nancy was flicking over the pages of her diary and finally spoke to the telephone which, as usual, was on 'hands free', "Yes, that's fine," she closed her eyes briefly in anxious anticipation, at the prospect of cooking for so many and trying to seat them around a small kitchen table, it was their turn, "Do you want to meet here?" She almost gasped in relief when Sarah replied, "Adam has beaten you to it. Apparently he knows the owner of a Sikh restaurant on the Narborough road that is little more than a house but he assures me that the food is superb. All vegetarian though. They are willing to let us have a room to ourselves and the cost, including soft drinks would be very reasonable. He assures me that no-one will leave hungry."

"Brilliant idea, and it's only a couple of minutes walk from our bus route."

"Excellent." She gave them the address and then thought to add, "Actually, when I said I'd spoken to everyone I didn't include Mr Calder. It seemed more of a business agenda than one to welcome a new member. What do you think?"

Graham made to speak but Nancy beat him to it, "I think it would be good to include him. We can show that the group isn't just talk, we aim to achieve things."

Graham was nodding vigorously, "Do you want ush to contact him? If he can't make it we'll still have the meeting though."

"Good thinking and yes please, I'd appreciate it if you made contact, just let me know if he says yes in case they need to know numbers for the food. Oh, dammit, I forgot to tell you the time. Is seven OK?"

"No problem, and I'll get in touch with Harvey." There was little more to add and Nancy soon ended the call. She had been dreading having to play host and welcomed the postponement. Nevertheless, the next meeting was unavoidably theirs.

Harvey was delighted to hear from them and brushed their thanks for the lunch away, promising that everyone enjoyed the occasion, including Esther who was propelling everything from cereals to custard across the kitchen with her spoon. He thought of them having to catch a bus and offered them a lift, but Harding had beaten him to it with an arrangement to collect them at six thirty.

The rest of the week passed by without incident and when Graham finished his shift at teatime on Friday he walked across the front of the store to see if there was any sign of Nancy and Timothy. He was delighted to see them both in the cafe area with mugs in front of them and exchanged waves before heading to the staff room where he could shed the heavy, high visibility clothing he was required to wear. He made his way into the store and sat down opposite Nancy and next to Timothy.

"Timothy, I'm delighted to shee you."

The boy looked up and smiled, "Hello."

Graham grinned and nodded at the foil wrappers on the table adding, "I am also delighted to shee that you two haven't eaten all the Kit Kats." He dug into his anorak pocket and retrieved three more bars, "Fancy another one?"

The reticence shown a week earlier had gone and Timothy didn't hesitate, "Thank you Mr Parsons."

"Who told you my name was Parsons?"

Cautiously, Tim replied, "Er, Nancy."

Graham leaned towards him conspiratorially, "See thish happens all the time. It'sh OK for you to call Nancy, Nancy but there you are calling Graham Mr Parshons. We men need to know where to stand so you go ahead and call me Graham. OK?"

Tim responded with a nod and sought refuge in the cavernous top of his mug of hot chocolate.

They allowed a minute or two to pass before Graham asked, "Sho maytee, how have things been thish week?" The body signals were clear and his heart sank as the boy shrugged and without looking up murmured, "OK."

Clearly, nothing had changed and Graham felt a rising concern. He'd given the boy some hope last week and in the light of Sarah's experience had less to offer him now. "So, the're shtill picking on you." Said more like a statement than question. Tim gave another small, eloquent shrug but said nothing. Graham lowered his head towards the boy, "I'm sorry maytee. I did have a word with that lady I told you about and she had a word with the head teacher but she said that they needed to know who was being bullied before she to do anything to shtop it. That would mean telling her your name."

Tim continued to stare at his drink but was slowly shaking his head. Graham could certainly identify with the desire for anonymity and had expected it, "I know maytee, you don't want to do that."

He looked with Nancy and shrugged his shoulders, his expression clearly seeking input from her. Their meeting had such an air of intensity that she scanned the tables around them to make sure that no-one was showing an interest before leaning forward, "Tim, have you spoken to your Mum about the bullying yet?"

He looked up immediately and said "No," and dropped his gaze just as quickly. How could he explain things he didn't understand yet knew with absolute certainty. He would need to be many years older to understand his mother's store of resentment and hatred, stocked daily with the bitterness of being alone, without the partner she thought would support them for life but who walked out instead, to set up home with her friend; *former* friend, leaving her with the small box of a house and the kid. She didn't want another partner or the renewal of faith and trust a new relationship would entail. In any event who would want her with 'baggage', the name she had heard someone give to another man's child.

Instead, she sustained her inner self with an emotional gruel that blighted any love she might have once had for Timothy. He came to represent the great yawning flaw in her life and as a result *his* life was an emotional desert, devoid of love, care, a hug, kiss, a smile of encouragement or kind word. He was fed and clothed, period.

Her ex's father, Timothy's grandfather, still called and weathered the 'chill' for the sake of his grandson.

One thing was certain, Tim couldn't go home and cry, or share, or expect support.

They sat at the table in troubled silence until, for want of anything better to do Graham patted the boy on the shoulder as a gesture of support. The darkness didn't come but as contact was made Graham was engulfed with a sickening despair that caught his breath and forced him to lower his head in submission. He had never experienced a void like it, an isolation that defied measure, but he knew one thing with absolute certainty and more dreadfully, he now understood the *motivation*. This child was preparing for suicide again.

Nancy recognised the signs and shuffled across to be opposite Graham and take his hand. She didn't say anything but he was deathly pale and a sheen of moisture had appeared on his brow. He seemed lost in thought for a short while but returned to the present with a smile and squeeze of her hand. She didn't know how poignant her love and support was at that moment or how it emphasised the lost state he had just experienced.

He made a decision, "Timothy, I'm going to tell you something now that is very, very secret." He waited until the child looked up before tapping the side of his head and continuing. "Do you remember when I told you about how I can shee things." Timothy nodded, his expression confirmed that he was still a wary but worthy custodian of the secret. "Well I think there is something elshe you should know, but," His forefinger appeared between them, pointing upwards, "It is very, very shecret too. Do you promish to keep it to yourshelf?"

It was the continuance of a very special experience, one he had never known before. No thumps, pinches, threats or petty theft; he wasn't the runt. Someone was treating him with kindness and respect and he was being trusted with something very secret; not a kid's secret but one involving grown-ups. He nodded and continued to look at Graham as he spoke, "I promise. I didn't tell anyone about your other secret."

"Good man! I knew you could be trushted. Shometimes I can see things but I need help to put them right. That help comes from a shpecial group of people who know about my gift. There are only a few people in it but there is a doctor, a policeman and a lady who worksh with children who are being treated badly. That lady tried to help but becaushe she couldn't be shpecific about *who* was being bullied no-one wanted to help. See, the lady wouldn't mention your name because you wanted that kept secret. Do you undershtand?"

Timothy nodded but said nothing.

"Now I want you to trusht me because that group of people are meeting next week and I will talk to them all about you. One way or another we *will* short this out for you, I promish. Do you trusht me?"

Graham would never know for certain whether he saw or sensed it, but a spark of hope appeared in the child's darkness when he nodded in confirmation.

"Good, then in that cayshe we can meet up again next Friday, just like today, and we can tell you what'sh been decided." He paused before carrying on, as though he'd had an afterthought, "That also means that you have to take care of yourself. Promish me, no tablets or anything like that."

Tim was still nodding, "I promise Graham."

"Well done maytee, we'll short it out, you see."

They didn't discuss the matter very much after seeing Tim off for two reasons. Firstly, it seemed enough, at least for the moment that they should raise it at the meeting on the following Tuesday evening. Secondly, they had a bigger than usual shop to do. They were hosting Jimmy for the weekend and were determined to make it a success.

Dinner was a quick and easy pasta bake and since there was little worth watching on television they decided to make an early night of it so that they would be in good form for the visit. But once under the covers they both discovered a need for the physical comfort of lovemaking. Gently giving and demanding without haste but with a mutual aim of nurturing the other's senses toward the matchless bond of simultaneous completion. Later, Graham lay on his back and wondered at the physical side of their relationship. They had first made love only five months earlier but since then a voyage of exploration and discovery had granted them a closeness he could never have dreamed of; had never known before, in twenty three years of marriage to Ann. He wondered if she had discovered as much with her new partner and rather hoped she had.

But that night the dream returned.

* * *

He was awake, unable to sleep yet afraid not to. He was holding something soft and yielding to his chest, tightly, and knew the warmth of a hot water bottle down near his feet. There was still light in the sky but the day was clearly over and the sounds of traffic were fading, allowing the sounds from a television downstairs to become clearer. They were a comfort and more. He sensed that they were important and needed to continue. He felt tired but knew that sleep wouldn't come. Feelings of loneliness and fear remained with him from the last dream just as he remembered the tiny sounds that seemed amplified, clearly audible in spite of the television downstairs. The programme ended and another began. Thank you, thank you, it was something worth watching. Sleep began to seep into his consciousness as though sanctioned by the comfort of an acceptable TV programme.

He sensed a sudden and frightening snatch into wakefulness, his pulse racing as he tried to focus on his surroundings and whatever was wrong. Silence. His heartbeat felt like moths' wings as the silence rose up over him like a cold wraith and once more he knew a dreadful sense of threat yet knew what it was to be defenceless. A door downstairs opened and closed; he knew then that a click of a light switch would be followed by the creak of the bottom step. He stopped breathing.

* * *

The dream blurred, leaving him in a terrified limbo until finally, reluctantly it seemed, it let go and Graham clawed his way out of bed gasping for air. His pyjamas were soaked just as he knew that his side of the quilt would be.

Resigned to another night of shelter under a dry towel he made his way to the bathroom and whilst there took the opportunity to pre-empt the night-time demands of a middle-aged prostate.

They left the house together the next morning; Graham to work and Nancy, via two bus journeys, to pick Jimmy up. They'd telephoned him two days earlier, on Thursday evening, to confirm that his weekend stay with them was still on. With a mother's intuition Nancy had insisted on making the call to allay any anxieties Jimmy might have had. Her insight was acknowledged when she finally, in spite of capricious bus service, pressed the visitor keypad at the home.

Pat Ensor greeted Nancy like a friend, with a hug and patent warmth. She took a half-step to one side, revealing a boy whose grin connected his ears, "Hello aunty Nancy."

Nancy opened her arms and cried out, "Jimmy! My God, look at you, I think you've grown in a week!"

With hugs exchanged by all, Pat sought control, "Right then Master Everard, shoes and jacket if you please. Then pop into the kitchen for a glass of squash before you go. Nancy and I will be having a cup of tea." He disappeared upstairs and Pat linked her arm in Nancy's, guiding her towards the kitchen door, "Your telephone call last Thursday was inspired. He was getting himself into such a state as the week wore on, you can imagine the sort of thing, moody, tantrums, sulks, disobedience. Your call worked instantly. From that moment he turned back into the excited and delightful little boy we saw last Sunday night." She paused then, with one hand on the kitchen door, "You know, I don't see many children change as much. He was in a very bad place before he met you two. It would be nice to think his Mum could have comfort from that."

Nancy murmured something between thanks and agreement but was too moved to add more.

Pat produced two mugs of tea and a tin of fig roll biscuits with a note of apology, "If I get any with chocolate on they're gone in a flash and these are treated with scorn, which means the grown-ups get a look in. Even these don't last long though." As if on cue Jimmy ran into the kitchen and dropped his jacket across the back of a chair before addressing the glass of orange squash Pat had put out for him. Holding the glass with one hand he reached into the biscuit tin and removed two. Pat looked at Nancy and raised an eyebrow. He was desperate to go and for a while, stared at the steaming mugs, willing the teas to chill. Grown-ups talked such a lot and were sooo boring, yet he dare not interrupt with a request for haste. Finally, he placed one hand on top of the other and rested his chin on them, while maintaining a steady beat on one of his chair legs by kicking his legs to and fro.

Pat reacted first, "I think Jimmy is ready to go now." She turned to look at him,"Go and get your things; we'll have a last check for anything you've forgotten and you can get on your way." He pitched himself off the chair and ran from the room. As soon as she deemed him to be out of earshot Pat asked Nancy, "Look, I nearly forgot to mention it but Jimmy does have accidents at night. Do you want to borrow a mattress protector?"

"No, thanks. We've already bought a couple. Somebody, Sarah or perhaps you, has already mentioned it." Jimmy ran back into the room with the single strap of his black canvas satchel across his body and over the shoulder. The satchel was full to bulging with a variety of small toys and a change of clothes, all duly sanctioned by Mrs Ensor who helped him into his jacket en route to the front door. Nancy laughed, "You're just like Chocks, if you were on a lead we'd be pulled along by now." At the mention of her name his face lit up, "Is Chocks coming with us?"

"No, sorry, not this time. We're off to the city centre today." He nodded his understanding but his disappointment was evident. Nancy thought back to their last outing, when she'd expressed doubts about taking a dog and thought 'Did I ever get that wrong!'.

The bus was in sight before they even reached the small queue at stop sign which they agreed was an auspicious start to their trip. Little was said on the trip but he sat next to the window paying avid attention to the world passing by. The morning was spent buying a few oddments Nancy had on a shopping list and visiting shops that would take a long time to describe when he sat with Mrs Ensor on the following Monday. One was a gadget shop full of designer tools and toys, many of which were 'hands on', like the radio-controlled truck. In *Boots* He was delighted to find the nail boards Mrs Ensor had asked him to look out for and dug the one pound coin he'd been entrusted with out of his pocket before Nancy had chance to find her purse. After carefully counting the twenty one pence change he put it back into his trouser pocket where it would remain until he handed the goods over.

One store claimed to be offering thousands of ex-catalogue items at outrageously cheap prices and a glance inside suggested that they really did have a large range, from bicycles to back scratchers. The photographic section was contained behind a counter where the goods were stocked in glass cabinets but on the counter lay a stacked display of pocket binoculars at a clearance price of only fourteen pounds. They both tried one and while Nancy thought they were well-priced and reasonable quality Jimmy was enthralled, viewing the inside of a shop on the opposite side of the street. Compared to the plastic ones he had tried to use on Beacon Hill they were fantastic. As they left the shop Nancy put the box in her bag and announced, "That, young sir is going to mean doing the drying up after each meal this weekend." He was nodding furiously before she had finished and added, "And I'll do them next weekend as well!" before realising his temerity in assuming they would have him for another weekend. They walked for a while in silence until Nancy noticed his embarrassment and perceived it's cause. She could offer no guarantees without agreement from Graham but she did ruffle his hair and give him a hug. That would do for the moment.

Suddenly it was lunchtime time and both were famished. At Nancy's suggestion they went to a pizza restaurant that offered a lunchtime special comprising of one visit to the salad bar and modest choice of pizza's laid out in buffet style on an 'all you can eat' basis.

The salad bar was a delicious selection of many things but the bowls were quite small and only one visit was allowed. So Jimmy was at first anxious and then delighted as Nancy demonstrated how to double the bowls' capacity by inserting a boundary wall of over-lapped cucumber slices around the edge of a full bowl. They were both giggling as they inched back to their tables and he was secretly delighted when a youth at the next table called to his companion, "Hey, look what the kid's done," The companion replied, "Wow, that's neat!" Since drink refills were free his intake of fizzy pop was excessive, but who was counting. Finally, they started on the pizzas which were, well, just pizzas really.

Nancy had planned on catching a bus out to Freemen's Park but since the weather was reasonable and they had an excessive amount of food and drink to work off they agreed to walk there. Lunch, with Nancy's anarchy, marked a threshold in their relationship, from which he began to truly relate to her, initiating conversations and even trying his hand at telling jokes; badly enough as it turned out for the attempts to be as funny as the punch lines might have been, if he'd remembered them. Within fifteen minutes they reached the cinema complex and settled for the relatively modest levels of gratuitous violence, obesity, anarchy and cruelty to dogs by watching 'Garfield the Movie'.

By four o clock they were back in town waiting for a bus home and reviewing the funnier moments of the movie. Since the same bus passed Graham's workplace they decided to continue their journey and pay him a surprise visit. Whilst there they would partake of what Nancy explained was a routine drink and *kit Kat*.

He was delighted to see them and since his shift ended just ten minutes later he was able to join them in the cafeteria where he listened to a joint account of their day in Leicester. Jimmy wrestled his satchel up onto his lap and produced his binoculars for Graham's appraisal, directing him in various directions towards a variety of subjects and relishing the approval that followed. Nancy pushed her biscuit along to the child and shrugged at Graham, "I was showing off at lunch by demonstrating how to double the amount of salad you could get in a bowl and what with that and pizzas I'm still stuffed."

"Well don't expect any sympathy from me; not when I had to put up with a cheeshe batch!" He looked at Jimmy and added, "Thanksh to you we are having one of my favourites tonight. Sausages, mashed potatoes and onion gravy, followed by shyrup pudding."

Jimmy grinned and nodded in appreciation. Graham had remembered their first meeting in hospital where that meal was cited as a favourite, though Nancy scolded, "Graham! That was going to be a surprise for when we got home."

"Shorry," he winked at Jimmy, "But half the enjoyment is in the antishipation. Now we can all look forward to it."

Nancy sighed, "Well if we don't start back you'll be having them for breakfast, so move it oh wise one."

* * *

The sky was beginning to show signs of light and the dawn chorus had begun when Nancy and Jimmy sat at the kitchen table with hot chocolates and a packet of chocolate *hob nobs*, his favourite biscuits. He looked pale and shivered slightly, though he was well and truly cocooned in Graham's dressing gown which almost covered his feet.

Nancy had been woken an hour earlier by shuffling noises coming from the guest bedroom. At first she thought their guest was getting up to go to the toilet; they had left the landing light on for that reason, but then she recognised the sound of linen being dragged from the bed. She crept out of bed and gently pushed the door to Jimmy's room open to find the child standing by the side of his bed, staring up at her in horror. His hair was tousled and he was crying in shame. His pyjama bottoms hung in sodden folds as he tried to pull the bedding onto the floor with the jerky movements of someone only just awake.

"I'm sorry Aunty Nancy, I didn't mean to do it." He flinched as she dropped down on to her knees beside him but fell against her when she wrapped her arms around him. "Shhhhh, don't be sorry, we can sort this out in a jiffy." She held him for some time, gently shushing and stroking his back until the sobs eased, but then the chill of wet clothing began to take effect and when he began to shiver it was time to get him into warm clothes. Pat Ensor had thought to pack a change of pyjamas and Nancy made light work of changing the bed. The routine nature of having him help to pull the sheets straight helped to soothe his anxiety and after wrapping him up in Graham's dressing gown Nancy suggested a hot chocolate drink and biscuits.

Jimmy didn't know how to stop wetting beds just as he didn't know how to stop feeling sad when he thought of his mum and his dog, Sally. He didn't understand many of the things that were happening in his life but he *did* know that Nancy was the best Aunty in the world and he loved her, loads.

When she tucked him back into bed the sky was light but it didn't hinder his return to dreamland, where this time Chocks waited to chase him through the bluebells.

Sunday morning's blue sky surrendered to a sullen grey in keeping with the forecast which also gave a seventy per cent likelihood of rain. All this information was passed on to Graham when they took a cup of tea up to him. Jimmy sat in bed between the adults and listened to their suggestions, though Graham did break off to moan at them for bringing biscuits, "It'sh all well and good for you but I shall be shleeping on gravel tonight."

Nancy rolled her eyes dramatically for Jimmy's benefit, "Well why don't you sweep the crumbs off the sheet before you get into bed, *Grandad*?"

"Shouldn't have to, but if you musht eat them here, try dunking the damn things firsht."

"I'll dunk you in a minute."

Jimmy might have been at Wimbledon for the way his gaze passed from one side to the other yet their banter held no anxiety for him. Instead he relished being included and waited for an opportunity to join in. It soon came.

"So, you make the crumbs, you take them,—away."

"I'll clean them up Graham."

"Hah! At lasht, a voice of reason. Thank you Jimmy, you'll have your work cut out though, she's a messhy eater."

Nancy had the last word, "You shouldn't have bothered young man, he gets enough pampering in this house. Now can we please get back to planning our day?"

An indoor venue was obviously preferable in view of the weather and they opted for the National Space Centre followed, if they had time, by a visit to the neighbouring Abbey Pumping Station Museum which was a favourite of Graham's.

Because it was Sunday and a cloudy one at that, the place was crowded but Jimmy was enthralled. They all agreed that the centres' building looked like a giant pupae ready to produce a jumbo jet-sized butterfly but the interior was filled with all manner of space equipment and planetary displays, together with a host of 'hands on' gadgets for kids of *all* ages, including Graham.

It was late afternoon when their slot came up for the 360 degree cinema and was a fitting finale to the day. The seats reclined to a position where the audience could look at the ceiling in order to watch an astonishing film depicting the universe, from birth to present day with a mixture of theory and reality where for example images from the *Hubble Telescope* were used. In spite of the significantly loud commentary Graham fell sound asleep as soon as the lights dimmed and snored loudly throughout the twenty six minute show. Once again, Jimmy was in the middle and couldn't decide whether to wake him, though he did find it funny. In the end, chortling with delight, he nudged Nancy and pointed at Graham whose mouth had fallen open, adding further resonance to the din. She leant over and spoke into his ear, "Don't worry, he does that every time."

It would be the first thing he related to Pat Ensor that evening, when they sat down to write another 'thank you' letter.

The three of them got off the bus and walked towards the care home in silence. Plans had already been made for the following weekend so all that remained was to deliver him back to the home. It could never be *his* home or even just *home*. No matter how well equipped or how lovely the staff were, it would always be an institution and Jimmy's heart sank with every step. This time he hugged them both and hung on tightly for a little while. Nancy knew enough to realise they should leave quickly and let Pat Ensor settle him back in, but they all felt miserable. As they walked along the pavement his small face appeared at one of the bay windows and as they waved he blew them a kiss. Graham suspected that Jimmy was crying but Nancy *knew* he was and looked away rather than have him see her tears.

Chapter 9

Once again, Adam Harding collected Graham and Nancy for a group meeting. They clambered into the car and after exchanging greetings he nodded at the carrier bag Graham rested on his lap. "What surprise do you have for us tonight?"

The reply was accompanied by a smug look, "That's shecret." He thought for a moment and added, "Well no actually, it's 'any other business'."

"Huh, well if you're going to go all procedural I've lost interest already. Keep your plastic bag."

He went on to describe how good the food was where they were going and explained his reasons for choosing the venue, "As the groups' only bachelor I didn't want to waste half the evening showing you my art collection or for that matter having one of you damage any of the regency furniture, and in any event, it's the chefs' night off."

"That sounds reashonable to me and if it's halfway decent Nancy and I will use it for our turn."

Harding smiled, "I think that's a good idea and in all seriousness, I do hope you enjoy it."

They were able to park within thirty yards of a small Victorian building that might originally have been a small shop with living accommodation above. Now it carried a sign saying 'Sardaar Vegetarian Cuisine.' Adam lifted a box that clinked of alcohol out of the boot and led them towards the door. A tall Sikh in a black turban and suit met them at the door. He gave a small nod of welcome and spoke in a soft, sincere voice, "Mr Harding, madam, sir, welcome. We have your room prepared for you."

They were standing in a room that couldn't have been more than thirty feet square with vinyl covered tables that extended out from each side wall. He gestured towards a door in the far corner, half hidden by a tall glass-fronted refrigerator that contained a wide range of goods, savoury and sweet.

Harding responded with a small bow and spoke in an unexpectedly quiet voice, "Surinder, my friend, I thank you for your efforts tonight." The tall Sikh smiled, "You are most welcome."

They climbed a steep set of stairs that were obviously not meant for public use and were directed to take the door on their left as they reached the small landing. A corridor disappeared off towards the back of the building and two other doors lay at the other end. Nancy suspected that the room they entered was normally used as a sitting room since a large sofa was pushed up against the wall. The centre was dominated by a long table that was covered by a white paper cover embossed with a lace-like pattern and laid with cutlery and wine glasses for six people. Harding was deafened by their silence and grinned, "Trust me, you will experience some of the finest vegetarian cooking to be found tonight." He wrestled a corkscrew out of his pocket and pulled two bottles of wine from his box, "It's BYOB, red or white?"

Moments later they heard someone climb the stairs and Calder stepped through the door, breaking into a smile when he recognised Graham and Nancy. Introductions were made and a glass of red selected before he drew their attention to the obvious. "I didn't know what to expect tonight but from the smells coming out of that kitchen I'm glad I didn't eat anything before I left."

Adam smiled, "That's what I've been saying. You're in for an experience."

Two sets of footsteps preceded the entrance of Sarah and the Doctor. Sarah greeted everyone with her usual vivacity and helped herself to the wine before Harding had chance to offer, though she added the two bottles they had brought to the box.

Surinder Singh appeared bearing platters of warm poppadoms before returning to the door and taking two dishes of accompaniments from two outstretched arms. Adam suggested getting on with the business of the meeting since they had a larger than usual agenda.

Sarah cut in, "I have no problems with that, our meetings are informal enough to accompany a meal but you've just raised an interesting point. We don't actually have a printed agenda; until now it's been more of a free for all."

Doctor Williams disagreed, "That is not the case Sarah, I seem to recall that at the last meeting you managed to bully us into an alcoholic haze under the guise of 'Any other business."

"Nonsense Donald, those were special circumstances, but now we could do with some structure. Any volunteers for secretary?" The room fell silent save for the cracking of poppadoms, until Nancy came up with the solution, "Why don't we start each meeting off by making a list of the things each member wants to discuss and then prioritising them. The ones we don't get around to will be less important and might wait until the next meeting."

The idea was accepted by all and Adam produced a sheet of paper though writing down his own list of topics before passing it on, saying, "Looks as though the ladies have organised us at last; makes me think of the Churchill story where one of his advisers forecast that women would be running the country by the year such and such. He replied, 'Still?'."

It was Nancy's turn, "Tosh!"

Surinder reappeared and cleared the table and placed the dirty dishes into the same arms that had delivered them. He remained at the door until the 'arms' delivered a number of fragrant savoury dishes which he transferred to the table with graceful elegance. Fresh plates and cutlery were delivered with the bowls of basmati rice and variety of breads before everyone dived in. Adam was called upon to identify some of the dishes and an appreciative chatter surfaced with each new tasting. Once the meal was properly underway the agenda reappeared and Adam paused to read the list out aloud. Surprisingly, an accord was reached first time and their first formal agenda, in order of consideration, read;

- » Welcome new member
- » Working practices
- » Current case
- » Journal
- » Updates on the children.
- » Any other business

* * *

Sarah began by addressing Harvey, "Well the first item is straightforward, the decision to invite you in was unanimous so the welcome is too. It's nice to see you here Mr Calder."

"Harvey please, and thank you for allowing me in, as you all no doubt know, I have a personal interest in Graham's abilities, though I still don't understand them."

Sarah lowered her head slightly, "Right oh, Harvey it is, but for what it's worth neither do we, though we have seen his gift at work."

The Doctor raised his hand slightly, "Sorry to complicate a straightforward item because I know you have been cautioned already, but it bears repeating. This whole affair is secret and must remain so."

Everybody at the table nodded including Harvey, "Aye, and I've honoured my promise to keep it that way, to the extent of breaking a promise I made to my wife when we married, of never keeping secrets from each other."

Harding referred to the agenda he had tucked under his plate, "Fair enough, the next item is the one I brought up at our last meeting. Graham's propensity for getting himself into bother requires the restraint of some working practices and there aren't many on my list but they are all there *because* of past events not in case of them." He pulled another sheet of paper from the inside pocket of his jacket and pressed it out flat on the table. It read;

WORKING PRACTICES

1. Don't do anything alone, get back-up
2. Protect evidence

3. Act within the law

4. The more members that know about actions the better. Brief everyone

5. Stay out of the police station

6. Stay out of hospital

Twenty minutes of animated discussion followed and voices were raised to interrupt and get a word in. Graham's adventures were re-visited to illustrate the need for such rules, but an observer would have noted that their anxieties diminished in the face of laughter and awe as each member retold their experiences of him.

Apart from an odd attempt to defend himself Graham remained silent, happy to have them as friends, to share an otherwise lonely secret. Adam's tales always caused hilarity with descriptions of the string of confrontations with Graham in the police interview room that left him confounded. Someone who not only lied, very badly, but managed to walk free each time, *and* con a lift home in a patrol car. When the time came to accept the list as a mandate five members voted for the idea. Graham abstained and received a prompt scolding from Nancy.

Surinder and the 'arms' returned to replace the empty platters with more, filled with new things to try. Before leaving he asked if anyone would care for a repeat of anything but they all declined, with declarations of surfeit and appreciation.

Graham took over for the next item, and as always his understated narration made his stories *more* shocking rather than less. When Timothy's tale came to an end he added a reflection, "There is something about thish case that frightens me more than it should. What he'sh going through is wrong enough, though I don't think he will try to kill himshelf now." He paused then and gazed at the table in front of him without focus, "But remember that when I firsht met him he was taking a large box of paracetamol home to do jusht that. A seven year old child was about to kill himshelf." He shook his head as if to clear the thought and continued, "I can't pin it down but I think something bad is going to happen to Tim if we don't do shomething for him."

It was Sarah's turn, and she began with an apology that was instantly dismissed as unnecessary. Having closely minuted her meeting with the head teacher she was able to give a blow by blow, word for word account of it and went on to give her own views. "First of all I must confess to losing my temper in the face of such disdain and unwillingness to help, yet with the benefit of hindsight what could she do? There I was, a stranger, unwilling to disclose the source of my information yet asking her to take action against one of her staff." She sighed audibly and looked around the table, "So I think I'm speaking for Graham as well when I ask for ideas please." Graham nodded, "Yesh, definitely."

Adam began on a cautious note, "I could always call in and see her but once again without any evidence as such and she would realise there was a connection between you and I. It *might* prompt her into taking action but it's just as likely to suffer the same fate as your attempt. What we don't want is for her to react badly enough to submit formal complaint about us."

Others murmured agreement and the doctor added, "The same would apply if I turned up, perhaps claiming to have had a report from one of the nurses. It wouldn't take much to determine who the boy's real GP is and I, or we, would be in a very difficult position, trying to explain away a bluff. What about the parents? Could we prompt them into action." Graham told them that it was a single parent family and described Tim's reaction to their suggestion of doing just that. For some reason the child feared involving his mother more than the bullying.

Harvey was the next to speak. "In this case, nothing short of hard evidence will do so why not have Timothy describe what's being happening?" He held up his hand to head off several responses and to indicate there was more. "Not in person. Record him and disguise the voice with a cloth over the mike or some such device." Silence followed as each member considered the idea.

Harding nodded, "Hmm, fits in the modern day ethic of keeping abused children out of the courts and using filmed interviews instead, but this time we'd have to do it without identifying the child."

The idea appealed to Sarah as well, "Do you know I think that might work. At any rate I'd be prepared to go back and see the head with the tape." She glanced around the table until she reached Graham who still looked anxious, "What do you think Graham?"

"The idea is a good one but we are still strangers to thish child. We've only shared tea and biscuits with him on two occasions so we can't hike off shomewhere to do a recording without frightening him or looking sushpicious to others." Nancy had realised the same but already knew the answer, "How about a hike to the far side of your car park?" She read his quizzical look and carried on, "All we need to do is take our drinks and biscuits over there, along with our portable music centre. It's got a tape deck with a recording facility we've never used but there's definitely a button marked 'record'. *And*, I'll bet that if we record it outside, with distant traffic, birdsong and other background noises, his voice will be difficult to identify."

Sarah agreed, "Also remember that she isn't his form mistress so she won't know the voice that well."

Graham grinned, "I think I'd better find out how that recording button worksh."

Nancy addressed Sarah, "We've already told him about you. You're the nice lady who went to see the head teacher and will do so again, with the tape, so do you think it would help if you were there. For the sake of authenticity."

"Yes I think that's a very good idea. I would be able to tell the head, honestly, that I was present when it was recorded and if it's raining we can sit in the car."

Arrangements were made and with lighter spirits they moved on to the next item. Sarah referred to her list and announced, "Journal," before casting her gaze around the table for a culprit. Graham had ducked down beside his chair and reappeared with a carrier bag which he placed on the table. "Lasht year someone suggested I write a journal." As he spoke he pulled five school excercise books out of the bag and continued, "Here it ish. But don't expect Dickensh, will you. It's been a long time since I wrote stories and it's taken ages."

Each member took a book and began reading passages, sometimes to themselves and others, where they thought the content merited sharing, they read aloud. The book recording his most recent activities was only partly full and for that reason was allowed to be returned to its owner but the squabble about who would have what and when could only be resolved by drawing matchsticks. Two more draws determined the order for the remaining members, excepting Nancy and Graham, and all promised to protect the books with their lives. Each would pass them on to the next in line as quickly as possible.

Sarah was the best source of information on past cases having spent an hour on the telephone that afternoon. She withdrew a notebook from her handbag and began, "Sam Pearce is very happy and doing well at school. He regularly sees his mum who, I'm told, has entered into another relationship that seems no better than the last one. His father, Tony, has managed his new custodial role magnificently; they seem more like friends than father and son."

The doctor spoke, "Couldn't agree more." He looked at Harvey, "Tell you what, if you write this information down you'll be able to relate it to the stories you read about in Grahams' journal." Harvey nodded his appreciation of the idea and dug another piece of paper out of his pocket.

Surinder entered the room and after ensuring that everyone had eaten enough, cleared the table of dishes and cutlery. The 'arms' appeared once more and were loaded before disappearing for a short while, returning with a tray bearing cups, saucers sugar, milk and a large cafetiere filled with a very fragrant coffee. Moments later the 'arms' offered a large tray of Indian sweets which were borne to the table and the diners were once again left alone.

Nancy began to distribute the coffees while Sarah continued, "James Everard has been a troubled little boy, which is hardly surprising when your mother is kicked to death in front of you, but he has just been befriended by a couple who have changed his life. I spoke to the warden today and she is so excited by the change in him. No sign of running away and he is mixing with the other children to an extent she'd never thought likely. Of course, his new friends are Nancy and Graham.

Laura Green's arm has mended and she has been fostered by a lovely family in Leicester Forest East. Similarly, Kirsty Randle has been fostered though the scarring on her back is permanent. Her father is already out of prison but thankfully, wants nothing to do with his daughter.

Mr Tunstall, the solicitor, is still inside. His wife has moved to a smaller house and reduced her working week to spend more time with Adrian. I fear he is going to need more help but at least his mum works with me now and together we can provide timely support.

For an update on Graham's last 'client' I call upon Harvey."

Harvey gave her a smile of appreciation, "Thank you. She is the light of our lives. Inquisitive and forever smiling, just like her mother used to at that age." A fleeting look of pain accompanied the memory but he continued, "The kidney damage is not threatening and other than that you would never imagine she was so close to death just a few months ago. Graham already knows that I've found it difficult to take all this in and sitting here tonight listening to five intelligent people discussing his telepathy as though it was normal has shaken me. But, I *have* to believe it and therefore I have to admire and respect what you are doing, and thank you for allowing me to join. I hope I can be a useful member."

Harding smiled, "Bank on it, we'll find something for you to do."

Sarah agreed, "Here, here on that. But if we have no more to say on the subject there is just 'Any other Business.' Anyone have anything else to raise?" After a short silence she continued, "In that case I would like to know how much we owe you for this meal Adam. It was absolutely superb."

Everyone voiced their appreciation. "I'm glad you enjoyed it but my reasons for bringing you here were entirely selfish. I'm no cook and I live under bachelor conditions. This is my way of feeding you."

"Nonsense, we can't have that. Please, let us pay our way."

Harding waved a hand, "No I'm just pleased you enjoyed it."

Graham spoke up, "In that cashe, I have a proposal to make. Rather than have to cater for these meetingsh why not use these facilities every time?"

Williams was the first to agree in what became a unanimous vote, "I'm up for that."

"In that cashe, we must shtart the way we mean to carry on and pay our way." The majority held sway over a minority of one and the surprisingly modest bill was shared.

At home that night Nancy and Graham shared a sense of relief at not having to host the next meeting in their house. Their small house, small kitchen, small table, small budget, in fact small everything would not now be tested.

Doctor Williams had won the first loan of Graham's journal and on discovering that his wife had gone to bed he made a hot chocolate and retired to his study, intending to read a few pages of the first volume. It was as startling as their first meeting, in which Graham's gentle and unassuming manner made the impossible sound plausible. His style of writing mirrored the same modest, self-effacing manner which, paradoxically, made his accounts of abuse more rather than less appalling.

Williams gasped audibly when he read the account of Graham's first encounter; when he *merged* with Jimmy and watched the boy's mother being kicked to death by his father. The lack of emotion was intentional, the doctor knew, from his association with Graham, but every detail had been included, leaving the reader in a state of shock.

The doctor could vouch for the veracity of Grahams next passage since he was personally involved. Somehow the fates decreed that when he identified young Sam's wounds as abuse he ignored normal working practices by not contacting the authorities. The wounds had been inflicted by the mother's partner and his natural father had brought him in for treatment but something strange about the natural father's account of a rescue by someone named Graham, *and* the guileless answers from the child that gave him pause. He would reflect on the matter later yet failed to pinpoint exactly what detail persuaded him to break the rules, but Sam's father honoured his promise and returned the next day with Graham.

The conversation that followed would remain forever the strangest in the doctor's life and yet something about it made the fantastic sound authentic. What the journal lacked in grammar and punctuation was more than made up for by its detail and he noted how accurately their meeting had been chronicled.

He closed the last journal at a quarter to four and sat back in his chair staring ahead without focus. The absolute silence seemed to settle on him like a cloak allowing his memory to snatch at the episodes Graham had described. Doctor's need to shield themselves from emotion, to protect themselves from the grief and suffering they deal with each day, so this GP was startled to reflect on how many times his eyes had watered, how profoundly he'd been affected. What on earth was this thing they were dealing with and for that matter what *should* they be doing with it.

He sat for a little while longer, pondering on the who, why's and what's but found no answers and instead his aching bottom and back prompted him to head for his bed, knowing though, that sleep would elude him.

* * *

A few miles away, two nine year old friends fell into their own beds, exhausted. Their efforts over the previous months had been rewarded by a lavish allocation of merit points at the new level. Paul Croft had always led in the game but ensured that his friend Andy Maynard kept up and now, finally, they had made it to the top level. They'd cracked it.

Sometime in the summer of 2002 a computer game called 'The Department' appeared on the market in timely fashion, given that it featured an imaginary secretive government agency formed for the sole task of fighting terrorism. Just months earlier, in 2001, New York had suffered the very real 9/11 terrorist attacks and there was a huge market for anything that embodied western values and the combat against a fundamentalist threat. It was an overnight success.

It was banned, internationally, five months later.

Players selected a codename and began their training at a camp sited in a remote corner of a military base in Arizona. As rookies their *strategic worth* was a meagre ten credits that would allow the owner to do little more than buy a coffee or newspaper. A significantly long training programme followed, involving the use of firearms, explosives and unarmed combat in a variety of scenarios including assaults on hi-jacked aircraft and buildings, hostage rescues from terrorist camps and an escape from 'hostile' forces.

One of the favourites was to be part of a special forces attack on an imaginary terrorist cell holed up in an Afghan cave system. There, the key would be to capture a terrorist rather than killing him, which entailed getting close enough to use a taser, usually by ambush. His worth, because of the interrogation potential was mirrored in a very high credit allocation.

Each player would only be allowed one attempt at each task and their success or failure measured by the allocation or removal of credits to their *strategic worth*. A certain number of credits were necessary to move up to the next level and the only way to correct an inadequate worth was to restart the game.

The following modules included 'Strategic Planning and Practice', 'Covert Ops' and 'Surveilance', where failure in any one would still send the player back to the beginning. The whole thing was pressured but eventually, after many more modules and missions the successful player was granted 'Agent' status. Every successful player would be subjected to a welcome speech from the head of *the Department*; a sincere, homespun, all-American patriot who pointed out that prefixes like 'special' or 'secret' were not deemed necessary for members of a discreet and very secret agency tasked with the defeat of a secretive and deadly enemy.

Each agent would then begin his career with relatively straightforward modules, or rather missions, such as tailing and monitoring terrorist suspects, where additional credits could be earned by broader observations and conclusions such as spotting a courier or suspect vehicle. Thwarted attacks and defused bombs attracted high scores but the identification and elimination of a human bomb, before they despatched themselves and the fifty other people in the surrounding area, merited the highest score in the game so far.

Always, the aim was to accrue credits though the 'why' would not be known until a player reached the necessary level, which was very high indeed.

Then, quite suddenly, the player's screen would go blank and remain so for over a minute. Any attempt to do anything else with the computer was blocked. An electronic voice would begin explaining that the Agent had proved him or herself worthy of further selection though more detail could not be provided until they had contacted the control unit with the code that had appeared on the otherwise blank screen. At that point they would be given a new ID and a further password. The programmers had wisely realised that their game might go viral and credibility would rest on each agent having a unique ID. The solution was simple and automatic. Any player submitting the correct codeword through to the dedicated website would learn that their future ID was simply a number, the next one allocated in sequence by the programme. For example 'Agent Daniel' might be given the ID 'fifteen' and would be known in the game and in the user website as just that, '15'. It said a lot for the complexity of the game that after three months of soaring sales, only two hundred and eighty numbers had been allocated.

The password required for the next module was provided with the new ID and placed the player at the top of the tree, where he or she would be party to and occasionally able to influence top political decisions in the game.

At this point in the agent's 'career' another feature was introduced whereby credits could be 'spent'. For example, individuals might be faced with a risky decision where the stakes were high and measured in the number of credits required for the gamble. Success added to the pot and failures were costly.

But there was another module, quite separate from everything else which required the highest stakes of all and which caused the authorities so much embarrassment, in that it took them five months to discover it and ban all sales. None of the sales literature or packaging mentioned the module, which was embedded in the more generalised and innocuous *Intelligence* section. Access required lateral thinking to a number of questions, using the sort of slippery guile one would expect from the likes of Sadam Hussein or Idi Amin when faced with investigative reporters.

It was called the 'Special Treatment cell' which, after successfully answering the *eligibility* questions required a very heavy stake in credits to gain entry. Once inside the player could choose from a selection of suspects and from then on direct the interrogation, beginning with questions and answers but ultimately continuing with a selection of tortures that beggared belief.

The simplest might have involved the use of a cosh or taser, or even removing finger nails, but the choice went on, and on. So much so that some of the content must have been educational in the worst possible way to the wrong people. Success, and therefore a substantial award of credits, lay in obtaining information. Failure was usually determined by the prisoner's premature death.

Ironically, experts would later agree that most individuals would be shocked and repelled by the modules' content if seen in isolation but the insidious tempering that occurred during the passage through the game dulled such sensitivity. Teenagers and extreme racial bigots seemed to be the most susceptible.

Five hugely successful months of sales combined with a ban served to ensure that an underground market would flourish. It became a redneck's bible.

Chapter 10

Friday the thirteenth was just that.

They parted that morning for their workplaces having arranged to meet at the store when his shift ended when they would need to shop for the weekend, since Jimmy would be staying again. But first they would persuade Tim to make a recording on the music centre Graham was taking in with him. New batteries had been fitted and they'd learned how to operate the recording device.

The afternoon brightened and by the time Sarah arrived it was warm enough to ensure they could sit outside comfortably. Nancy arrived moments later and suggested they wait for Tim in the cafeteria, as usual, while Graham finished his work period.

He changed and hurried through to the ladies as soon as he could but was surprised to find them alone. There was no sign of Tim.

After another thirty minutes and cup of tea they decided to call it a day. Graham was particularly unhappy in spite of reassurances from the ladies who expressed certainty that he would turn up on the next Friday if not before. He reminded them of how anxious he was in the meeting and cursed himself for not getting Tim's home address, but eventually he agreed to begin the shopping while Sarah headed back to her car.

Even so he was too distracted to offer any opinions on what they should eat that weekend and Nancy knew better than to try and shake him out of it. He wasn't being selfish; his concern was for another and worse still a child. It was enough to struggle home on the bus with the shopping so Nancy waited at the store exit while he took the music centre back to his locker. It could wait there until the following Friday.

They were both tired and slumped into the only pair of seats left on the lower deck of the bus for the short ride home. Each had a large shopping bag on their laps and shuffled into comfortable positions. Graham sat next to the window and hadn't paid any attention to the two boys in the seat ahead though he became aware of a smell of paint as he rested his elbow on the window sill and his hand on the back of the seat in front. The boys were whispering to each other and the one in front of Graham thought of something amusing enough to whisper into his companion's ear before throwing his head back in laughter. Graham made to snatch his hand away when the boy's head made contact but he wasn't quick enough. This time the darkness engulfed him.

* * *

It began with timid fear but things were being said that he couldn't grasp though the threat was clear. Fear became horror by degrees.

He felt thumps and kicks and knew he was somewhere alone, without any possibility of help. He was being forced to kneel and then lie flat on his front, crying now, and pleading but all he could hear was laughter. Then hands were holding his head down under water, the smell of mud and cold wetness filing his senses, as his heart began to race and he heard his own mewling. With rising terror he felt his body surrender to the need for air and sensed the agonising inhalation of muddy water. The accompanying convulsion caused the attackers to release their hold and when his head came clear of the water he choked up the foul smelling mess. Things were being said throughout but though he tried, nothing was distinct enough to understand. He was sitting up saying 'please' over and over again when suddenly, something struck the side of his chest forcing the breath from his lungs and leaving him with an agonising focus of pain where the piece of fence post felt sharp enough to crack a rib. More kicks and thumps, shouting now, his hair grabbed to shake his head violently. On and on.

He could see little for tears but knew he was still pleading for them to stop. He felt them lift his hand and felt two cold coarse surfaces before he looked down, just as a foot stamped on the two house bricks used to sandwich his small hand. He tried to snatch it away but only half succeeded before other hands held his arm down, just as the foot descended again. This time his hand was only part of the way inside the bricks and he clearly heard the crack of three fingers breaking. He had descended into a hell he couldn't understand but his scream had made his torturers pause and take stock, though not for long. He could hear something rattling, like a marble in a can and had managed to make it to his knees when hands grabbed his hair again and forced his head back. Still more shouting and still he didn't understand what was being said. Suddenly, the hands that were holding his hair moved forward over his forehead and fingers dug into his eyes, wrenching his eyelids open. The rattling stopped and a hissing began just before his eyes seemed to explode in pain. He heard a feral, penetrating, unearthly scream before sensing his scramble forward, away from the hands and the agony. He felt the hands try to find a grip and finding purchase on his sweater but he was still moving forward, dragging them with him as he made it to his feet with the strength and primal urge of an animal fighting for life. They let him go, suddenly, just as he sensed his foot fail to find solid ground and his body fall forward into water. This time he was barely aware of the cold water, set against his injuries and adrenalised terror. Time stretched on as he floundered in shallow muddy water, sobbing until finally he heard footsteps running away. More time passed, he was shivering and knew he needed help. Using just one hand he groped his way to the bank.

* * *

He came to with a start, his head resting on the shopping bag and aching, terribly. As before, the hideous length of his nightmare was contained in just seconds real time. Nancy was saying, "I thought you were having a little noddy off there. . . ." She stopped as soon as she saw his expression and the waxy sheen on his face. She whispered then, "What is it love, what's happened?"

"It'sh Tim." He was looking around, trying to get his bearings before catching sight of his hand, resting on top of the seat in front. His mind raced as he tried to remember something. It must have been something to do with Tim, something he said. He cast back to their first meeting, after his grand dad's whistle had been stolen. The conversation came back to him piecemeal;

* * *

"One of them is.. ....'s brother. She's in my class."

"But they didn't jusht take your whishtle did they Tim. I know how much they frightened you. What elshe did they do? Come on maytee, shurely you know we're friendsh."

* * *

And then he knew, with awful certainty, who the boys in the next seat were. He looked at Nancy with dread, "Oh God, no."

* * *

"They said they were going to take me in for questioning and then they would do me in."

* * *

Before Nancy could respond Graham lunged forward and grabbed the boy in front, who yelled in surprise. "Hey, what you doin?"

Graham leant forward as far as the shopping bag allowed and whispered hoarsely, "Where have you left him."

The boy wriggled furiously and answered at the top of his voice, "I don't know what you're on about, leggo of me. Help." His plea was not aimed at anyone in particular though his companion had clambered off his seat to stand in the aisle and other passengers were beginning to take an interest.

Graham improved his grip on the boys jacket and collar before continuing, "Where have you left Timothy Dexter?" The boy began to shout a further denial when Graham snatched his head back. He barely heard one of the passengers call out, "Oi mister, what are you doing with that kid," or noticed Nancy's hand on his arm, in a gesture that called for caution as he whispered again, though loud enough for the people in neighbouring seats to hear. "Tell me where you left Timothy, or shall I shpray paint in *your* eyes."

The boy in the aisle gawped in shock and the boy in Graham's grasp paused for long enough to understand what he had heard. Comprehension prompted a frantic struggle to break free and he yelled for help. The man who had already spoken rose from the second seat in front and spoke directly to Graham as the other boy scuttled past to be blocked from view. "Is he related to you?" The captive boy answered for him, "No he ain't and 'e's hurting me." His struggles eased with the prospect of help but the grip on his collar remained constant. The man continued to speak to Graham, "Then I suggest you let him go. That's assault that is." By now every passenger was taking an interest and the bus was slowing.

Graham didn't acknowledge the man's input and continued to speak into the boy's ear, "Jusht tell me where you left him you evil little sod."

"What the hell is going on here?" The bus had stopped and the driver was pushing past the boy and man in the aisle. His only concern was keeping to the timetable and when he saw Graham and his captive his solution was the usual cure all, "Right you pair, either pack it in now or get off!"

Graham addressed the boy again, "You aren't going anywhere until you tell me where Timothy is."

The boy started to struggle again and wailed, "I don't know nothing, leave me alone."

"Right, that's it, off, the lot of you." The driver put on his most belligerent look and pointed an outstretched arm towards the front of the bus.

This time Graham snatched at the boy's collar, "*Tell me*!" Nancy put her arm on his, "Graham, love," but the boy yelled at the top of his voice, "Narghhh, let me go, bastard."

It was enough for the first boy, who had sidled clear of the group to make a run for it. The doors were stilled closed and he scrabbled at the chrome emergency release lever until they folded back with a hiss of air. He fled without a second thought for his partner. Curiously, his flight, which implied that he'd gone for help encouraged the driver to make his threat, "I've had enough of this, I'm calling the police."

This time Graham did respond, "Yesh! Call the police quickly. Tell them there's a child badly hurt and this *animal* knows where he ish." He had pulled at the boy's collar as he spoke but this time received no response. The tableau remained in place for a few moments while each cast member tried to interpret the situation and their respective roles, all except Graham, "Pleashe, call the police, nine, nine, nine."

Paul Croft realised he was in trouble and *had to* get away, especially now they were threatening to call the police. The grip on his collar had tightened again as though the bloke behind knew what he was thinking. He hadn't even seen him yet. Desperate, he tried to turn and face Graham and called out in a tone that signalled surrender, "He's by the canal."

Graham hadn't expected the boy to turn towards him or provide the information and in his surprise allowed the grip on the boy's collar to slacken slightly. Enough for a desperate twist and wrench to succeed in breaking free. Before anyone could react he was out of the door and running.

The driver was the first to react, "Right then, perhaps we can get on, my bloody timetable's gone down the toilet."

"Wait, I'm getting off." Graham pushed at Nancy and added, "I'm shorry love, he can't be far away. I'll get on the tow path by the shtore and search from there." Nancy tried to argue, "Graham, wait, please let's go and look for him together, you mustn't go on your own." He shook his head, "No not with all thish shopping, I need to run, I *know* I do!" He looked at the driver and asked, "Can you remember where those boysh got on?"

"Er, yeah, the stop before you."

Graham had twisted around to deposit his bag of shopping on the seat and Nancy swivelled to one side so that he could squeeze by but as he did she looked up anxiously and shook her head, "Please love, I'm scared, please wait."

He dug a hand into his pocket and retrieved the portable telephone Harding had given him, pressing it into her hand as he bent and kissed her forehead briefly, "Don't worry, I'm not going to take any risks, but telephone Adam on his mobile, the number'sh in there and anyone else you can think of." He was moving down the bus now, sidling past the driver who by now had surrendered his timetable to the drama that was unravelling before him and which was amplified by Graham's parting words, "Oh, we're going to need an ambulanshe as well."

"Bloody hell." The driver shook his head and ambled back to his cab.

In the time it took for the bus to reach Nancy's stop her fellow passengers sat in silence, pretending to mind their own business but enthralled, as she spoke to Detective Sergeant Harding. "Adam, there's another one, we need your help. All I know is that the boy we spoke about needs help. I don't know exactly, but he's by the canal just past Graham's store. What? Yes he's in a real state and just dashed off to search for him." She appeared to hiccup but observers saw her tears as she continued, "I know, I tried to stop him but he just wouldn't listen, he also said we'd need an ambulance." A pause, "Thanks. No, that's all I know. OK I'll dump the shopping at home and wait for you, thanks Adam."

Everyone sat in silence as Nancy stowed the telephone in her handbag and soon the bus slowed in its approach to her stop. As she struggled to her feet the man who had tried to get involved with Graham's interrogation of the boy leapt up and carried one of her bags off the bus. He waited on the pavement until she joined him and asked, "Have you got far to go love, I can easily catch the next one."

She smiled gratefully, "No, thanks. She pointed at her house, I live just there."

He scratched his head and wore a look that managed to exhibit a mix of guilt, embarrassment, care and intrigue, "Well whatever's going on I hope it sorts itself out. Good luck luv." With a nod and smile she hoisted the two bags off the pavement and hurried away. He stepped back on to the bus and gave the driver a perplexed shrug as the doors hissed closed behind him.

Meanwhile Harding had established via control that a patrol car was within a mile of Graham's house and gave the appropriate instructions. Rather than waste time in going to collect Nancy he set off for what he knew would be a scene of crime. His usual buzz of excitement was chilled though, for Graham's call outs always involved children and more often than not injured ones.

As the bus doors closed an excited chatter took over but it was swiftly silenced when, within yards, the bus was forced to pull into the curb again, so that the patrol car blazing with blues and twos could dodge past them and shudder to a halt outside the small semi-detached house Nancy had indicated to her would be Samaritan. An officer leapt from the passenger side and approached Nancy, responding to her nod by taking both bags and allowing her to hurry forward towards the house, scrabbling in her handbag for the keys.

The driver's vocabulary remained unchanged as once again he shook his head in wonder, "Bloody hell."

After all the physiotherapy and excercise Graham's gait was almost normal, until he tried to run and then the shambling, stroke-like weakness of his left side became evident. The job had done wonders for his stamina but made few athletic demands so that by the time he reached the store colleagues were startled to see him gasping for air and trying to run in an odd lop-sided fashion. He couldn't speak but the look on his face was eloquent enough. One of the car park attendants watched him cross the car park and clamber awkwardly over the fence before disappearing down the embankment towards the canal tow-path. The unspoken messaging was enough for him to shove his column of trolleys back into the nearest bay and set off in pursuit, tapping his pocket as he did so, to check for his mobile telephone.

Graham tripped and rolled down the bank into one of the muddy puddles formed by the earlier showers but scrambled to his feet regardless. No-one was in sight and there would be few boats in use at that time of year. After a few hundred yards the opposite bank was dominated by a derelict Victorian mill with foundations that disappeared underwater. The filthy brickwork was broken up by gaping steel-framed windows bearing tooth-like shards of glass, adding an austere chill to an already cold day. One of the store trolleys lay on its side half-submerged, a mindless act of vandalism that doubtless added to all manner of navigational hazards along this stretch. There were no houses, just scrubland and derelict industrial units with an air of neglect that dissuaded most walkers from using the place. All these things Graham noticed, in a peripheral way but by now he could do no more than walk. His throat and chest were on fire as he struggled for air and the sight of so many things dumped into the canal made him begin to fear the worst.

Running footsteps caused him to turn and wave when he recognised his colleague but as he turned back he saw a black dog in the distance, caught in the narrow corridor of light from a low bridge as it tried to move along the tow-path. It seemed to be limping badly, to such an extent that it fell over on to its weakened side, but Graham forced his attention back to the task in hand. He continued to scan the canal and both banks as he struggled on until the distance to the bridge closed and his arc of sight passed over the dog once more. It had struggled back to its feet and was making some sort of sound, that was too indistinct to identify but when it rolled over again it brought the opposite limb over to nurse the injured one and in doing so ceased to be a dog, to become a young child that had been trying to crawl along on its hands and knees.

The colleague caught up and had started to speak when Graham howled in anguish and broke into a run.

"Arghhh nooooooo, pleashe God, nooooo." In his breathless state it was a waste of valuable oxygen to call the boy's name but as they drew near they could hear a keening sound that neither man would ever forget. It defied description and fell way shy of being human, but it signalled a pit of suffering that contained a dreadful mix of fear and pain.

When he heard approaching footsteps he,- it, cringed in fear. Graham would later reflect that the image was so inhuman he still thought of the poor creature as 'it' as he drew close.

Tim fell on to his side and looked towards the approaching footsteps before curling up into a defensive position. In that moment Graham glimpsed a small face that looked like a pantomime burglar with the black eye mask and dropped down on his knees to consider the muddied form that continued to make the unearthly sound. Gently, feeling his way around the injuries he could see, Graham eased an arm under the curled up child, murmuring words of comfort, "Shhh now, you're shafe, it'sh me Graham, I've got you. Shhh now." He slowly gathered Tim up into his arms and squatted back on the ground so that his lap would serve as a seat and both arms could be used to form a protective shield. The colleague interrupted, "Graham, what do you want me to do?"

He nodded at the bridge, "The Polishe are coming, could you bring them here pleashe." As the man left they heard the first siren but Graham sat there with Tim in an isolation of despair. The boy showed little sign of comfort, but the man who was nursing him, who'd promised to help and failed, looked up at the sky and fell apart."

Two uniformed officers were the first on scene, where they found the victim cradled in the arms of a man who was gently rocking to and fro and weeping openly. Several times they heard him repeat the same words, "I'm shorry, sho shorry. We were too shlow." While one officer reported in, the other ran back to the car for some sort of cover for the child. On his way he passed 'breadbin' Harding and gave him directions.

The detective squatted down in front of them and inspected the child, who was shivering and looked a mess but seemed to be showing signs of comfort inside Graham's embrace as indeed and at last, he was. Moments earlier Graham's voice had penetrated the fog of trauma, carrying with it the certainty of rescue.

Harding asked, "Is this Timothy?"

Graham nodded, "There were two older boys; one of them hash a sister in Tim's Class. They said they were going to queshtion him and do him in."

"Yes, I remember you saying." Harding gently patted Graham on the shoulder and pushed himself to his feet before addressing two 'uniforms'. "Right, you two, seal this side of the canal off for the moment, just in case. Put a call in for the Soco and stand by to help him. If he needs more help he can contact me." They headed back to their car but both were perplexed by the detective's behaviour. It was as though he had expected to find the adult male with the injured child. Not only did he fail to show surprise but he seemed to know the bloke on the ground, with a strange cleft on the side of his forehead *and* the child's name. As they made their way back to the patrol car for rolls of the blue and white tape they met the ambulance crew who were being shown the way by

Graham's colleague. He had waited for them at Harding's request. The car Nancy was in had been directed to the location by control and pulled up moments later. She had been listening to the radio reports from the scene and leapt out of the car, dodging around the two officers who looked as though they were preparing to block her way and ran towards the canal bridge. Each of the uniforms considered the situation, noting that she had arrived in a patrol car and the driver seemed unconcerned by her entry into a crime scene. Ergo, why should they.

Someone would later point out to Graham that he shouldn't have moved the victim before establishing the injuries, in keeping with the example shown by the medics when they ran down the bank beside the bridge. He remained in Graham's arms while they carried out an initial assessment, easing answers out of the child with the comforting care of professionals. Nancy moved slowly around the group to establish a line of sight with Graham who had regained some control though when their eyes met he nodded slowly and another tear welled from the corner of each eye. Very soon, the medics felt able to transfer Tim to the stretcher and Graham clambered to his feet. He was watching them place wet pads onto the boys eyes and secure them with tape when Nancy moved in and held him tightly, feeling his silent sobs of distress, "Oh Nanshe, they sprayed paint in his eyes, he can't shee."

The ambulance crew made Tim comfortable, wrapping him in a red blanket before securing him to the stretcher. As they carried him away, still comforting with a gentle chatter, the adult-size stretcher seemed to emphasise Tim's small frame.

Harding's voice interrupted their thoughts, though it was soft enough for only the three of them to hear. "You, my friend have just saved that boy from Gods knows what. If you hadn't done what you have we might have been taking a body away from here in a day or two's time. As it is, they might even be able to save his sight." He stepped into Nancy's view, I've spoken to the medics and told them you're close friends. They'll allow you to go in with him, and whilst you're there see if you can get something to help

Graham. I'll follow on later." She gave him a smile of thanks and they hurried after the stretcher.

'Now' he thought, 'I have work to do'. He telephoned Sarah next and after providing her with a brief summary obtained the information he needed. Minutes later control furnished him with Angela Tenson's home number.

Her husband answered on the fourth ring. "Tenson, good evening."

"Good evening sir, is Mrs Angela Tenson there please."

A cautious "Ye-es, may I ask who's calling."

"Detective Sergeant Harding sir, it's a matter regarding one of her pupils."

Moments later a female voice, equally cautious, "Hello?"

"Ah good evening Mrs Tenson, DS Harding here, Leicestershire Constabulary. I need to trace one of your students but via an indirect angle I'm afraid."

"How so?"

"Well all we know at this stage is that the student concerned attends your school and has a younger sister who does too. Her form teacher is a Mrs Stretton."

"I think I need to know what this is all about."

"I'm not at liberty to divulge much yet I'm afraid, we haven't located the victim's parents, but I can tell you that one of your students has been attacked and injured, he's on the way to hospital now. We believe that the student we are trying to identify can help us with our enquiries, but there is a need to identify him quickly."

She felt a cold leaden weight of dread but forced herself to focus, "How quickly?"

"Within the next thirty minutes would be good."

"I'm leaving now, give me your number." She scribbled it on a notepad and ran for her coat and keys, leaving her husband with just enough information to avoid concern and ensure that he would finish preparing his meal. She considered the two glasses of wine drunk while cooking the dinner and guessed she would be border line in a breath test but another anxiety prevailed. Clearly, something dreadful had happened and she had an obligation to do all she could. *Obligation!* Was that the word she should have considered when that child protection woman came to see her? It could have happened to any child but God forbid it was him. She wracked her brains for a name but it wouldn't come. At the school she left her car parked across the school gates and unlocked the adjacent pedestrian gate. As soon as the alarm had been disabled she ran into her office and retrieved one of Sarah's cards from her desk drawer. Short of issuing a general memorandum to all staff about bullying she had done little else, though there was a faint recollection of writing a name on the back of a card. The one she held was blank but there were two cards, the second had been dropped on to her desk with a threat of consequences. She flicked through the cards in her draw and because it was face down, saw the name first. Just one word; 'Mary'. Damn! The teacher, not the pupil. She offered up a silent plea, 'Please, please let it not be him.'

Within ten minutes she had located two sets of siblings that fitted the criteria but of the two elders one was currently excused games because of a broken wrist. She telephoned the detective with the information and he expressed little interest in the injured student, which left just one, Paul Croft; his sister, Linda was in Mrs Stretton's class. She gave him the home address and waited for him to continue, "Look, Mrs, er, Tenson, there is some additional information you'll have that will save me some time, though I must ask you not to divulge this name to anyone until you see it in the news."

"No problem, go ahead, what do you want to know."

Her spirits sank as he spoke, "Would you be kind enough to give me an address for Timothy Dexter please?"

* * *

Nancy sat on one of the casualty departments plastic chairs and rested her head on Graham's shoulder, "We're spending too much time in hospitals, you and me."

Graham gave a 'huff' of agreement, and rubbed the side of his head against hers. They sat in a silent, mutual comfort then, against a background of beeping monitors, squeaky wheels, groans, moans and cries until they were startled by the voice behind them, "Hello you two." As they separated to turn towards her, Sarah placed her head in the gap and hugged them both. "How is Timothy?"

"We don't know yet but they promised to come and tell us when he's out of theatre." He glanced at his watch and saw that it was past eleven.

"Doc's on his way in and so is Harvey but Adam has gone after the kids that did it. He's got an address for one so we should hear something soon. Meanwhile, who fancies a coffee?" They pooled their ten penny pieces before Sarah and Nancy headed off to find a machine, just as a lady on the opposite side of the waiting room rose from her seat and walked to the desk. Graham hadn't paid any heed to her but now, with nothing else to occupy him she became the focus of attention. He first noticed her creased raincoat and the lank fair hair that seemed to shelve onto the collar in disarray. Her legs were so thin they made Graham think of *Popeye's* partner, *Olive Oil.* She wore black tights and her shoes were nicely polished brown lace-ups. He wondered whether she might in fact be wearing stockings and quickly dismissed the thought. Sexy, she wasn't.

His passive scrutiny ceased when he realised that the feet had turned around and were heading towards him. Looking up he noted that she had a pale, pinched look with a down-turned mouth that resembled a permanent grimace. The frameless spectacles that rested on her small nose completed the image of a Beatrix Potter mouse, a very sour one.

"Excuse me, I've just been advised that are you the gentleman who discovered my son, Timothy Dexter?"

Graham smiled slightly and nodded his head, "Yesh."

"Then I'm indebted, thank you for all you have done."

Graham repeated the gestures and added, "You're welcome, I hope he'll be alright."

"Yes indeed, though please, don't feel you need to hang around here, I would be most happy to telephone you tomorrow with news."

"Oh no, I really would like to hang on and see how he is."

"Well of course, if that is your wish, but the nurse tells me that when he comes out of theatre he'll be too woozy to know what is going on so I have decided to go home now, I have an early start tomorrow."

Graham's jaw dropped slightly and he continued to nod as she continued, "They will no doubt contact me if anything of importance crops up and I've left a message telling him I shall visit tomorrow evening." She held out her hand, "Once again, thank you for your kindness." He shook her hand but couldn't bring himself to stand as he watched her lips twist into what might have been a smile. She bade him goodnight and left, passing Nancy and Sarah in the corridor. Nancy asked, "Who was that?" and without meaning to, Graham snapped, "You mean *what* was that?"

He allowed a short pause before continuing, "*That* is the besht cashe I have seen for spaying at puberty, before nature could have gifted her with a child."

Sarah looked puzzled as she conjured with his pronunciation, "Do you mean sterilisation?"

"No, I chose the correct word."

An hour later the group had an impromptu meeting in the hospital cafeteria which was closed for business but the seating area remained open, with a vending machine to hand for hot drinks. Only Harding was absent, for obvious reasons. Doctor Williams knew the surgeon and had spoken with him when he came out of the theatre. Tim was comfortable but Williams relayed the long list of injuries to the group. Thankfully, most were relatively minor, including the broken fingers and bruised ribs but they couldn't determine the full extent of damage to the eyes. The attackers had used acrylic spray paint at very close range and a substantial area of each eyeball had suffered burns. They had cleaned him up and would now wait and see. Almost the whole body was bruised, some parts severely, and whilst they had taken photographs, it would probably be necessary for another set to be taken the next day, when the full extent of bruising would be more evident. Lastly, he had brought up foreign matter from his lungs which suggested an intake of some sort, possibly muddy water and a course of antibiotics was thought prudent.

Sarah had made a point of sitting next to Graham and gently leaned against him so that she could speak quietly, "Nancy tells me this one hit you hard."

He shrugged, "I'm OK now. It was the firsht one since I'd packed up lasht Christmas, *and* I'd made promises to him that I couldn't keep. Now that I've met hish mother I realise how alone he is. I think he musht live in a world without any love or friendship. He turned to her then, "I'm beginning to undershtand how suicide became an option."

They sat quietly for a minute or two until Harvey made an observation they all identified with, "You know, this feels like Graham's been out on some sort of operation and we are here for the debrief."

They all nodded though Sarah added, "And to acknowledge what he's managed to do yet again. Save a child."

Nancy was sitting on the other side of Graham and nudged him with her elbow, "Yes, well done for that, but you bloody well did it again, didn't you?" She turned to the others, "We agreed working practices five minutes ago and today he ignored most of them." This time she punched his arm with enough force to make him wince, "When will you learn luv? We nearly lost you last Christmas because you charged into a situation on your own and today you leapt off the bus leaving me with two bags of shopping and a mobile telephone."

Graham had already given the matter some thought but the answer remained the same as always, "I didn't think. All I could *feel* was Timothy, who was injured and," he paused, looking for the words, "And *dying* inside." The group was silenced then, as each member tried to imagine that depth of despair.

Harvey moved then forward, "OK chum, how about bringing us up to date."

Graham explained how they had waited for Tim to turn up at the store cafeteria of Friday, when they intended to make a tape recording. They sat in silence as he told the rest of the story, his voice catching with emotion when he described the form he took for a dog and the dreadful cries it made.

This time Harvey was shaking his head, "I still have to pinch myself to make sure I'm not dreaming this. You are quite remarkable Graham; I'll go home tonight and remind myself of that when I kiss Esther 'night night'."

Williams spoke. "Well, hopefully Adam has caught up with the culprits by now and with Timothy in safe hands we just need to address the recurring problem of the media. Any suggestions?"

Sarah responded, "Well my first tactic would be to avoid any contact for a start."

"But if they do get a whisper Graham's going to find himself under siege."

Harvey raised his hand slightly, "All they have at this stage are two boys, hopefully in custody, who could have been overheard talking about their actions on the bus. Graham took it from there, and after bullying the victim's location out of them, contacted the police. The rest is a matter of Police record."

The Doctor nodded, "Sounds like a plan, and your point is well made, the press will first seek information from the Police so maybe we should leave it at that until Adam tells us what the official line is."

A consensus was agreed and everyone except Graham stood to leave. Williams called out, "Oh bugger, I nearly forgot, I've brought the journals for the next one to read. I knew most of it but it didn't make the experience any less stunning. Great job Graham." He held the carrier bag up and added, "It occurs to me that Harvey is the least well informed so do you think he should be the next to read these." They all agreed, forgetting the order that had been agreed in the last meeting and Harvey wasted no time in claiming them. It was past one o clock and they were all tired. Nancy rested her hand on Graham's shoulder, "Come on love, you need to get some sleep."

"He placed his hand on hers and looked up at her, "No, I'm shtaying here. Tim needs to see a friendly face when he comes round, but you go back and get shome rest, you're picking Jimmy up in the morning."

She had forgotten all about Jimmy and their arrangements for the weekend, "Look, with all this going one surely we could postpo . . ."

"No!" Once again he'd spoken more sharply than he'd intended and softened his voice as he continued, "These weekendsh mean the world to Jimmy and we couldn't expect him to understand what'sh happened tonight. He'd rather play *Monopoly* all weekend than be left in the home. Go on, I'll catch a taxi home." She saw the sense in what he was saying, better that one of them should be at least partly refreshed to play host to their young guest. She kissed him and turned to Williams who had been waiting and now said, "Right, well I'll get you home Nancy but we'll just call down at the recovery room on the way out and clear Graham as a visitor. They're always a bit chary about non-relatives." He looked at Graham, whose clothes were still muddied from holding Tim, "Though I would expect them to have you change into a gown. See you old chap."

The chillers and refrigerators humming were the only sounds left as he sat and replayed the episode in his mind. He knew that he should feel elation at having rescued the child but as he pushed himself up from the table he only felt sadness. Would life change for Timothy or was his role in life already determined?

Williams was right, he was asked to don a gown and wash his arms and hands thoroughly. He was then directed to an alcohol dispenser for a final treatment to his hands before the nurse swiped her card through a box beside the double doors which opened electrically. They walked down a short corridor into a small ward that contained six beds. Three were occupied by patients who were hooked up to machines but clearly asleep. Two beds were empty but the sixth, nearest the large office window was softly lit by a diffused neon light above the bed head. A card just beneath it bore the name, *Timothy Dexter*, who lay on his back fidgeting and turning his head from side to side. The small noises he was making confirmed that he was having a bad dream. Graham paused to consider the tubes and wires that connected Tim to the paraphernalia around him and the pads that were held over his eyes by a gauze bandage. But easily the most shocking was the bruising. His arms lay on top of the covers and were covered in purples and yellows; so many that it was difficult to see where some started and others finished. He didn't know how long they had been standing at the foot of the bed but finally his reverie was interrupted when the nurse explained, "He came around from the anaesthetic without any problems, but he's still woozy so we're keeping an eye on him." She nodded towards the office as she spoke and added, "If he feels sick use that," pointing at a small card bowl that had been left on the bedside locker. She returned to the office and gave him a small smile of encouragement as she sat at the desk behind the glass.

Graham sat quietly at the bedside for some time, gazing at the injuries and trying to find a way of shaking the despair. Eventually he shook himself and leaned forward, to whisper, "Hello maytee." Timothy remained in the same troubled place and showed no reaction until Graham repeated himself. All movement stopped and he sensed the boy's tension as he waited for another signal.

"It'sh me Graham, from the shtore." He rested his fingers across Timothys', "I've come to keep you company. Nancy shends you her love and has kept your *Kit Kat* for you." For a while there was no response until Graham felt movement under his hand and watched as the smaller hand appeared and settled on top where they closed around two of his fingers. He slept on but this time without noise or movement. Each of them comforted, in different ways.

But Graham's ease didn't last. He drifted in and out of a doze that began to fill with images and emotions.

* * *

One by one he relived episodes of the child's life. The end of the first school year, going home with a whole years' worth of paintings sandwiched between two pieces of card. Miss had told them all how proud she was and that they should hang their work at home. He felt the certainty of approval and praise, trying to guess where the pictures could be hung; where best for guests to admire them. He knew the journey home as time of joy and didn't want it to end. He tried to fight it but soon he felt the confusion and pain of seeing the portfolio flicked through and discarded. None would be allowed up on the wall. It was the next morning when he discovered his work in the dustbin.

Blinded by so many flashbulbs, he listened to the applause of many parents who minutes later collected the cast of the Nativity play from the classroom that had served as the changing room. He watched children being hugged and congratulated with promises of a MacDonald's or pizza in recognition of their performances when he felt his own hand snatched towards the exit. The cold walk home held no praise. Just a critique and concern about the embarrassment he caused by forgetting that line.

Recently, he had thought to please his teacher by writing a story over the weekend. He was proud of it until one by one his spelling, grammar and punctuation were ridiculed. There was a silence as the pages were torn in half and thrown onto the fire. A single tear moved down across his cheek as he watched his whole days' work turned into a fluttering, fragile film of ash.

Every Christmas was the same. A small stocking of presents and braised beef for dinner, each accompanied by a an attack on society's exploitation of Christ's birth. Mother would get maudling drunk on sherry in the afternoon and television was unwelcome. After washing up from lunch he would wait until teatime and eat a lonely tea of pork pie and crisps.

They went on, each episode a corrosion of self esteem and each time his spirit became colder and weaker.

He did not know love, yet knew he needed something.

* * *

An hour later Tim stirred again, but this time seemed restless and uncomfortable. Graham waved at the nurse who was wading through a pile of paperwork and caught the movement out of the corner of her eye. She checked the monitors and her patients' temperature before pointing at the card bowl. I should standby with that in case he's feeling a bit sickly. It'll happen suddenly but don't worry, it's perfectly normal."

He had only just set the bowl down on the bed when Tim moaned slightly and sat up. Thanks to the nurses' warning the bowl was positioned quickly enough to catch the lot, or at least almost. She returned immediately and smiled at Graham as she settled Tim back down, "There, I was right and no spillages I see. Well done you."

As he turned his attention back to Tim he couldn't help thinking, 'No wonder people fall in love with nurses!' Fingers were re-engaged and after a few moments Tim croaked, "Are you Graham?"

"Yesh maytee, I'm here."

"My throat's ever so sore."

There was a jug of water and glass on the top of the locker but Graham decided to check, "Hang on then. I'll see if I can give you a drink." He crept into the office and received permission, though 'for sips to begin with rather than glugs.'

With that task over Tim seemed to be fully conscious though Graham found himself at a loss for something to talk about. Certainly not the attack, he was certain. Momentarily he thought of Nancy and hoped she was getting some rest, ready to entertain Jimmy and then it came to him, he would tell a story.

A story that told of a young prince who lived in these times but in a distant ice-covered land. He was the apple of his mother's eye but hated by his stepfather who arranged for two evil men to kidnap the boy and transport him here, to England. His mother was distraught when they told her a tale of how he had strayed from the group and been taken by three huge wolves. She would spend the rest of her life mourning her loss. He'd gone into great detail when describing the prince's mother, the palace and the countryside until he realised that the grip on his fingers had eased and Tim's regular breathing signalled sleep. Graham allowed his own eyes to droop when suddenly the grip returned and Tim said, "Go on. Please."

He chronicled the long trek by dog sled, horseback, cart, car rail and ferry until they reached England, where they caught a train for the last leg of their journey to a city in the centre of the country where no-one would think to look for him. There he was abandoned, on a bench in Abbey Park, close to the bandstand and with no more than a small canvas bag containing a few clothes and a stale ham sandwich. The Police found him and placed him in a big old Victorian home that was run by the kindest and funniest lady anyone could wish for. But it wasn't home, away from the land he knew and the mother he loved. He became so very unhappy and ran away time and time again until once, when it was raining very heavily he ran out in front of a car and his leg was broken. From then on Graham stopped making things up and though Tim didn't know it, the prince became Jimmy Everard, whose friends Nancy and Graham with their dog Chocks, joined him in all sorts of adventures. There had been a few breaks while Tim dozed so that the arrival of morning teas spared Graham the task of finding a credible ending, though they agreed that more adventures were due before the tale could end.

They both had a cup of tea, though Tim needed help to line up his feeder-style beaker. Afterwards they sat quietly for a few minutes until Tim turned to face where he guessed Graham was sitting, "Thank you for rescuing me."

"Heyyy. That'sh the least a friend should do." After a pause he added, "They'll never do that to you again Tim, take my word for it."

He described how the ward was beginning to come alive, and thought to pardon himself for the unintended pun. He also sought Tim's pardon for having to leave, knowing that it would be a stretch to get home, change and make it to work in time. He promised to return as soon as he could with Nancy and some sweets, thanked the nurse who appeared to be signing off to a colleague and dashed for the door.

At that moment the real Jimmy Everard, was struggling into his socks at the home before racing downstairs to wolf down breakfast and wait for Nancy.

* * *

At around ten o clock the previous evening Detective Harding had been accompanied by the police Child Protection Officer, Pat Geary who had been briefed on the situation and voiced her concern, "I'm not sure where I fit in to this; I'm normally programmed to deal with vicious parents not their kids."

Harding sighed, "I know, but as our CPO you might manage to stop me from beating the shit out of these lads. It will be a new slant on Child Protection and you would be saving my long and inglorious career from an ignominious end."

"That was a lot of big words."

"Listen and learn young lady, listen and learn."

They pulled up alongside a row of modern semi-detached council houses built in the nineteen seventies when it was fashionable to have homes facing each other across areas of grass and shrubs with pedestrian access only. Vehicular access was at the rear in an enclave that served half of the houses and half of those in the neighbouring close in a contemporary 'back to back' fashion. The enclaves were sufficiently quiet and discreet for all manner of criminal practices to thrive, from hub-capping to storing stolen goods in the garages that still had doors. At best it became a dumping ground for car wrecks. They left the patrol car out on the main road, on double yellow lines, with the impunity bestowed by having an orange one on each side of the car. It would have been culpable folly to park a police car in an enclave.

Bill Croft was a wiry 53 year old who worked nights at one of the local transport warehouses. The work was hard and shifts lasted for twelve hours but that meant he only worked four nights a week, giving him nice long weekends for his carp fishing. Since the fishing required him to bivouac at the lakeside for at least one night his family saw little of him. His friend George shared his interest in fishing and they would spend hours contemplating their rod tips and discussing such world affairs, the *Tiger's* run of bad luck and whether they'd even hang on in the Premier League. Terrorism and immigration, with little to distinguish the two in their opinion, also featured regularly as did beer prices, and the mammary glands depicted on that morning's page three. They accepted that there was little need to understand things like high finance and foreign policy since the politicians would muck that up anyway.

He had often told George about his lad's new computer game that was all about fighting terrorists. The actual game play seemed terribly complicated and way beyond him, which by default, afforded his son Paul a certain kudos, since *he* was doing really well. Both George and Bill thought the kids could probably do just as good a job of sorting the fundamentalists out as the berks at Westminster. In any event, they couldn't do any more harm.

His wife, Josie, was less impressed by the amount of time Paul and his mate Andrew spent on that damned computer, but with an absentee husband and father she acknowledged the value of any-thing that kept him out of trouble and her way. As for opinions, on international politics and terrorism, Bill had more than enough for both of them. Paul had raced in from school, or rather from his friend Andrew's well after seven and taken his meal up to his room, which was nothing new, but it enabled her to settle down with Linda and a box of chocolate mints to watch the Friday quiz show. Linda had always been more *companionable* than Paul and their 'Girls nights in' were a ritual of great comfort. That evening was no exception.

When the doorbell rang Linda was curled up on the sofa with her head resting on her mother's shoulder, a position she relin-quished with the reluctance of a disturbed cat.

"Good evening, Mrs Croft is it?" Harding smiled and offered his warrant card for inspection.

"What is it, what's happened?" She couldn't bring herself to put her suspicions into words but deaths, accidents and other bad things usually triggered a visit by the police. In that moment she could only think of Bill or her parents, the rest of her family were either dead already or accounted for.

"I am DS Harding and this is one of our specialists, WPC Geary, may we step inside please Mrs Croft?" In his customary way Hard-ing was already crossing the threshold as he spoke. Once inside he stopped to allow Mrs Croft to lead him into the lounge where a young girl sat curled up in the corner of a sofa, watching television.

Josie began to repeat her question and thought to protect her daughter from any bad news, at least for the time being, "Linda, love, pop up to your room for a minute, I'll call you back down in a bit."

Harding stayed any movement by raising his hand, "Ah so this is Linda," he turned to her mother and added, "I would like to speak to both of you if I may. And Master Paul, is he in at the moment?"

Josie was beginning to feel flaky with the tension and responded to anything that might bring some sort of order to the proceedings, "Yes, he's upstairs, I'll go and get him."

"No, not for the moment, thanks Mrs Croft. Please sit down and I'll explain." Josie sat down beside her daughter who had uncurled into a similar formal sitting posture. Adam sat in the only easy chair and Pat occupied a dining room chair at Linda's end of the sofa.

"What time did Paul get in this evening Mrs Croft?"

"About an hour, perhaps two hours ago."

"Hmm, so would that be before or after seven, say?"

"Oh it was definitely after seven, he often stays back at his friend's house, Andrew Maynard that is. He grabbed his tea and went up to his room. He's probably stuck on that computer again."

"Did he seem different at all, upset perhaps, or disturbed."

"No, no more than usual, but why? Has he done anything?"

Instead of answering Harding turned to Linda who visibly wilted, in spite of his smile of encouragement, "Linda, you're in Mrs Stretton's class aren't you?" He returned her nod with one of his own before continuing, "So you would know a boy called Timothy Dexter." Another nod. "Do you know him very well?" This time she shook her head.

Pat asked the next question, "So you didn't bully him then?" Linda turned to face the uniformed lady and shook her head again though a little less certain. After a moment or two she said quietly, "No."

"A lot of children did though, didn't they?" This time the time taken to reply was much longer, and took the form of a timid nod.

Harding followed through quickly, "Paul and his friend did, didn't they?" This time the girl turned towards him and then looked up at her mother with a look that held a silent plea for guidance. Even perhaps, a sanction to tell the truth. Silence reigned as Josie struggled to interpret her daughter's look. She said the only thing she could think of, "Answer him Linda."

The girl turned back to face Harding, the inner struggle clearly evident, "They were only playing."

"What did they do to him Linda?" This time it was Pat who asked and the girl swivelled around to answer, "Nothing much, they just called him names and things."

"What things Linda, what did they do?"

Linda rested a forefinger on her lower lip and looked upwards to demonstrate an attempt at recollection. "Just pushed him and things." Her questioners said nothing and her attempts to protect her brother failed to weather the silence that followed. Both hands fell into her lap and she looked down, "And they stole his whistle." The last was said so softly the adults barely heard it but Harding responded just as softly. "That wasn't all though, was it Linda. They were planning to do something to him weren't they?"

All little sisters eavesdrop and spy on their elder brothers, it's a given, but Linda's spirits sank as she realised how much trouble she was getting involved in. She was given a small respite when her mother interrupted. She had listened to the questions in stunned silence, more particularly since her daughter answers to the questions seemed to imply a certain 'fit' with their line of questioning. Clearly, their focus was on her son and she wasn't prepared to let things carry on without an explanation. "Look, you've done nothing but ask questions since you got here but you won't answer mine. Now it's obviously got something to do with Paul, so I want to know what, before we go any further."

He didn't show how annoyed he was by the interruption and spoke gently, "Mrs Croft, I understand your concern and I apologise for appearing to be secretive. If I can just ask Linda one or two more questions I will tell you everything, I promise." He allowed a few moments to pass before repeating his assurance, "I promise."

Josie was unused to dealing with anything like this and couldn't articulate her anxiety quickly enough to influence the moment. Intead she sat in silence as the chubby detective addressed her daughter again, "Linda, what were they planning to do to Timothy?"

Linda fidgeted in her seat and stared resolutely at her slippered feet. "They were only playing." Again the silence. "It was only a game." Silence. "They didn't mean anything, s'just a game."

Josie broke the silence that followed. She might not know how to deal with the Police but she knew when her children were holding back and her daughter's prevarication was beginning to frighten her. It was time to sort things out. "Linda, love, you must tell us what they were going to do this lad Timothy." She rested a hand on the girl's arm in support, "Come on love, what was it?"

"Interrigation."

"Pardon?"

This time Linda looked up at her mother, "Interrigation, that's what they called it."

Pat leaned in towards the girl, "Thank you Linda, that was brave of you and it was the right thing to do. But what do you think they meant by that. How do you think they set about it." She kicked herself for using the tense she had in the last question but the girl didn't seem to notice. The mother did though and was sitting bolt upright, eyes widening in comprehension. Harding was going to give her a bollocking for sure just as Josie was going to demand an explanation. Her daughter answered first, "Dunno, it was just interrigation, for the game."

Harding had also seen the signals and cut in before Josie could speak, "What game Linda." She shrugged her shoulders, "Dunno, it's on the computer and they'd got to interrigate someone."

Realisation finally took hold and Harding leapt to his feet. "Pat, please explain to Mrs Croft why we are here while I go and have a word with young Paul." He had left the room with such haste that half of the sentence was called from the hall as he began climbing the stairs. When he reached the landing the room selection was easy. Only one door was closed.

He tried the door and wasn't surprised to find it locked, "Paul, your mum's sent me up to have a word with you, open the door please, immediately." He placed his head against the door and could hear movement of some sort but nothing that suggested an approach to the door and as he prepared to shout again he heard the unmistakable beep of warning from a computer. Harding's weight was more than enough to send the flimsy bolt flying off the other side of the door and because the curtains were closed and the room in darkness it was easy to locate the computer screen with the figure hunched in front of it, attacking the keyboard in a frenzy. The screen turned blue and a single message appeared though Harding didn't attempt to read it, the boy's intentions were clear; probably wiping the hard drive. He ran across the room and did the only thing he could think of; he ripped the plug from the wall.

"Hey, what're you doing? Who are you?"

"I've come to find out more about this game of yours, Paul, the one I imagine you were trying to wipe. We have techies that can recover that sort of thing but it'll be a different sort of recovery to the one Timothy Dexter's struggling with right now. Why did you do it Paul?"

"Don't know what you mean, you could have damaged me computer doing that."

The detective moved around the boy and sat on the neighbouring chair. In that light, his dark eyes might have been those of a shark for all the comfort they offered, "Well, see, I'm going to arrest you now and take you back to the nick for an interrogation of your own. Do you want your mum to come or are you going to sweat this one out on your own?"

Paul wilted, he couldn't turn away yet couldn't bear to continue being held in that scrutiny. Finally he wrenched his head around and stared at his computer screen. There he found his confidence again, "I don't know nothing about Timothy Dexter, what's 'appened to him anyway?" There was no response, and he grew bolder, "I bet some of the bigger lads 'ave beaten him up and we're getting the blame, just 'cos we borrowed his whistle. You could 'ave damaged my computer doing that."

"Master Paul, you are not being helpful enough for my taste. In fact you are beginning to irritate me and that is a very silly thing to do. Who's your friend."

Paul continued to stare at his monitor but leaned back in his chair and folded his arms across his front, a barrier gesture, "Which one, I've got lots".

Harding glanced around and saw the mobile telephone on the edge of the desk. He snatched it up and checked the call register, noting the number that had been called just thirteen minutes earlier. Reference to the contacts section identified the owner as 'Andy'. He stood and beckoned Paul to do so as well, "Come on, we can continue with this down at this station.

"You can't do nothing till me Dad gets home."

Harding bent down, his face uncomfortably close to the boy's and spoke quietly, "If you ever get a halfway decent handle on our beautiful language and in particular double negatives you will find that your last statement tells me I have to do *something* since you told me I cannot do *nothing*." He moved closer still, their faces almost touching, "But here's the thing, I need *you* to do something. So get out of that chair you little shit and get your arse downstairs, NOW!"

Paul bolted for the door but stopped when Harding called after him, pointing to the fleece that lay on the bed. "Take your jacket, it can get cold in the cells." It was enough, Paul grabbed the jacket and left the room howling, "Muumm."

'Mum' had heard enough from the woman Police officer and her daughter to know that her son was in trouble. But he was still her child and she would stay with him. Even so, Paul was shocked to find his mother waiting with another officer, her coat and shoes on, ready to leave.

Harding spoke first, "Mrs Croft, I am sorry you're having to deal with this, truly, but I hope you understand that we have a job to do." She was still in shock but couldn't bring herself to offer any support for the people who might be about to wreck their lives. He nodded his understanding and continued, "Paul's friend Andy, you mentioned his name earlier, do you know his address please?"

"That'll be Andrew Maynard. They live two blocks away, at number two twenty I think."

"Muumm!" Paul was shocked by his own mother's treachery and sat next to her in sullen silence during the journey in to the station, listening to the fat Detective give instructions for other policemen to raid his friend's house to collect him and his computer. In passing he did wonder how many game credits this lot was going to cost.

Mother and son were checked in and left to stew in an interview room while Harding and Geary set off to the canteen for a cup of tea and debrief. At the same time Andrew Maynard and his mother were being escorted from their house to one of the two patrol cars parked outside. Thankfully, his father was still down at the Fox and Hen, where he would probably end the evening with a fist fight. It was almost a ritual really. 'Still' Janice Maynard thought, as an officer placed a hand on her head when she slid into the back seat, 'It'll be one of his regular opponents instead of one of these coppers.

That would be a great topic for the nosy bleeders round here as if this wasn't enough.'

The officers hadn't told them much but were resolute. There was no question of them refusing to accompany them down to the station, but by the time Andrew and his mother were escorted into the Police station she knew more than anyone, other than the three participants. She had literally beaten the truth out of him in the back seat of the patrol car. One of the officers later admitted that had it not been for the seat belts she would have probably bent him over her lap and slippered him. As it was Harding met the blubbering nine year old after his mother had flung him against the desk in front of bewildered duty officer. She was in a fearsome mood, "Here, take him. He's yours now, I've given up!"

"Mrs Maynard I presume?" She whirled around and regarded Harding from head to toe and back before asking, "Who's asking?"

Harding had seen all that he needed to and recognised a need to get this pair into an interview room and on tape as soon as possible. "I'm Detective Sergeant Harding and you, I believe, could do with a cup of tea."

Taken aback by such hospitality her reply was short, "Er, yes, right. That's just what I need."

"Then please follow me," He stretched out an arm, "You too Andrew, I dare say a coke would be your first choice." Drinks were ordered and an interview room found. As soon as they were seated mother son and Pat Geary watched the detective insert tapes into a machine and listened as he cautioned the boy in a soft voice, void of threat. He didn't pause, "Andrew, you know why you're here so I'm not going to waste time going into detail in front of your mum. Just start at the beginning, tell me about the game and how you came to do what you and Paul Croft did with Timothy Dexter this evening."

He'd read the situation perfectly. Mum had beaten any denial out of the boy on the journey and the promise of sparing his mother from more an ordeal and therefore him from more punishment was enough to do the trick. Andrew told his story.

An hour later Harding and Geary left the room to start on Paul Croft. They stopped off at his desk on the way where two notes had been left. One had been sent in by the officer at the hospital and gave a full list of injuries sustained by Timothy. "Sweet Jesus, look at that." Pat took the list off him as he read the other note before screwing it into a ball and lobbing it in the direction of a bin. Taking the list off her he added, "Seems they've located Daddy Croft and he's not happy, follow me."

Bill Croft was as pissed off as an angler could get. Conditions were perfect and some heavy weight fish had already been caught around them. Then there was some bloody nonsense about bullying which, even if it was true, should be down to the school to sort out, not this bleeding lot! Coppers were afraid of sorting real crime out these days; kids like his Paul were much safer to deal with.

They found him pacing the corridor just along from the interview rooms. He was determined to have his say before they joined Paul and Josie.

"Mr Croft?"

"Yeah, are you the joker who's in charge of this fiasco? Nice and safe here at the station on a Saturday night innit?"

"Mr Croft, do you know why we've brought your son in?"

"Yes, of course I know and since when did the Police deal with school bullying."

Harding handed the list over, "Please read this before you say anymore." He watched Croft's eyes widen as he read the long list or injuries and continued, "Those are the injuries meted out by Andrew Maynard and your son on Timothy Dexter earlier this evening." He held up a hand to stay Croft's denial, "We already have a full statement from Andrew and we're on our way to speak to Paul. So now, tell me Mr Croft, what would you expect the Police to do about those injuries, or better yet, what would you have us do if someone had done that to Paul?"

They watched a mix of emotions pass across Croft's face but the standpoint was predictable. They would deal with things as a family and that included seeing off any external threat, official or otherwise. It didn't take long for Harding to hear the words he expected.

"We want a solicitor."

Chapter 11

By the time Graham got home he knew he would be late for work and had Nancy telephone the store to at least assure them he was going to get there, eventually. While she was making the call he raced upstairs to shed the muddied clothing and take a shower. When he returned to the bedroom Nancy was sitting on the bed. She had put clean clothes out and a fresh mug of tea sat on his bedside table.

She asked the obvious, "How is he?" Graham had been leaning against the bed, struggling to get a sock on. As soon as it was in place he fell on to the bed and his shoulders dropped. His voice mirrored far more than physical exhaustion, and when he turned to her his eyes were full, "That child is in a far worse shtate than you could imagine." He shook his head in despair and two tears laid tracks. Nancy turned and quickly crossed the bed on her knees to hold him, shushing and rocking gently. In time they fell back and lay together as Graham told her of his dreams in the hospital. There was no doubt, whatever, he had seen a little of the child's dormant store of torture and denial. "How is it, that a child becomes a victim at school when he's already suffering sho much at home? Is there shomething the kids see in him that makesh him a target?"

Somehow Graham managed to survive the day and arrived home in time to enjoy a glass of wine before dinner was served. Jimmy, with a modicum of prompting from Nancy, described their day which included lunch in Leicester at a new sandwich bar that sold a range of funky new fillings. They had also completed a tour of the charity shops because Nancy had needed to replenish her stock of romantic novels. Jimmy was tasked with finding some

DVD's to watch though in truth he was delighted just to be with her. The Salvation Army shop had a large circular basket filled with odd balls of wool, and Jimmy held a lurid purple one up with a gasp of disgust. Nancy had been worrying about the lack of activities, particularly since Graham would most likely be too tired to do anything after work and the variety of bright colours in the wool basket brought back a happy childhood memory. With little more than a 'trust me', Jimmy was persuaded to join her in the selection of enough different coloured balls of wool to fill a large carrier bag. She refused to give a reason for the purchase though on the bus journey home they did hold different balls up to see which colours looked best together. Once home and sustained with a cup of tea or glass of raspberryade they sat on the sofa with the bag of wool and a drum of knitting needles.

At that point in his tale Jimmy disappeared into the lounge and returned with two squares of knitted wool held up for inspection. "Look, Aunty Nancy's taught me how to knit and we're going to make a blanket, a great big one."

Graham took a square and examined it, "Hmm, I'm impreshed. How many of these have you got so far?"

"I've done these two and aunty did . . . " He placed his squares on the table and cast his eyes up. Fingers stood to attention as he completed his mental count, "Eight."

"Wow so you've done ten already. How many do you need?"

Nancy answered then, "Seventy, for a good single blanket, so we're already a seventh of the way there."

Dinner was eaten and Graham retreated to the lounge while Jimmy and Nancy washed the dishes and was sound asleep by the time they joined him. The clicking of needles soothed him into deeper slumber but once his lower jaw dropped into fly catcher mode and the snores became Olympian their giggling woke him. His grumbles disappeared as soon as he realised that their favourite talent show was on television and it served to keep him conscious, at least until Jimmy's bedtime. They left Nancy downstairs and parted at the top of the stairs with a night night hug. The gentle comfort of his quilt soon delivered him into a deep, deep sleep.

* * *

He was back in a bedroom he recognized and was afraid again, desperate for the sanctuary of sleep but kept awake by the need to hear the sounds from downstairs. The television, or perhaps the radio. Movement from one room to another and a sense of relief at the sound of the chair springs signaling the occupancy of a grown up. But there had been another sound that held no comfort at all, of glass on glass and of ice cubes falling from their tray into the sink. As time wore on and in spite of his tiredness, other sounds; of a door crashing open, crockery or glass being dropped on a tile floor, an oath followed by a dismissive laugh. He knew they chronicled the descent into drunkenness. Now the sounds of the television became important. He knew that his fear was in some way governed by the continuance of those sounds, they had to keep going.

Eventually sleep came to rescue him from the exhaustion of shallow breathing and a thudding, fearful heartbeat.

A cramping fear swept over him. It seemed only moments since he'd fallen asleep but must have been longer because his heightened senses heard the sharp rustling sound downstairs. His heartbeat began to ease as he recognized it as 'white noise'. The television programmes were over and the set was still on; which meant a reprieve. He was asleep in the chair.

But then the door handle creaked in its downward arc and the cloying dread engulfed him. He squeezed his eyes together and prayed for the visitor to leave. Instead a weight settled beside him and as his body rolled forward a hand rested on his shoulder. He screamed for pity and pleaded to be left alone, yet made no sound. In the silence hands began reaching under the bedclothes.

* * *

His bedside light had been turned on and a small hand was stroking his head. Just as before, the dream had left him soaked in sweat, though in the reality of his own bedroom he had whimpered, cringed and cried. Slowly, he focused on the hand that was soothing him and looked out from beneath his quilt. Jimmy stood at his side, his expression serious and concerned, "Don't worry Graham, I have bad dreams too."

He looked thoughtful and rolled his head onto one side to align it with Graham's, "Would you like me to help you change the bed?"

Later, when Nancy joined him, Graham told her about his dream, "It'sh the shame one and each time they get a little worshe and more frightening."

Nancy had already rolled over onto her side, facing away from him, "Then I think we should get you something to help you sleep. These dreams are just that, which is why you can't identify anything and they're brought on by all those real experiences you have. Now just try and put it out of your mind and you'll sleep easier."

"Humm." He wasn't convinced.

* * *

Harvey set the notebook he was reading down on his lap once again and stared ahead. How could anyone rationalize what he was reading? For that matter how was his acceptance of the journal possible. Yet a detective, doctor and senior social worker, all apparently sane, believed every word and more importantly bore witness to much that had happened. With a small shake of his head he returned to the text, in Graham's rounded style of handwriting.

Audrey sat across from him, watching the television, and Harvey from the corner of her eye. Whatever he was reading, it wasn't the diary of a former shop manager as he'd claimed. He was a tough business man with the brusque, no nonsense characteristics of a Yorkshire man, but he couldn't lie for toffee, at least not to her. Just as she knew he was lying, she knew that he was being affected by what he was reading. Earlier, when she had asked to see it he apologised, saying that he had given the author an undertaking to keep it to himself. Now, after hours of seeing him register such shock, yet silently discreet in an obvious attempt to keep it from her, Audrey wanted some answers. She was from Yorkshire farming stock and had never been afraid of this old bull.

"So what's in there then? No bullshit this time if you please"

Harvey looked up, startled, "I've told you, it's a diary." He wriggled slightly in discomfort, "Honestly, but you're right, it isn't from a manager. I'm sorry for the fib, but I have been sworn to secrecy and it's a promise I need to keep."

"Well I do know it has something to do with Graham," she waved a hand as she tried to remember the surname, "Oh whatever his name is, the one who helped save Esther and came here for lunch a couple of weeks ago." She saw his puzzled expression and pointed at the exercise book, "His name is on the cover."

"Please love, trust me on this one, I've given my word." He stood up and headed into the kitchen, "I'll finish it in here and have a nightcap while I'm at it. Can I get you anything?"

"No, I'm fine, except that I don't like secrets Harv, we don't do things that way."

As he walked towards the kitchen he bent and kissed the top of her head, "I know pet, but this isn't my secret, it belongs to someone else."

Any concern she felt was lost to the incredible an hour later. She dropped the television sound down a couple of notches to make sure that she wasn't hearing things and that her husband *was* weeping, openly, in the next room. The sound stopped suddenly, as though he suspected she had heard but it didn't lessen the shock. The Harvey Calders of this world simply didn't do that sort of thing. He might have promised to keep that damned thing private but she hadn't and tomorrow she was going to do all she could to get hold of it.

Harvey shakily poured himself a large scotch and sat back down at the table, staring at the orange cover of the exercise book. He had read the passage with growing shock and horror but after a pause, he felt compelled to read it again, and lost control, completely. He would later realize that he'd read a unique account of the neglect and starvation that almost killed his grand daughter. It went beyond an eye witness account, way beyond. It was an account from within. One Esther might have given if she'd been able, telling of the aching hunger and thirst that eventually became the dull listless prelude to death in the dark stinking corner of her cot, where she became too weak to hold her head up.

Graham had added to details gleaned from Harding, of the terrible death her mother had suffered when crack cocaine induced a convulsion when she was in the bath. Claire, his daughter. Her injuries suggested that she had been trying to tear imaginary bugs from her skin which almost certainly caused enough terror to bring about a cardiac arrest.

All that Harvey knew already, from the coroners hearing but this was on an entirely different level.

The following morning he was quieter than usual, due partly to a hangover but Audrey persuaded him to set off as arranged and not let his friends down. Men were so predictable. Sundays mornings were for golf and a couple of pints in the clubhouse. In the meantime, secret things, like the carrier bag containing orange exercise books would be hidden under his side of the bed. With those retrieved all that remained was for her to make a large cup of latte before settling down to read. Audrey Harvey was about to embark on an incredible journey.

* * *

Linda Croft had been a silent witness to the shock and recriminations that had continued since the Policeman came for Paul. Often, she would be sent outside or up to bed before her parents began to discuss the mess her brother had caused. Some of the things they talked about left her confused or bewildered and in her isolation she could think of only one thing to do that might help. It didn't take her long to find what she needed in Paul's bedroom and a large padded envelope from the odds and sods drawer in the kitchen.

She was at a loss then and for want of anything better to do walked over to the nearby row of shops and sat on a bench to wait. It was a Sunday and most of the shops had closed at lunchtime but her isolation didn't bother her.

Sometimes the fates warm to such things, though Alice Taylor, a resident at the nearby Orchards Care Home wouldn't have thought much of them when an hour later her mini-stroke prompted a call for an ambulance.

It was exactly what Linda had hoped for and she trotted in the direction of the siren, just a couple of streets away.

Alice was stabilised and installed in the ambulance in short order but when the driver opened his door he saw the package that had been left on his seat, addressed by a young hand.

TO TIMOTHY DEXTER AT THE HOSPITAL. VERY IMPORTANT

"Ben, come and look at this."

His partner poked his head through into the cab and considered the package, "Posties as well now are we?"

The envelope had only been folded over so that they were able to check the contents which raised two smiles, "Nice thought, I hope it finds Mr Timothy, his ward sister will be delighted!"

Evening visiting was over and even though his mother had warned him that she was unlikely to make it his heart skipped a beat when he felt someone move alongside his bed, but then his spirits sank as he recognised the nurse's voice. She bent over and whispered into his ear, "Someone has sent this in to you Timothy, but if you must try it, blow very gently won't you." With that she folded his hand around his granddad's big shiny whistle.

A short while later the ward heard a small, timid peep. It could just as easily have been the Queen Mary.

* * *

Harvey had returned from the club just after two and was faintly surprised to find the house empty though he wasn't concerned, they never bothered with traditional Sunday lunches and ate their main meal at night. He made himself a cheese and pickle sandwich and went through to the lounge to watch the golf on television. As usual, lunchtime television had a soporific affect though he felt thoroughly refreshed when he woke forty minutes later. He wandered back into the kitchen just as his daughter, Lucy walked in through the back door, with little Esther in her arms. "Granpa!" The toddler reached out her arms and transferred from one to the other with the ease of a baby ape.

"Hey Dad." Lucy gave him a peck on the cheek and headed for the kettle, "Want a drink?"

"Er, yes please, I was just about to make myself one. Where's your mum?"

"No idea. She telephoned me just before lunch and said she had to go out and would I look after Ess. Seemed a bit distracted to tell you the truth. When I got here she just thanked me and disappeared. I had to get Esther ready and lock up. She's had a sleep by the way"

"Perhaps she's popped down to Fosse Park, to do some shopping."

"Hmm, could be. Actually, she might be taking something back, she had a carrier bag with her."

Harvey allowed the words to sink in with a growing dread, "Excuse me a second." He left the room casually before taking the stairs at the run, though he already knew that the journals would be missing from beneath his bed. 'Bugger!' he thought, 'should have put them in the car.' He went back downstairs and had a cup of tea with his daughter. There was nothing else he could do but wait until Audrey had finished reading and heaven only knew how the conversation would go then.

Lucy left shortly after and Harvey played with Esther, keeping an eye on the television and clock. Teatime passed by and Esther had been bathed and put to bed before Audrey returned. As she walked through the lounge towards the kitchen Harvey turned and smiled, "Hello love."

She gave him a small wave and continued on to make herself a drink. He listened intently as she filled the kettle and switched it on, followed the process of making a cup of tea, just one he noticed and finally decided to join her when a chair was dragged out from beneath the table. The carrier bag containing Graham's journals lay on the work surface. He poured himself a scotch and was delving in the freezer compartment for ice cubes when she spoke.

"You bastard." She said it so quietly and matter-of-factly he wondered whether he'd misheard her.

"Pardon?"

She took a sip of her tea before replying, "She was my daughter as well you know."

He understood immediately and spoke softly, "I know love, but I gave my word to the man who wrote those."

This time she stood and turned to face him. He saw then that her eyes were red and swollen and she was trembling, but her scream shocked him more, "That's the point you thoughtless bastard! How DARE you promise anyone to keep something like that from me. I was her MOTHER for fuck's sake!"

They stood facing each other as her words sought purchase in his thoughts. He realized how wrong he'd been and how he should have refused to accept them rather than agree to keep the truth from Audrey. "My God, I'm so sorry love, you're right. I'm so sorry you had to read that on your own." They held on to each other then, for a very long time. Each had already spent their tears and needed comfort.

Later, they sat at the table and jointly considered passages in the journals. It was past midnight when they finished and Audrey shook her head tiredly, "You are certain that this is true, not science fiction."

He didn't hesitate, "Yes, if you met the others you would realize how bright and down to earth they are and don't forget, most of them have actually witnessed Graham's gift at work. So yes, I'm convinced, but a little scared because of it. It's, well it's so *unworldly.*"

Audrey nodded, "I know, I couldn't see how I could believe in it until I realized that if it hadn't been for Graham we would have lost a granddaughter we didn't even know about, as well as our daughter, *and* he was nearly killed doing it. I will never tell anyone you know that, but if it will help, I will never let on to the others in your group that I have read the journals, provided you never, ever keep that sort of secret from me again."

Harvey took her hand, "I swear love, though I'm inclined to 'fess up to the group too."

She patted his arm, "Right then, it's bedtime, though God knows what my dreams will be like tonight."

Chapter 12

School assembly had been a quiet affair as the students and staff listened to Timothy's plight. They closed with a prayer for his swift recovery and return to school. Angela Tenson delegated the morning's schedule to her deputy and retreated to silence of her office where decisions needed to be made. She also expected another visit from Sarah Whiting and rather than risk a confrontation on the telephone she gave her secretary permission to grant any spare slot in the appointment book if Sarah called. She did, and arrived promptly at eleven thirty.

They shook hands and both sat down, waiving niceties as Sarah cut to the chase. "Last night, when I saw Timothy come out of surgery I wanted to come here this morning and thump you." Tenson began to speak but was silenced by Sarah's raised hand and tired half-smile. "But then I thought about our last meeting and that maybe you were as unhappy with your behaviour as I was with mine. A fist fight today would be even less appropriate. This time I would like to try again, in a spirit of co-operation, even though I still can't divulge my source." She held her hand out palm downward in a calming gesture, "Please, this is not a threat but if we can't do something about what happened here I will go to the press and refer to our meeting, which is recorded in your appointments diary and my detailed minutes. I shall simply say that I was notified by an anonymous caller whose information proved to be correct." She saw the head trying for an opportunity to react and continued quickly, "I know, I don't sound very co-operative but all I'm trying to do is give you a perspective to consider. You're initial reaction was entirely understandable, I realise that now, even if I didn't at the time, but just consider how the press will question malpractice by a form teacher who has been teaching for so long."

The head teacher sat back in her chair as the implications of Sarah's last sentence became clear. Only one person would be blamed for allowing that to go on for so long, if it were true. With that poor child in hospital conclusions would be made and besides, who knows what else would come to light.

She was a professional and extremely good head who never backed away from self-scrutiny. If that teacher *had* been using practices from the nineteen fifties she, as head, should have been aware of it. The irony was that a bad head could have ducked and dived their way out of it. Angela Tenson was too good a head teacher for that.

Sarah spoke softly, "I'm sorry I don't mean to be high-handed again, truly." She was looking at the head but lost her focus to moisture, and added weakly, "There were so *many* injuries and they don't know whether they've saved his sight yet."

Tenson was moved by her visitor's struggle for control, and connected with what the woman had said. After all, she had obviously been to the hospital. Glancing at the business card in front of her she paused in thought before acknowledging to herself that their previous meeting had been a disaster. It was time to get on with the necessary. She looked up at Sarah, "I'm going to say something now that I would like to keep off the record." She paused to allow Sarah time to consider and give a nod of agreement. "I haven't slept much since last Friday and whilst I could argue enough of a defence against a professional enquiry, I know that personally, I will never forgive myself for not doing more, something specific, after our last meeting, instead of behaving like a petulant amateur." She waved away Sarah's attempt to ease her perspective and with a slight smile asked, "Mrs Whiting, may I call you Sarah?" She received a nod and reached for the telephone, "Let's start over shall we. There's a lot to do and I promise to listen this time. Tea or coffee."

From then on they shared a common aim. They needed to get to the bottom of what had happened and to make sure it couldn't happen again. Though neither would have guessed it they were to become firm friends.

* * *

Graham and Nancy grabbed a hasty lunch on Monday in order to catch a bus in time for afternoon visiting at the infirmary and were startled to discover that Timothy had been discharged that morning. Since they were not relatives the staff could not provide any more information about his progress or his address so further contact was out. All they could hope for was another Friday afternoon rendezvous. Saddened slightly to have missed him, they headed home with the consolation of knowing that he'd recovered enough to go home himself. 'God help him' thought Graham.

* * *

Two days of discreet enquiries followed, in which staff were encouraged to air concerns they'd had for a long time. Like all questionable procedures some had decided to ignore them whilst others feared to question what they saw as established practices. Those who taught in neighbouring classes had gathered a fuller picture from the scraps they had learned over time and now voiced their concerns by citing actual examples. Shouting and shrieking to levels that bordered on abuse, children standing and weeping in front of the class that was being encouraged to chant accusations, yet at other times the class would sit woodenly in utter silence while Mary was working at her desk.

But the gentle probing and encouragement of a few children, in the safety of the head's office, was more upsetting. Somehow, their poor grammar and simplistic narratives leant greater weight and poignancy to the intelligence they provided.

Mary had been aware of the sidelong glances and how talk stopped abruptly when she entered the staff room. She wasn't stupid and guessed it had something to do with that pathetic little Timothy. Nevertheless, she still felt her pulse pick up as she read the note delivered to her in class, asking her to call in and see the head after school that day.

* * *

"Please sit down, I'm sorry you haven't managed to be first away this afternoon." The elder allowed that punch to pass without reaction but sat down and readied herself for more.

"Mary, I want to discuss some of the practices you have been *guilty* of for God knows how long now."

"I beg your pardon!"

The head continued as though Mary hadn't spoken, "Practices that do not belong in the modern classroom, in fact do not belong in any civilised environment."

"I'm not going to sit here and listen to this nonsense, if you want a witch hunt pick someone else." Mary stood and headed for the door. "It's your choice Mary, you either sit down, *now,* or I call the police and have them talk to you about practices that cultivated a regime of bullying that went out with Tom brown's schooldays and which resulted in grievous bodily harm to one of your students. Conspiracy or Incitement to violence I think they'll call it. I'll make sure you're arrested rather than see you go out of that door now."

Mary had listened to the threat with her back to the head and turned slowly, "If that happened you would be finished too. Your career would be over, gone."

"That would be a tiny price to pay if it meant I could stop you and don't think I'm not ashamed, bitterly ashamed, for not conducting this meeting before now. That said, I can start a new life but I hope you're not too settled in that village of yours. A conviction for those *crimes* would make you a pariah."

Mary focused on the head's telephone and considered her options. With an exaggerated sigh she sank into the chair, "OK, I have no wish to get in the way of your *remedial* measures, what do you have in mind? But before you start let me add this. I know that you wouldn't want this school dragged through the media and you're threats are just that, no more. So what do you propose? A change of class, closer supervision or a transfer?"

Angela rested her elbows on her desk and wrapped one hand in the other, her eyes had the impassionate gaze of a wolf and her voice a chilling certainty, "I propose to install our most experienced teaching assistant in your class for every minute that you are and she will be told why. I will sit in on your classes at least once a day at random times and in the meantime I require you to give me your preparation for classes in advance. I can tell you now that they will be unsatisfactory and I anticipate a completely new regime of longer hours and commitment to be put in place. I will not be saddened when, given time and influence, either a nervous or physical breakdown forces early retirement."

Each held the other's gaze but only one held the aces. She continued, "Any infraction, no matter how slight will force me to consider your influence in Timothy's life and at the very least report it to the LEA. Alternatively, you might wonder how attractive early retirement could be. Go home and think about it; you have a week of sick leave to make your mind up."

The older woman stood slowly and sneered, "You don't think yo . . ."

Angela's voice remained measured, controlled, "Get out of my office please, now."

The elder turned to the door and had begun to open it when the head called after her, "Mary." Sub consciously she knew, though had yet to admit it to herself, that her exit from that office represented her exit from teaching and she refused to turn and face her executioner, though she did pause as the head continued;

"It's not nice being bullied is it?"

Chapter 13

Life returned to normal for the next week, at least as far as it could for Graham who still received 'hits' that told him of petty cruelties so many children suffered. Often as a result of thoughtlessness or distraction rather than overt cruelty. For the most part he shrugged them off in favour of his own sanity.

Nancy collected Jimmy from the home as usual and discovered that knitting had swept through the entire place. There were brightly coloured squares everywhere, with a full blanket hung on the wall of the entrance hall, in pride of place. Pat Ensor, the warden, was delighted. Apparently, Dr Bernardo's charity shops around the Midlands had cleared their stocks of wool and promised to sell the finished products, provided any of the knitters could be persuaded to release them.

They had tried to make contact with Timothy but his mother's telephone number was ex-directory and because of a huge workload Sarah had passed the file on to a colleague. She promised to let them have the number as soon as she could. Graham had already decided against calling at the house. Somehow, he knew his mother would react badly.

The following weekend drew near and the forecast was good; the agenda even better. It was a bank holiday Monday which gave them a three day weekend, since those holidays were taken on rota and it was Graham's turn to have the day off.

The battlefield centre at Market Bosworth was advertising a mediaeval event with a craft fair, a campsite of the period, sideshows and a jousting tournament. Lunches were available in the restaurant but there was also a hog roast for those more inclined to picnic. Bus 153 to Market Bosworth would leave them a two mile walk to the centre, part of which would be on an old gated road.

Provisions were still required, not least of all the '*Wagon Wheel*' biscuits that had found favour with Graham and Jimmy. Nancy was considering whether to ration them when she arrived at the store on Friday evening and found Graham sitting on the low wall that ran along the front of the car park, basking in the evening sun. "Wake up Tarzan, Jane wants a cup of tea please."

Graham looked up and smiled lazily, "Ugg, you want bishcuit too."

"Of course, a *Kit Kat* if you please." She stopped short and their smiles faded, "I wonder how he is?"

They headed into the stores and past the checkouts to the caf-eteria. At first, neither noticed the small boy waiting by the tray dispenser. He was wearing a new red anorak and startlingly white trainers but as they drew nearer they could see that one eye had a patch and he wore a pair of heavy-looking spectacles. His face still bore bruises and the fingers of one hand were bandaged into a splint. Nancy's heart melted when he used that hand to wave at them.

"Maytee! It ish *shooo* good to see you, we've been so worried."

Timothy wore a solemn expression, "My mum said I must thank you for saving me."

Nancy cuddle him, "Nah, don't worry about that, he was a bit late anyway, just like tonight. Have you been waiting long?"

Torn between good manners and honesty, his head described a circular compromise between a nod and shake. She ruffled his already tousled hair, "Enough said, let's get you a hot chocolate and *kit Kat* shall we?"

Within half an hour they had re-established their friendship and this time, telephone numbers were exchanged. Breaks and bruising were healing nicely but the eyes had been damaged. At best spec-tacles would be necessary in future, and whilst hopeful, the final call remained to be made on the eye still bearing a patch. Most importantly, and with great pride, Tim extracted a large silver whis-tle from his jacket pocket. How it managed to reach him in the ward remained a mystery though he was happy to run with the possibility of magic.

They agreed to continue their Friday night ritual and parted company in high spirits. Graham and Nancy said very little on the bus journey home, they didn't need to. Timothy had turned a bright light back on for them.

That night Graham telephoned Sarah to pass on their news and stop her from attempting to contact her colleague. She was delighted and chuckled at news of their hot chocolate and *Kit Kat* meetings. They chatted about various things and were consulting diaries to agree the next group meeting when she suddenly told him to hang on, returning minutes later and slightly out of breath, "Just had to check with Stan, to make sure he hasn't got anything planned. Why don't you bring Jimmy down to the farm for the afternoon on Monday, we'll show him around and let him meet some of the stock, drive a tractor, that sort of thing."

"That shounds wonderful, hang on a mo', I'll check with Nancy."

Sarah called loudly, "Hang on, I've also had another thought, but it's very much up to you, for God's sake don't feel obliged, but would you like to invite Timothy too."

Graham spoke quietly and with feeling, "I think that'sh a wonderful idea, thank you."

He checked with Nancy but only out of courtesy, her enthusiastic response was expected. It was only eight o'clock so they decided to telephone Tim straight away. Nancy made the call which was answered promptly by Mrs Dexter but in silence.

"Hello, is this Mrs Dexter please?"

"Who are you?"

Nancy was slightly shaken by the tone of voice, "Oh, er, I'm sorry, this is Nancy, Graham Parson's partner, we've become quite good friends with Timothy. May I speak to him please?"

"He's in bed. Perhaps I can help?"

"Yes, well I suppose so. We have been invited to a picnic next Monday at a friend's farm and after his experience we wondered whether Tim might like to join us." There was a pause in which

Nancy's misgivings grew, this was not what they had expected. The response when it came was cool.

"I don't think that's a good idea. I am still grateful for your partner's actions, but I believe an outing like that would be, . . . *inappropriate*. I understand you have been purchasing drinks for him at the supermarket which seems an unduly generous thing to do for a child you had never met before." There was another pause before she continued, "Thank you for calling, it's enabled me to ask you not to do so again, goodbye."

Graham was standing at Nancy's side hoping to say hello to Tim and instead watched her jaw drop in shock. The murmur of the voice at the other end had ceased and the call ended but Nancy continued to hold the receiver to her ear, trying to make sense of what she had heard. Eventually, she returned to the lounge and repeated the conversation to Graham who was as shocked as she was. They sat in silence until Graham attempted to rationalise things, "OK, let'sh look at it from her point of view. She never knew about the pillsh or what we did to stop him, let alone about my what not." He pointed a finger at his head as he spoke, "So maybe it does seem a bit shtrange for two adultsh to be buying him drinksh."

After a few moments Nancy gave a resigned nod, "Yes, but it looks as though we're the only friends he has and that's taking his own mother into account as well, if what you felt was right. The poor kid is going right back to zero."

Graham closed his eyes in concentration and within a moment or two leapt from his chair. "Nope, I know what we'll do." He was halfway out of the room when he turned back towards Nancy, "Remember, a problem is jusht a solution hiding!" Nancy rolled her eyes in mock disdain but she felt more like crying as she recalled the dreadfully cold dismissal.

Sarah's first reaction was the same as theirs' but she soon agreed with Graham's take on the matter. His solution was simple provided Sarah wouldn't object to taking the case on. After that, she would be able to validate Graham and Nancy's involvement and vouch for them. Details were agreed and Sarah promised to go and see Mrs Dexter during the following week. This time the telephone was in conference mode and Nancy's shoulders dropped in relief at Sarah's closing sentences, "Well done again you two. Monday's out, obviously, so let's make it the following Sunday. Tim will be there then, I promise, even if I have to bring him here myself."

She turned to Graham and hugged him. "Well done you."

"Phah, it wush nothing!"

She held him at arm's length, "Hmm, you're pretty good now but I wonder if you were even brighter before someone dented your brains."

His expression was sombre when he moved back into her embrace and deftly pressed a fold of her skirt under the edges of her panties, pulling her to him, "All *that* did was to shend them three feet lower, now get up those shtairs, we've got some thinking to do."

After that the weekend went from strength to strength. The weather was perfect and Jimmy was smitten by the mediaeval event. The paraphernalia, jousting, costumes and tall stories were a joy but it had been a very long day. The walk back to Market Bosworth seemed far longer going back and on the bus home he fell against Nancy in a deep sleep. In his hand, clutched tightly, was a cardboard tube that contained a copy of the 'Everard' coat or arms, bought at the heraldic tent. It proved he was someone special and tomorrow they were going to the Fosse Park shopping mall for a frame to hang above his headboard.

For the first time in years, Graham looked at the sleeping child and wondered how things might have been if he'd had a child of his own. One thing he did know, he or she would have a great store of childhood memories to sustain them in leaner times, ones like Jimmy had put into his own store that day.

* * *

Sarah stepped past the thin, rather drab lady who had invited her in. As they walked though to the lounge, Mrs Dexter voiced her concern, "I have some difficulty in getting time off work, but you said in your telephone call that this was rather urgent." She gestured for Sarah to sit on the wooden framed settee and sat in the armchair opposite, waiting for an explanation.

The seat cushion had risen up on either side of Sarah's ample backside and she could feel the support straps beneath. She prayed they would withstand her weight but couldn't shake the imagery of being trapped in the debris with her knees beside her ears. "Yes, thank you for seeing me Mrs Dexter. I'm sure you would echo my concerns over what happened to Timothy and agree with the need to act promptly." The woman opposite gave a nod of acknowledgement but remained silent. Sarah forged on, "Bullying is unacceptable at any level but when it becomes a matter of criminal injury the relevant authorities, including mine, are required to act. Initially, I need to obtain as much background information as possible and that might mean a few meetings with yourself and Timothy. I would like to learn more about his home life, what he does in his spare time, what you two do together and that sort of thing. Perhaps I might see his bedroom before I go."

"You may not. All that is extremely intrusive don't you think?"

"I understand why you might feel that but what happened to Timothy is most unusual and it may be that something in his behaviour might have made him prone to victimisation."

Mrs Dexter spoke slowly, precisely and with the warmth of wet fish, "So you're saying that Timothy is responsible, at least in part, for the attack on him?"

'No you are, you loveless harridan' thought Sarah but she furnished a smile of understanding and explained, "No Mrs Dexter, that is not what I am saying. I have only one aim, which is to come up with some answers and make sure that this never happens to your son again."

"As you say, he is my son and I assume full responsibility for him."

'And for what he is,' thought Sarah who was growing to dislike Mrs Dexter more by the second. "Is there a Mr Dexter?"

"There is."

It was like pulling teeth, "What does he do for a living?"

"I have no idea."

'Then take a guess, just for me.' Sarah managed to contain the thought by writing it down on her pad rather than articulating it. "So you don't exchange that sort of information."

"Mrs," she made a point of referring to the visiting card, "Whiting, I'm not sure whether this is any of you business but my *ex*-husband and I have exchanged little more than solicitors' letters for the last five years.

Sarah automatically checked Timothy's date of birth and guessed that the last exchange of bodily fluids had probably occurred nine months before that. "Oh, I'm sorry to hear that, then I take it you receive maintenance payments for Timothy."

"No I do not, at least not very often which is why our solicitors continue to communicate."

"Was the split up a difficult one?"

"Is there any other sort?" She paused before surrendering more information, "He took up with another woman. They live in Leicester Forest East."

'No surprises yet' thought Sarah. "Then do you have a job."

"I do."

"What is it please, and what does it entail, for example how many hours a week do you work, what holidays do you get and what is your salary?"

After an exasperated sigh Mrs Dexter replied, "I work forty two hours per week as a receptionist at the medical centre on Hangar Street and my salary is none of your concern, though rest assured, I do not receive state handouts."

"And holidays, outings, that sort of thing?"

Suddenly, Dexter stood up and glared down at Sarah, "Look, this has become tiresome. Your questions are unwelcome and in truth you have yet to provide an adequate reason for getting involved. I think your time would be better spent with the thugs who attacked my son. Maybe their home lives would be more entertaining for you. As for this meeting, it has just finished. Neither I or my son are any of your concern."

This time Sarah, took a moment to compose herself, nothing would be achieved by losing her temper though she so wanted to.

She remained seated, "Please Mrs Dexter, I *am* here to help and I am here because the law requires me to be here."

"We do not require your help thank you. Please leave."

"With respect Mrs Dexter, I believe you do need our help and I am certain of an *official* need to be here."

"Then we shall have to agree to differ. Please leave."

Until then neither woman had shown any emotion but it was time to take control of the meeting and show a little metal, "Since my file opens with your son's plan to commit suicide I consider this case to be one of my higher priority ones. I do not wish to leave yet. Please sit down."

She was immediately ashamed of herself for such a brutal delivery but at last saw a flash of emotion and shock pass across the Mrs Dexter's face. It was only temporary, "I assume you have some evidence of that?"

"I do. Thankfully someone caught him purchasing enough paracetamol to do the job and not only prevented it but became a friend to your son. I understand that since then they've met each week for a drink in a cafeteria. You see, this file had been opened before the attack on Timothy and I had already spoken to his head teacher."

At last, Mrs Dexter was lost for words as she tried to make sense of it all, and to consider the links. "This man, the one who's been buying Timothy drinks, surely you people would see that as an unhealthy thing to be happening."

Sarah smiled slightly in understanding, "Yes, often we would, but I actually know Mr Parsons and his partner Nancy, they are foster parents and are two of the nicest people I know."

"But they even telephoned me inviting him to a picnic on a farm somewhere. I told them no."

"I can understand that Mrs Dexter, and I think I would have done the same, but this whole episode is one of remarkable coincidences. The farm belongs to my husband and I and I'd invited Mr Parsons, Nancy his partner and Jimmy, the child they foster. They were so delighted to have seen Timothy out of hospital and on the mend that we agreed to include him as well."

Mrs Dexter was stunned and sat in silence, trying to follow the connections. "Then, is this meeting an arranged affair. This is beginning to feel like some sort of conspiracy."

"No, just coincidence. It goes further actually, the Police officer in charge of the case, who I might add is determined to see those boys punished for their actions, also knows Mr Parsons very well and would be happy to vouch for him. His name is DS Harding. Telephone him, he would welcome your call I promise."

She gave Dexter a much warmer smile, "But you know, there is a final and compelling coincidence you should consider. Mr Parsons saved your son's life *twice*. You do see, don't you, that we must be involved. If we did nothing and Timothy did anything dreadful in the future we would be held to account. All of us."

Dexter spoke in a much smaller voice, "What do you suggest."

"Well, let's go back to square one, where I can ask you to call me Sarah, you can then tell me to call you Alice and we have a cup of tea together."

Alice nodded and began to get out of her chair but fell back, as her face folded in tears. Weeping was an indulgence she hadn't succumbed to for so many years.

Sarah did what came naturally, dropped on to her knees and held the weeping woman.

The next hour passed quickly and much of the information Sarah gleaned fitted perfectly with what Graham had told her. The atmosphere was much warmer but some of the old Alice still came through. Sarah made her final request, "I would like to see his bedroom please Alice, they can tell us a great deal about a child. Their hobbies, interests, tastes, that sort of thing."

Mrs Dexter looked at Sarah thoughtfully before conceding, conditionally. "Very well, I'll go and make sure he left it tidy. Please wait here until I call you."

"No, please. Mess in a boy's room is normal, *very* normal."

It wasn't in Timothy's case. The bed was neatly made and the walls were entirely bare. No posters, calendars or any personal expression. Just a pastel green emulsion. A lightwood single wardrobe stood next to a small desk, made of the same material. Pens and pencils were stored neatly in a pot mug. Alice must have sensed Sarah's shock, "I insist on tidiness and decorating is expensive enough, without blue tack and sellotape making it necessary every year."

Sarah replied gently, "But what would Tim like it to be? This is his space, where he could express himself. Find an identity, of his own."

Alice shook her head in confusion, the whole meeting was more than she could take in. Sarah rested a hand on the woman's shoulder, "Don't worry, you are going to be one of my very favourite cases. There's lots' of help and oodles we can do together. But that's enough for now, I need to leave you to think about things." She reached the bedroom door and turned back, "Oh there is one other thing and please trust me on this one Alice, you must not, on any account confront Timothy about his suicide attempt. It could have disastrous results. We'll leave that one to the experts." She held the other woman's gaze until she received a nod of commitment.

Another smile, "Chin up."

Alice murmured her thanks and they headed downstairs where Sarah gathered her paperwork together, "There is one other matter. Since Timothy was unable to make it last Monday we postponed the farm picnic until next Sunday in the hope that he could make it then. What do you think?"

"Well, I suppose so, if you think it would be OK."

"Not only do I think it would be OK for Timothy to go but I think you should come to."

"Oh no, I couldn't possibly. We hardly know each other and anyway, Sundays are the only day I have to clean the house."

Sarah would have none of it, "Good, that's settled then, housework is eminently miss-able. We would love to see you and just think of what it will mean to Timothy. You'll have chance to meet up with Graham and Nancy as well and judge them for yourself."

"Humph, apologise more like."

"Don't give that a second thought. Do come, please."

She was exhausted and wanted time alone now. She said yes to end the meeting more than anything else but was still charmed by

Sarah's delight. "Splendid, I'll pick you up at two o'clock and bring you back in the evening."

Sarah felt justifiably pleased with herself as she drove away. Mission accomplished and without a hint of Graham's secret. She chuckled to herself, the omission didn't matter, Alice wouldn't have believed it anyway.

She went back to her office and began her report. Timothy needed help, of that she had no doubt, but now there was the question of Alice, who needed help as well though she wouldn't admit it. This was going to be a long term job and a *very* thick file. Just the thing for Sarah to get her teeth into. It was gone six thirty when she reached a natural break in her narrative, though the late hour didn't matter; she had an important meeting to attend.

Ironically, the meeting was at the Golden Pheasant, where over a year earlier she had met with Dr Williams for lunch and he had related a ridiculous story about a chap with some sort of telepathy with abused children. That meeting had felt a little clandestine just as this one did.

Williams, Harding and Calder were already there though judging by the levels of beer in their glasses, they hadn't been waiting long. Calder was the first to greet her, "Hello, Sarah, what can I get you?"

She pulled a stool up to the table and pointed at their glasses, "They look good, I'll have one of the same please." Apart from a little small talk they waited until Harvey returned with her drink but then addressed the topic immediately. Doctor Williams began, "At some point we will need to decide whether to tell Graham about this meeting, though it still feels a little underhand to discuss him in his absence."

Harding, who had suggested the meeting responded, "Well let's think of this as a support group meeting rather than a conspiracy. I wanted to speak to you all because I'm worried for him."

The others nodded and Sarah added, "This last business has upset him, that's for sure. I spoke to Nancy and she said the he is putting it down to the long break since he was last *active*." Her slight emphasis on the last word made it clear that she was referring to his telepathy, or 'hits'.

Harding nodded, "And small wonder he wanted out of it after last Christmas, that episode nearly killed him. It's taken some time for him to begin again and make no mistake, he saved the child's life." As he was speaking he pulled a sheaf of large photographs out of a brown envelope and kept them face down, "Just so we understand a little of what Graham goes through, I've brought these to show you. They were taken at the hospital and you must not discuss them with anyone since they are evidence and the matter is still *sub judice*."

He handed the photographs to Sarah who gasped as soon as she turned them over, "Imagine that child's fear, confusion and dreadful suffering and remember that Graham didn't just witness that mess, he actually *experienced* the horror of it too. I hadn't really thought of it in that way until I saw the state he was in, holding the kid at the crime scene." Harding shook his head in wonderment, "He had broken down completely and kept saying he was sorry for being too slow. I suddenly realised that Graham had done more than just witness the attack, or be shocked by the injuries; he had actually suffered the attack too, at least to some extent."

Sarah sat in silence, her hand over her mouth as she thought of the images she had just seen. The Doctor had just finished scanning the pictures and handed them to Harvey before looking across at Harding, "And you're afraid for him." It was more of a statement than a question.

"Yes, I am. It made me reflect on all those cases last year and how he must have suffered."

They paused to consider his revelation in a silence broken by Harvey, "Sweet Jesus." He shook his head and handed the sheaf back to Harding, "Imagine how it would be for a Doctor to share that sort of suffering as well as treat it."

Williams grimaced, "I wouldn't be practicing, I can tell you that much!"

Sarah looked at Harding, "Well Adam, you've been considering this for longer than we have. Do you have any proposals?"

Harding huffed, "Not one. This is about a secret held by this little group. Now I don't know about you lot, but I think that's a little bizarre. I realise that as a group we've been able to put his gift into practice without compromising his secret but it occurs to me that we should formally accept that we're here to protect him too. I don't know what to suggest but I do know that if Graham continues in that way he's in for a complete breakdown. I was hoping we could do a bit of brainstorming tonight, I mean, it's not like mending a puncture or pulling a tooth is it? This is new ground"

They all nodded in agreement but the following hour was fruitless. All manner of ideas were suggested, discussed and dismissed. Harvey's idea of giving Graham and Nancy a holiday would be helpful but eventually they agreed that the 'hits' would continue wherever he was and Williams added with some chagrin that with Graham's luck their hotel would be next door to a Romanian orphanage.

Finally, Sarah came up with a plan, the only reasonable one, "Look, this isn't going anywhere and I think it's because we're trying to come up with a remedy without having the patient at hand. We're all agreed about the need to ease Graham's suffering so let's try talking it through with him. It's time for another group meeting."

If nothing else, they had identified the problem and had a plan. The next meeting was set for the seventh of June.

As they walked to their cars Harvey called over to Harding and Sarah, "I've finished the journal, so it's between you two now, who's next?"

Sarah glanced at Harding and said, "It looks as though I'm in for a busy weekend, will you have time to read it?"

"I should have loads of time this weekend, it'll help to pass the time." The prospect of a divorcee on his own with nothing to do prompted an immediate invitation to the picnic but he declined, since at least part of the time was committed to bringing his flat back to a biological norm. Harvey handed the carrier bag over with a warning, "I grew a little older reading that. I'd thought of it as a gift, now I don't know how to think of it. Perhaps it's more of an affliction."

Chapter 14

Sarah was tired. It had been a long week and instead of heading home a smidgeon earlier, or at least on time, this Friday saw her in the supermarket stocking up for Sundays' picnic. She was relieved to settle into her car seat, the overfilled shopping bags behind on the back seat, but knew there was one more job to do that night. She dialled out on her mobile and waited for some time before her call was answered, "Hello, is that Mrs Dexter, Alice?" The elongated pause confirmed her suspicions, but she continued to sound buoyant after Alice had confirmed it was her, in a distinctly non-buoyant tone.

"Great, I'm glad I've caught you though sorry it's a little late, I've just finished shopping for Sunday." She continued without pause, denying any opportunity to respond, "I know, or at least I'm pretty sure you've decided not to go but I'm calling now to say how important it is that you *do* join us. I shall be calling for you as arranged but it would be improper for me to take an unaccompanied child away for the day so early in our relationship, so if you don't come I shall have to explain to Timothy why he can't."

"That is blackmail Mrs Whiting and I simply cannot give up so much of a Sunday."

Sarah noted the absence of first name terms and decided to land another blow, "Alice, I invited you because I would like you to join us but make no mistake there is another agenda and I will not hide it. Timothy needs help and friends as much as the breath in his lungs right now, and that begins at home. Bluntly, we need to show him how much there is to *live* for. Do I make myself clear."

"Now you're threatening me."

"Please Alice, don't even think like that. Tim is being invited because we would like him to join us, not because we feel a need to do so and the same applies to you. An afternoon out would do you the world of good but imagine how much your support would mean to Timothy." She softened her voice, "And when you see him running around and laughing you'll be able to celebrate his happiness. Two weeks ago you could have been mourning a terrible loss." She allowed a few moments to pass before lightening the mood, "Besides, I need a fellow grown up I can teach how to drive the tractor."

The imagery of that must have caught a nerve because Alice emitted something between a huff and a giggle. "I really don't think that would be a good idea." There was a pause before she conceded defeat, "Very well then, if I can be sure we'll get back in good time."

"Absolutely, once you've all finished the milking and mucked out the pig pen. Just joking. It'll be fun I give you my word."

* * *

An hour earlier, in another store, Graham and Nancy answered all sorts of questions from an excited Timothy. His hair was still tousled and he was still painfully thin yet the most affecting feature was still the patch over one eye. Nancy's heart melted when she saw him though she hid her feelings as he accepted her welcome hug. A hot chocolate and *'Kit Kat'* followed in short order. They had only visited the farm at night and couldn't provide much in the way of information, though they did describe the recalcitrant 'Chocks' and her bad breath as well as the family car which was a farmyard in transit.

They all went home in high spirits. Not even his mum's refusal to discuss the picnic could taint Tim's excitement.

That Friday night marked the beginning of the first weekend he had taken off for months and even then only because his inspector had told him to. There had been no murders that week but there was a premier league home match at the 'Walker' stadium which was costing far more than it should, and policing was a matter of economics nowadays. He micro-waved a shepherds' pie and since the butter had only just come out of the fridge, settled for the entrap-ment of butter lumps within two slices of bread as an accompa-niment. Since he could eat the meal straight from its container he congratulated himself in adding only one fork to the pile of dishes that covered the sink and drainer. After watching the news for five minutes he switched off, disgusted. He wondered once again why good news couldn't attract ratings.

In the end he ran out of choices. It was either Graham's journal or the cleaning. He wasn't sure whether he wanted to read the jour-nal but at least that choice could be accompanied by the bottle of '*Antiquary*' he'd got in the cupboard.

Bad choice.

When he came to in the armchair it was mid-morning and the staleness of his surroundings was amplified by the heat of the day. Dust motes danced in the beam of sunlight the ill-fitting curtains allowed in. His head throbbed and when he allowed his tongue to explore its surroundings he thought of sweaty socks. He scanned the room and soon found the journals piled on his table but the bottle and glass were out of sight, at the side of his chair. With a groan he rested his head back on the chair, he'd been right to treat the exercise with some ambivalence, after all, he had a better idea of what to expect. He'd been responsible for much of the police work arising from Graham's encounters and had read the journals as a participant rather than an observer. Like most coppers he used devices such as black humour to detach himself from the horrors they had to deal with, but somehow such things never quite worked when kids were involved. They were his Achilles heel.

He struggled to his feet with a small groan and shambled into the kitchen where the washing up waited, it seemed, in silent con-demnation. By the time coffee began to trickle through the percola-tor he had started his search for the washing up bowl. He 'numbed out', refusing to re-visit the stuff he had read and in that state dish washing seemed the right thing to do. From behind, his trousers hung baggily from his hips and his shirt tail was hanging over the waistband in similar fashion. Both limp and creased. 'Bugger it' he thought, 'I hate days off.'

* * *

Graham and Nancy enjoyed a modest lie-in on Sunday, at least until Jimmy tottered in dragging his new over-blanket with him. The dozens of knitted squares were of such bizarre colours they actually worked together. When they had collected him from the care home there was a sign on the gate which bore a photograph of a blanket with the words, 'For Sale. Hand-made knitted blankets. Large choice. £5 each.' Someone had since put a line through 'large', due Pat Ensor explained, to the unexpected demand and depleted stocks. The kids were still in a knitting frenzy, particularly after learning that a reporter from the *Leicester Mercury* was calling in on Monday. Needless to say, Jimmy had selected and stashed his favourite in the hope Nancy would buy it. A given.

Sarah had already telephoned to say that Timothy *and* his mother were joining them though they agreed that it would be better to collect them first. Getting into a car full of strangers might be too intimidating. In spite of doubts Graham agreed to treat Alice with an open mind. Sarah didn't go so far as to detail her official assessment of the woman but had argued for the positive of mother and son sharing a day out.

At twenty past two the large wretched-looking Peugeot pulled up outside the house. As they walked up the garden path Graham pondered how long they had been without heavy rain and couldn't remember. Yet the sides of the car were covered in fans of dried mud. A black foul-smelling smoke poured from the exhaust though at that point his appraisal was interrupted by a call from the car, "Come on you lot. Autumn will be here at this rate!"

Nancy called back, "We're not the ones who are late, you said two o'clock."

Sarah responded cheerfully, "I know, I lied."

Graham nodded towards the rear of the car, "The shmoke is new."

Sarah waved a hand dismissively, "Yes, Stan said something about jets, I'm not sure, but it'll probably sort itself out."

The car had a third row of seats which folded up out of the floor of the luggage area. They were quite small with little legroom but ideal for the two boys. Timothy sat huddled defensively in his seat but Jimmy was having none of it. He'd been told that Tim had been hurt by some bigger boys and promised to take care of him. "Hello, my name's Jimmy and you are Timothy." Tim nodded cautiously before Jimmy continued, "Hey, if we called you Timmy we could be a pair. You know, Jimmy and Timmy." He grinned and nudged his new friend, "See?" From then on Jimmy was relentless and by the end of the journey a two-way conversation was in place.

Meanwhile, Alice sat bolt upright in the front passenger seat looking more like a crash dummy than a person. Introductions had been made but her reluctance to turn in their direction made conversation extremely difficult. Somehow though, Sarah managed to mediate with a cheerful selection of topics. No-one could speak for Alice, distanced as she seemed, from the human race, but the remaining adults were delighted to hear the growing chatter from the rear seat. As they pulled into the farmyard the matted bundle of black and white fur barrelled out of a barn towards them. "Chocks! See, I told you, that's Chocks. She's great." He had been addressing Tim but patting Nancy on the shoulder urging her to exit the car quickly and drop her seat to let him out. Chocks rarely wasted energy on barking but her tail had a mind of its own and was signalling delight at seeing Jimmy again. He dropped to his knees and hugged her without paying heed to the halitosis or the noxious fumes given off by whatever she had rolled in earlier that day. Timothy joined him for an introduction but limited contact to a light two-fingered stroke to the top of her head. "She smells."

Jimmy replied with the authority of an old hand, "Nah, that's because she lives on a farm, see?" He pointed at a pile of manure behind another barn. Tim simply wrinkled his nose.

Sarah had cocked her head, listening before she could be certain. "Stan's still rolling the new grass in the Watery Lane field. I know! Come on you lot, it's not far." They all trouped after her, passing through a large brick outbuilding via two tall archways. A sweet smell of hay filled the air and on one side a thick-set young man was working on a small *Massey Fergusson* tractor. Sarah waved at him and addressed her guests, "That's Mathew, my eldest. I'll introduce you properly later."

Mathew looked up and smiled, "Afternoon everyone."

They all said hello and hurried after Sarah who had disappeared out sight. Eventually, gasping slightly, they caught up with her, side-stepping cow pats and nervously monitoring the herd of bullocks sheltering under the trees in the distant corner of the field. They could hear the tractor by now but needed to cross two more fields before they saw it, pulling a large roller across a field of grass and clearly following a line. The driver waved as he reached their end of the field and stopped the huge green machine, knocking the engine into tick over. Sarah walked over as he opened the cab door and exchanged a mix of words and gestures. He looked at his watch and nodded an assurance before Sarah gestured towards her guests and said something else which was rewarded with a grin and nod. She hurried back to the group and explained, "Sorry folks, Stan thought he'd have finished by now, but he's only going to be fifteen minutes or so. Time enough for us grown-ups to have a cup of tea and you two to join Stan on the tractor." Both jaws dropped, but not for long, Jimmy exclaimed, "Ye-eah," whilst Timothy nodded continually.

Half an hour later the grown-ups were having tea in the garden and watched over the low brick wall as the tractor swept into the yard. The two boys were squeezed into the cab on either side of Stan, bouncing around like two loose saddlebags but as soon as Stan helped them down they raced over to describe the adventure. Each took a turn to add something until finally, out of breath, they finished. Sarah rewarded them with a glass of home-made ginger beer.

Every adult there welcomed the interruption for their conversation had been stilted. They had tried to involve Alice but her responses were conversational cul de sacs and to ask more questions would have made things feel like an interrogation.

Soon, Stan joined them, scrubbed up and changed out of his overalls into jeans and a short-sleeved shirt. Introductions were made and when asked, he described what he had been doing and how new grass needed bruising with a roller to make it throw off side shoots. He was softly spoken and eloquently described their farm and activities but social chatter was beyond him. With nothing more to add in agricultural topics he took the boys off to explore. Sarah was telling them about her younger son Andrew who was at agricultural college when the sounds of laughter reached them. It continued, at times hysterically and the grown-ups decided to have a look. They rounded the far end of the house and in the heat could hear and smell the chickens before they saw them. In the shelter of the brick barn stood a slightly ramshackle chicken shed which was connected to a large wire enclosure. Stan was standing at the entrance with his arms folded and back to them, his large frame shaking with laughter as the two boys stalked the chickens inside. Each time they would creep towards their intended victim, arms outstretched, until it was time to pounce and each time the chicken dodged away from them, with a small quark of irritation.

He turned to greet the others and explained, "I've promised six eggs to the one who brings me a chicken." Just then and probably because of his limited vision, Tim lunged for a chicken and tripped over an exposed root. This time, albeit fleetingly and because of the unexpected trajectory he actually caught the bird but released it almost immediately when he struck the ground, winding himself. His prey gave out a much louder squark and ran away, ruffling its feathers in alarm while Jimmy laughed hysterically, pointing at the splinted hand, "It looked like you were going to spank it."

Tim pulled himself up into a sitting position and he cast around for his spectacles. The bruising around his chest had almost healed but the fall had made him aware of it and his new friends' laughter hurt him even more. With his glasses in place he looked across, scowling yet ready to cry, but then he saw something he hadn't expected, subtle signals he could read easily. Jimmy was still laughing, but openly and without a sneer or jibe. None of it was at his expense. There was no malice, no wish to demean or embarrass. In fact, his new friend was trying desperately to applaud him amidst the fits of laughter. For the first time he could remember, Tim grinned back in acknowledgement of the comedy instead of cringing in shame.

Sarah took Nancy by the elbow, "Nancy my dear, would you be kind enough to help me set the picnic out please?"

Alice overheard and offered to help as well but Sarah chuckled as she replied, "No, that's fine, you stay here with Graham and Stan in case first aid is necessary, though I'll take you up on your offer when we clear up."

The two women returned to the house and began emptying the fridge of a startling variety of meats and accompaniments but it was clear that Sarah wanted a chat. Still delving into the fridge and without looking at Nancy she asked, "Jimmy thinks the world of you two you know. How are you managing?"

Nancy didn't need to think about her reply, "Wonderfully. Do you know, we had a dry night last night and his relationship with Graham is, well, amazing. Their like two best friends and sometimes I wonder who is trying to look after who. I don't know what we'd do with our weekends without him."

Sarah straightened up and looked at Nancy, her smile had gone. "That's what I wanted to speak to you about." She paused and looked down, "Although he isn't one of my cases I have kept an eye on him and Pat Ensor at the home telephones me regularly. Your weekends have changed Jimmy beyond measure but the authority can't afford to keep him on that basis."

Nancy started feel a chill of fear as Sarah dropped her shoulders and sighed, "I said that I would break the news, but the thing is another couple want to apply as full time foster parents and the authority have earmarked Jimmy for the placement."

Nancy covered her mouth with her hand, "Oh Christ, I can't believe it."

Sarah grasped Nancy by the arm, "Listen, that doesn't mean that you won't get to see him, I'm certain something can be worked out, but it won't be as often, that's all." Nancy shook her head slowly and Sarah added, "I'm so sorry. It's either that or take him on yourselves." She stroked Nancy's arm in a gesture of support and they returned to the task in hand. Once everything was assembled they called the others in, made the boys wash their hands and carried everything out to the table on the lawn. Predictably, Nancy was quieter than usual and whilst Alice showed some signs of relaxing, conversation remained tediously polite. Graham seemed to be hitting it off with Stan but the boys were like long lost friends, their constant chatter and giggling carried the event.

Once the picnic was over Sarah stood at the door and yelled for Mathew. Almost immediately, they heard a tractor start and moments later the small tractor they had seen him working on appeared from the barn, towing a flat bed trailer that had a row of straw bales along its centre. A short set of steps appeared and they all climbed on for a sedate tour of the farm. Mathew drove and Stan dealt with the gates while the boys shrieked in delight as the trailer rocked over the uneven ground. Sarah provided the commentary as they came across pheasants, a hare, a badger's set and anything else thought worthy of comment. Twenty minutes into the tour, when they were on their way back to the house she noticed Alice had turned to face the rear and after a few moments made her way down to that end of the straw bales and sat beside her, startled to see tears.

Embarrassed, Alice brushed them away and smiled apologetically but said nothing. Sarah asked, "I hope you didn't find this too terrible. It's been a pleasure having you and Timothy has had a good time, I'm sure."

Alice realised her tears had been mis-interpreted and said, "Oh yes, thank you," she faltered and waved a hand dismissively, "It was just, memories."

Sarah moved a little closer and said, "Go on, share, please."

The other woman gave her a wan smile before returning her gaze to the rear, "I was five years old and we went to an old-style steam fair with so many things to see and do. They had a cart similar to this though it was pulled by a horse, a great big one, a Shire I should think. I remember thinking it was the happiest day of my life, which is ironic really." She sighed, "Two days later both my parents died in a car crash and that was the worst day in my life."

Sarah reached across and took Alice's hand, "Thanks for telling me that, five is no age to be left on your own. Who took care of you?"

"An Aunt and uncle. He was a gamekeeper on an estate in Derbyshire. They had no children."

Sarah imagined the sudden abandonment, a life of isolation in the middle of an estate and the emotional void from a couple who had no children of their own. They would talk, another time but for now she squeezed the other woman's hand and said, "You know what?" Alice looked at her, waiting for more, "I think today has been a pretty special one for Timothy. I certainly hope so."

Just then, as if on cue both boys laughed out loud and Alice glanced back at them before replying, "I think so too."

By the time they reached the house it was time to head home, though Sarah dashed indoors and returned with a dog-eared book which she shoved down the side of her seat. They were just driving off when Stan came running out of the house, waving a box in the air. He opened the tailgate and said, "I nearly forgot my promise." He presented a carton of eggs to Tim, "You didn't actually bring the chicken to me but you would have done if you hadn't tripped up. Well done." Tim settled back in his seat with the carton in his lap, a grin on his face and a bunch of memories in the bank.

The journey home was much noisier than earlier where even the adults joined in a discussion about the wildlife they had seen. Predictably, the journey seemed so much shorter. They dropped Alice and Tim off first since this time the journey had to be extended to drop Jimmy off at the home. Sarah got out of the car and gave Tim a hug when he thanked her. She turned to Alice then and gave her the book, "I love poetry, the state of that book tells you as much. Sometimes poetry says things I can't put into words myself. Let me have this back when you're finished, but I do hope you enjoy it." She leant closer and whispered, the one by Eugene Field is one of my favourites. It makes me realise that a child's love is one of the purest things we can ever know."

The next leg of the journey was silent. Graham's move to the front seat seemed to exaggerate the loss of two companions particularly when Jimmy declined Nancy's invitation to move forward and join her. At the home Jimmy was reluctant to get out of the car and dragged his feet along the path to the door. As they reached it he looked up at Graham and asked quietly, "Couldn't I stay with you for another night, please."

Graham dropped to his knees and tried to sound upbeat, "I'm shorry maytee but we have to go to work and stuff." He drew jimmy forward into a hug, "You watch it'll be next weekend before you know it."

When they eased apart the brave nod spiked Graham's heart, but the child's silent gaze nearly broke it. At that moment the door was swept open by Pat Ensor, who gave her usual welcome but Jimmy dodged past her and ran upstairs without glancing back.

Sarah had watched from the car and said nothing when they climbed back in but as they pulled away Graham shook his head, "That was awful." Sarah glanced in the mirror and saw Nancy looking at her from the back seat, shaking her head.

After dropping them off Sarah had chance to consider the days' events. She'd hoped for such a happy occasion, at least for her friends, Alice and Tim were always going to be unknowns, but her chat with the Jimmy's case officer on Friday bore news that had to be passed on as soon as possible, not least of all because there may have been mention of it at the home and both Graham and Nancy would have seen that as treacherous concealment on her part.

If that wasn't enough, she had behaved stupidly with Alice. It might just have been an uncanny coincidence that the trailer ride should have caught a nerve and there was no doubt that she was incapable of showing love or emotion, from Sarah's own observations and particularly Graham's, but she had no right to pull that stunt with the poetry. She had no psychiatric qualifications or authority, yet, and she grimaced at her attempt at justification, life was full of circles and improbable twists. She'd wager that Alice at five years of age was torn from a loving family life to an emotionally austere life with a childless couple, living in the middle of a country estate. "Oh for heavens' sake!" she called out in the car, "You'll be trying to write another *Polyanna* story at this rate. You stupid woman!"

She was certainly right about life's improbable twists. The Dexter's were the only ones to return to their home in better spirits than they had left with. Timothy was full of it, desperate to recap on the day's highlights and for once Alice allowed him to, as they shared a pot of tea.

After he had gone to bed she did the unthinkable and poured herself a glass of sherry from a bottle that had remained almost full since the previous Christmas. There was nothing worth watching on television so she picked up Sarah's book of poems which was in fact a small scrapbook. On the cover, written in felt pen were the words, 'My Favourite Poems,' and Alice wondered how old Sarah was when she started the collection. It was an eclectic mix that included Wordsworth, Keats, Dylan Thomas, Robert Frost, Kipling and many she hadn't heard of. Many were sentimental but she skipped through until she found the one written by Eugene Field, entitled '*Child and Mother*'.

Intrigued by Sarah's earlier comment Alice settled back in her chair and read on;

Child and Mother

O mother-my-love, if you'll give me your hand,
And go where I ask you to wander,
I will lead you away to a beautiful land,—
The Dreamland that's waiting out yonder.
We'll walk in a sweet posie-garden out there,
Where moonlight and starlight are streaming,
And the flowers and the birds are filling the air
With the fragrance and music of dreaming.
There'll be no little tired-out boy to undress,
No questions or cares to perplex you,
There'll be no little bruises or bumps to caress,
Nor patching of stockings to vex you;
For I'll rock you away on a silver-dew stream
And sing you asleep when you're weary,
And no one shall know of our beautiful dream
But you and your own little dearie.
And when I am tired I'll nestle my head
In the bosom that's soothed me so often,
And the wide-awake stars shall sing, in my stead,
A song which our dreaming shall soften.
So, Mother-my-Love, let me take your dear hand,
And away through the starlight we'll wander,—

Away through the mist to the beautiful land,—
The Dreamland that's waiting out yonder.

Alice read it twice more and in the silent seconds passed before she gagged and heard a noise that stemmed from somewhere deep within her. She tried to draw the words back into focus but couldn't. Instead she curled up tightly into a foetal position and surrendered to the sobs that wracked through her body. Her mind's eye didn't see a mother, instead it saw a happy, carefree five year old girl, secure and loved, suddenly and without reason abandoned. Her life fills with grown-ups who say strange things and weep, yet though they cuddle her there is no love. Nothing makes sense, who is Jesus and why has he taken Mummy and Daddy away? Night and day pass without notice until one day a man and woman come for her. They call themselves Aunty and Uncle yet she doesn't know them and cries when they make her leave so many toys in her bedroom and take her away. They have a small house in a big wood with lots of pheasants, but they never laugh or tickle her, the way daddy did.

Later, exhausted and drained of tears she uncoiled herself and picked the book up from the floor where it had fallen. She felt utterly spent and read the poem once more with a dulled mind. The words still carried an awful weight but she had no emotion left. She rested her head back on the chair and closed her eyes, forcing herself to remember an earlier childhood before the unhappiness of her life in the woods, where joy was unknown, supplanted by the gratitude demanded of her by her guardians. They were not cruel people but had chosen not to have children and therefore found an enforced parentage irksome. Their income never stretched to include holidays or days out except an occasional visit to friends, usually on the same estate.

Gradually and without malice, they broke the young spirit the fates had charged them with.

Alice's journey through her past stopped suddenly and her eyes snapped open. She cast back to that afternoon, at the easy way Sarah had with her family and the fondness Graham and Nancy had for Jimmy. The way he related to them and how they held hands so automatically. Above all, she couldn't ever remember seeing Timothy laugh like that.

She read the poem once more and looked up towards his bedroom with a soft groan, "Oh Tim," she murmured, "What have I done."

* * *

Graham's shock at Jimmy's distress was nothing compared to his reaction when Nancy relayed Sarah's news. "They can't do that! The poor kid will jusht run away again."

Nancy countered, "But look at it from the authority's point of view Graham, thanks to us he's stable now but they must find permanent homes for kids, not just let them out at weekends."

Graham shouted at her, something he never did, "Bollocksh, they have no idea what that kid went through and he'll become a runaway again, mark my words!"

"Don't cuss at me like that! It's not my fault and whether you think it's wrong or right get used to the idea, because they are already considering a couple for the job."

He continued to shout, "The shtupid sods! They have no idea."

"Well fine, let's go down to the offices and tell them how we know what he went through. That'll guarantee we get struck off the list!" She held up both hands, palm outwards to signal an end to the conversation, "This is not the way we should be discussing this. I'm going to bed. Let's see if we can avoid yelling at each other tomorrow." With that she disappeared into the kitchen and returned minutes later with a mug of hot chocolate and book. "Goodnight!"

* * *

Sarah climbed into her side of the bed with a tired groan. Stan was barely awake but asked, "Had a good day then love?" She leaned over and kissed his forehead before settling back onto her side, "Mmm, I've had better.

Timothy ended the day as a champion. Wholly unaware of the dramas surrounding him he dreamt only of handling great tractors with ease and routinely catching chickens for appraisal.

Chapter 15

"I'm shorry."

"So you bloody well should be." The words were much harsher than they sounded, her softened tone indicating a tacit acceptance of a truce.

Graham had heard Nancy wake and dress but remained in bed with his eyes closed, trying to make sense of it all. Finally he donned his dressing gown and followed her downstairs, his hair still tousled from sleep. "You know, I shall mish him, a lot."

Nancy placed a mug of tea in front of him and sat opposite. "So shall I, but Sarah said something that made me think." She held up a hand to signal caution, "First of all she feels sure that we will be allowed to see him still, but not on such a regular basis." Graham shook his head violently and tried to speak but Nancy continued, "Yeah, I guessed you'd feel that way. It'd be worse than not seeing him at all, but she then said it was either that or take him on ourselves."

Graham looked up at her, eyes widening in comprehension. Nancy grinned, "Well I'm up for it, if you are."

"Oh Nansh, wouldn't that be wonderful!" He took her hand and added, "Shometimes I wondered whether we could, or should, but well you don't think it would trigger . . . " Nancy cut him short, for she had seen the connection long before. They knew Jimmy through Graham's special ability, the same one he'd acquired when he held her own son at the point of death. "I've been there and thought about it a lot, but no child will replace Christopher." She shook her head slightly, hanging on to control, "Jimmy is another person and I know I won't be looking for a substitute."

She looked at him then, at the cleft in his forehead, the pale white scar down the same side of his face and the bags under his eyes. How could she have fallen in love with such an odd-looking man? But she looked at those bright eyes with such a store of compassion and the cheeky grin that spoke of his special take on life. She felt very lucky to have him.

He clapped his hands together, "Well that's settled then. We musht telephone the foster people today." He leaned over and kissed her before heading upstairs to get dressed. She picked up his half-finished drink and poured it into the sink, he'd need a fresh one after he'd showered and dressed and they could make some plans. Still smiling at the thought, she turned to find him at the doorway to the lounge, looking serious. "There is one problem." Nancy said nothing but held her head to one side awaiting more.

"Well, the way I see it, we could do an even better job for him. I mean, in giving him a complete home; Mum, Dad, that sort of thing." He shrugged his shoulders and shuffled uncomfortably.

"I just wondered, erm, would you marry me?" He glanced down at the floor, embarrassed, "Actually, I was using Jimmy as an excushe, it's for me really."

She walked towards him, grinning, "Well as proposals go that's a tad shy of romantic." She wrapped her arms around him and added, "But it will do." A kiss and hug sealed the deal before Graham flew upstairs to shower and dress while Nancy prepared to leave for work. Ordinarily she'd have already left but a realisation occurred to her and threatened to drag her spirits back down. When Graham came back downstairs he found her sitting at the kitchen table, obviously waiting for him. "There is one minor detail you've forgotten."

His smile froze, "What?"

"You still have a wife, remember?"

He'd had almost no contact with his wife Ann, since she had left him almost a year earlier and set up home with the deputy head teacher of the school she worked in. She had taken their life savings but left him with the house and most of the furniture. Nevertheless, they were still married though legally separated and Nancy went on to add that bigamy was not an option.

Graham's face cleared as he waved her concern aside, "No problem. We can apply for the divorce in twelve months time, I've checked. After that it only takes six weeks." He grinned and shrugged his shoulders, "Eashy peashy."

"How do you know I'm prepared to wait that long?"

This time his expression implied that the answer was obvious, "No problem, I'll just make you my sex shlave and you won't have the will to leave."

She rolled her eyes, "Oh, right, well I hadn't thought of that one, *master*." Even so, she was reassured by Graham's research. He had known about the dates and they were already living together anyway. She stood and kissed him, much longer than usual, before heading out of the back door, though as she turned to close it thought of something else, "Just one thing. If I end up with a leather collar you'll get the sharp end of a riding crop sunshine."

* * *

Sarah had slept badly. Sunday had been a disaster in which she'd inflicted pain, anxiety and discomfort on her guests. She had already resolved to make an appointment with Alice as soon as possible, to get her poetry book back and arrange for professional help, no doubt made all the more difficult now after her amateur sleuthing. She winced when she thought of Nancy's reaction to the news of Jimmy's probable placement with other foster parents, and in particular that gaze in the car mirror. A signal to shut up and allow her to break the news to Graham in private. Sarah was a professional and as such was feeling pretty inept.

Halfway to work she realised that Chocks hadn't been at the back door for her bowl of tea that morning. She sighed, life was getting quite shitty.

Although she couldn't know it, the day had more bad news in store for her, though with the finesse of a short-lived change for the better in the morning. She had barely settled down at her desk with the first coffee when the telephone rang. It was Alice, who tried to say thank you in her painfully correct manner. Sarah allowed her to continue until there was a pause, long enough for Sarah to say, "Hello?"

Alice finally began again, "I'm not very good at this am I?" She gave a self-deprecating huff, "Mrs Whiting, Sarah. Yesterday was a lovely day and I wanted to say thank you very much. In fact it was a wonderful day and Timothy thought so too." She was trying so hard.

"Oh my dear, I'm so glad. The truth is I'm relieved too. I thought we might have overdone things for you."

"No, not at all, in fact there's something else." This time the pause continued for longer and Sarah was just about to speak when she heard a tiny sob. Alice was weeping.

Sarah spoke so very softly and with the empathy only one woman could have for another, "Take your time." She could imagine Alice looking up and shaking her head, struggling to regain her composure and eventually heard what sounded like a gulp. "I read your poems. How did you know the *Eugene Field* poem would have such an effect on me?"

"Intuition and an ear for children who are hurting, or used to. I thought you it might strike a chord, though it was presumptuous of me and I expected to be apologising to you this morning."

Alice made a noise that might have been a chuckle, "Perhaps you're right on both counts." Another pause, "In fact that brings me onto another point. Last week, during your visit, it was clear that you were concerned about a number of issues."

Sarah tried to ease the woman's angst. "Don't worry, we can sort everything out together. I can be your guide and you can learn, but deep down you are still a good person Alice."

With a delicious dichotomy that almost caused Sarah to laugh out loud, the new Alice replied in the way the original would have, "Then I should like to start as soon as possible please."

Appointments were made and Sarah came off the telephone with a lighter air. An hour later she received another call that was just as good. It was Nancy telling her of their decision to take Jimmy on full-time. They had spoken to the fostering agency who were delighted, though the news was being withheld from Jimmy until that afternoon when they planned to visit him and break the news themselves.

Soon after, Stan telephoned to say that he had found Chocks in a corner of the hay barn where she had made a cosy bed for herself, and the puppies that must be due within the next day or so.

'See' she told herself, 'shitty days *can* get better'.

She was wrong.

It felt like Christmas day. Graham and Nancy strode up to the care home gate and pressed the intercom button with a flourish. It took longer than usual and the voice didn't sound like Pat Ensor's though she was obviously shocked to find them there. Her anxiety was clear but the buzzer sounded to signal the opening of the lock.

As they approached the door it was flung open by Pat Ensor, whose expression mirrored the tensions they had heard. "Is he with you?"

Graham's jaw dropped, "No. What'sh happened?"

Pat thrust her hand back through her hair, "He's run off again. I should have seen the signs, he was so unruly last night and this morning he spent most of the time by himself." She sighed and waved them in, "We've notified the Police of course, but there's only so much they can do." They followed her into the kitchen where she filled the kettle and continued, "The wholesalers were delivering some supplies and the driver had left the gate open; he was struggling with a sack trolley. Anyway, Jimmy was gone like a flash."

Graham was beside himself, pacing back and forth, quite unable to think beyond the horror of losing Jimmy. It was left to Nancy to act and she turned to Pat, "We need to make a couple of calls, may I use you 'phone please?"

"Yes, of course, you know where my office is." Ten minutes later she returned to the kitchen and sat before the mug of tea that had been set down for her. This time she was careless of any indiscretions as she spoke to Graham, "Sarah is in a meeting at the moment but will find us as soon as she can get away. Adam is making enquiries and will come back to us shortly. He seemed quite upbeat though, kids his age are usually found quite quickly, apparently teenagers are the ones most difficult to track down."

Pat murmured her agreement but there was little to add. Searching seemed futile in a city the size of Leicester though Graham suggested making a list of places he might go to. The first place they thought of was obvious. 38 Randall Avenue, their home. Hurriedly, they called a taxi and agreed to compare notes later. Within forty five minutes they were home, searching the garden and surrounding area but there was no sign of him.

Adam Harding telephoned with news of the Police action. It was being treated seriously because of Jimmy's age and the photograph supplied by Pat Ensor had been copied for all on duty officers who would check with the city traders and snack bars. In addition, copies had been given to the Transport Police and the service bus operators for distribution to their drivers. "There's not much more I can do Graham, though I made sure they've pulled me into the loop if there's any news. Don't worry, we'll find him."

Graham sat with Nancy at the kitchen table, though neither spoke; each lost in thought. Eventually, he suggested they carry on with the list for want of something positive to do. It was a poignantly long list that included the many places they had taken him too, though none held any real promise. For one thing, he wouldn't have known how to get to many of the places, let alone have enough for the fares.

Sarah arrived at five o'clock, her usual sparkle absent as she acknowledged their distress with big hugs. They showed her the list and she immediately hustled Graham into his jacket, "Come on. If Nancy stays here to take calls we can check these out. They may be long shots but at least we'll be doing something which is better than moping around here." Nancy found a couple of photographs they had taken on their outings and thought good enough to frame, though as she waved them off she realised how forlorn their chances were. Their best hope lay with the authorities; he couldn't have got far.

* * *

He'd managed around four miles as the crow flies, with the change he had accumulated from his weekends away that paid for his bus fare into the Haymarket. There was nothing left to pay for a lunch and his stomach grumbled as the fast food restaurants exhausted fumes of pizza, burgers and chips onto the street. He ambled over to the fruit market and joined the lunchtime crowds, buying ingredients for the evening meal. There his height and stature enabled him to palm two apples and keep them beneath the stall, out of sight though his pulse was racing so hard his chest ached. He slipped away and sat on a bench in Granby Street to eat his spoils and watch the world go by. Most of the afternoon was spent window shopping in *The Shires* shopping centre but teatime brought fresh demands for sustenance. He considered asking someone to take him back to the home but couldn't face the thought of Mrs Ensor's censure and his heart sank when he considered Graham and Nancy who only wanted him for weekends. Still, he was so hungry

At that point he was distracted by the young man who passed him, wearing a suit and obviously a city worker. He had pushed a pizza box into the top of a litter bin that was too small to take it and as a result the box concertinaed in a way that opened it, to reveal two unwanted slices of pepperoni pizza.

He relished every mouthful and dismissed any thoughts of returning to the home. At the Clock Tower he saw a sign for the railway station and headed in that direction.

Leicester Railway Station is anomalous, with its huge Victorian frontage of brick archways and cobbled dropping-off zone within. Once inside the entrance though, it adopts the scale of a small suburban station with a small concourse that only accommodates one small coffee bar and seating area. A couple of other snack bars and a news agency are housed in units that face onto the area. In the far corner two staff stand at a row of gates that resemble those found in the London Underground and allow access to a footbridge that spans all platforms. On this day, the two on the gates, a young man and woman had only two issues in mind. His pitch for her favours and a shared hatred of anyone attempting to sneak by without a ticket, in the way that kid tried to, claiming he was meeting his mother. The guard told him to go and wait outside and took no further interest in him.

Jimmy had studied the arrivals board and opted for London, but his plea to be allowed through to meet his mum was hopeless. He sat on a seat in the small area of tables and chairs, just short of the gates and hoped for an opportunity to present itself. An hour passed by and the aluminium seat began to make his bottom ache. Shuffling around, to face the table, he was startled to see a middle-aged man seated opposite, drinking a cup of coffee and reading a newspaper.

Their eyes met and the man gave a small nod of acknowledgement before disappearing behind his paper though Jimmy could see from the way those eyes were set that the man had smiled. They were kindly eyes, beneath a head of light grey hair. Discreetly, from the corner of his eyes, Jimmy saw that the man was dressed in a light jacket, brown trousers and a pair of white trainers.

As time dragged on, the man reached forward for his mug, replacing it in the saucer after a sip without looking away from the text he was reading but eventually, the paper was lowered, folded and placed on the table. He looked at jimmy and asked, "Are you waiting for someone?"

Jimmy nodded but said nothing.

"Well you've been waiting a long time, are you sure they're coming?"

Again jimmy nodded but this time felt a need to establish why he was sure, "I'm waiting for my mum."

"Ah, so is she late?"

Another nod.

"Oh dear, I am sorry, why do you think that is."

This time Jimmy shook his head, "Don't know, p'raps she missed her train."

"That's so easily done, though I'm glad it's warm. You might have been frozen, waiting for so long. I take it she is coming up from London."

"Yes, she always comes from there."

The man glanced at the arrivals board and gave Jimmy a reassuring smile, "Well in that case you shouldn't have to wait much longer. The next one in is due in ten minutes."

They spent the next ten minutes getting to know one another though in the usual way of things the youngster found it easier to answer questions than ask them. By now, Jimmy's need to get past the barrier was joined with a need for more food. Either way, he wished the bloke would go away.

Suddenly, the concourse was filled with a phalanx of people heading out towards the exit. As the last few stragglers passed them the man said quietly, "Don't worry young man, she's bound to be on the next one." He glanced down at his cup and retrieved the malt biscuit that had accompanied the drink, "Here, have this, no point in them taking it back and I'm about to have dinner." He grinned, "My wife goes to Keep Fit on Mondays so I take the chance to have a cheeseburger, chips and milkshake before I go home."

His expression changed to one of concern, "Goodness, look at me, I'll bet you haven't eaten yet and I'm talking about food when you've got another hour to wait. Please forgive me. You see, she'll be on the next one." He smiled then, with a warmth that cheered Jimmy, "Well, it was pleasure meeting you Jimmy, cheerio."

Jimmy returned the smile, "Bye, bye." He watched the man walk out of the archway onto the cobbles, where he dodged a car that was swinging into one of the bays. On the London Road, where he was little more than a silhouette he paused, as if in thought, before turning back towards the concourse. He wore a slightly vexed expression as he approached the table and began apologetically, "Jimmy, I can't help noticing that the next London train won't be in for another hour and that will no doubt be way past your mealtime. I would be most happy for you to join me for a cheeseburger, fries and milkshake, just over there in Granby Street. It'll only take half an hour then you can come straight back here and I'll head off home."

"I haven't got any money."

"Good Lord no, I meant it as my treat. It's nothing, honestly."

Jimmy paused, unsure of what to do but his hunger helped his reasoning. With a nod, he slipped off the chair as the man said, "Splendid. It'll be nice to have some company for a change, oh by the way, my name is Donald."

* * *

Patricia Geary had been cursing football and its fans ever since they left the station. Her colleague, PC Andrews had only been serving for six months and listened to her politely though he hoped they could find something else to talk about soon. Monday nights were often boring and long. Pat's real gripe was that as Child Protection Officer she had better things to do than pound a beat. Sadly, with budgets taking precedence over everything, the chief Constable had chosen to allow time off in lieu rather than pay overtime to the huge force required for last weekends' home match at the Leicester City's ground. He then decreed that the time taken off work had to be on a midweek day as allocated. The shortfall was then made up by pulling officers across from less sensitive areas, though Pat was most vocal on that last point. A child, who watched his mother being kicked to death last year, was missing from the care home and where was she, the city's CPO? Walking around town all night. Great!

It was only a quarter to eight and they had already circled the city centre once. There were very few people about. Most were waiting for next weekend or reserving funds for summer holidays. They glanced in at the Indian restaurants that were virtually empty, though the burger bars and takeaways still seemed busy. Grease pockmarked the pavement and the nearby lampposts obviously served as supports for last Saturday's drunks when they threw up a third of a week's wages.

Pat continued to moan, but something began to niggle. Andrews took the opportunity to mention a film he had seen recently and she showed a little interest out of courtesy, realising perhaps that she had monopolised the conversation thus far. In fact she was not at all interested and allowed her mind to wander, through her outstanding files, upcoming cases, watch lists.

"Oh Fuck."

"What?" Andrews had turned to see Geary running back the way they had come from.

She called over her shoulder, "Come on, quickly."

He had barely caught up with her when she dived into a burger bar, her head moving from side to side, frantically. As he entered he heard her shout at the person behind the counter, "The elderly bloke and small boy, which way?" The man pointed in the direction of Chatham Street, a small one-way road opposite. She pushed Andrews back towards the door, "Up there, quickly." One young boy and a middle-aged man, around five foot nine, grey hair, medium build. His name is Colin Speers and he's on the register."

They saw them as soon as they entered the street and for a moment it looked as though the man was going to make a run for it. Pat made sure that he realised the futility of such an action by yelling his name and besides the PC was going up the slope like a racehorse.

The boy didn't hesitate though, and fled around the corner out of sight, a large plastic carrier bag bouncing against his leg. Andrews did the right thing by collaring Speers but by the time Pat reached the end of the street there was no sign of the boy.

After cautioning Speers she said, "Right, down to the station."

Speers looked startled, "Why? I've done nothing."

She turned back to him, pushing inside his personal space, "You done more than enough to warrant a long chat with your probation officer. I take it that wasn't your son?"

* * *

As soon as she heard of Harding's interest she called him, "I really couldn't tell sir, he had his back to the street and Speers was facing me. Took me a while to make the connection though. 'Course he's refusing to say anything but I am certain there was a reaction when I showed him the photograph; just a flicker and then he denied all knowledge." Harding told her to leave Speers stewing in the interview room and head for the canteen where he would join her in ten minutes time for the mug of tea she was about to treat him to.

Shortly after, he dropped into the seat opposite her. From his ragged breathing she deduced he had hurried. He eased the mug of tea to one side and looked at her, "Thank you Pat, that was a good collar, we'll have to get you out on the beat more often."

She replied evenly, "I seem to recall asking you to fuck off once before sir."

He chuckled, "You did, and I shall accept this request in the same good humour as last time." He stopped smiling then, "Because this one is important to me, for reasons I won't bore you with. What I want you to do now is go back in there and initiate a full interview process, tapes and all. When I enter just do as I ask and play along, alright?"

* * *

Speers knew his rights and knew they wouldn't hold this one together. Everything was too flimsy and the Crown Prosecution Service wouldn't let it through. He favoured Pat and her colleague with nothing more than a disdainful sneer. The tape machine continued to record her questions but evidenced nothing in reply.

Suddenly the door burst open and Harding made his entrance. He looked at Pat, pointed at the tape machine and without a word drew his forefinger across his throat. Speers had barely begun to protest when he heard the stop button pressed down. Harding pointed at Andrews and barked, "Out."

Once the door closed behind the PC Harding began, "Right, me laddo what shall we call you tonight? Mr Speers? Don't think so. Child molester out of retirement? Nope too formal. How about Perv, still with the pair of nuts they should have taken away years ago." Harding held up his hand to halt Speer's indignant reply, "Or how about Sick Little Bastard." He glanced at Geary as if startled, "I know, we'll just call you 'Unlucky'."

Speers sat back in his chair and waited. He was puzzled by the detective's words, and a little anxious too.

Harding sat on the corner of the desk and folded his arms across his ample midriff. "Seems you've picked a celebrity this time. When I say celebrity I'm referring to the television coverage Jimmy received tonight and it'll be in the newspapers tomorrow morning. I will be interested to see how the media treat it after the 'leak' occurs. See, besides reporting that he ran away from a children's home this morning they'll want to include a few details about his background. Things like him having to watch his mother and pet dog beaten to death, just last year. This kid has been in a hellish place, the public sympathy will know no bounds and the story is going to be front page stuff. Can you imagine what the public reaction will be like when they're told who's helping us with our enquiries?"

He slipped from the table and dropped to one knee, his body pushed well into Speer's zone, forcing him to lean back. Harding rested an arm on the table and held his wrist with the other hand, continuing in an almost conversational tone, "See, I know this boy and what he's been through, then and since." He glanced at the stilled tape machine, "So the rule book just left via the window." This time he locked eyes with his prey, "You're mine now. There won't be any protection inside this time. The isolation wing will be full, promise, and they welcome people like you with open arms, and flies. It'll be that or the shiv at shower time."

He stood and addressed Geary, "Lock him up, we'll find Jimmy tonight with or without this creatures' help and once we've got an ID he's away for a long time, trust me."

As he moved towards the door Speers whispered hoarsely, "I've done nothing. Just bought him a burger. What do you want from me?"

Harding nodded at Geary but addressed Speers. "Everything, I want you to positively identify the lad and tell us everything he did, said and signalled."

* * *

There is a distinct and penetrating nature to the sounds made by a police radio, the one in the car that is. Sudden bursts of static and the sharp 'cuts' made when a transmission ends. George Cope certainly thought so when a patrol car parked beneath his bedroom window. He peered blearily out and saw two officers peering into next doors' windows. 'Blimey' he thought, they must be looking for Jimmy. Next door was empty and still for sale so they would have no luck there. He rapped his window and with a series of hand and arm signals indicated that he was heading downstairs to meet them. As he moved towards the door he gathered his dressing gown up and prodded the sleeping form in the bed, "Get up girl, we've got company."

One of the Police Officers was waiting on the pavement when he opened the door and called out, "It was too late to do anything so we put him up in the back bedroom."

* * *

There was no elation at Randall Avenue, just an exhausted relief. Harding, Sarah, Nancy and Graham sat at the kitchen table nursing mugs of hot chocolate that had been laced with rum. They had listened with growing horror as Harding described the paedophiles' attempt to take off with Jimmy. Speers detailed all that he could remember Jimmy talking about, which wasn't very much, though he did speak about his dog, Sally. He'd gone on to say that she was buried at the old house and Graham remembered telling him as much. More as a long shot than anything, a patrol car was sent out to have a look and bingo. The neighbour had found Jimmy wrapped up in his multi-coloured blanket, next to the small wooden cross that marked Sally's grave and taken him inside. Jimmy had spent a lot of time with them when he lived next door and since it was so late they gave him a drink and put him to bed.

Speers was severely shaken though allowed to go. The CPS would have wanted a stronger case and in any event, Jimmy had seen enough in his young life without being subjected to another circus.

Chapter 16

The following morning, as soon as Nancy returned from her cleaning jobs, they travelled by bus to the care home.

This time a very different Pat Ensor greeted them both with a hug, "Well, thank heavens that's over. Come in, I'll put the kettle on." Once seated at the table her mood changed though, clearly shaken she voiced her concern, "My God, it doesn't bear thinking about, that was such a close thing. Creatures like that seem to have a knack of finding the Jimmy's of this world." She paused before quietly admitting, "I don't know what I'd have done you know." She caught a flicker of movement at the door and called out, "Jimmy! In here if you please."

After a few moments a shame-faced James Everard eased around the doorway, his shoulder maintaining contact with the door-frame. He stayed there until Pat called him forward, turning to Graham and Nancy to add, though for his ears rather than theirs, "Needless to say, this young man is still in the doghouse." She then addressed him directly, "I believe you have something to say to them."

He'd remained halfway between the door and table, his head bowed, though his words were clear, "I'm sorry for running away."

Graham's mother had been an expert at extracting public confessions and pleas for forgiveness, often where an unfortunate aunt or uncle would be as embarrassed as he was. The memory was clear and still felt uncomfortable forty years on. He addressed the ladies, "Would you mind if we had a private chat together pleashe. Man to man short of thing."

They found some plastic garden chairs near the swings and sat in the sunshine. Graham didn't prevaricate, "Did you know we came to see you yeshterday?" Jimmy nodded. "Do you know why?" This time a shake of the head. "We came to ask you if you would like to come and live with us properly, not jusht at weekends."

Jimmy stared down at the ground with an aching heart. They were there today to explain how he had spoiled it all by running away. He began to hurt then, in ways he could not hope to explain.

"*Would* you like to come and live with us?"

In utter disbelief, Jimmy looked up at Graham and nodded, silent tears tracking down his cheeks. With a tiny sob he whispered, "Yes please."

Once again, Jimmy's silent tears seemed to mirror such a noble spirit in the child and Graham's heart melted. He pulled Jimmy to him and into an enclosing hug, his own eyes filling, "Then you shall."

A short while later Graham eased Jimmy away but continued to hold him at arms' length. "Maytee, I will only have this one chance to say these thingsh to you so you musht listen. That man, the one who bought you food last night, was a *very, very* bad man who was going to hurt you. We know this because he has done it before and the Police caught him. Do you undershtand how lucky you were last night when the Police lady recognised him." Jimmy nodded firmly though Graham wondered how any child could comprehend that sort of evil.

But there was one thing he needed Jimmy to understand fully. "Maytee, if you come and live with us you musht promise one thing. Never ever runaway from us. Listen carefully Jimmy, because if you did it would break our heartsh and they would probably refuse to let us have you back. Do you undershtand."

Jimmy continued to nod but added a quiet, "Yes Graham." After a moment or too he asked, "Can I come and live with you today?" Graham stood and gestured towards the house, "I don't know, we'd better go and make some arrangements." As he began to walk a small hand took his, and received a reassuring squeeze for the trouble.

The two ladies were still in the kitchen and Graham made his announcement, "That's it then, we have an undershtanding." Both ladies clapped and Nancy opened her arms as Jimmy ran towards her. Graham continued, "But don't think it will be easy. Pocket money will need earning, that meansh either the washing up or drying *every* day of the week and the pay will be loushy." Jimmy looked up uncertainly and saw Nancy grinning, it was just Graham, being Graham.

It was simply a case of planning after that. There were a few formalities, not least of all to ensure that a significantly increased fostering allowance was put in place. Nancy wanted to make sure they had all they needed at home and so it was agreed that it be business as usual until Saturday when he would be collected for the last time. Just three days more in the home.

That night each member of the group was welcomed by the tall, softly-spoken Surinder at the Sardaar Vegetarian restaurant on the Narborough Road. As before, they were directed to the private room upstairs.

The aromas from the kitchen were as wonderful as before and before long the platters were delivered to the table. Adam had bought the wine again but this time they would share the cost as they would for the food. Calder and Doctor Williams listened to the other four relate the events of the previous three days, beginning with Jimmy's reluctance to go back to the care home on Sunday. They were all delighted to hear about the child's future but unnerved by the thought of what might have been. Sarah put it into words, Pat Geary is a damn good Child Protection Officer and we owe her a great deal, but she shouldn't have even been on duty last night, let alone on the beat in the city. I think a guardian angel was at work, don't you?"

Williams piped up, "Well he's got two more now." He smiled at Graham and Nancy, "So you'll be thinking about schools, designer label trainers, ski trips, family holidays and heaven forbid, adolescence before you know it."

Nancy chuckled, "Designer labels and holidays will have to wait until the lottery win comes up I'm afraid, but a home and family will get him started."

Graham rallied defensively, "I reckon I could get some more time in at the store as well, eshpecially now my arm is stronger."

Williams smiled at them, "You two will manage, I know it."

They chatted about a number of other things as they ate, including the previous weekends' picnic and Tim's continued improvement. Sarah decided to omit any detail about Alice. Besides being unprofessional she decided that what they had shared should remain private.

Once coffees had been served Harding suggested they deal with the agenda. Graham asked, "What agenda, I haven't got one."

All but Nancy showed varying degrees of embarrassment as Harding explained, "Ah, well we owe you a bit of an apology Graham, because we had a meeting last week, about you, or rather our concern for you." Graham said nothing but his impassive expression made them all feel uncomfortable. Sarah explained, "We are all rather fond of you Graham and we have come to realise how upsetting these experiences are for you."

Harvey added, "Lord knows, I found your journals harrowing enough and that was without any participation." There were murmurs of agreement around the table and Harding followed through, "I've seen most things and have my own way of dealing with them but violence involving kids has always been the toughest. Your reaction when you found Tim was entirely understandable, but I, we, feel that you can't keep suffering in that way without doing yourself permanent harm.

Williams added, "We didn't come up with any answers mark you. Couldn't really, without including you in the discussions, though I have been thinking about it since."

Sarah said, "So here we are. You are with us and our aim is to ease some of the suffering you go through with these 'hits'."

It was Harding's turn, "The way I see it, there needs to be a way of reducing your exposure, either by reducing the frequency of your 'hits' or lessening their intensity somehow. For example, we can all try and be more supportive, more accessible."

Harvey, "Or try to find some way of switching off, maybe by taking time off."

Williams added, "Well medically speaking you could try a mild sedative, perhaps intermittently, so that you have periods of peace."

Graham had continued to gaze ahead, unfocused and with no sign of reacting but Nancy sensed how angry he was. Suddenly he cast a look around the table and responded, "You lot have no idea do you?"

Nancy quickly reached across and took one of his hands before leaning across his shoulder and murmuring, "Love, they are all thinking *about* you not for you. They care."

He looked down at Nancy's hand, sighed and seemed to deflate somehow. In a much quieter voice he said, "Yes, I see that." He looked up again and added, "This *thing* I have doesn't cause me pain in the way you think. Tim wash a special case because I think I," he glanced at Sarah, "We, could have acted quicker and avoided what happened. I felt to blame for what happened to him. Normally, when I have a 'hit' I feel the pain, fear, confusion and all manner of things the child is experiencing as if I *was* that child and yet in a shtrange way my mind knows not to react now, or at least not as a victim. That way I can act; get help or try to shtop it and that is what you musht understand. If I became a hermit for one week a month or took drugsh and missed just one case like Tim's or any of the others a piece of me would die too." He glanced at Nancy and shook his head, "I didn't choose to have this connection with children and for a time I didn't want to live with it. But I have it and now," he sighed, "Well now I daren't live without it."

The group sat in stunned silence until Nancy articulated their thoughts perfectly, "This is weird. We've been sitting here discussing the matter as if it was a matter of overwork or stress. This is something we can't even begin to understand yet we're dealing with it so *normally*.

Williams huffed, "I'll second that. We don't seem to have achieved anything by this meeting."

Harding disagreed, "Yes we have, we've achieved a great deal. We must carry on supporting Graham but be guided by him too. He's the only one who can measure his experiences. Oh, that reminds me." He passed the carrier bag containing the journals over to Sarah, but addressed Graham, "Please please continue keeping a journal."

Everyone agreed and pressed on with their own views and reactions to those records. Amidst that chatter Sarah's mobile rang and she left the room to take the call. A few minutes later she returned and secured Graham's and Nancy's attention. The others fell silent as she spoke, "Now you would no doubt be responsible for the clearing up, training and excercise so think about this carefully. It's Stan's idea not mine; that was him telephoning to say he's in the barn acting as midwife. Anyhow, the question is, do you think Jimmy would like a puppy?"

Graham's reaction was explosive, "Yesh! You bet he would." He leapt up and hugged Sarah before turning back to Nancy, "I'm sorry love, do *you* want a dog?" She chuckled, "As if I dare so no after that reaction."

"Well you'd better bring him down to the farm next weekend and he can pick one from the litter. It should be weaned in about ten or twelve weeks' time, you can have it then."

"Thank you Sarah, thank you sho much!"

Harvey addressed Sarah, "What do you plan to do with the rest of the litter?"

"Oh, we'll sell them, or at least find good homes for them."

"Well I know a little girl who would love a pet dog as well."

Sarah beamed, "Wonderful, in that case you had better bring her along at the weekend too. How about bringing Graham and company with you, it'll save me having to turn out."

"Yes of course," he turned to Graham, "I'll give you a ring to confirm details."

Williams spoke to Harding specifically, though for the group as a whole, "Huph! And I thought the meeting was going so badly! I think we should close on a high don't you?"

* * *

The store manager suffered a moment of panic when Graham asked for more time. He remembered the nightmare of trying to find someone to fill the vacancy for a car park attendant before

Graham turned up. The trolley and car park work was split into part-time slots for a very good reason. Since so few people wanted the job the existing bank of employees provided cover for sickness and holidays, but the only way to give an employee extra hours would mean bringing them indoors and that would mean one less part-timer and that was counter-productive. On the other hand Graham was a good worker and incredibly popular with the staff.

In the end they reached a compromise. His job in the car park would be advertised and as soon as the position was filled an indoor post would be found with a five day week. They would review things in three months' time if nothing had developed. In the meantime he could have an extra day per week indoors, shelf-filling.

Next door, beyond the thin partition wall the manager's PA, Angie made another executive decision. When appropriate, she was the soul of discretion, necessarily so, since she could hear every word spoken in the office next door. Occasionally though, she would learn something that she deemed to be 'sharable'. So it was on this occasion and by lunchtime staff were patting Graham on the back, saying how much they looked forward to seeing him inside.

Timothy turned up on Friday as usual without his eye dressing and with a big grin. He would need spectacles for the rest of his life but both eyes were functional. Over drinks in the cafe he presented a note of thanks from his mother, which closed by expressing the hope that Tim and Jimmy could see more of each other. That prompted the news of Jimmy's full time placement with them and a promise to organise something soon. Tim's excitement grew as they re-lived parts of the farm visit and time slipped by easily. Suddenly it was time to go, yet Tim had so much more he wanted to say. Reluctantly, he parted company with a promise to meet next week but within yards thought of one vital piece of news. He ran around Nancy and blocked her path, "And guess what? Mum is letting me decorate my room!"

The bulging satchel and two carrier bags placed by the front door contained all his worldly possessions, save for the clothes he was wearing. Like his luggage, he stationed himself next to the front door, waiting for Nancy. This time, instead of heading into town to do some shopping they were going straight back *home*. He was only six years old, and heading for seven, but he knew enough to cherish that word

When Nancy arrived she presented Pat Ensor with a bouquet of flowers and accepted the offer of a cup of tea. Both ladies were excited by his prospects, discussing the many plans and arrangements that were now necessary but he was quite unaware of it; he just wanted them to stop talking and get him out of there. Yet when they finally left he hugged Pat tightly and even submitted to a kiss from her. He might have hated the home but she had been a bit special.

On the bus he held Nancy's hand and stared out of the window, his heart bursting and grin constant. When they reached home Nancy directed him upstairs to put his clothes away though the real purpose was to have him find the small plaque Graham had fixed to the bedroom door. It read,

Jimmy's room
Please knock before entering

Nancy had argued against the sign but Graham insisted. It had been a long time since the boy had somewhere he could treat as his own.

The remainder of the day was spent doing chores and small insignificant tasks but it held a dream-like quality for Jimmy who would sit for a while in the lounge before wandering up to his room or relocating to the kitchen where he would sit at the table to draw or read a comic and chat to Nancy. After lunch she announced that they were going to visit the farm again, as soon as Graham got home. "Great! Will Tim be there, and Chocks?"

Nancy was emphatic, "Chocks will definitely be there but I don't think Tim will. Some other friends are going, in fact you'll be in their car. They'll have a little girl with them, her name's Esther." Jimmy absorbed the information and hoped he wouldn't be required to play games with a little girl though he certainly wasn't going to raise a discordant note on that day.

Eventually, they heard Graham open and close the front door before calling out, "Is he here yet? The lawn still needs cutting and the front of the houshe still needs painting."

Jimmy looked at Nancy and rolled his eyes upward. She nodded, "Yeah, I know."

"Da da!" Graham burst into the kitchen with his arms stretched wide. Jimmy was ready and allowed himself to be wrapped into a hug before shuffling across to allow Graham to join him at the table.

Time was short since Graham had telephoned Harvey on the way home from work and expected them to arrive any minute. In fact, they had only just donned coats and shoes when they heard the gate hinges announce an arrival. Both Harvey and his wife Audrey stood at the door though Audrey explained, "The plan was for all of us to go to the farm but that's six people in a car with five seats, though actually that will work quite well." She looked at Nancy, "If you don't mind Nancy, you and I can stay here and have a chat."

Harvey looked at them apologetically, "Listen, I can pop back and pick you up, it won't take long to make two trips."

Audrey sounded like the archetypal Yorkshire woman having to deal with a recalcitrant male, "It *will* take too long H and you know it. What time do you plan on getting Esther to bed tonight? Anyway, I really do want to chat with Nancy." She caught her appointed host's eye as she spoke and Nancy realised it wasn't a casual sugges-tion. She had wanted to see Jimmy's face when he saw the puppies but clearly, it wasn't to be. She remained silent until Harvey surren-dered and the reduced party had been waved off before suggesting a cup of tea.

Audrey put her arm into Nancy's and said, "That would be lovely. I have a fair amount of ground to cover with you and I've brought these to share." She opened her bag to reveal a bottle of champagne and a box of *Harrods* cookies, "I've been saving these for something special."

* * *

Jimmy was agog. He had never been in a *Jaguar* before and was enjoying a sensory overload. The smell of leather and the quiet purr from the engine that had enough power to push him back into his seat. The radio was playing music that came from all directions yet still permitted them to speak normally.

Esther continued to prod him with a crayon until he looked at her drawings which were little more than random lines but he was polite enough to feign recognition of the cows, tractor and dog she offered up for appraisal. In no time they arrived at the farm. Sarah came out to greet them as did Chocks, who barrelled through the adults to get at her young friend. Jimmy hugged her as usual before encouraging Esther to stroke the matted fur.

Suddenly, Chocks turned and trotted off towards the barn on the other side of the yard. The adults had been watching and Sarah spoke, "I think you'd better follow her. She wants you to see something." Jimmy so wanted to run after Chocks but good manners dictated that he should keep pace with Esther since it seemed that he had somehow assumed responsibility for her. Moments later though, the whole group stood at the barn entrance, peering into the gloom to see where the dog had gone. As their eyes adjusted they saw a small enclosure in the corner formed by wooden planks. Chocks briefly poked her head up into sight as if to confirm her location and her movement triggered a little chorus of mewling sounds.

The grown-ups held back and allowed the two children to move forward. Esther grasped Jimmy's hand as they both crouched and crept towards the enclosure though when she was able to peer inside she snatched her hand away and held both up tightly against her chest. She gasped and turned, "Grandpa, she got babies!"

Jimmy had no words for what he was experiencing and sank to his knees, gazing at the six tiny bundles of black and white fur nuzzling at Chock's tummy. He didn't know what he could or couldn't do but took the risk of reaching over them and stroking her head. A wag of her tail and the lick of his hand was enough to show her welcome and trust. Things had been said behind him but nothing registered until Esther tried to climb into the enclosure. That broke the spell and he moved forward, ready to protect them from the toddlers' incursion but Harvey lifted her back, explaining how tiny and fragile they still were.

Sarah reached in and lifted one out for them to inspect though Jimmy watched Chocks anxiously looking up at her pup. It's head bobbed as though it was too heavy to support and just as Esther stroked the shoulder it began to cry. She snatched her hand back and looked at Harvey in case she'd been to blame but he picked her up and chuckled, "She just wants to get back to her mummy."

Jimmy asked, "Why hasn't it got any eyes Aunty Sarah?"

"Oh their eyes won't open for another ten days or so yet, but then they'll be all over the place. Chock's will find it hard to get away from them, at least until they're weaned and that won't be for another twelve weeks or so. Hopefully we'll have found new homes for them all by then."

He didn't dare ask.

Sarah set the pup down and watched as it latched on to one of Chock's teats. Satisfied that all was in order she clapped her hands and said, "I'm thirsty, let's adjourn to the house shall we."

As they left the barn Graham glanced back to see Jimmy sitting beside the enclosure with his knees drawn up beneath his chin. It was clear that he was foregoing drinks at the house and would remain there for as long as they would let him.

There is a certain joy in giving, particularly when the gift is so profoundly significant. Graham struggled to keep his voice steady when he crouched down and whispered in Jimmy's ear, "If you're going to stay here and keep Chocks company you may as well pick which one will be yoursh."

Jimmy could hardly believe his ears. He was going to have a dog again. All to himself. He looked up, "I'll look after it, I promise."

"I know maytee, I know, but make shure you get a good look. Nancy is going to want a full description."

* * *

Nancy soon recalled how easy Audrey was to get along with particularly when their conversation was so well lubricated. There seemed to be so many things they were able to discuss and over half the bottle had been consumed before Audrey announced that she had something important to talk about. She paused to fully recall what she'd planned to say, which had seemed so much easier when she was sober.

"Tell me, does Graham ever tell you fibs or hide things from you?"

"No, at least not that I'm aware of." Nancy chuckled then, "'Course I wouldn't know if he was hiding it from me would I."

"Yes, true! But then what if you caught him out doing it."

"Well then I *would* know."

Audrey paused for thought and shook her head, this was getting too complicated. "Tell you what, I'll stick to my side of the story. Harv' hasn't kept things from me either," she inclined her head towards Nancy who was recharging their glasses and tapped the side of her nose with a finger, "Or at least as far as I know. He did recently though, about a very important thing. Had to give him a bollocking."

"FFfppff." Nancy burst into shocked laughter just as she had been taking a sip of wine and both of them giggled at the fan of spray that lay across the table, but Audrey's next comment had a startlingly sobering effect.

"He hid Graham's diaries." She saw the effect her words had and grasped Nancy's wrist, "Oh don't worry, his secret is safe I promise you, but I did read them. Had to really, they contain the only record of my granddaughter's suffering and I needed to know about that, to understand what she went through d'ysee?" She looked into her glass and her focus glazed, "But hell's bells, those diaries went to places I couldn't imagine. Does he really see those things, and feel them?" Nancy nodded. "Then God help and bless both of you. I need another drink."

They took another swig of champagne and Nancy grabbed a cookie before replying, "When he began to get these visions, we call them 'hits', his wife thought he was going nuts you know." As she spoke, she'd dunked her cookie in her drink and was absently swirling it around. Audrey eyes were drawn to the spectacle but she listened politely as Nancy continued, "O'course, he isn't but we must keep it a secret. He's terrified of the press."

Audrey nodded, made to speak but instead nodded again, before she began to laugh. The more she tried to stop the worse it became. Desperately, she sought control using any mechanism she could; turning away, delving into her handbag for a tissue to wipe the tears away, checking for her keys, anything, but every time her gaze fell on Nancy or her wineglass she dissolved into hysterical laughter. Nancy waited patiently for her guest to regain some control which she did, eventually. Falteringly Audrey explained, "Nancy, you have been dunking very posh biscuits in a Champagne that cost over eighty quid a bottle as though you did it every afternoon and I think that is one of the coolest things I have ever seen. It was delicious and you know what? I'm enjoying this afternoon more than you can imagine. Please, do let us be friends."

Nancy grinned at her guest, "That's just the champagne talking. I'm not very interesting."

Audrey wasn't laughing or smiling when she answered, "Never say that lass. You and I share more than you know. My upbringing was as poor as it gets; I take nothing for granted, even now, and I can never forget that true generosity is more often found in groups that can least afford it. But there I go, getting sanctimonious, or sentimental, not sure which, but see, I share something else with you. We have both lost children and Graham has helped us deal with it." She looked down at her glass, "God, I'm starting to sound like DH Lawrence. Give me another drink, I need to work on Mickey Mouse."

Nancy upended the bottle, "Oops, do you fancy slumming it with some discounted Chardonnay."

Audrey peered at Nancy with one eye closed, "Go for it."

It was so easy to chat on about all manner of things and at one point the talk moved on to holidays. In particular the ones they most remembered as children. Times when families who had never met before would join up on the caravan site for a game of cricket or rounders. When a roast beef dinner in a seafront cafe would cost the equivalent of fifteen pence and was thought to be the height of sophistication. As they exhausted their stores of childhood memories Nancy asked, "Are you planning on a holiday soon."

"Oh, not until the middle of November. Neither of us much like crowds so we'll head off to Florida then." She smiled and added, "We've done the Disney World and Theme parks several times so these days we rent a cottage down on the Gulf coast, on an island called Captiva, it's beautiful. Mind you, anyone who hasn't been before should try Disney World, it's a real eye-opener. Where are you going?"

Nancy waved a hand dismissively, "Oh we not going anywhere this year."

"You are now lass."

Nancy furrowed her brow, "Pardon."

"I told you Harv' has stopped keeping secrets from me. I know that you're giving Jimmy a home, and o'course I know Jimmy's background. Harv' also told me you weren't going on holiday and I wasn't having any of that. Pour some more wine, you're going to need some."

She produced a business card from a pocket and set it down on the table, in front of Nancy. The background was an impressionist beach scene with a band of sunlight playing across the sea. The vivid blue print declared, *Distant Worlds Travel* and someone had written *Arnold* across the bottom, beneath the address and telephone number. Audrey picked up her replenished glass and winked at Nancy, "Cheers."

Nancy took a sip and waited for more. Audrey nodded her understanding, "We've used these people for years and I've briefed their Florida specialist, Arnold, so he's expecting you."

"Audrey, we couldn't even *borrow* enough for a holiday like that."

Audrey giggled and playfully slapped Nancy's arm, "Silly, this is my treat. You just buy the T shirts."

"No! We can't do that Audrey. Thanks, but no thanks."

Audrey rested an elbow on the table and sighed, "I've had too much to drink. I'd thought this out so thoroughly at home and I've bloody well forgotten what I was going to say now."

She closed her eyes and waved a hand in the air, "Hang on, it's coming back." In spite of her embarrassment and anger Nancy couldn't help laughing.

Audrey spoke, "Tell me something Nancy, and no holding back now, how did you feel when Graham told you about holding your son when he was dying, Christopher wasn't it?"

Nancy was knocked off balance momentarily but the answer came easily, "I cried, then I hugged him and thanked him. I also think I began to love him from that moment on."

Audrey chortled, "Well I couldn't stretch to that! He'll have to make do with a holiday." She regretted her brevity immediately and held up a hand to stay Nancy's response. "OK then imagine this. If you'd had two children and Graham had at least managed to save one life, how deep would your gratitude be then?"

"Bottomless."

Audrey nodded, her eyes filling with tears sourced from emotion and alcohol, "Then I'm getting off lightly, and you lot are going to Florida."

Nancy shook her head and tried to speak but the older woman grasped her arm and spoke softly, "Please lass, don't fight me on this one."

"What about Harvey, what does he think?"

"For a start off men don't *think*, they do and this is my gift with my money."

"So he doesn't know about it."

Audrey grinned conspiratorially, "Ah, I know what you're thinking. You're thinking that I am keeping this a secret and you're wrong! I shall just be a little late telling him." They both guffawed.

Silence reigned then and they looked at each other until Nancy finally succumbed. With a small wail she reached across and hugged Audrey. In time they broke apart, each wiping their eyes. Audrey broke the silence, "Now where is that wine. Have you anything we can eat with it?"

Nancy thought for a moment and replied, "I've got some custard creams."

Chapter 17

Graham readily admitted to a limited experience of foreign travel and Nancy said she had none. He and his ex had only ever been to Majorca, cocooned within the comforting embrace of a package tour operator. They had answered all sorts of questions the travel agent put to them, covering all aspects of holidays; good and bad until the chap on the other side of the desk clapped his hands and said, "You guys are in for a holiday of a lifetime, believe me.

Arnold was a truly gifted travel agent who genuinely shared his clients' excitement. He thought back to last week and his meeting with Audrey who sought an intriguing mix of package holiday and independent travel. This would be just as he and Audrey had planned and he had already sourced a deal for them that ticked all the boxes yet remained within the very generous budget Audrey had given him.

Delightedly, he began setting out an itinerary for them, "OK, the dates are set for the middle two weeks of November and you need to start in Orlando where believe me, you will need twelve days. It won't be enough to do everything but I promise you, it will be enough, you'll be exhausted. It's not just Disney, you will want to visit Universal Studios, Seaworld, the Space Centre at Cape Canaveral and maybe even 'Wet n Wild' which is a funky sort of water park. All these trips will be part of your package that includes transport to and from the hotel and almost all admission fees.

You will stay on the Disney World complex which is amazing and will give you priority access to all their theme parks. Places like the *Contemporary Resort* or *Polynesian Resort* are amazing but you might find them a bit formal, while the Caribbean Resort is very relaxed. I know you'll love it. Lots of pools, places to eat, it's great.

After twelve days you will be flown from Orlando down to Fort Myers which is on the beautiful Gulf Coast. There you will get a chance to relax and spend some time on the beach. You will stay at the *Golden Horizon Suites* at Fort Myers Beach and whilst your package includes escorted transport to the hotel I understand that Harvey and Audrey Calder will be meeting you. Either way, you will be well taken care of.

Your flight out is direct but from Heathrow, though I'm told '*the group*' have your transport there in hand. Coming back you will fly from Fort Myers to New York before catching the overnight flight back to London. Again, no worries, there will be someone to escort you through the process at New York."

He looked up at their bemused expressions and chuckled, "Don't worry I'll print off a copy of the itinerary for you and Audrey left this." He passed over a Guide book for Florida and added, "The library will have guides as well." With a dramatic flick of the wrist he tapped his keyboard and waited for the printer to produce a sheaf of papers which he tamped and stapled together. "Oh Lord, I nearly forgot, we'll have a thousand pounds' worth of travellers cheques ready to collect one week before you go, though do take a credit card as well, as back up."

They left the office in stunned silence until Nancy hit the nail on the head, "This is how lottery winners must feel."

*　*　*

The following two weeks disappeared in an excited blur. Jimmy could barely cope with his good fortune. A new life and home would have been wonderful enough but now he had so much more in store and spent hours studying the many Florida guides they had borrowed from the library. During that time they visited the farm, with Nancy, who recognised Jimmy's pup from the description he'd given. A bitch, it carried a little more white than the others but was still very obviously a Border Collie. Their eyes were open by that time and Jimmy was allowed to hold it, cupped in the fold of an arm and gently 'shushing' when it cried for its mother. Esther had yet to pick hers and would do so when the pups were ready to be parted from Chocks.

Eventually though, they exhausted the subject of Florida and the more mundane aspects of life re-asserted themselves. Jimmy had settled into his new school where, remarkably, a friend was already in place. Since the seating arrangements had been changed by the new teacher, he and Timothy sat together and became firm friends. Mrs Tenson taught them twice a week and had given Graham and Nancy a hard time of it when they sought permission to take him out of school mid-term for a holiday. The point had to be made, but Sarah had called in for a coffee the previous week and told her of Jimmy's background. A holiday with his new family seemed more important than ten days in school. She had been struck by the coincidence and strength of his friendship with Timothy Dexter and had mentioned it once in class. Tim answered promptly, "Jimmy's dad is Graham, the man who saved me at the canal. He knew what those boys had done to me."

Later, in her office, Tenson had chance to consider the connection. When Timothy was in hospital Sarah Whiting had continued to keep her informants' details secret but in the course of her briefing, which included detailed information about the bullying by peers and a teacher, also mentioned the suicide plans that were foiled by an observant store employee.

Last week, Sarah had described the association between Graham and Jimmy as one that started in Hospital, though she also detailed his complete history which was even worse than Timothy's. She had gone on to say how delighted she was with the new foster family.

Tenson considered the link and wondered at the coincidences. Graham Parsons seemed to have saved the life of one boy and given a home to the other. A store employee had blocked Timothy's purchase of *Paracetamol* and Mr Parsons worked at a store. And now the boys were firm friends; curious.

* * *

On Saturday, the first of July, Graham experienced another serious 'hit.' Minor ones, representing undue severity of punishment or thoughtless but relatively minor acts of neglect occurred all the time and Graham consoled himself with the thought that they would survive, if only to become careless parents themselves. This one was different.

He had seen the family leave the store, both parents and two boys. One marched alongside the trolley and was having a lively conversation with his father. The mother was also alongside but an older boy had fallen in behind. He looked rejected somehow, the posture was all wrong and Graham began to sense mistreatment of some sort. He followed them at a distance that enabled him to be nearby as they finished transferring their bags into the car. As the father began to push the trolley towards the nearest shelter Graham reached out, "I may as well take that for you shir." The 'hit' occurred instantly with a rapidly changing sequence of images; the shock of a blow from a fist, the ritual of a well known wide leather strap or the thick rope with a knot at the end, or the slicing agony of a cane. He was suddenly overcome by a feeling of surprise and betrayal as he caught an image of the cane being passed to the other son and the punishment continuing.

Only seconds had passed but it was time enough for the man to start the car and begin moving away. Trembling, Graham snatched a pen from his pocket and wrote the car number down. After a little thought, he telephoned Sarah and described the hit, adding apologetically that he had done no more than take the car number. He passed that on and Sarah said she had an idea and would get back to him.

A call to Harding initiated a check at vehicle registration at Swansea to establish the name and address of the owner, followed by a check of criminal records. He drew a blank there but provided Sarah with the information he'd obtained. She in turn had checked the welfare records and come up trumps. The family had been subject to a fairly intensive period of visits that had gradually ceased after the second partner and father of the youngest boy had left for pastures new. The departments' concern centred around the older boy whose injuries had been noticed by his games teacher and reported to them. The man's name was the same as the registered vehicle owner so evidently, he had returned and was continuing to abuse his stepson.

Within a couple of days a home visit was organised and the injuries they found were appalling, though within the boundaries of normal clothing and out of sight. Sarah isolated the younger boy from his father to discuss his role in the punishments. She spoke so knowingly that he gave up any attempt at denial.

Later, Sarah spoke to Graham on the telephone, "You know, the most surprising thing was that whilst the mother must have known that the punishments had occurred, I'm certain she had no idea of the scale of them and more importantly her partner's recruitment of the boys' own brother to administer some of them. I would be very surprised to see the man there tomorrow, judging by her reaction but I have to refer this case for appraisal now. Do we leave him there and monitor things or do we move him. It'll be close, either way."

The episode was ground-breaking so far as Graham and the group were concerned in that they'd discovered a new modus operandi that fitted with their wish for him to act without risk. The same strategy would be employed several times more that year.

* * *

Parenting is more often a 'seat of the pants' experience than the science one might suppose. Each week issues cropped up requiring decisions and accommodations, often unforeseen though in hindsight they should have been. So it was that the school holidays were just ten days away when Nancy realised a need for a childminder. She worked until eleven each morning and Graham didn't work on Mondays or Tuesdays so they only needed a minder for three mornings a week but it was proving impossible to find someone. Jimmy argued that he could manage perfectly well by himself but she would have none of it. In the meantime, Jimmy and Tim's friendship had extended beyond school and after accompanying them a few times and with Alice's agreement both boys were allowed to walk to each other's house. It was Alice who came up with the perfect solution. A neighbour took care of Tim during the school holidays and had agreed to take Jimmy in as well, at a very modest rate.

For the most part though, the new family became stronger each week. Their own social worker submitted glowing reports and the additional incomes, from Graham's extra day at work and the full time fostering allowance enabled them to have grander excursions on Sundays, often accompanied by Tim and on a couple of occasions, Alice too.

Her own life was changing and her relationship with Sarah had warmed remarkably as they plotted a new course for Tim and for that matter, both of them. More out of friendly discussion than recommendation, since it was wildly beyond Sarah's remit, Alice began to acknowledge what a strange upbringing she'd had and spoke to her GP about it. He had always regarded Alice as a bit of a 'cold fish' and recognised the need for some counselling, just as she had. It would take time but every step counted.

The greater bulk of folk took their annual holidays in July, once the schools had broken up and Thursday the twenty first had been very pleasant. The store was exceptionally quiet and the weather lovely, leaving Graham and his colleague Colin with little more to do than chat. For the sake of appearances they wandered around the car park with litter pickers but remained close enough to gossip. At five o clock, half an hour before their shift ended, they heard a squeal of rubber and turned to see a silver Renault weave from side to side as it advanced into the car park until suddenly it straightened and hurtled towards them. Anxiously, Graham and Colin moved toward each other, perhaps hoping that the mass of two bodies might represent and unacceptable level of damage to the car, but at the last moment it swerved through an arc that ended with the passenger door in front of them. The window was descending as the driver called out, "Graham, get in boy, quickly." Doctor Williams sounded rushed, frantic even, but Graham still had thirty minutes to go and said as much.

Williams was beside himself, "Listen, this is urgent, I have a case you need to see. They're at the surgery now but they think

I'm making an emergency house call. Please, we need to get straight back."

Graham looked at his watch to make sure of the time before replying, "Look can't you keep them for half an hour?"

"Get in man, I'll have you back here in no time." Graham showed no sign of giving in and Williams became desperate, "Graham, if you don't get in this car now I shall throw you in!"

Colin came up with the solution, "He seems like he means it mate, why don't you go. If anyone asks I'll say you've gone home with a headache, with the sun an' all. It's hardly busy is it?"

Graham thanked him and ran back to the locker room to get his jacket. Within minutes he was hanging on to the overhead grab handle as Williams sped back to the surgery, briefing him on the way.

"Her name is Shelley Caldwell, eight years old. Her mother has just brought her in with scalding to the neck and shoulders, claiming that she had pulled a mug of fresh tea off a high shelf by accident. But the track of the burns are all wrong; you'd expect a fairly vertical spread whereas the affected area seems to suggest some horizontal movement too. The scald itself isn't too serious and won't need hospital treatment. I've tried probing but both mother and daughter are playing it close to their chests."

The brakes exceeded all of Graham's expectations by stopping the car before it barrelled through the wall of the surgery. He had hardly opened his door when Williams pulled him out of the car by his elbow. "Now listen, I'm going to have the nurse come and collect Shelley to apply a dressing but she will sit her next to you while she goes to make sure a room is available. I shall tell her to give you at least ten minutes. Meanwhile, I shall keep the mother with me on the premise of making an accurate incident record."

As Graham was being hustled through the entrance lobby he thought to ask, "What about your other patients?"

"Same explanation, 'emergency home visit'. They're being seen by the other partners."

Graham sat where he was told to and Williams marched down a passage to enter one of the far doorways. He re-appeared after a few minutes and pointed Graham out to the nurse who had followed him. Nothing more was said as they entered another door-way, obviously Williams' consulting room. Shortly after the nurse re-appeared, holding the hand of a young girl who was holding a plastic bag against her neck with the other hand, half- hidden by her long blond hair. The nurse was explaining something to the girl though Graham couldn't hear what was being said but as they drew near the nurse addressed him, "Excuse me sir, but would you mind keeping Shelley company for me for a few minutes please, while I go and prepare things for her."

"Of courshe not." He looked at the girl who seemed a little bewildered, "But I must tell you now, I'm no good at sewing heads back on." She looked at him, startled and he grinned at her before continuing, "Hello, my name is Graham and I can see that your neck is perfectly shecure. In which case I can do something usheful and give you a game of noughts and crosses. What'sh your name, no let me guess." He rolled his eyes upward in feigned concentra-tion before announcing, "I know, it's Shilley!"

The girl looked back at him with a slightly cross expression, "No it isn't, it's Shelley."

Graham touched the side of his nose with a forefinger, "Ah, in that case you can be Shelley and I will be shilly."

The nurse tried to keep a straight face as she eased Shelley onto to the seat beside him. Graham asked for some blank paper and after providing them with a handful, she disappeared into her treatment room.

It didn't take long to establish a rapport and though she had never played noughts and crosses before she was playing like a 'pro' within five minutes. Eventually the nurse re-appeared and escorted Shelley back to have her wounds dressed. Halfway down the corri-dor Shelley turned and gave Graham a wave which was returned but the moment she moved out of sight he sank back in the chair and closed his eyes. Throughout their game they had sat closely enough to make contact and he barely managed to hide his reactions.

Soon, he became aware of someone sitting beside him and opened his eyes to see Williams staring at him. "What do you think?" he whispered.

"She's a frightened little girl. I *think* it was about a chocolate bar she ate. She had started to run away when the mug was thrown at her but it was shtill close enough for the mug to break. I think she was cut on the back of the head because I felt a panic around her to shtop the bleeding. Perhapsh before bringing her here. Oh, it was the father."

Williams placed a hand on Graham's shoulder, "Thank you Graham, thank you. I'll organise a cup of tea for you, but would you mind hanging on, in case I need more. I'm going to telephone the authorities now."

Graham gave a nod of thanks and added, "There was the broken toe as well."

Williams had already left his seat and returned to it, cautiously. "Broken toe?"

Graham waved a hand and explained, "There were lotsh of things but some were stronger than others. I felt the fear or shock and the suffering. She was sitting on a sofa I think, and had drawn her feet in but there was a shout and he stamped on her foot."

"How do you know it was her father?"

"Oh that's easy, I can tell by the feeling of shock. Somehow, it'sh different when a parent or relative does it. Anyhow, it hurt for a long time, weeks I think." He pointed at his right foot, "The one next to the big toe."

Williams sat back in his chair, startled and wondering what he could do. Moments later Graham continued, "Then there was the ladle."

"Pardon."

"He used a ladle to beat her. I couldn't tell why but it was recent because it still hurtsh."

"Where? I mean, where on her body?"

Graham spoke as though an excuse was called for, "Oh you wouldn't have seen anything, it was on the legsh and bottom." They both recalled the pink jeans she had been wearing.

Before moving Williams asked, "Anything else." Graham shook his head but added, "No, but there are lotsh of things there."

The nurse had finished putting the dressing on the scald by the time Williams entered the treatment room. He took a quick look and smiled, "Thank you Carol." He took her outside into the passage and said, "I need you to sit in and take some notes for me please. I need to have a chat with Shelley and your record of what is said and seen may be required by the authorities." They heard someone calling Shelley's name and Williams raised his hand to signal silence, "I'll sort that out first."

He strode out of the room to find Shelley's mother walking slowly along the passageway and softly calling her daughter's name. She saw him and said, "It's been such a long time and I need to get back. Where is Shelley?" Williams took her by the shoulder and guided her back to his consulting room, though on the way he called to a receptionist for a cup of tea to be organised. "I'm very sorry it's taken so long but a scald dressing takes much longer than most. Please, sit down and I'll be back shortly."

He hurried down to the treatment room where Shelley was attempting to show the nurse how to play noughts and crosses. "I wouldn't even try nurse, Mr Parsons says she's far too good at that."

He smiled warmly as he drew a chair up and sat in front of the girl. He made a show of inspecting the dressing and murmured 'fine' as he gently lifted the long blond hair around the scald site. Sure enough, an inch or two away from the scald and hidden by the hair, was a three quarter inch cut that had stopped bleeding but was obviously recent. As he described his findings Carol recorded them on an A4 pad and to her credit, hid any surprise when he grasped the girl's right foot and removed the trainer and sock. The second toe was clearly mis-shapen. Taking it gently between his thumb and forefinger he said lightly, "My word Shelley, that must have hurt for quite a while." She nodded gravely. "I think he ought to watch out where he's stamping his feet in future, don't you." She stiffened slightly, clearly anxious, but he had spoken so matter of factly he must have known all about it. She nodded again. "OK just a quick once over and we're all done. Stand up and drop your jeans down for me."

Carol had noted all she could, though the business of the big toe had surprised her. Now, as Shelley stood with her jeans around her ankles she was really baffled. She knew where this was going now that the evidence was in sight, but Doc seemed to know exactly what he was looking for. He eased Shelley round so that her back was facing him and continued dictating. Gently easing her underpants to either side he saw over a dozen round bruises spread over her buttocks and thighs; the expression 'Blue Moons' sprang to mind. They looked old enough to be pain-free now but he guessed that seven or ten days ago they hurt like hell. He finished his examination and asked Shelley to get dressed before turning to Carol, "Nurse, I need you to wait with Shelley for a little while longer, would you take her along to the meeting room please, and perhaps pick up a cold drink on the way." With that he headed for his consultation room.

"Thank you for your patience Mrs Caldwell, we've applied the dressing and established that abuse has occurred." He noted her brow knitting in confusion and continued quickly, "Ordinarily I would call the welfare services and a Child Protection Officer would contact you but in this instance I'm tempted to call the police Child Protection Unit who have the powers of arrest and can take Shelley into care immediately. What do think you could say that would change my mind?"

"I don't know what you mean."

"Well, let's start with today. The mug of tea was thrown at her, with enough force to cut her scalp. Then there's the toe, stamped on and broken, then left to heal itself which is why it is now permanently deformed. Lastly, there are more but these will suffice, there is the attack with a ladle of all things. I can't imagine how painful that was but I can do something to stop it happening again."

Mrs Caldwell gazed back at him in stunned silence, her usual excuses discredited in advance. Eventually she seemed to slump in her chair and looked down before saying quietly, "He's a good man, really. Sometimes Shelley does things to make him mad, but he's always brought a wage home, the kids have never gone hungry." He began to speak but she looked up sharply and added, "It hasn't happened often and Shelley couldn't cope in a home. Please believe me, we do love her."

Williams looked down at his blotter in thought and was reminded of that last time he had considered this sort of issue. That time he had let his heart rule his head and failed to notify the authorities, instead he gave the parties an opportunity to justify being allowed to sort things out for themselves. Part of that process had involved meeting Graham and he discovered things he'd never thought possible. Even so, he'd been censured by his partners for failing to observe the working practices for suspected child abuse cases and this one was beyond suspicion. The question was, Police or Social services.

Somehow, the thought of Shelley being removed from her home and family into protective custody persuaded him to opt for the Social Services but he needed to make sure of one thing.

"Mrs Caldwell, I believe you in that Shelley hasn't been the victim of gratuitous cruelty, but your husband cannot continue to mete out these punishments, or attacks more like. You may take Shelley home and you may be sure that a Social Services Child Pro-tection Officer will be contacting you, soon. Her job will be to help you both become better, no, civilised parents. But in the meantime, if Shelley suffers so much as a scratch I shall do all I can to have your husband put in jail. Is that clear?"

Mrs Caldwell began to weep with relief as she nodded her acceptance of his terms.

He gave her a tissue and used a softer tone, "I'll go and get Shelley for you, probably best she doesn't see you upset. Oh, there is one more thing, she has no idea about this development and you must not discuss it with her, is that clear too?"

She was weeping openly now, struggling to wipe her tears away with a trembling hand. but she nodded and murmured, "Thank you Doctor."

Surgery had closed by the time Shelley and her mother were shown out and Williams apologised to Graham profusely before asking for yet more time, "I must just make some notes, while it's still fresh see. I won't be long I promise, then I'll give you a lift home. Have you telephoned Nancy by the way."

Graham nodded glumly as the Doctor hurried back into his room and Carol approached. She was carrying a bag and clearly about to head home but as she drew near, sat beside him. "Hello, I'm Carol."

Graham smiled and they shook hands, "Hello, I'm Graham."

"Forgive me, but I have to ask. All this thing with Shelley seemed to be organised in some way. What happened out here."

"Oh, we jusht chatted. I learn a lot from kids you know, we communicate well." He shrugged his shoulders and added, "Bit of a gift really."

* * *

Colin sat in the locker room, changing out of his work clothes and trying to explain to the man who was there to take over from him. "It was weird. This bloke drove at us, screeched to a halt and told Graham to get in, he'd got a case for him to see at the surgery. Graham said no, of course, he still had half an hour to go, but the bloke insisted. In the end I told 'im to go, it was dead quiet 'ere anyway. Next thing they're going out of the car park like the *'Italian Job.'*"

His colleague shrugged and said, "Dunno."

Colin continued, "I reckon Graham's a bit of dark horse. P'raps he's a marriage guidance counsellor or something."

Meanwhile, Graham sat quietly in the surgery waiting room. He'd read the magazines and in the absence of anything better, tried to take a nap. Eventually, Williams called him to the consulting room where two large scotches were being poured. As he entered the doctor advanced towards him, "Look, I am truly sorry for taking up this much of your time, and also for shouting at you in the car park. Bit excited you see." He handed Graham the glass and added, "I didn't have much choice really."

Graham replied, "Shpeaking of choice you should get some more magazines for out there."

"Ah, yes, well the patients don't usually wait as long as you had to. Cheers anyway."

They both sat while the Doctor confirmed all that Graham had told him. "You know, it is ironic that I should be the last to witness your special abilities first hand. It's no longer such an abstract issue for me now."

Graham smiled and nodded before asking his question, "Would you mind driving a little shlower when you take me home?"

* * *

He had only been able to give Nancy the scantest details when he'd telephoned to say he was going to be late and because it would have been inappropriate to discuss things in front of Jimmy they waited until bedtime. He cherished the comfort Nancy gave him by cuddling up closely as he told the story, but his head ached and he was so very tired, too tired to discuss things after he had finished.

Nancy kissed him gently and whispered, "Go to sleep my knight, I'm here to watch over you."

* * *

He was back in the bedroom that frightened him. The night was stiflingly hot and he had thrown off his covers, yet sleep still eluded him. In its place a heightened awareness of household noises became surreally significant. He knew it was a Saturday by the sound of bottle on glass downstairs and from the television programmes. He also knew the same fear, once again and desperately sought the sanctuary of sleep, yet he also knew that sleep offered no protection. Downstairs the fridge door clumped open and the clatter of glass signaled the removal of another bottle from the carton.

Consciousness returned in the shocking sense of silence, save for one terrible sound. All noise from downstairs had ceased but the tiny creak of his bedroom door handle was deafening. Time slipped into slow motion as a floorboard creaked and a weight settled on the edge of his bed. This time the hands were bolder, searching, intrusive and undeniable. The smell of beer and sweat was overwhelming and the endearments were sickening. He knew he was resisting yet his hand was grasped even tighter, painfully so, as it was taken down to a dank, forbidden tumescence that was so wrong, so wrong. Please daddy.

"Please Daddy!"

* * *

The bedside light on the other side of his bed had come on. He was wide awake yet had no recollection of calling those two words out and waking Nancy.

He'd been crying though.

She moved across the bed and held him tightly, shushing and stroking.

"Oh Nansh, it's the same dream and I *know* it'sh not me but I feel such fear!"

"Easy, easy, you've had a bad day and it's triggered a recurring dream that's all."

"No! It'sh more than that, much more." He tried to describe the sounds from downstairs, their significance and the sound of the entry into his bedroom. His loneliness and fear; how the experience had been extended to something unclean and corrupting."

"Stop it Graham, now! You cannot afford to let what happened today, which was based on fact, let your dreams take you to places like that. Tomorrow I want you to ask the doctor for some sleeping tablets. Yes?"

He shook his head in confusion but finally said yes. They kissed tenderly and he rolled over on his side, facing away from her. She gently stroked his back in the way he so loved and within minutes heard his gentle snore.

She lay awake. There would be no more sleep for her that night.

Chapter 18

The following morning Colin was determined to be cool about the whole thing. Graham would either tell him all about it, or not, his choice.

By ten o'clock he'd run out of patience and trotted over to the other side of the car park where Graham was picking up litter. "Come on then, give. What was all that about yesterday."

Graham shrugged his shoulders, he'd already thought about what he might say, "Oh, nothing. Just sorted itshelf out really."

"What. Sorted what out? Come on man it sounded really important."

"Nah, it was case of mishtaken identity. The Doctor thought I knew the patient."

Colin wasn't *Mensa* material but he knew bullshit when he heard it. "So who was the patient, male, female, old, young?"

"A young girl."

"And."

"And what?"

Colin sighed, "Jeez, you're making this hard work. I *hate* it when people do that, so now I'm going to chase you all the way down the tracks. Come on, give, every detail."

Graham realised how pathetic his preparation had been and decided to stick to one of his basic principles, of telling the truth or at least as far as he could, "She was a young girl and the Doctor suspected that her father had injured her. I didn't know her sho I couldn't be the go-between they wanted me to be, or anything like that. Anyway, it all worked out I think. I went home as shoon as they organised a lift for me."

Dismayed by the absence of high drama Colin trudged back to his side of the car park where he pondered on the matter. He couldn't put his finger on it, but something didn't feel right about Graham's story.

At pretty well the same time, Sarah was quickly scribbling notes as she listened to Doctor Williams on the telephone. At one point he said, "I must say, I'm glad you've been given this case. There is so much I can tell you without fear of compromising Graham, for example how I came to know about the earlier injuries."

She chuckled, "Yes, well by the time I've put some weight in this file the question of discovery will be well masked. Incidentally, how was Graham?"

"Took it all in his stride. Seemed happy to take part and he dealt with the information he gleaned very well. Phlegmatic would best describe it I think."

"Good! I'm delighted, and relieved."

"Who's taking them to the airport by the way?"

"I'm not sure, everyone's volunteered, apart from the Calders, they'll already be over there. We can sort it out nearer the date when we'll all know what our diaries look like and Adam thinks we should have a group meeting before then, as a sort of *bon voyage* do. In the meantime they're coming to collect the pup in six weeks time."

"Wonderful, so it's an exciting time for them."

"Yes, I'm sure, but come on we'd better get back to business. I have an abusive father and a conveniently nescient mother to see very soon."

There was a significant pause before Williams spoke, "You know, this weekend I'm going to do something I haven't done for a long time."

"What's that?" Sarah asked, though she knew the answer.

"I'm going to go to church," another pause, "Because I don't know who else to thank."

The Doctor was right on one count at least, they *were* excited. The guides and plans for Florida were re-visited almost daily and when that subject was exhausted they would move on to dogs, and in particular 'Susie', the name Jimmy had chosen for his puppy.

In just over a weeks' time, on the first of August, Graham's store were to start their end of season sale which included a very acceptable range of summer wear, so they arranged to make their selection on the previous day, Sunday. Graham had made arrangements for the list of items with details of colour and size to be left with the department manager who would bag them up before the store opened on sale day.

Things settled back to normal very quickly at work, where the mundane became the norm once more. Again, Graham had stayed fairly close to the truth when he announced their holiday plans at work, by saying that a wealthy relative had paid for the trip to celebrate Jimmy joining them on a full-time basis. Some of the staff had already been there and would stop by at lunchtimes to give him tips on what to do and where to eat. They seemed almost as excited as he was.

In spite of the clothing sale the following week continued to be quiet but they were warned by the old hands to standby for a hectic one ahead, when families would be back from their holidays.

Graham and Colin sat on a low wall, out of sight of the office and chatted about everything and nothing, as men often do when they have nothing better to do.

The car park was barely an eighth-full without a single trolley out of place when they watched an elderly Ford Fiesta being driven to the far corner where it was stopped, next to a litter bin. There was a couple in the car and the driver, a man, got out and removed a large black plastic sack from the boot. It was too large to fit into the bin so he dumped the sack on the floor and leant it against the post. Without checking to see if they had been observed, he jumped back into the car and drove back towards the entrance at speed. Colin gasped and looked at Graham in disbelief, "Will you look at that. It's fly-tipping, that's what that is, and it's against the law."

Graham smiled, "No, 'fraid not, but he has been very cheeky. Of course, there could be shomething in that bag that *would* make it illegal." They ran through a host of possibilities that included illicit cash, drugs, secret documents and arms,—military or human, until Graham volunteered to go and check.

It made quite a change to be able to amble across the expanse of tarmac without having to dodge the traffic yet as he approached the sack a feeling of unease developed. To begin with he handled the sack with caution, easing it from one side to the other in case a tear or cut might have exposed some of the contents. They were soft, that much was certain and not very heavy. He would have wagered that they were clothes but he still exercised caution in the way he untied the string at the neck. Eventually, the string fell away and he eased the top open. Sure enough, there were clothes in there and he could smell wool, soap and something else, baby powder perhaps. He reached in to move the top layers, hoping to find documents or some other means of identifying the source;

* * *

He was crying in the darkness. All he knew was thirst, hunger and a need for comfort. Downstairs the television had grown louder and louder so he knew that he needed to cry even louder and rock his cot to and fro so that it banged against the wall. On and on and on.

Exhausted and desperately thirsty he paused expectantly as footsteps hurried upstairs. Relief turned to terror so quickly as a heavy hand grabbed the front of his pyjamas and snatched him out of the cot, banging his knees painfully against the headboard. He heard the yelling and felt the material of the jacket pinch painfully under the arms until his back and head struck the wall, driving the breath from his lungs. He knew fear then, at a primeval level, as a face came close and continued to yell. Moments later a great crashing blow to the midriff smashed his spine against the wall in an agonising explosion of pain. The hand released his jacket and he was allowed to fall to the floor. The room returned to darkness as the door was slammed shut but tears or cries wouldn't, couldn't come. The pain was beyond measure, just as the attack had been so unexpected. He could still hear the television but now he could hear his own whimpers, though they didn't seem as though they belonged to him. Eventually he could only hear the television and it was growing cold, very cold, but the pain wouldn't ease. He continued to stare at the doorway, bordered by a tiny band of light and waited fearfully. After a long time, or so it seemed, he grew even colder but then the pain finally began to ease.

There was a moment of fear, panic even, though he didn't know why but moments later he felt himself falling as if into a ditch and without any effort climbing up the other side into what felt like a field of wonderfully ripe wheat, moving very gently and basking in a glorious golden light. A profound sense of peace and wellbeing overwhelmed him. All pain had gone.

* * *

He opened his eyes and heard footsteps running towards him as he ran a quick physical audit. It was a 'hit' and he'd blacked out again, falling across the bag of clothing as though he'd claimed possession. A shadow fell across him and Colin spoke, "Graham, are you OK? What happened, you just keeled over. I called Linda," there was a pause, "Yeah, she's on her way now."

Graham rolled off the bag and sat up, "No need, I'm OK."

As though she had heard him Linda, the stores' appointed first-aider called out as she hurried towards them, carrying a green holdall, "Graham, stay where you are!"

The last thing he wanted was fuss and Linda's urgency was enough to stir Graham into action. He struggled to his feet was dusted himself down as she reached him. "For God's sake, I told you not to move."

"I'm fine, honestly, it was just the heat. I'd hurried over here and in these jackets it's like a shauna."

She bent to retrieve a small bottle of water from her bag, "Take that off and drink this, slowly. Then I'd like you to go to hospital for a check up."

"No. Trust me, I only fainted through the heat. Pleashe, I really do know how I'm feeling."

Linda looked uncertain but eventually realised he was serious, "OK, I'll do you a deal, I won't call the ambulance if you promise to see a Doctor, today."

Graham hid his relief by countering her offer, "Tell you what, if I lie back down and closhe my eyes will you have to practice your resuscitation technique on me."

"She smiled slightly and held his gaze as she spoke, "Colin, nip back to the store and get me the defibrillator would you. Graham here wants some shock treatment."

Graham grunted, "Blooming technology, takes all the fun out of being ill."

She smiled openly then, "Come on, let's get you inside anyway, in the cool."

Colin moved towards the black bag, "Yeah, I'll see to this then come and join you."

Graham held out an arm, "No, leave that where it is, pleashe." He saw Colin's surprised look and was aware of Linda's sudden interest. "Don't ask me what but there's shomething odd about that lot, I don't think we should touch it." Colin stepped back quickly in case he had missed something Graham had seen, like wires!

Graham added, "it'sh probably nothing, 'cos it's only clothing, but I'm going to speak to someone becaushe of the way they dumped it. It felt wrong." As he spoke he removed his telephone from his pocket and gave them a small wave, "You go on, I'll follow in a second." He turned away from them and hit a speed dial number.

Harding was sharing the interview room with a young Detective Constable and a much younger car thief who was treating him with utter disdain when he felt his telephone vibrate. After a glance at the caller ID he called a halt to the interview and went outside to take the call. "Hi Graham, everything OK mate?"

Graham began to shake as he tried to speak, but words wouldn't come out. He leaned against the fence and gasped, trying to ignore the sudden headache.

Harding hid his anxiety when he said quietly, "It's OK, there's no rush, take your time."

Moments passed until finally he could whisper, "There's another one, it's the worst. He's dead."

Harding called the DC out of the interview room and briefed him on what needed to be done with the young thief. As he strode down to the canteen he realised that if the DC made an utter balls up it wouldn't make much difference. The kid would have only been given community service anyway.

Meanwhile, he wasn't prepared to wait for a crew and car to turn up, it was teatime and he knew where to find one. The two he found in the canteen were taking a legitimate break and said as much but Harding cut them short, "Tough, you're mine now and I have a triple nine to deal with. Come on, chop, chop!"

Colin and Linda had walked slowly back to the store as directed though she retraced her steps smartly when Graham slumped against the fence. As soon as she was within earshot Graham smiled and waved, "With you in a moment, jusht waiting for someone." He waved again, dismissively, so she made her way back to the store and joined Colin. They discussed whether to call an ambulance anyway but as Colin pointed out, if he was going to refuse their help it'd be a waste of time. They waited and watched the small figure in the distance as a police siren approached. Neither thought much about it until it grew louder, much louder and suddenly it stopped. The patrol car entered the car park slowly and crept along the front of the store until a figure in the back seat pointed across the car park. Clear of blind corners and possible pedestrians the car swerved around and sped towards Graham. They watched as a portly figure clambered out of the car and ran to Graham where he rested a hand on a shoulder. Graham pointed at the bag and the man holding his shoulder turned to the two uniformed officers who were standing by the car. They ran to the boot of the car and withdrew two traffic cones and a roll of something. It only took moments to establish a crime scene with plastic tape; in its centre lay the black plastic bag. The plains clothes officer helped Graham into the back of the car and joined him, closing the doors to allow the air conditioning to take effect but after a few minutes they were joined by another patrol car and the store manager who had walked across to them.

Inside the car Harding saw the approaches and spoke quickly, "Listen Graham, so far we only have a bag of children's clothing dumped suspiciously. That is all, do you understand?"

Graham paused to consider the strategy and nodded his agreement. Harding got out of the car and gave the two newly arrived officers a description of the vehicle used to dump the bag and sent them to interview shoppers as they left the store. With luck someone may have seen something when they arrived.

"Hello, is there a problem?"

Harding turned and recognised the manager, "Ah, just the man. May we adjourn to your office please sir, I'll explain everything on the way. I don't know whether you remember me, but I need to have a look at your car park tapes again if you wouldn't mind."

They left one officer guarding the taped-off area while the other was instructed to find Linda and Colin and take statements.

As they made their way back across the car park the manager thought to ask, "Was Parsons involved again?"

Harding's reply was prompt, "As your car park attendant I'd expect him to be. Wouldn't you?"

Once in the office Harding explained that they were keen to trace the couple who had dumped the black sack. The manager looked a little puzzled, "I'm bound to ask though, what are they suspected of?"

Harding hadn't expected the question, at least from this chap and thought quickly, "We're concerned about the way that clothing was dumped. It would have been far more normal to have taken it to the tip."

The manager was still unconvinced, "If they only had one bag of clothing and they lived locally why *not* dump it here, or in a litter bin anywhere."

Harding responded, "I can accept that if they had dumped it here as part of a normal shopping visit, but instead they fled the scene." He held up a hand to stay any further comment, "But let's hope we're wrong, hey?" He headed off further comment with a tight smile, "Must crack on then. The tape if you would, please sir."

Harding gave the manager a receipt and was set to ask for Graham and Colin to be called to view the recording, but reconsidered, "Would you mind if we ran this tape past all of your staff please? People are creatures of habit and I wouldn't mind betting that these two shopped here on a regular basis."

The manager shrugged, "No problem, we can set a monitor in the staff room and send them in to view the tape in batches."

Graham had wandered back into the store to find himself besieged by curious staff members. His head ached terribly and he experienced a sudden and desperate need for solitude. The toilets were the only place he could think of and once there he locked himself into a cubicle. That was when the shaking started. He leant against the wall and folded his arms around himself, tightly, but the shaking wouldn't stop.

He had no idea how long he'd been there but someone shouting his name finally penetrated the fog he was in and brought him back with a start. "Hello?"

Colin spoke from the other side of the cubicle door, "Oh, so it is you in there, thought you'd nodded off again. That fat detective wants to speak to you."

"No, I'm fine. I'll be right there."

Since they had a fairly accurate idea when the dumping occurred Colin was able to identify the car but the distance and filthy number plate made recognition impossible. Curiously, the man and woman in the car were visible, at least enough for identification purposes. Colin was sent to find Graham and soon returned with his colleague trailing behind. Harding was startled by Graham's appearance; the poor man had aged, with a grey pallor and haunted bloodshot eyes. The detective took Graham's arm and led him to the monitor where once again, the car was identified. A Constable was asked find a quiet corner to take a statement from Colin and Harding led Graham out to the car park where another officer was instructed to take him home. He spoke quietly enough for only Graham to hear, "Go home and rest, I'll telephone Nancy to let her know what's happened and I'll check with you later on." He squeezed Graham's shoulder and helped him through the rear door of the car before addressing the driver, "38 Randall Avenue, no chatter just deliver this chap to his house and get back here quickly please."

Nancy was waiting for him and opened the front door as he walked down their path. She was just as shocked by his appearance but said nothing as he stepped past her into the house. As soon as the door was closed she stepped forward and wrapped her arms around him. The gesture was enough. He fell against her and let go, the gentle silence of their home broken by his sobs.

Back at the store six people had recognised the couple as regulars but couldn't provide a name, though two mentioned that they'd seen them with a toddler. As soon as the last staff member had seen it Harding had the tape rushed down to Headquarters where the 'techies' were waiting for it. He knew one of them well enough to get drunk with on occasion and had telephoned him with a plea for priority. It was a forlorn thought, he knew, because they were always under pressure and there was always a backlog. The reply confirmed this, adding that nothing short of a murder could jump the queue. It was then that Harding realised how vulnerable he was, using significant manpower and resources for what would be seen as a dumping of discarded clothing. He was the only copper who knew it for what it was, a murder enquiry, and had no choice but to keep blagging it. The 'techie' was still on the line and called out to see if Harding still was. Bracing himself he took a further step into deep water, "How about the murder of a toddler? Would that get past the queue?"

The 'techie' didn't hesitate, "Yes, defo, but when and where was this."

"Well that's the problem, at this moment in time I have nothing more than a bag of toddler's clothing a security tape of a car and a tip off. But, the source has never let me down and my only hope right now is for you to do your magic on the tape and get me a registration number."

"Where's the tape?"

"On its way in, with your name on it." Harding heard a gasp of resignation before, "This is going to cost you a bottle of good stuff and more as the need arises."

"Done deal mate, I'm on by the finger nails this time, thanks."

Colin and Linda sat in the staff canteen, discussing the adventure over a mug of tea. She had him describe what happened when the blue car appeared and how Graham had volunteered to go over and check the bag, but then keeled over after he had opened it. After that they shared recollections until Linda stated the obvious, "What made Graham think it was important enough to call the Police and how come they're making such a meal of it."

Colin shrugged his shoulders, "Perhaps because of what happened last time, you know, that little girl with a broken arm. Maybe 'e's got a special cred with the Police, like they listen to him more than they would you or me."

Linda snorted, "I wouldn't have thought so. But the way they're treating it you'd think someone had been murdered."

"And it's not just the law y'know?"

"What do you mean?"

Colin wriggled slightly, settling himself down to relate another tale from just last week; when a Doctor came screaming into the car park and desperately sought Graham's help with a case. In the interest of dramatic value he omitted to include Graham's explanation for what had happened.

* * *

"OK, I'm on my way. Can't treat him of course, but I can make damned sure he gets treatment if I think he needs it." Harding signed off from the other end and Williams snatched his car keys off their hook. As he marched out of the house he wondered what it must be like to share death and pictured the effect it might have had on Graham, he muttered, "You poor bugger."

He arrived at the house at a little after seven and recognised Sarah's car parked at the kerb. At least Nancy was getting some moral support as well. Inside he found the two women sharing a bottle of wine; another glass had already been put out for him. Jimmy was in the lounge watching television.

Nancy said, "This one knocked him about. I got him to take a sleeping tablet and he's just gone off. All being well he'll be out for a few hours now."

They all turned as the back gate swung open and Calder stepped into view. Nancy jumped up and opened the door but Calder seemed to be embarrassed. "Look, you've got enough help I can see, I just called round to make sure you were both OK. I'll get off, but please give me a ring if you need anything."

Nancy was alarmed, "Harvey, please, come in and have a drink with us. Adam may be calling in soon as well." She saw his hesitancy and said, "Please Harvey, I want you to join us."

Another glass was found and Williams telephoned Harding who confirmed that he was on the way *and* could buy a couple of bottles of wine on the way, via the back door so as not to disturb Graham. When he turned up, half an hour later he briefed them with the limited information he had but beyond the discovery of children's clothing there was little to add. Nancy gave him her chair and pulled a small stool out from beneath the work surface. Conversation eased as the wine took effect and Adam was pressed for more details about this type of investigation and what would normally happen now.

He gave a wry chuckle, "Well one of the first things I would expect to find on a file would be a detailed statement from the person who reported the crime. Every detail they could remember, who, what, when, where. And in Graham's case, *how*!"

It served to lighten the mood further and shortly after, Harvey rationalised the situation, "You know, I have no doubt that this child has died, but there is nothing any of us could have done to prevent it. More importantly, thanks to Graham, the Police have got a head start on catching the killers."

Harding nodded, "People have been known to get away with things like this you know. Bluntly, a toddler's body can be disposed of far easier than an adults'."

Nancy seemed distracted for a moment and Sarah reached across and grasped a hand, "Nancy, having us here must be wearing you out, we'll leave you in peace."

"No!" Nancy didn't mean to shout and couldn't say anymore. She looked upwards, her lips pressed tightly together and her eyes filling as she fought for control. She succeeded, eventually, and looked around the table, "The best place I could possibly be right now is with *the group*. You are the only people I can share this with."

Williams said brightly, "Well I'll open another bottle then."

Nancy smiled, "And I'll get Jimmy to bed. He must wonder what's going on."

She was still upstairs putting Jimmy to bed when Harding's telephone rang. He wrestled it out of his pocket, glanced at the caller ID and pressed the green button, "Yes mate, what have you got for me?"

Thanks to the copying and digital technology at their disposal they had identified the first three letters and next two numbers, leaving just ten numbers for each year the model was sold to work on. Vehicle records showed that of the fifty numbers it could be only one belonged to a blue Ford Fiesta. Harding scribbled a name and address down and made for the door, saying, "We've got an address. Save some of that wine for me."

* * *

The house was in the middle of a terrace and was the only one in total darkness. The row of houses had a vehicle access at each end that connected to a dirt drive behind the row, wide enough to allow the passage of cars and parking. He tried the neighbours who were a young couple and keen to help, confirming that the couple next door had a toddler and that they'd left suddenly, just that afternoon, without a bye or leave.

Suddenly, Harding was faced with waiting until daylight before they could even *try* get a warrant, but on what grounds? In any event, before they got that far his inspector would want an explanation for his profligate waste of resources. 'Christ' he thought, 'I'll be back in uniform with this one.' But then the young man made a comment, "Ah well, the board will be up tomorrow, our Landlord doesn't hang about."

Harding asked, "You both have the same Landlord?"

The young man chuckled, "He owns half the row."

"Do you have an emergency number?"

The Landlord was an accountant and extremely disinclined to venture out at that time of night. He told Harding to meet him there at ten am the following morning. Harding was in too deep to worry about the consequences and told the landlord that his property may well be the scene of a murder, telling him, in no uncertain terms that ten am tomorrow would be at least twelve hours too late.

Twenty minutes later Harding struggled out of his car as headlights approached. As an accountant *and* landlord a BMW 5 series was *de rigueur* though after one look at the dishevelled Harding and his equally dishevelled Sierra the man asked to see some form of ID.

Once the landlord had unlocked the front door Harding placed a hand on his arm, "If you don't mind sir, I'd prefer to lead. First impressions and all that." He paused at the threshold and focused his mind, as he'd done so often before when entering vacant properties. With the absence of humans he needed to use all his senses to acquire the information they left behind.

The first signal was emptiness, he had no doubt the property was empty. He could smell grease and the sickly sweet smell that signalled personal neglect. The light switch failed to meet its obligations and realising the likelihood of the meter having no credit the landlord said he would get his lamp. Harding stayed where he was until the large hand held lamp was placed in his grip. Behind the door lay a few pieces of junk mail and from where he stood he was able to pan the beam across most of the ground floor. At some point a centre wall had been removed to provide a large lounge instead of the original living room and parlour. The space was largely empty save for a broken dining chair and the remains of a Chinese take away in polystyrene cartons that littered the fire grate. Three pale patches on the carpeted marked where the three piece suite had been.

He moved forward cautiously and peered into a narrow kitchen where neglect was more evident. The cooker was covered in blackened grease and the fridge door hung open to reveal oddments of food that looked life-threatening.

Upstairs he cast the beam around and saw there were only two bedrooms and guessed that the bathroom was downstairs, built as an extension beyond the kitchen. The front bedroom was almost as empty as the lounge. Here though a small wardrobe stood against the wall, its door propped up against the adjacent wall. A voice behind him said, "That'll cost them, if I can find them. It's on the inventory as perfect."

Harding didn't say anything as he glanced around at the full ashtray and bits of litter. That done, he side-stepped the landlord and walked along the landing to the other bedroom door. This time he paused once more to place his senses on high alert. This had to be a child's bedroom and as such could be a crime scene. He pushed the door wide open but remained where he was.

It was spotless. Even the carpet had gone.

He sighed, more out of a dark relief than anything else. Until then he had no more to offer the world than the information gleaned from Graham, but now at last he had something to work with. "Outside sir, if you please, this is now a crime scene."

An hour later with the electricity back on and the owners' permission to carry out a search, Harding stood in the child's bedroom staring out of the window as flashlights swung in arcs along the drive behind the houses. They looked a little like fireflies. Behind him, a SOCO in a white suit had started to collect fragments for analysis and a uniformed officer appeared at the doorway.

Harding recognised him, PC Crowe, a good lad with promise. "Evening Crowe, what can I do for you."

"Sir, we're drawing a blank. It looks as though we need daylight, I'm sorry."

Harding had turned back to the window and showed no sign of hearing what had been said. Instead he gazed outside and asked, "If you had killed a young child where would you go?"

"Hell sir."

Harding glanced back and saw that the young officer was serious when he added, "Turn myself in there sir."

Harding nodded, "But supposing you wanted to hide the body, where would you go then?"

"Over there sir." Crowe pointed to the absolute darkness beyond the access lane.

"What's there?"

"Woodland sir, quite a bit of it actually. They've never built there because it's owned by some trust or other."

In daylight the woods would have been an obvious, but he kicked himself for not recognising the absence of street lights out there. "Right, I want you to go back to the station and get the bag of clothing I booked in earlier. Use the blues please, I want you back here by the time our dog handler gets here."

"Yes sir."

"And Crowe," the young officer paused as Harding continued, "*I'll* decide if we wait for daylight, understood."

As he spoke the white suited figure kneeling by the wall gave a small grunt to signal a discovery. He stood and turned to Harding with a triumphant grin and held up a small plastic bag that contained dark fragments. "If I'm not mistaken this is blood. Course, we won't know whose until we get other samples to check it against."

It was after one when Harding telephoned and he'd planned on breaking the connection after five rings in case they were all in bed, but Nancy answered very quickly. She didn't bother with trivia, "Hi Adam, what news?"

He sounded tired, no, more than that, there was a weariness in his voice that went much deeper, "Is every one there?"

"Yes, in fact they were just getting ready to go."

"OK, have them hang on would you, I'll be there in fifteen minutes."

When he got there the group had reformed around the kitchen table, clutching mugs of tea. He placed a litre bottle of whisky on the table and addressed Nancy, "Got a glass please?"

They saw the faintest tremor of his hand as he poured a huge measure, after which he held the bottle forward for anyone to join him. They'd all had far too much to drink that night so declined politely as he took his first mouthful.

A moment later he looked around the table and spoke, "We found his body buried in the woods behind the house, a couple of hundred yards away." He paused then, to collect his thoughts, "The parents have done a runner and left the house looking like a tip, but the kiddie's room has been stripped bare, literally. The coroner said it was too early to be sure but death was probably the result of a massive trauma to the child's midriff, just as Graham said."

Graham walked into the room, dressed in a paisley patterned dressing gown and with the haggard look of someone just out of bed. He gave them all a little wave, "Shorry, been eavesdropping." He pulled a glass out of the cabinet and pointed at the bottle, "I'll have some of that if I may pleashe Adam."

Nancy began to speak, "Love, you shouldn't be mixing . . ." He placed a hand on her shoulder, "I know, but trust me, I need a drink." He accepted her offer of a seat, assured everyone that he was feeling OK and suggested they get back to their discussion.

Harvey was the first to speak, "If the injuries were internal there wouldn't have been much in the way of evidence so why would they strip the bedroom so completely?"

Harding nodded, "There would have been some blood loss but as you say, much of it would have been held within the body cavities, until death occurred at any rate. I reckon they've headed off to somewhere distant, Scotland perhaps, and they will start a new life as a childless couple. Provided there's no close family to question the child's whereabouts who's to know he ever existed. Who would ever check the birth registry?"

Williams asked, "So how come they dumped a bag of clothing in a car park when they'd gone to so much trouble clearing his room."

The detective refilled his glass before replying, "I don't know. There would have been a pile of stuff to clear out. Toys, carpet, bed and they probably took them down to the refuse tip. Perhaps they overlooked the clothes and remember, it was a pretty safe bet dumping the sack where they did. There was nothing in there to trace back to them and let's face it, no one could factor someone like Graham into their equation."

Nancy asked, "So what happens now?"

"Well there'll be a nationwide alert out for them first thing tomorrow and we'll be interviewing the neighbours to see what they know. Then I reckon the *Crimewatch* people will want to feature it on their programme, particularly since it involves such a young child."

He turned then to face Graham, "But what about you my friend, can I ask you the same question."

Graham smiled, "I'm OK, really. I wasn't prepared for anything like today. In the last meeting what I said about being part-removed from the experience was wrong, at least this time. Today I actually experienced death and I have to tell you the experience itshelf is beautiful.

He described every second of his journey and added, I will never fear death now, but," he took a breath and shook his head, "The journey there can be a terrible one." He took a gulp of whisky and gasped before continuing, "How can anyone share an infants' violent end without *ageing* spiritually."

Harding suddenly realised that he and Graham shared a special sort of kinship. Poor Graham *knew* what had happened to the kids he came across but when Harding stood at the side of a shallow grave and saw the small form that lay there he could only imagine what he or she had gone through and sometimes imagination could be a terrible thing. Tonight they were treating their personal demons in the same way.

Williams had enough empathy to understand too and poured a measure of whisky into what remained of his tea.

Graham looked around the table and grimaced, "I sheem to have put a bit of a dampener on the occashion. Would anyone care for some cheese on toasht?"

Harding didn't hesitate, "By God, that *would* hit the button!" One by one they all succumbed and a long-suffering Nancy began work. She was soon joined by Sarah and within twenty minutes they had all been served. The men continued to drink the scotch while the ladies finished off the half bottle of wine to have made it into the fridge earlier on. When Nancy offered Harding her last piece of toast he snatched it off her plate with a grateful smile. The midnight feast served as a wonderful 'firebreak' and conversation eased into happier topics, not least of all Florida.

When there was a pause in the chatter the detective raised his glass towards Graham, "I'd like to propose a toast, to our new and unique arm of the law." As they raised their glasses Graham added, "And the red stripe taxi company. They brought me home again today."

"Well I'd like to propose a toast to us all." Sarah looked around, "To Graham's Gang."

Chapter 19

Nancy telephoned Angie at the store before nine to say that Graham was feeling ill after hearing the news and was remaining in bed. The news of the murder had already broken and Angie said that she had expected the call but sent her best wishes. In truth, he was hung over and since the sky was lightening when they finally went to bed, he was also exhausted. Harding had slept on the sofa and the others shared a taxi home.

It would be a quiet day for them. It needed to be.

* * *

It took a little over two weeks to catch Alan and Amy Bates, just days before it was due to be featured on the *Crimewatch* programme. The Police had withheld the vehicle details in the hope that the couple would continue to use it, which proved to be the case.

The Devon Police had sited an Automatic Number Plate Recognition, or ANPR camera on a bridge over the dual carriageway at Newton Abbot, aiming to catch traffic offenders. The number would be taken and a link with vehicle records would show whether the vehicle was taxed, the owner was disqualified, a fine not paid and many more, all before the vehicle had reached the next traffic island where a large group of traffic police lay in wait.

Needless to say, they were startled to see the message that appeared on the screen relating to the blue Fiesta that had passed by and delighted to include the capture of two murder suspects in the days' bag.

They were both working at a hotel in Brixham, she as a chambermaid while he sweated at general duties in the kitchen. Since the hotel was large enough to have staff quarters their personal possessions *sans* furniture were soon located and moved to the station before Harding and his driver arrived the following morning.

He saw them separately and whilst not overly bright, Alan Bates had a heavy, muscular build that must have been acquired in a gym.

He denied any knowledge of a child, but beyond that said very little. Harding read the signals, an affected slouch in the chair, a cynical half-smile and an attitude that implied disdain. Yet he couldn't maintain eye contact and looked upward, to the right when answering the few questions he chose to.

Amy was extremely pretty, with cropped blond hair and bright green eyes, but like her husband a bit dim. To begin with she was quite chatty, readily confirming her name, age and background; even admitting to doing a runner from the house in Leicester. Harding eased the conversation toward their child and she reacted immediately, saying, "I don't know nothing about any child," with a deceptively puzzled and guileless smile. They had obviously been rehearsing.

Harding sighed, "Are you saying you've never had a child."

She made an exaggerated show of surprise and replied, "No, 'course not, I haven't seen no baby."

Harding leaned forward and spoke quietly, "Well I have actually, once we'd brushed the soil and leaves off his body." He saw her smile slip slightly and continued, "Did you see Steven before Alan disposed of the body, or did you both bury him?"

She folded her arms across her chest and slouched back in her chair, clearly determined not to say anymore.

"Thing is, he might have looked reasonably OK because the injuries were almost all internal, so I'm going to give you a blow by blow account of what happened.

Your child had been crying for ages and no matter how high you turned the television up his crying could still be heard. Eventually Alan lost it, ran upstairs into the back bedroom, grabbed the boy by his pyjama jacket and snatched him out of his cot. He slammed the child against the wall, knocking all the wind out of him. But he then thumped the child in the stomach, with every ounce of strength he had. See, we can tell that from the injuries." He pulled out a sheet of typewritten details from his pad and waved it in the air, "The Coroner's report, I'll read the list to you."

"You're just trying to scare me."

Harding ignored her and began to read aloud, "OK so we have a minor fracture to the rear of the skull, massive bruising to the abdomen, that's stomach, a ruptured spleen, which is why he bled to death and a ruptured intestine. There's quite a bit more but they were the killers."

He waited patiently as she continued to hum loudly with her hands clasped tightly over her ears, drowning out his voice. She wouldn't have heard anything but the tape will have recorded it.

Finally, he placed the document on the table in front of her, stopped the tape and made his way to the door, nodding at the Constable who had driven him down there and was now the second officer in the interview room.

She stopped her din as he opened the door and he spoke quickly, "OK, you win, no more gory details. There's no need, our doctor will take less than thirty seconds to tell whether you've ever had a child and the blood match will confirm who that child was. Either way you're nicked, it's just a question of what we nick you for. Accessory or killer. Think about it, I'll send a cup of tea in."

After arranging for her drink he wandered outside into the car park for a cigarette and deliberation. They had a body and a whole bunch of circumstantial evidence but nothing to prove conclusively that these two had committed the crime. All he *could* prove was that they had fled the scene and they could come up with all sorts of reasons why they'd done that. Enough to unnerve a jury anyway, who often identified with dimwits who plead ignorance.

Strange though, how they had erased him from their lives so completely, there must have been some feeling for him if he'd reached seventeen months of age.

He then considered the facts Graham had provided him with and couldn't therefore be shared. In the first place, there was only one attacker and from the damage one punch caused, it had to have been the man. The child had been left to die. He didn't know how long that had taken but it must have been a while and that implied that there was no-one else in the house to check on him. So why didn't she do something when she did discover the body? And how could she chuck away every trace of her child's existence? Well, not everything; he held that thought for a few moments, to flesh out an idea.

He had no doubt that he could wear the woman down, eventually, but the stunt he planned might cut to an end-play immediately. It had to be worth a try.

He strode into the interview room and the PC fired up the tapes again. Harding sat opposite Amy and placed a brown paper package on the table. "Now I don't want you to say anything just now because I'd like to tell you what I'm thinking at the moment." He wore a kindly expression and spoke gently as he continued, "I think that *if* you'd had a toddler you would have loved it. Loved buying presents at Christmas and loved that first pair of shoes you had him fitted with. I reckon you'd have kept those.

Wouldn't have all been sunshine I know but he would have been yours, your blood. Then something terrible happens and he's gone, in a flash. But everything that might have reminded you of him is destroyed or thrown away. If you were that mother I'd feel sorry for you, there would be a gaping big hole left in your life."

He gently pushed the parcel across to her, allowing the wrapping to fall open and reveal a pale blue cot blanket, folded inside out so that the soil marks were hidden. He wanted her to be reminded of a child asleep in his cot, not buried in the woods. "I'm sorry love, this is the only thing of his we have."

He knew he'd struck gold as soon as she reached forward to touch the blanket, it was time for the *coup de grace*, "He was wrapped in it when we found him."

She gagged as she tried to contain the sob, "Alan said that Stevie fell out of his cot and must have fallen awkwardly 'cos he was dead by the time Alan went up to check on him." She was shaking now and tears streamed down her face. Harding spoke quietly, "It's OK Amy, tell me in your own time."

Minutes passed as she sat with her head bowed, weeping, but eventually she became aware of the silence and scrutiny of the two men. She pulled her sleeve down over the heel of her hand and wiped away the tears and snot.

"I'd gone to Bingo and when I got back Alan was going mental. He said that people like you would never believe the likes of us and we'd end up going to jail for the rest of our lives, pretty well."

"He lied to you Amy. From the list of injuries we know what happened, and they could only have been done by someone as strong as Alan." Harding allowed a pause before asking, "Did you both bury him?"

She shook her head, "I couldn't do it, but Alan told me he'd said a prayer over his grave."

"What about his things?"

"I couldn't do that neither, I went into the city while Alan took it all down the tip."

"And the bag of clothes?"

"Oh yeah, that. When I got home I found a load of clean clothes in the airing cupboard that Alan had missed." The recollection brought more tears but she recovered quickly, "The tip was closed then so we put them in a plastic sack and took them to the supermarket. They've got bins there, only the bag was too big and we had to leave it by the side."

Harding felt an overwhelming pity for her. Nature had denied her a reasonable IQ and she would probably spend her life being manipulated, but he felt sure she'd been a reasonable mother and now the fates had robbed her of that too. He spoke as kindly as he knew how when explaining how the young officer next to him would take a statement. He left them then, to go and speak with the killer.

Chapter 20

Graham came through the experience better than the group had expected, thanks largely to their support and his new family. Jimmy had settled in wonderfully and daily routines fell into place quite naturally. But notwithstanding those, the prospect of a Florida holiday and a new puppy still held sway. Jimmy had been encouraged to borrow books from the library to help him prepare for *Susie's* arrival and they had already paid her two more visits at the farm.

It had seemed such a long wait yet suddenly, it seemed, it was Saturday the third of September, the day before they were to collect her. Nancy and Jimmy visited a pet shop on the Welford Road to purchase a basket, two bowls, collar and lead, leaving Graham to purchase the food at his store. It was a sound strategy, since Graham would have winced if he knew how expensive a puppy was and that was before they'd paid the vet's bill for all the jabs.

Sarah collected them the following morning at a civilised time of ten o clock which Jimmy regarded as criminally late. As soon as the car had stopped he leapt out of the car and headed across the yard towards the barn. Chocks met him halfway expecting and receiving a hug and fuss.

As if on cue, Susie gambolled out of the barn and ran out of legs on the turn, rolling onto her side. She was soon up, prancing towards him and grabbing his proffered fingers in needle sharp teeth. Jimmy called out, "Yeow!" laughing though and rolling the pup onto it's back. Chocks lowered her head and sniffed her young as though slightly put out by such a trespass into Jimmy's affections.

On the way home Susie began to cry for her mother and Jimmy held her in his arms giving as much comfort as he knew how. There is little more to say about the rest of the day that could adequately capture the magic and lifelong memories a young boy would bank as he bonded with his dog, though Graham's enthusiasm waned a little when Nancy made him get up in the small hours to comfort the crying animal.

One thing was certain, Jimmy and Susie would, and did, become inseparable.

Nancy cemented her friendship with Audrey Calder by meeting up on a couple of occasions, once for coffee and the other lunch, at a nearby Garden Centre. Unsurprisingly, Florida featured highly in their conversations even though the trip seemed so distant.

Meanwhile, Graham enjoyed a period of calm. His speech therapist continued to achieve improvement and his s's were gradually shedding the 'h's.

He still had 'hits' but none that caused serious concern. It was as if he'd been given a time to prepare for his holiday, though in truth they had read all of the guides they could find and were in a state of limbo.

That is until the third week of October, when a large envelope arrived by registered post containing their tickets and a confirmed itinerary. There was so much to read and take in. Arnold had scribbled an additional note asking them to call in and collect their travellers' cheques which they did the following day. They each signed half in his presence and he explained how to use them. Graham couldn't hide his relief, "It's just like writing a cheque."

Arnold grinned, sending folks like this off to Florida for the first time was so much more fun than sending seasoned travellers to more exotic destinations; the excitement was infectious. "There is one final thing Audrey thought of and sorted out with me last week. These will get you started without having to worry about cashing a travellers' cheque." As he spoke he passed two envelopes over, one, with Jimmy's name on it. They opened the other one and found two hundred and fifty dollars in cash. Nancy gasped, "Oh my goodness."

Arnold chuckled, "Now promise me you'll spend every penny."

* * *

Finally, the day arrived. Susie had gone back to the barn for the duration and the three of them dressed and assembled downstairs in an anxious silence. Their tea went cold as once more, passports, money and tickets were checked and the cases weighed again. As arranged, at five o clock Harding pulled up outside and grinned as he watched the clumsy exodus from the house.

Moments later they were on their way. Graham had a small half foolscap sized leather bag that held their money, credit card wallet and passports which he checked yet again as they headed for the motorway. He settled back in his seat and gave a sigh of relief, glancing over at Adam who was grinning broadly. "Jusht checking." He said defensively.

They beat the worst of rush hour and the road works south of Luton were trouble free so that by six forty five they were within five miles of Heathrow and saw a Jumbo jet taking off. Conversation dwindled in an air of nervous expectation.

Instead of dropping them off at the entrance Harding insisted on parking the car and helping them through check-in. The queue seemed enormous but soon disappeared and they found themselves at the high counter. Jimmy watched their luggage snatched away on the conveyor and wondered if they would see it again but his concerns fell away as Graham led them back to thank and bid Harding farewell. He stepped back and waited for a few minutes after they had disappeared into the security check area. Satisfied that they were well and truly in the travel sausage machine he found a parking machine and was startled. Having paid the *Heathrow* parking fee he made his way back to the car, feeling robbed.

* * *

There are many 'firsts' in life that are never forgotten and one of them might be a six year olds' first sight of a Boeing 747 being readied for him to board. Adults still gawk at the monster but to Jimmy it beggared belief. After a quick look around the shops they waited by the jetway for over an hour though Graham looked like someone awaiting some sort of surgical procedure, his rucksack resting on knees that were locked together.

At last they began boarding. Jimmy sat next to the window and for the next nine hours, became a pilot. Graham sat in the middle out of consideration for Nancy's nervous bladder. She had already determined where the nearest toilet was. Doors were closed and the business of take off began. They watched the safety demonstration avidly and before they knew it the engines were throttled up and they were pressed against the back of their seats. It seemed to go on forever and just as Graham began to feel certain they had run out of runway he felt the front of the aircraft rise and eventually, the ground fell away. Nancy tried to release her hand and he realised he had been squeezing it tightly, trying then to make light of it by saying, "Thought we were going by road for a minute."

Nancy was struggling to cope with the experience in her own way, which didn't include laughing at his attempt at humour.

The drinks, meals and films all added to the adventure but ultimately transatlantic flights are boring, even for first-timers, though that and their aching backsides were forgotten as the aircraft began its descent. Once low enough Jimmy stared at the huge shining trucks he had only seen on television before. All the roads seemed straight and the buildings light in the sunshine, but everything was surrounded by great areas of water and greenery.

Once again they were fed into the sausage machine, along glass-sided passageways, escalators and moving walkways until they were confronted by the queues at immigration. After a long period of shuffling along long lines of taped aisles they were called forward by a man sitting in a glass cubicle. Graham noticed two things; how neatly pressed his tailored shirt was and how serious he was.

Officialdom always made him nervous and when he was nervous he often did or said silly things. The man took their passports and the immigration forms they had been given to complete on the aircraft. As he began to thumb the first open he asked, "What is the purpose of your visit."

Graham didn't hesitate, "To visit Mickey." There wasn't so much as a flicker of response and Graham's anxiety climbed.

"Will you be staying together."

Again, mouth in motion before brain in gear, "Nah, if I can get a decent price for them they can go."

This time the officer slowly looked up from the passports and gazed at Graham. The look was a twenty four carat sphincter clincher and Nancy wanted to beat her partner soundly. Eventually, the scrutiny of their passports continued as Graham stood in cowed silence.

The local tour representative was waiting for them and once the whole flock had been assembled, she herded them outside to where their bus waited. They were startled by the sudden change from air conditioning to an all-enveloping warmth but it was only temporary. They would come to realise how arctic the Floridian air-conditioning could be.

Twenty minutes later they arrived at the pink and turquoise resort and left to queue at another check-in. Most of the passengers remained on the bus and were obviously staying elsewhere. The check-in was slick and they were startled by the amount of information they were given in such a short space of time, including directions to their room which was spacious, with two double beds, a bathroom and toilet.

They had arrived at last.

* * *

Each day was filled with incredible experiences, for them all. They would leave a ride thinking that nothing could top it yet the next one did just that. Even the junk food was wonderful.

As hotel guests they were allowed into the parks half an hour before the general public and each day ended after ten o clock when they fell into bed, exhausted. Jimmy often fell asleep at lunch time, over a half eaten hot dog but he wouldn't countenance a longer break back at the room. But by Thursday they all needed a break and decided to spend the next day chilling out at the huge water park, *Typhoon Lagoon* which offered a mix of water slides, swimming pools and beaches. They were partly influenced by their tour guide's offer of an excursion on Friday evening to a small theme park and speciality shopping area called *Old Town*. Friday nights were especially favoured because of the huge procession of classic and custom cars that passed through there. They also decided that an excursion out of Disney world would be worthwhile too.

Old Town proved to be that, in a pseudo sort of way. Timber built speciality shops and restaurants were fronted by wooden boardwalks and sure enough, at nine o clock a procession of gleaming cars and trucks passed down the 'street' between the shops. Huge, glistening motor cars of bygone times edged past the huge crowds before disappearing beyond the variety of pleasure rides at the rear of the site.

The Disney experience was unique and remarkably sophisticated in such a benign, friendly way but they also enjoyed Old Town for its simplicity. Graham had also noticed a convenience store on the opposite side of the highway and was determined to pay it a visit.

Half an hour before they were due to catch the bus back to the hotel he left them on a mission to buy some soda at the right price. Thankfully, there was a pedestrian crossing at the set of traffic lights nearby though the hike over eight traffic lanes startled him, to the extent of questioning the wisdom of his trek. Nevertheless, he was there now. On the concrete apron that sloped up to the store entrance. Cars were parked with their noses just shy of the large step up to the doorway and he noted how tired some of them looked, the open windows evidencing derelict air conditioning units. As he walked towards the entrance a huge black man, tall and overweight, marched out of the door with a pack of beers under one arm. He slammed the door behind him before making for one of the wrecks, a Chevrolet Graham noted, with its windows open and a woman's arm hanging limply out of the passenger side.

Inside the shop a small figure was screaming as it tried to open the sprung door and in his distress the child failed to counter the effect of Graham opening the door, falling out onto the concrete. Graham was appalled and bent to help him up, "Hey maytee, I am shorry."

* * *

He only knows that his mom told him he could have a candy bar when his daddy stopped at the store. He doesn't know how bad he's been by taking too long to choose one and runs after his daddy who has paid for his beer and snarls at him before walking out of sight. He runs after him; into the next aisle and hangs on to a trouser leg but he is shaken like a rag doll until he loses his grip and is thrown across the shelves. He's frightened and needs the security of that trouser leg but when he takes hold again the flat of a hand sweeps down and knocks him across the aisle into a display of beer packs. He's stunned, crying uncertainly. Daddy has disappeared again and he runs as fast as his two and a half year old legs will carry him. This time Daddy is waiting around the corner and lashes out with a roundhouse kick. His feet fly out from underneath him and his small frame is carried across the aisle to collide with one of the refrigerators. He is wailing now, failing to understand the punishment yet still needing to stay close to Daddy who this time is watching his tottering approach and waits until just the right moment to whip open a refrigerator door. The impact knocks him backwards with enough force to lift him off his feet and plant him on his bottom three feet away. He sits there, stunned and bewildered as his nose bleeds onto his T shirt. The sight of blood makes him cry louder and suddenly he sees Daddy walking out of the door. His fear of being abandoned is total, overriding everything and when he struggles to open the door his cries become screams."

* * *

Graham came to, still bending over the crying child and whilst he knew the 'hit' would have only lasted seconds it was enough for the child's father to think he was interfering. He felt the sheer strength of the man as he was pushed out of the way, "Git mister, an' mind your own business." A great hand grabbed the child and threw him towards the car, "Now git in the fucking car yo little shit."

Graham would have chased after them normally, trying to make a scene and get help but here it felt different, and he was frightened. He was hyperventilating, he knew, but couldn't do anything about it, yet as the car backed away and turned towards the highway the woman's hand was casually raised to give him the finger.

There was only one thing he could think to do in that moment and he scrabbled in his bag, pulling the pen out in time to scribble the vehicle number onto his hand. He sat and looked at the number and just didn't know what he could do. Get shot probably, he thought.

He was still shaking when he went into the store but couldn't help himself. The bank of tall refrigerators lined one wall and he knew which door to try. As soon as he touched the red spots near the base of the door flashes of the 'hit' came back to him. He shook his head, trying to make sense out of the gratuitous assaults and worse, the mother's crude gesture as they left. He knew that this time he would have to come to terms with the idea of doing nothing and began to make his way to the packs of soda. Posters announcing the special offers covered the upper walls, right up to the ceiling where the red light on the camera blinked at him.

He grabbed a pack of cokes and joined the queue at the counter where an elderly man was taking money. Eventually the sodas were placed on the counter and the man rang the sale up on the till. Graham handed over a twenty dollar bill and asked, "Excushe me but are you the manager?"

"Yessir, at night times at any rate." He handed over the change.

"Can you tell me," Graham gestured to the far corner, "Are those cameras on all the time?"

The clerk answered but with an edge of caution, "Ye-es, sir, all the time." He gestured to the queue and said, "Now if you'll excuse me."

He had picked up the next customer's purchase when Graham said more forcibly, "Look, I think your cameras have jusht filmed something you will want to know about. Please! May I shpeak to you for a couple of minutes."

The manager looked at him uncertainly but finally decided to grant the request, shouting across at a youth who was filling shelves to take over at the till. Even so as they moved to one side he explained, "Sir, we are very busy right now. Say whatever you have to say but do it real quickly please."

Graham grabbed a paper napkin from the doughnut display and copied the number from his hand. He looked at the manager and asked, "Do you have any children?"

"Yep, three, and eight grand children."

"Shome little ones then?"

The man nodded, not sure where they were heading and clearly desperate to get back to the till. Graham spoke slowly and clearly, sensing that he was only going to get one shot at this. He pointed at the camera, "If you check the tape from that camera you will see a truly disgushting example of child abuse that occurred ten minutes ago. Please, I beg you, check it out and think of your grandchildren.

If it had been one of them you would be telephoning the police, right now, I promishe!" The thug of a father *and* mother drove off in this car." He passed the napkin over and gently held the manager's arm, you will be upset by what you see, I promishe you."

The manager watched the funny looking Brit leave the store, and wondered if he'd been the subject of abuse at some point, but there was something about the way he'd spoken.

After checking the queue he saw that the store was emptying. "Shaun, I have to go out back for a minute, call me if you need me."

The youth called back, "Sure, OK."

Fifteen minutes later the manager walked back into the store, in complete shock. Shaun watched anxiously as he wandered to the front window and waited, until the first police car arrived.

Nancy was furious, the bus was waiting in the car park, full except for him. The guide said nothing but once they were rolling she switched the mike on and addressed everyone. "Hi folks, I hope you had a good time. We'll have you back to your hotels on no time but in the meantime I need to give you guidance on what to do if we are forced to leave without you."

Graham shrank down in his seat and noticed that across the aisle, Nancy swivelled to look out of the window she was sharing with Jimmy.

They were so thankful to be one of the first to be dropped off and since they had agreed to avoid any arguments in front of Jimmy Nancy waited until he had run on a little way, towards their room.

She walked closely and hissed, "I have never been so embarrassed. I kept hearing things, like 'There's always one', or 'Should just leave him, it's not fair at this time of night'. I could have curled up and died! And then you turn up with some bargain pop just to make sure they understood how important your delay was!"

"Please love, there was a good reason."

"No! There wasn't, because you should never have gone all the way over there in the first place, so just shut up and give me time to get over it please."

'Sod it' he thought as she hurried away from him to catch Jimmy up.

Jimmy was soon tucked up in bed and Nancy was in the bathroom when Graham wandered over to deliver the usual nightime kiss on his forehead. "Night night, God Bless." As usual "Night night Go'bless" came back by return but this time Jimmy twisted and looked up from his pillow, "Did you have one of your bad dreams?"

Graham smiled gently and nodded his head. "It's gone now. Let's all have shweet dreams tonight, eh?"

Jimmy grinned and nodded his agreement.

Nancy came out of the bathroom and clambered into bed without a word. Saddened slightly, Graham picked up the book he was reading and made his way to the bathroom. Half an hour on the throne should see both the other two sound asleep.

* * *

The following morning found them refreshed yet needing a break from theme parks. They had thought that *Typhoon Lagoon* was going to be relaxing but it proved to be every bit as exciting and exhausting as the previous five days. Their own complex had a forty five acre lake with beaches and self-drive boats, an island strewn with hammocks and a variety of swimming pools. The atmosphere *en famille* had thawed somewhat and they agreed to spend the day on the complex. The rest would be therapeutic.

Just after lunch they made camp near the largest of the six swimming pools having found that swimming in the lake was forbidden. Jimmy's disappointment waned when Graham implied it might be due to alligators or snakes and an hour at the helm of a boat more than made up for the loss. Now, as they watched him use the water slides and cannons Nancy asked a question, "Jimmy said you'd had a bad dream last night. How much have you told him?"

Graham huffed, "I don't tell him anything about my hits, but last year, when I saw him in hospital, I *did* tell him how I came to see all that he did. Since then I think it's something we've shared and maybe he recognises the signs."

"So last night was a 'hit' then?"

He sighed, this was supposed to be their holiday of a lifetime but he wasn't about to spoil it, for any of them. At that moment he was so sick of the thing and spoke truly, "Yes, it was, but I really don't want to talk about it."

They took turns to read then, while the other either monitored or swam with Jimmy. By teatime things were back to normal. The holiday had been derailed at *Old Town* and Nancy put them back on track with an observation, "This is a one-off, an experience we'll never have again, let's not spoil it by squabbling."

By eight o clock that evening they had eaten and returned to the room for an early night. Jimmy was washed, brushed and into bed first but Graham bagged the next bathroom slot. He was only in there for fifteen minutes but by the time he stepped back into the bedroom Jimmy was sound asleep and Nancy sat in front of the television, her hand over her mouth in horror.

They both listened as the newscaster finished off with, "Whilst the District Attorney is indicting the father on the evidence to hand the Police would welcome an opportunity to speak with the British tourist who alerted the stores' manager to this awful act."

Nancy looked up at him and whispered, "I had no idea, and I should have had. I'm so sorry, so very sorry. This holiday means so much that I let it blind me to what you were going through last night."

They sat next to each other and held hands while Nancy trolled through the channels for the next newscast. The one she had watched was a local channel but an hour later they were startled to see it on CNN. The newscaster began by saying that they had just received a report from Orlando, Florida of the most appalling example of child abuse. Thanks to a caring store manager and his security camera tapes the man responsible was in Police custody. She went on to warn viewers of the graphic and upsetting content of the film to follow. The security camera captured everything, in astonishing detail, except for the blurring of the man's face since it was *sub judice*, and all exactly as Graham had seen it.

The truly dreadful moment, that took world audiences by the throat was the image of the toddler still running after his parent after being so brutally assaulted by the man so many times.

Nancy let her head fall on to Graham's shoulder, "Is that what you saw?"

He was still too shocked from seeing it all again and could only nod.

Fifteen minutes later the telephone rang, a piercing and unexpected intrusion that threatened to wake Jimmy. Nancy snatched the receiver off the hook as Graham watched, and said, "Yes?"

She began to weep a little then and a short time passed until she was able to speak. Graham heard more noises from the receiver and Nancy said, "Yes it was. Oh Harvey, I'm so pleased to hear your voice."

On the other end, in their rented house on Captiva, Harvey spoke, "I couldn't believe it but Audrey knew immediately and made me call you."

"How did you know our number?"

"We're in Florida. Who doesn't know *Disney World*. The number is everywhere, and we knew which resort you were in. But how is he?"

"Fine, we're just a bit shocked really. I suppose we didn't expect it to happen over here."

Graham had been listening to half the conversation and began waving urgently. Nancy said, "Hold on a moment," and looked at Graham who whispered, "Ashk what we should do about the Police. They're looking for me."

Harvey had heard him and responded instantly, "Keep your heads down! If you even whisper anything about this the media will be all over you. They've already said that there's enough evidence to nail this man so there really isn't any need for you to get involved." There was a pause before he continued, "Listen Nancy, you must carry on with your holiday as though this hadn't happened. Trust me, if the Police don't need additional evidence they're not going to commit any time to finding Graham."

Her spirits had been climbing throughout the call, "Harvey, this call has been so helpful. Being able to speak to you like this is such a relief."

Harvey chuckled, "Good. Well take this number and call us anytime. It's late, so get to bed, I'm sure you've got a busy day tomorrow and you can tell us everything next week."

She wrote their number down and ended the call before springing up and hugging Graham. "I feel so much better knowing we've got someone over here who knows everything. He said stay away from the Police and get on with our holiday."

Graham nuzzled her neck and said quietly, "Sounds good to me. Shpeaking of sounds, how quiet do you think we could be?"

She grinned, "Very."

He allowed her to push him gently down on to the bed and under the covers. Nancy climbed in after him, on her knees and kissed him before whispering in his ear, "Just don't scream when the time comes OK?"

She began to trace a gentle, loving trail with her lips and tongue, down his body to where she could give him an exquisite gift and take him on an unforgettable journey. He didn't scream, quite.

The following morning they decided to head back to *Epcot*. They had seen everything in the *Futureworld* section of the park with its themed pavilions with rides that were beyond anything they could have imagined, but they had yet to see the other half, called *World Showcase*. One of the guides they had brought over with them recommended this area for Sundays, since the additional number of weekend visitors gave rise to long queues at the larger rides. Over breakfast Graham read aloud from the guide, " . . . the World showcase arena, which invites you on a Global Adventure across a collection of international pavilions." Another day, another plan.

Just as they were leaving their room the telephone rang. Graham ran back and answered it, expecting Harvey to have thought of something else to mention. "Hello."

There was a slight pause before he heard Sarah, "Graham, we've just seen the lunchtime news, about a little coloured boy beaten up by his father in a store. Please tell me you weren't involved."

Graham had a vision of Sarah, her usual exuberance transferred to frantic anxiety and laughed out loud. "Yep, 'fraid sho."

"Oh good grief! Can't you take a holiday from that as well?"

"It's not something I can switch on and off."

"No, of course not, I'm sorry. Just a bit anxious that's all."

Something occurred to him then, "Are you saying it was on the UK newsh?"

"Yes, at lunchtime, I think they used it as a 'filler'. I've never seen anything like it. Seen the results often enough, obviously, but to see it actually happen. It's when they mentioned the British tourist that my heart skipped a beat. How are you?"

Her mention of lunchtime reminded him of the five hour time difference. "I'm fine, in fact you just caught us, we were just setting off to the *Epcot* park for the day."

"Oh my dear, you cannot imagine how relieved I am to hear that. Go on, get started. Every minute counts, we'll have hours to talk when you get back."

He chuckled, "OK, we'll get started, but Sarah?"

"Yes."

"It was lovely to hear your voice too."

* * *

The huge *Epcot* golf ball was as astonishing as ever but this time they strode on and caught a boat across the lagoon to the other side of the park. There, a huge arc of dedicated spaces bordered the lake, each representing a different country and offering ethnic experiences.

'*Mexico*' offered a boat ride around a smoking volcano while '*Germany*' offered a biergarten with Bavarian music. There were eleven countries represented though Jimmy's favourite was '*Norway*' with its turbulent '*Maelstrom*' ride. All held a mix of rides, films, shops and restaurants, including the '*UK*' where Graham treated himself to a pint of very well kept *Bass* bitter.

It was mid-afternoon when they entered *'Canada'* which offered a 360 degree film of the country. There were no seats, just bars across the floor space at waist height. It was a huge dome filled with a dramatic journey across Canada. The motion in the film was all-encompassing and a viewer would lose their balance and fall over had it not been for those rails; which is why the twelve year old girl in front of them should have been using one instead of succumbing to vertigo and falling against Graham.

He had no time to formulate a thought but the leaden fall in his stomach was eloquent enough, 'Oh God, not again.'

* * *

This was different. He was frightened and crying yet there was no pain. Above all he wanted to shout something, to someone, to help them somehow. At the same time he wanted to shout at someone else, to stop and to go away. There was a sense of hatred then.

The sounds came soon after. A swish followed by a crack, and a scream. He caught the image of an arm being raised and a piece of thick electrical cable. The swish and scream occurred again followed this time with words, shouted, "Bastard, bastard, bastard. Say it. Bastard. Go on say it, I'm a bastard."

He felt as though he was dying inside somehow. He couldn't move, he knew that, yet there was no physical pain.

And then the image appeared, of a young person, draped over a stool wearing just a T shirt. A pair of trousers and underpants lay on the floor.

He felt a numbing empathy for the figure and a deep love. He glimpsed a small penis between the bare legs and knew a most profound sympathy for the boy's humiliation and shame. Three livid welts ran across the buttocks, each bearing a necklace of bloody droplets. Swish, crack, scream. This time he saw the black cable sweep down and away, leaving a fourth red line.

He knew then that he was being made to witness the attack.

And as he slipped away from the 'hit' he realised who he was.

* * *

The lights came up and a few people applauded. Nancy glanced over to Graham to remark how good it had been and saw him leaning against the rail, bent over as though he was resting from a long run. She groaned, "Oh no, please no."

As soon as she grasped his shoulder he seemed to rally, looking around frantically. The audience was disappearing through several exits that acted like horizontal sand timers and he began to struggle forward in a desperate bid to find the girl.

If it hadn't been for the clumsy man trying to force his way through the compacted mass of people and treading on Laura's heel with enough weight to pull her shoe off Graham would have missed them but as he stepped outside he saw her at the side of the passageway on one knee re-tying her shoelace. Next to her stood a middle-aged man who was enormous, in every sense. Around six foot six in height and with the build of an Olympic weight lifter. His T shirt covered his torso like a second skin.

Graham cut across the phalanx of people and given the man's size addressed him first, "Pleashe excuse me but may I have a word with your daughter, pleashe?"

The man had a voice that carried every bit as much menace as his appearance, "What about?"

Graham wavered, should he just back away this time? He knew instantly that it wasn't an option. He *had* to do something.

The girl had stood up and taken the man's hand. Graham crouched slightly and spoke to her, "You must tell someone, about the whipping." He felt the man tense and continued quickly, "No-one should make you shtand and watch that sort of thing."

The man spoke, "Come on hon', let's get outa here."

Graham followed, his voice raised slightly in desperation, "Listen, pleashe, I know you have to watch him being whipped, with a piece of electric cable and I know how much it upsets you."

By now they were outside in a passageway that ran alongside a building and the crowd had already thinned down to a trickle of stragglers. The girl glanced back at him with a frightened look, but said nothing. He tried one last time, "You love him don't you? Yet you're made to watch him shuffer like that?"

It all happened so quickly. In a blur of movement his eyes and brain failed to keep up with, he was lifted and thrown against the wall. There was a frightened shout from one side and the grizzly bear that was holding him spoke quickly to the approaching Nancy and Jimmy, "Keep quiet, stay still and he won't get hurt."

He turned to Graham who was pinned to the wall by a forearm across the throat and gasping for breath. The giant wrenched the leather bag from his hand and rifled through it with his spare hand before retrieving the room key and charge card.

"OK, I know where I can find you," he glanced at the card again, "Mr Parsons. Now if I even see you again I'm gonna come and hurt you. A lot. You understand what I'm saying?"

They appeared from nowhere. Two pairs of men in Disney uniforms were walking towards them at a pace, yet not quickly enough to attract attention from any other guests. Grizzly glanced at them and eased away slightly with a friendly smile. "You even dream of whingeing and I'll rupture a kidney before those flunkeys can twitch." This time he laughed out loud as though they'd shared a joke, "You dig?"

One of the approaching men asked, "Is everything OK gentleman."

Grizzly chuckled and patted Graham on the arm and muttered "Smile rabbit." Chuckling then as he turned to the men who by then had encircled them. "Hell yes, we were just talking about the show and how giddy it can make you." He turned to Graham and gave a small wave, "Well we'll get along. Been nice meeting you, have a great vacation." As he walked past the Disney spokesman he grinned and gestured toward Graham, "Brits, don't you just love their accents."

The Disney staff remained where they were until Grizzly and the girl were out of sight. The same man addressed Graham, "Is that right sir, you look a little shaken."

Graham shook his head, "No I'm fine, honestly."

After enough of a pause to signal his disbelief he conceded to Graham's obvious wish for discretion. Moments later he gave an order for the team to disappear again leaving Nancy to move forward and grasp Graham's arm in support. He was trembling but glanced at Jimmy's stricken face and knew he had to salvage the situation.

He pushed himself away from the wall and said, "I would like another pint of *Bass* and I reckon Jimmy could do with another *Mountain Dew.*"

As they headed towards the United Kingdom area Jimmy moved from his usual station at Nancy's side to take up position on Graham's other side and held hands. That gesture gave Nancy an idea. For the rest of the holiday they would insulate Graham in this way and maybe avoid anymore 'hits'.

Graham sank half of his pint in one and sat for a moment in thought before making his observation. "'Courshe I had him just where I wanted him. It's lucky those men arrived when they did. He'll never know how close he came to being mincemeat."

Jimmy hid his mouth behind his hand and waited to see what Nancy's reaction would be.

It began with 'humph' and titter which was enough for Jimmy to laugh out loud. The holiday was back on track, *again*!

Even so, an early night was called for. Tomorrow they were booked on a trip to *Seaworld.*

* * *

It was after ten o clock when *something* struck the door. It couldn't have been human, it sounded too much like a battering ram for that.

Graham leapt out of bed and wondered whether to use the telephone to call for help or answer the door but his very British aversion to causing a fuss and the security bar on the door persuaded him to try the latter. It was a Disney complex after all and they'd have wall to wall security people here in a trice. As he reached the door he turned to Nancy who was sitting up in bed and pointed at the telephone, hissing, "Be ready, jusht in case."

He opened the door as far as the security bolt allowed and peered through the gap. It was Grizzly.

Graham almost voided both bowels.

Grizzly waited for a few moments, perhaps for Graham to say something but finally, with a shrug, he said, "I need to speak with you." There was a significant pause before he added, "Please."

Graham was aware of a number of things. Firstly, and miraculously, his boxer shorts remained unsoiled; his heart had stopped trying to bruise ribs and that Grizzly's voice lacked the menace it had held earlier.

The bar was removed and Grizzly stepped inside, bowing his head through the doorway. He wore a red cloth around his head, jeans and a denim jacket that was covered in badges. Nancy held the telephone receiver up in view as if she couldn't decide whether to use it as a weapon or to make a call. Their visitor raised a hand, palm facing out, "Nothing to worry about. I just need to speak with your man." He turned to Graham, "You'd best get dressed, where we're going only the women dress like that."

Graham shook his head, "We can talk here, surely."

"No we can't. Now git dressed." Another significant pause. "Please."

For the want of anything else to do or say Graham did as he was told. When he'd put his shoes on Grizzly added, "You'll need a jacket." While Graham went to the wardrobe he turned to Nancy, "Don't worry. I'll take care of him and bring him back when we're done."

He'd been feigning sleep but when they left Jimmy sat up in bed and held his arms out to Nancy, "That man frightens me."

She crept into bed beside him and wrapped around his slight frame, "Hey, don't worry, they're just going for a drink and a chat. He probably wants to say sorry for pushing Graham up against the wall at *Epcott*." She hoped it would be enough to ease the boy's anxiety; it had done nothing for hers.

Her pulse was clamouring for assurance too, but there was no one else there to give it.

Graham's pulse was still skitty as he raced to keep up with the man's extended gait, past the reception and into a car park designated for non-resident visitors. He suddenly realised they were walking to a huge motor cycle gleaming in splendid isolation as if no-one would dare to park near it.

"Here, put this on." A helmet was thrust into his arms. He managed to wrestle it on to his head and was aware of Grizzly's scrutiny as he struggled to do the strap up. Finally, his hands were knocked away and it was done for him. He was shown where to put his feet and told to get on and hold tight before the engine roared into life and they sheared away from just about everything he held dear, or at least that's what it felt like.

Grizzly wasn't wearing a helmet, though Graham did note the words 'Hells Angels' across the back of his jacket and recalled reading somewhere that in the US they ignored the law and were regarded as a major threat to civilised society.

Traffic was fairly light until they reached the I 4 freeway where they drifted over to the far lane and passed everything else on the road. Eventually, they took an exit into an area of neglect, with high security fences, car wrecks, gangs and prostitutes. Even Graham, a self-confessed innocent saw that much and could only wonder how much more stayed out of sight.

Suddenly they pulled into a lot that was occupied by what looked like an old fashioned and semi-derelict diner. The only clues that suggested it was still in use was a small neon sign saying 'Bar' and a few pick-ups and motor cycles parked outside.

Graham noticed two things as they entered the building. The smoke and the nipples. The latter belonged to the waitress that walked by with a loaded tray. She shimmied against Grizzly and said, "Hey Bob, are you going to tease these for me tonight?"

Grizzly half turned towards her and grinned, "Hell no Lucy, you know I can't afford your prices. Go find yourself a richer man girl." He paused then before pointing at Graham, "Now how about this fella. He's a wealthy Brit, come over here to check out the special relationship our president keeps promising them."

She sidled up to Graham, ignoring the violent shaking of the head. "Hon, you just found yourself one heck of a special relationship and it comes a lot cheaper than a cruise missile."

He would later put it down to any number of things, including, fear, heightened blood pressure, the unusual surroundings and of course the bare breasts but he couldn't contain the semi-erection that threatened to signal a tacit acceptance of her offer. He thrust a hand in his pocket to take the wilful member in hand, so to speak.

They walked to the back of the bar and sat down in a booth. Lucy was right behind them and set two beers down on the table. Grizzly glanced at the glasses and looked up, "Weren't they ordered by someone?"

She grinned, "They'll wait."

They both admired her deliciously ample and mobile bottom depart before Grizzly spoke, "I owe you an apology mister. My name is Bob, what's yours?" He had extended his hand as he spoke which Graham grasped with relief at the growing realisation he was going to see another dawn. "It's Graham."

Bob nodded and took several large swigs of his beer.

Graham took the opportunity to carry out a swift appraisal. The man was middle-aged, certainly but fitter than most twenty year olds would ever dream of being. His hair or what could be seen of it and his beard were peppered with grey. The arms, he already knew about, but the hand that was wrapped around the glass was huge and every single knuckle was skinned, the blood still shiny and still coagulating.

Graham tried to think of something to say that didn't include the weather. Finally, he asked, "Do you live around here?"

"Hell no, I drink here sometimes but I spend most of my time up at Daytona Beach."

There was another long, and for Graham painful pause before Bob spoke again, "How did you know about the whipping?"

Graham responded with a question of his own. "What did you find out?"

Bob gazed at him at said, "Listen to me, I have just apologised to a rabbit and that is a very difficult thing for me to do. Now I ain't gonna hurt you but I would like for you to answer questions in the order they are given."

Graham swallowed hard and considered his options. The only saving grace could be that this individual lived outside of normal society and would be unlikely to spread the word. He couldn't have been closer to the truth, but where to start.

Bob supplied the answer with his next question; pointing at the crease in Graham's forehead. "Someone do that to you?" Graham nodded. "Hmm, must have stung some." He looked towards the bar and called out, "Hey Lucy, another beer."

There was a another pause in which Graham wondered whether he should ask why Americans never say please in restaurants and bars but a glance at Bob's stare put him back on track.

"I need your sholemn promise to keep what I'm about to tell you shecret. An oath on your daughter's life."

"Why."

"Because if I can't be sure of that I think I'd prefer you to take me out into the car park now and beat the shit out of me. Either option would be as bad as the other."

Bob thought for a moment, "OK, let me promise you this much. I won't tell a soul, ever, and if I believe you that'll be the end of it. However, if I think you've fed me bullshit, well then we're heading out to the car park, you and me. That good enough?"

"Humph! You may as well get started now then, 'cos you're probably not going to believe what I have to tell you anyway."

"Just get started dammit! We ain't got all night an' I'll know if you're shittin' me."

Graham went back to the beginning and told Bob pretty much everything, though summarising when he was able. The whole story was as preposterous as ever just as Graham's gentle, unassuming manner made it believable. Bob had interrupted with questions a few times but for the most part he just listened. Finally, after almost two hours Graham shrugged his shoulders and said, "That's it."

"Shit, so you're the Brit tourist the police wanted to speak to about the kid in the 7/11? And you reckon you can see that just by touching them?"

Graham nodded, "Just like when your daughter fell againsht me in that domed cinema."

Bob began to shake his head. "Well you were right about one thing, it *ain't* believable. I'd sure like to meet this 'group' of yours, 'cept the pig of course." Even as he spoke he thought of the episode that featured him. Graham had been sure to include every detail, with imagery that matched the evidence he had actually seen for himself, the previous evening, even the number of lashes.

"Oh man, how can you expect someone to believe that?" He shook his head, "But then I saw the boy's ass with my own eyes and CNN actually *showed* the abuse actually happening to that other kid.

Graham waited a moment before speaking, "Can you answer my question now, pleashe?"

"What was it?"

"What did you find, when you saw your son?"

"He ain't my son but he'd been beaten, just as you said."

"Who did it?"

"My Ex's new guy."

"Have you reported it to the authorities?"

He glanced at his knuckles, "No need. He'll be in hospital for a while and then he's moving to another state, alone."

Graham was just sober enough to know better than pursue that one but *was* drunk enough to say, "He *ish* your son."

"Mister, you're going places you shouldn't."

Graham shook his head, "Pleashe, I am certain he is, I don't understand it properly, but there was something about the *feelings* I experienced from your daughter. I just know I'm left feeling they are full blooded brother and sister."

"Listen, my wife fooled around when we were married, got pregnant and tried to pass it off as mine."

"Sho that's why you take your daughter out on her own."

"I told him he could come but he backed off."

"I wouldn't mind betting you and your wife have rowed over his parentage quite a bit. Have you had the test done?"

"Now it's time to mind your own business."

The feelings Graham was experiencing overrode his fears when he next spoke, "That poor kid has probably grown up believing you have no feelings for him even though his mother keeps telling him you're his Dad. He would probably sell his soul to hear you call him 'son' but inshtead his stepfather beats the shit out of him until he admits he's a bastard."

The movement was so quick he didn't see it, but suddenly his shirt front was halfway across the table, along with his face, anticipating violence. Bob glared at him but eventually opted for clemency and threw Graham back to his side of the table before shouting, "Lucy, the bill."

She arrived promptly, bearing a slip of paper and Bob said, "Pay the lady."

"You didn't tell me to bring any money with me!

Bob looked at Lucy and shook his head, "Fucking rabbits." He paid the bill and gestured for Graham to follow him.

Outside Graham asked, "Why do you keep calling me a rabbit?"

Bob spoke over his shoulder, "You a biker?"

"Er, no."

"Then you're a fucking rabbit."

As always, the journey home seemed quicker than the one going but it was long enough for Bob to consider all that had been said and to regret rough handling Graham yet again. In the resort car park he took the helmet back and said, "Graham, tonight has been a strange experience and I still need time to think about it, but I regret grabbing at you like that and I'm still grateful for the information about the boy." He paused then and his shoulders slumped. In an exasperated tone he said, "You've really put a burr up my ass. Just how certain are you about him being my son, and before you answer I gotta tell you, I *will* bear a grudge if you're wrong."

"I'll pay half of the cost of the test."

Bob nodded and asked, "How long are you here for?"

"We're going down to Fort Myers Beach next Thursday, *The Golden Horizon Suites,* then we go back to England on the thirtieth."

"Well, whatever, I am still sorry for any discomfort I caused at *Epcott* and I'm grateful to you for the information." He made to get back on the bike when Graham spoke, "It'sh a good job you believed me."

"How's that?"

"Well if we'd have gone into the car park I'd have been beaten the shit out of you." Bob paused and suddenly Graham's bladder felt overly full. Slowly, Grizzly kicked the bike stand back out and rested his machine on it. As he turned back to face them both Graham and his bladder were delighted to see a grin on the man's face, "You know, I'm beginning to think it might have been a pleasure meeting you."

They shook hands and without another word Bob mounted his Harley and raced off.

* * *

Nancy opened the door as soon as he tapped it. It was almost three and it was clear she had stayed wide awake. "What happened? Is everything OK?"

"Oh yeah." He locked his hands together and added, "Bob and I are like this. Rock solid." He dropped his head on her shoulder, "Oh Nansh, I've spent most of the time scared witless."

They clambered into bed and with whispers, he told Nancy about his midnight excursion, including Lucy's nipples and offer. They agreed to treat it as an acceptable closure to that nasty episode at *Epcott*. It was easy then, to get back to the business of enjoying their holiday.

Somehow, they managed to get up in time to catch the bus to *Seaworld* and had yet another remarkable day. If Jimmy had been aware of what happened he showed no sign of it though he was put out when Graham fell into bed at eight o clock that night. Tomorrow they were going the Kennedy Space Centre.

Wednesday was spent in *Disneyworld* pulling in the features they hadn't yet seen along with a selection of 'must do agains'. Halfway through the day they were walking along Main Street hand in hand, towards the fairy castle when Nancy voiced what they were all feeling, "It doesn't get better than this!"

At teatime they grabbed a burger and curly fries at the resort so that as soon as they'd finished Nancy could leave them to play in the games arcade while she packed. Tomorrow they were heading for the Gulf Coast and meeting up with Harvey and Audrey.

* * *

Grizzly hit the door at ten o clock prompt. Fearful of waking Jimmy, Graham leapt out of bed and ran to the door, remembering to engage the bar before opening it.

"Bob." Bob indicated with a shake of his head and said, "Come on," before disappearing out of sight.

Graham crouched over as though he were trying not to void a bowel and hissed at Nancy, "What shall I do!"

Nancy thought for a moment before saying, "Go. I've a feeling he just wants another talk with you. It'll be OK, I'm sure."

Graham had started to get dressed anyway, since he couldn't imagine saying no to the man. He grabbed his wallet and was half-way through the door when Nancy whispered as loudly as she could, "But stay away from that Lucy!"

* * *

Lucy was behind the bar and called them over when they walked in. She looked down at her breasts before looking up at Bob with a grin, "Hey Bob, will ya look at them. They're real pleased to see you."

"Now you know that ain't true Lucy, you've turned the air con up too high again is all, though I do cherish the thought that it might have been me."

She turned to Graham, "Hey welcome back honey, have I ever been thinking about you and a very special relationship." Somehow she'd managed to make her breasts move in time with her words and the image of her gorgeous backside came back to him. He was beginning to feel uncomfortable again when she said, "Now then hon', don't you go putting your hands in those pockets tonight. Just show me you appreciate an *aware* sort of woman." She grinned impishly at Graham's back as he fled towards the same booth they'd occupied on Monday.

Bob sat opposite and said nothing until the beers had been delivered. He then slapped a receipted invoice on the table and said, "You owe me ninety dollars."

Graham read the invoice, from a laboratory in Tampa, that detailed the paternity test at a cost of one hundred and eighty dollars. He looked up, "Have you got the results?"

Bob nodded, "He's mine."

"That ish wonderful, I'm delighted. What did you do when you found out."

"First I cried. Then I went and got the Ex out of work and Tyler out of school. We went home and we cried some more. This is privileged information you understand?"

Graham nodded, "It won't go any further. What's next?"

"I gotta a lot of catching up to do and a heap of wrongs to put right. You know, the one whose taken this the best and the worst 'cos of how it's affected her is my daughter Chloe, the one you saw at *Epcott* and it made me think again about your connection. I reckon it was her hurt you felt, watching her brother get beaten like that."

Graham nodded again, "I'm sure you're right. Anyway." He opened his wallet and began withdrawing the cash. Bob quickly covered Graham's hand and exclaimed, "Hell no Graham, I was just joshing about the bill. I brought you here tonight to thank you."

Graham held Bob's gaze and withdrew his hand, "I am thrilled to be paying this, so take it, pleashe."

Bob nodded as Graham counted the notes out in front of him, "Yeah, I guess I can understand where you stand on that." He stuffed the cash in his pocket and leaned forward, "There's something else I need to say and you need to understand that I mean it. If you ever need help, specially *'specialist* help, you know what I'm sayin'? Here or in England, you call this number and say that Big Bob told you to. They'll know where to reach me. I've had a few days to think things over and I don't understand a lot of it even now, probably never will, but I do know I have a lifelong debt to you." He passed a folded piece of paper over to Graham and said, "Keep that safe." He seemed to shake himself then and said, "Right that's enough brotherly love shit for one night, Lucy! Two more beers."

From then on though, they were easy in each other's company. Graham repeated episodes that Bob wanted to hear again and learned a great deal about the Hells Angels, aka the 81's, aka the One Per Centers.

He was back at the room by two o clock this time, but extremely drunk. Bob handed him over to Nancy with a polite, "Goodnight ma'am" and disappeared. Graham was totally unaware of the exchange and allowed Nancy to undress and tuck him into bed. When she gave him a quick kiss he murmured, "Nishe chap that." and lost consciousness.

* * *

The pinkish beige airport building at Fort Myers was very different to Heathrow and Orlando, homelier and more welcoming. Since their flight had been internal they didn't have to run the gauntlet of immigration control and in no time at all had retrieved their cases and were walking out into the arrivals lounge to the welcoming arms of the Calders.

Audrey held on to Nancy tightly and whispered in her ear, "We've been so worried about you."

Nancy snorted and linked arms with her friend, "Worried? You haven't heard about our dust up with a Hell's Angel yet."

"Oh heavens no!" Audrey looked closely to try and measure any anxiety in Nancy's face. In a way they felt responsible for anything that happened on this trip and now something else had happened as well as the 7/11 incident.

Nancy grinned and said, "We had a few scares but it ended happily and believe me this story is one for the grandchildren."

Audrey smiled back uncertainly and said you must tell us about it but I'm damned glad you're down here now where we can keep an eye on you."

A tugging on her skirt made Nancy look down to find Esther, looking up expectantly, "Oh Esther, you must have thought we were forgetting you." Nancy lifted the toddler up, and hugged her, "Well look at you, you've grown so!"

Esther nodded her agreement and said, "I can swim."

Nancy caught Audrey's wink and said, "Well good for you, will you show me." The toddler nodded again and decided the encounter was over, struggling to be let down.

The Calders had rented an eight-seat minivan for the visit so that guests and luggage were easily stowed. As they travelled away from the airport they were struck by the sense of space and huge indigenous palms. Shopping malls in the middle of nowhere, a huge college stadium and all of it gleaming in the bright sunshine. Jimmy half-listened to Harvey's commentary but he was still more interested in the trucks, cars, Police cruisers and just about everything else that he had only seen on television before.

Graham sat in front with Harvey and would call out if they approached something interesting. He asked Harvey about the absence of traffic islands and the consequent waits, sometimes long ones, at traffic lights.

"I don't know why they don't have them though I suspect it would end up being a traffic anarchy, and heaven for the ambulance chasing lawyers. At least traffic lights are unequivocal."

They caught glimpses of waterways and marinas with gleaming white charter boats until they saw the white Fort Myers Bridge arcing up into the sky. Jimmy gasped as they passed over the shimmering blue waterway with boats creaming along in both directions. At the top the three new kids in town all cried out as the deep blue Gulf of Mexico filled the horizon. Below them a pier stretched out from the creamy coloured beach which marked the centre of the resorts' hotels and restaurants. The new arrivals had never seen anything like it.

They dropped down to sea level and turned right as the main highway kicked left. Within a few hundred yards Harvey pulled off the road onto the forecourt of *The Golden Horizon Suites*. They tumbled out of the vehicle into the balmy warmth and a uniformed man appeared with a luggage trolley, leaving them to enter the lobby. On the opposite side a wall of glass offered a view of a pool, beach and sea that lay just beyond.

Their room featured an area that contained a single bed in one half and a mini kitchen and bar in the other. A doorway led past the bathroom and toilet into a bedroom that had the same view as the lobby but from an ample balcony. The bed was enormous and on the side, next to the television stood a large vase filled with flowers and a note that read,

> Welcome to the Gulf
> It's time to party,
> love H & A.

* * *

Nancy had been standing at the balcony rail staring out at the sea when Audrey joined her. They stayed that way for a while until Nancy turned, her face streaked with tears, "This is the most beautiful place I've ever seen, I don't know how we can ever thank you enough."

Audrey's eyes were full, "Watching you now has done that and more, I promise you." A clink of glasses heralded the arrival of chilled sparkling wine and prompted her to add, "We stocked your fridge with a few bits and pieces, none of it healthy."

Twenty minutes later the Calders left them to unpack after arranging to meet at the *Shark bite* restaurant next to the pier for lunch. There they basked in the sunshine and ate burgers and fries washed down with icy beers that highlighted the humidity by leaving pools of condensation on the table. With a finesse that elevated the experience to the subliminal the restaurant sound system played a *Beachboys* album.

In the afternoon they drove over the three mile causeway to Sanibel. Jimmy gazed out in awe at the sparkling sea on both sides, just yards away from him. On the other side they turned right on the Periwinkle Way where timber built malls full of designer shops beckoned. Harvey explained that up until the previous year the road had passed between a corridor of magnificent trees but Hurricane *Charlie* came visiting and knocked the lot down. Soon they left the buildings and drove along the Sanibel-Captiva Road through lush sub tropical greenery until Harvey turned left at a sign that said Bowman's Beach. They parked in a sandy car park and walked through the exotic undergrowth and over an enclosed piece of water until they were confronted by a panorama of sea and sand with hardly a soul in sight. Jimmy had been too polite to say anything at the hotel when he was forced to get back into the vehicle instead of getting on to the beach, but this was worth it.

Harvey explained, "I've brought you here to enjoy the beach, obviously, but also to introduce you to the 'Sanibel stoop'." He pointed to the area around them which was covered in shells of all colours and shapes. "People come from all over to collect shells here."

There was so much more, the place seemed to teem with life and the water was heavenly. Some shuffled along in the water, watching the stingrays rise off the bed and undulate towards deeper water or watched the surface come alive as a predator hit a shoal of fish. Others 'stooped' for shells or simply sat and stared. Even as he took his photographs, Graham knew they couldn't begin to capture it.

Esther divided her attention between them all, though her favourite activity was chasing the flocks of sanderlings as they ran in and out with the waves' edge.

After the hustle and bustle of the theme parks the afternoon on the beach was an inspired choice but before long Harvey announced that it was four thirty and time to head back, adding that they must be back at the hotel before five thirty. Nancy asked why but Harvey would only smile and say, "You'll see."

Their return mirrored their earlier arrival in that Harvey went to the fridge while the others made their way onto to the balcony. Glasses were charged and they sat down to watch one of the truly wonderful sunsets that coast is famous for. For Nancy it wasn't just a sunset, it was a natural wonder.

Shortly after, the Harvey's left them to spend the rest of the day together and to do a little exploring on their own, though promising to collect them at eight o clock the next morning for a full day out. It was a delicate and thoughtful touch that allowed the three innocents to explore the shops and find somewhere to eat by themselves. The choice of restaurant was easy. As soon as they saw the log construction and the western-style stoop beneath the sign that said *Stuffed Hog BBQ* the decision was made.

The following morning Harvey drove them back across the causeway and shortly after the turning for Bowman's Beach they drove over a bridge onto Captiva Island. After a short distance they turned right and drove slowly down a drive towards a large single storey house. The front garden was sand dotted with all sorts of palms and fruit trees. They recognised lemons, coconuts and grapefruit but none of the others. A tennis court appeared on their left and they could see the swimming pool extending from the right hand side of the building, enclosed in a box-like structure of mosquito netting.

Inside they made their way through a huge lounge into a kitchen/diner of similar proportions. The smell of fresh coffee filed the air and the table carried a platter of sliced fruit, croissants and a jug of fruit juice. Audrey called Jimmy over and said, "After all that junk food you've been eating I thought you would like a healthier option this morning, though to be on the safe side I also bought these." His eyes lit up as she lifted a plate of sugared and iced doughnuts from behind the counter. With a wry grin she said, "Yeah, thought as much."

Two doughnuts and an orange juice later Jimmy looked set to go, but the adults hadn't even finished their first coffee. Sheesh!

Audrey came to his rescue and asked Esther if she wanted to show Jimmy how well she could swim. Within minutes both children were back in their swimming costumes and Esther stood fidgeting while her water wings were installed. A Patio door led straight from the kitchen to the pool so her grandparents felt easy enough to remain at the table. Jimmy could swim, quite well, but minutes later his style was being subjected to criticism and he was being told to 'do it this way.'

It was an opportunity for grown up talk and a report of what happened in Orlando, good and bad. Graham seemed less inclined to discuss his 'hits' because, as he explained to Nancy later, he felt obliged to dwell on the fabulous holiday they'd enjoyed thanks to the Calders'. Even so the encounter with Big Bob improved with the telling and wasn't without comedy.

Audrey laughed, "And we thought this would be a break from all that. It'll have to be the Gobi desert next year."

Nancy huffed, "Don't bank on it, he'll be talking to camels by then."

Harvey capped his hands together, "Right, well it's time we got a move on." He turned to Audrey, "I'll leave you to tidy up and Graham and I will launch the boat."

The shock of hearing that made Graham realise that he had no idea of what the Calder's had in store for them and hadn't even thought to ask.

They left by the back door and crossed a sandy back garden to a small wooden walkway that led through some mangroves before opening out onto a jetty which overlooked a waterway. The Gulf was on the other side of the island, three hundred yards away, but here the calm waterway separated them from another island only a hundred yards away, covered in mangroves and without any signs of habitation. On the right hand side of the jetty was another construction with a crane overhead. Beneath lay a gleaming white boat.

Graham's heart skipped a beat; their whole holiday had come to have the phrase embedded in it,—'It can't get any better, surely.'

Harvey launched the boat with practiced ease and moored it to the jetty just as Nancy arrived with two cool boxes and said, "Audrey told me to ask if you'd remembered the ice."

"Oh bugger it, no I didn't. Tell her we'll get some at Cabbage Key," and then under his breath, "I hope."

Soon they were all aboard, sun lotion, hats and fishing rods in place. Harvey cast off and they headed slowly past other jetties, many with boats left in the water. Their own boat was a twenty two footer with the helm and controls in a centre console allowing passengers to wander around the whole thing and select one of many places to sit, some of which enjoyed the shade from the canvas bimini top. As the mangrove island on their right petered out the houses on their left gave way to hotels, restaurants and a boatyard offering bait plus all sorts of water borne rentals. At last they turned to the right and headed down a line of channel markers, picking up speed a little until they reached a much larger marker. There Harvey turned left in the *Intercoastal waterway*, and told them to hold tight as he eased the throttle forward. The hundred and twenty *Mercury* horses on the back soon had them up on a plane and hurtling forward at twenty five knots. Graham stood next to Harvey, exhilarated, as he watched the low islands disappear from sight. Behind them a jewelled white wake marked their passage through the blue water.

After fifteen minutes or so Harvey suddenly cut the throttle and everyone lurched forward. Those who were hanging on were fine and that included Esther who had clearly decided to have Jimmy as her escort for the day and was hanging on to him. Nancy and Audrey ended up on their knees. "Harvey! What are the bloody hell are you playing at."

He smiled apologetically and pointed off to starboard, "Dolphins."

They drifted as three dolphins cruised through the water and gradually came closer. Cameras were clicking furiously but stopped when suddenly one of the creatures appeared at the side of the boat, no more than three feet away. It rolled on to its side as if to favour them with a grin. They saw another pass by under the boat and surface several yards away before the others followed it and the show was over.

Harvey throttled up again but within minutes eased off and headed left towards an island. He explained, "I thought you might like to visit a deserted island, well near enough empty to count. This one is Cayo Costa and it's a state park.

He beached the boat and they waded ashore onto the beach. No one spoke. Tiny waves continued to roll onto to the shore and they heard birds calling, but there was an emptiness that assaulted the senses. They were close to a channel that separated them from the next island and they strolled around the point onto the Gulf side of the island. Stumps of palms stood in silent testimony to the awesome force of hurricane *Charlie* but there was no sign of man, anywhere. No footprints, litter, just peace. Little was said as they gathered much better specimens of the shells they had found the day before. They also found lots of complete sand dollars and a couple of prehistoric-looking horseshoe crabs before once again and too soon, time ran out. Harvey rounded them up and herded them back to the boat.

Before pushing off he allocated the fishing rods according to experience. Graham had used a spinning reel before and to his surprise Nancy said the same, though they were at pains to point out that their experience was limited to the ponds back home. They were given lures to use and sent to the bow while Jimmy was promised tuition once they were in position.

They moved into the channel where a swift current from the Gulf confirmed the tide was on the flow. Once they were a few hundred yards into the Gulf Harvey cut the engine and allowed them to drift.

Then time became measured by the slapping of waves against the hull as a shrimp was put on Jimmy's hook and he was shown how to cast a little way upstream and allow the bait to 'trot' past the boat in the current. A fish hit his bait on the very first cast and Harvey had to repeat his tutilage several times for the instructions to penetrate the boys' exhilaration. Finally, as the fish appeared on the surface Harvey grasped the line and smoothly lifted it up over the gunwhale. With a quick flick the hook was out and another shrimp attached, but Jimmy was still kneeling on the deck staring at the fabulous shining mix of silver and yellow.

Harvey nudged him and winked, "There you go, but we'll need more than just one for the barbecue. Jimmy grasped the rod and set to while his tutor filled a bucket with water and dumped the snapper into it.

Graham was next, with another, slightly larger snapper then lines were hauled in and they motored back out to the Gulf. Everyone had been so engrossed they hadn't noticed the islands pass by.

Graham caught another before Nancy cried out in panic, her rod was bent over and she was struggling to hold on. Harvey ran forward and with quiet assurances, talked her through the fight. At one point she asked him to take the rod but he refused, though he did help her lift the road from then on. Suddenly they saw the fish and Harvey ran back to the console for the landing net. Five minutes later a thirty inch snook lay on the deck and Harvey quickly threw the anchor off the bow. They were perilously near the shallow waters that marked where the currents eased enough for the sand to settle. Nancy put her rod in one of the holders and sat down, trembling. Graham placed a hand on her shoulder, "Are you OK love?"

She looked up at him and said, "That was one of the most exciting things I have ever done."

Harvey had returned with a tape and announced, "It's a keeper! These taste superb, I promise you."

Audrey had been sitting with Esther, enjoying the spectacle but now she said, "You haven't got any ice and you're not going to get that in the bucket."

"No problem, we'll have one more pass and we'll head in. Until then I'll show you how we'll keep him fresh." The anchor was raised and they were positioned offshore for the final pass. Harvey had already tied a loop of rope that passed through the gills and out of the mouth. With a superior smile he lowered it over the edge and into the water near Jimmy, tying the other end of the rope to the guard rail.

He'd gone a little further into the gulf this time, now that he had a better feel for the current and all three anglers caught a decent sized snapper. He was unhooking one for Jimmy when Nancy called him. Within seconds she called him again, much louder. Puzzled he moved forward to her side. She was staring at the water ahead, transfixed, unable to say a word but as he followed her line of sight he saw the fin. There were two of them, both around eight feet long, grey and unutterably sinister-looking as they cruised around the front of the boat. He ran back and grabbed at the rope he had tied off, frantically hauling the snook back in. Jimmy's jaw dropped as the sleek grey shape slid beneath him. Even Harvey had been startled and he decided it was time to pack up and go find some ice. Once again lines were hauled in and they cruised north to another island called Cabbage Key. On the way Harvey attempted to pass it off as a fairly common incident but Audrey would have none of it. "The last time I saw you move like that was when Esther tried to clean your car with a wire brush."

Harvey bristled but he didn't argue the point. Eventually, he mumbled defensively, "At least it didn't get our dinner."

Minutes later they were all laughing and all admitted how alarmed they'd been.

They negotiated a narrow channel down to a dock that lay at the bottom of a grassy bank. At the top stood the Cabbage Key Restaurant where they were about to have lunch. A tallish slim, elderly man took the rope Harvey threw to him and tied it off before helping everyone step onto the coarse wooden planks. Harvey spoke to the man and handed over some money, neatly folded. When they got back they would find that the cool box had been filled with ice together with their catch, already gutted and cleaned. Harvey did know when to be generous in a culture that survived on tips.

After lunch they took a stroll across the island before climbing back on board. On the way back both Graham and Jimmy added to their store of memories by taking the helm, though once they left the main channel Harvey took over again. In relaxed fashion, the women went back to the pool while the men, Jimmy included, cleaned the boat down and hoisted it out of the water. Harvey then set Jimmy up with a rod, stool and a lidded bucket of bait tied to the dock but left in the water. Beers were retrieved from the house and the men sat at the end of the dock to offer tips and encouragement.

Jimmy lost count of the fish he caught. Most were catfish but he also caught small snapper, sheepshead and some rays. Harvey insisted on taking them all off the hook, pointing out the dangerous spines on the catfish and rays. During a quiet spell Jimmy recalled the shark's passage along the side of the boat and relished the prospect of telling Tim about it. That thought prompted another and he asked Graham, "Can I take a present home for Tim please?"

"Good idea maytee, we'll find something at the airport."

Before they knew it, dusk was falling and the mosquitoes had found their appetite. In equal but opposite measure Harvey lost his appetite for barbecuing since he would have been the only one outdoors and therefore the only item on their menu.

Plan B was put into operation.

Harvey filleted the fish and they piled into the van and drove back over the Blind Pass Bridge to a restaurant called *The Pink Pelican*. It was a timber building on stilts and inside the hewn timber furniture gave the place a rustic air. The Americans are relaxed about most things but the waitress, Sandy, who took them to a table took it further. It was difficult to pin down, but somehow it felt as though they were family. As they sat down Nancy gazed around at the furnishings and fittings with a grin, "This place is really funky."

Harvey had handed the bag of fillets over and moments later a pitcher of beer appeared plus a *Dr Peppers* for kids. They had been early and soon realised how fortunate that had been. Within half an hour the place was full and the atmosphere extraordinary. Well before then their catch had appeared on a platter and Sandy pointed out the blackened, grilled, mesquite-grilled and fried fillets, all with baskets of fries, salad and the trimmings.

They were halfway through the next pitcher when Graham proposed a toast, "To Harvey and Audrey, and another unbelievable day in the bank."

They all joined him in the toast and cheered. Audrey said, "That's a different way of putting it."

Nancy answered the implied question, "These days have been beyond anything we could have dreamt, full of fantastic things and once they're in the bank," she tapped her head, "No-one can take them off us, so each night we 'deposit' the day and its memories."

Audrey grinned and glanced at Harvey, "We are so pleased. Watching you discover things has been good for me too. Sadly though, it's your last night."

Nancy shook her head, "No, not at all. This may sound daft but it's all been *so* wonderful that we want to protect the memories, by going home." She shrugged, "As I said, daft logic."

Audrey remembered feeling that way many years ago, when they were just making ends meet and sharing the joy of two young daughters. She smiled, "I know exactly what you mean."

Chapter 21

Back on Captiva, just a few hundred yards away from where the Calders were staying, Grant Haddon pushed his head back and closed his eyes as he climaxed. Seconds before he had relished the sight of his violent penetration of the figure bent over the arm of their sofa and it had been enough to trigger his completion. He stayed in that position until his member became flaccid enough to push back inside his shorts.

Without a word, he turned and left the room, leaving his daughter to weep into the cushions and clean herself up.

The house was quiet without his two minders, the cook and her husband who acted as caretaker, all of whom had been given the night off

He settled into an easy chair on the stoop overlooking the ocean, rolling the ice around in his glass of bourbon. His wife, April was unconscious as usual by that time of day but he liked to keep his family with him these days, where he could keep an eye on them. They had a role to play now.

He sat back with a satisfied smirk as he thought about that and the why.

The fates had certainly smiled on him when they felled the current and, it seemed, entrenched senator with a stroke. He and his team had begun to prepare for the next elections, still five years away and knew they had a fight on their hands. Not now though. Mindful of Grant's support and the security his own tenure enjoyed when his ally secured the siting of a major Taiwanese factory in the State, the Governor decided to nominate Grant for the remainder of the current term as Senator.

In other words, he was in, without the need for an election cam-paign and with five years to do enough to ensure he was re-elected. They had spoken three days ago and Grant had accepted the role informally but protocols had to be observed, not least of all the internment of the dead senator which had occurred earlier that day. Tomorrow he would meet with the Governor and agree on the content of his acceptance speech, before the announcement was made on Monday.

He'd decided then to fly down to the house on Captiva and relax for a few days. Some of his team had come down with him to help prepare and were staying in a hotel nearby but for the most part he had enjoyed the peace of his surroundings.

Slowly, absorbed by the ritual, he formed a line of coke on the table beside him and once he drawn it in leant back to consider which one of the sparkling stars was his. Life could be so sweet.

* * *

The Calders dropped them back at the hotel by nine o clock so that they could pack and have an early night before their journey home the next day.

They couldn't sleep though, other than Jimmy who left for the land of nod as soon as his head hit the pillow. Nancy made two hot milks and they sat out on the balcony to talk about all they had seen and done. It hadn't just been a holiday, it had been a sen-sory overload.

At eight prompt the Calders drove onto the hotel forecourt where Graham, Nancy and Jimmy waited with their luggage and by eight thirty they were at the airport. Audrey always hated partings and they kept this one brief. Inside the travellers found checking-in to be much easier than in England and were delighted to discover that the aircraft they would be travelling to New York on had a three seat configuration next to the window so they would continue to travel together.

After the formalities they were comforted by being in the travel sausage machine once more. Tomorrow morning it would eject them into Heathrows' arrivals lounge where hopefully, Sarah would be waiting for them. In the meantime, they wandered upstairs. The check-in process had been so quick they were left with quite a wait and rather than risk there not being facilities beyond security Graham suggested having a coffee at first kiosk they found. It was surrounded by tables and they soon found a seat that provided them with a view of the lower concourse. The coffee was delicious and Jimmy confirmed that his plate-sized cookie was too.

Someone sat down in the seat behind him and from the movement and noise he guessed there were several people occupying the next table. Something was said, too quietly for him to hear but the person behind him slouched back in the seat and nudged him.

* * *

He passed through one experience after the other, there were so many. The early touching, fondling and molesting that became worse with time and tempering. He knew the crawling disgust of being made to masturbate the man and the terror and shame of that first rape. The clattering of instruments under a bright light and knees painfully slung onto chrome stirrups with such shame and confusion. It went on and on until he knew it was here, near the beach, one hand was pressing down on the head so that it was almost impossible to breathe. The other was tearing at underclothes and then a brutal invasion.

* * *

Nancy was shaking him, "Graham, are you alright." He'd been out for longer than usual for a 'hit' and she thought he'd nodded off, until he failed to respond when she called him. Eventually, she grabbed his shoulder and he came to, though still dazed. He rubbed his forehead to try and ease the pain before turning to look at the victim.

She was a teenage girl, very pale and with dark unkempt hair. Her clothes were all black and looked rather 'goth' but a small gold chain and crucifix stood out from such sombre surroundings. Opposite, a sandy blond woman sat nursing a glass of clear fluid and a thick-set man in a suit looked at him suspiciously. He swivelled around in his chair and startled the girl by speaking. "You

297

don't have to put up with it you know." She looked at him and his creased forehead as though he was a crazy.

The man leaned forward and spoke "Is there anything I can do for sir?"

Graham sensed the threat and smiled, he couldn't walk away from this one. "I'm so shorry, my name is Graham Parsons, I'm English." He reached forward and offered his hand which was ignored as he continued, "Would you be this young ladies father by any chance?"

"What is that to you, sir?"

"Ah, so you're not." Suddenly he felt angry. In the hit he remembered pleading with 'daddy' so the brute opposite wasn't the abuser. He turned to the girl and smiled and spoke quietly, "What's your name?"

She wouldn't look up but murmured, "Chrissy."

This time he lowered his voice further, "Oh my dear, you mustn't put up with it any longer. He shouldn't be doing that to you, he's your father and fathers don't do that sort of thing to their daughters, at least normal loving ones don't. He's in the wrong, not you."

He waited for a response but she wouldn't look up though a tear rolled down her cheek. The man opposite leant forward and prodded Graham painfully on the front of his shoulder, "Now butt out mister or I'll get security."

Graham stood and moved to one side before beckoning the man. Moments passed as the brute glared back from his seat. Finally, with a deep scowl he rose and walked over to Graham. The options had been considered and the man decided that it was time he did something. A good nine inches taller, the man bent slowly and engaged Graham with the blank gaze of an alligator, "What?"

"I take it you work for the girl's father."

The man continued to stare but didn't speak until Nancy stood up to take Graham's arm and things started to look too public. He spoke quietly, "Yes I do and you are being intrusive. Now I will warn you for the last time. Go or I call security."

Nancy pulled at Graham's arm "Come on love, you can't help this time."

Graham put a hand on hers, "Perhapsh not, but I can poke a stick in the nest." He turned to the minder, "I was wondering though, if you knew how many times her father had raped her or knew about the abortion she had to have. I think the whole world should know don't you?"

As Nancy had said, there was nothing more he could do. He walked back to his seat and picked up his bag, "Come on, let'sh go."

The minder watched them walk towards departure security and pulled out his telephone.

* * *

They had already arrived at the airport when the pilot informed him that his Gulfstream was grounded with a technical fault. A team was on its way but it was *Thanksgiving* and it would be at least a couple of hours before they would be airborne. Haddon was annoyed but he could at least make calls from the aircraft. He sent a minder with April and Chrissy into the airport to wait while he and his other minder followed the captain out to the aircraft.

When his mobile rang an hour later he looked at the caller ID and closed the call he was making on the aircrafts' telephone. He listened intently and asked a few questions before closing the call with, "Wait there." He sat quietly for a few minutes, drawing on his instinct for survival. Whatever happened this one needed to be dealt with; discredited, or disposed of.

With the inkling of an idea he pointed at his large black attaché case and spoke to the minder he was with, "Get that and come with me, we've got a problem."

They were already on the secure side of the airport and an attendant showed them through a door that led to the departures lounge. His minder had been told what to do and spent a short while in the toilets before they sought the gate assigned to the next New York flight.

Graham had finished telling Nancy all he had experienced in the 'hit', the times of fear, confusion and hatred. The nightmare of the clinic and even the time when she was being filmed. They held hands, knowing that he'd done all he could.

"Excuse me sir, may I have a word with you please?" Graham looked up from his seat at a tall, silver haired man, dressed casually but in clothes that yelled money. He was clean shaven and wore a serious, concerned expression, as he extended a hand.

In a voice that only Graham could hear he said "My name is Grant Haddon and since time is short I won't waste time prevaricating. The man I left to take care of my niece and her mother has just told me something I can barely believe. Please, would you grant me enough of your time to tell me what you know."

Graham shook the hand briefly as he stood up and listened to Haddon gesture to some empty seating in the corner of the lounge, "Please, may we talk in private," he gave a small shrug, "We're going to be discussing something no family wants to hear and this concerns my brother."

Graham turned to Nancy and said, "I'm jusht off to have a word with this man. We'll be over there." He pointed at the far corner and felt a hand on his shoulder, guiding him gently forward, "Thank you so much sir." He turned to his minder and said, "Karl, bring the gentleman's bag over for him."

As soon as they were seated they completed introductions and Grant spoke, "Mr Parsons, before we go any further I want you to know that if there is substance to what you tell me I *will* take the appropriate action, I promise you. Now please, tell me what you know."

Fifteen minutes later the summary of abuse was complete. Haddon shook his head in despair, "Oh my Lord, this is dreadful, but tell me who told you about this?"

"No one told me."

"Then how did you come to know all this?"

Graham considered his options. He could tell the Haddon the truth, given that he would be out of the country in a few hours and beyond reach or he could hold on to the secret and leave the man guessing. But if he did that nothing would happen, that much was certain and Chrissy would continue to suffer. After all, how could anyone be expected to act on those grounds. He sighed and held his hands in the air, palms upward as though cradling his secret. "Look,

I haven't time to go into detail but I have a sort of sixth senshe, a kind of *connectivity* with abused children and my time with Chrissy was appalling. Please, you must check this out and do something."

Haddon patted Graham's knee, "What you've told me is strange, you must admit, but I promise you I will act."

Graham looked across and saw that boarding staff were manning the gate, "I'd better get back to my family now."

"Yes of course, and thank you. Don't forget your bag." Graham took the rucksack from Karl and said goodbye. As he made his way back the two other men stared after him. Haddon spoke, "I can't afford to have someone like him on the streets. Make the call."

Graham smiled as he sat down, "Do you know, I think that man might do something about it. Good news eh?"

Fifteen minutes later Benny, in his bright orange jacket led the way from the external stairway into the jetway. His handler thought it unusual to be checking a line of passengers *boarding* a plane. Usually they just checked the baggage in either direction and lines of passengers as they disembarked, but they had received a call.

Benny didn't know or care about the change. His tail wagged as the first passengers appeared at the head of the jetway, boarding the flight to New York.

* * *

Things happened so quickly. Jimmy had been promised the window seat again and Nancy carried a roll of magazines to enjoy on the flight. They passed a sweet-looking beagle that was held on a leash by a uniformed officer and Graham chuckled at Jimmy as it tried to follow them, its tail wagging furiously, "He sheems to like you."

Uniformed officers suddenly surrounded them and they were escorted out of the door and down some stair, bewildered, frightened and pleading to be allowed to get on their flight. Nobody said a word as they were swept across the apron and through another door. They were taken through a maze of stairs and passages until at last they were shown into two separate rooms, one for Graham and the other for Nancy and Jimmy.

Later, no matter how he tried, Graham could not fully recall what happened. The nightmare seemed to keep getting worse. A man was asking him if he had packed his own bag, left it unattended or accepted anything from anyone. Vaguely he remembered saying 'no' before watching as his rucksack was emptied and he was more certain about saying 'no' when the officer held up a plastic bag of white powder and asked if it was his. He remembered saying 'no' time after time until some other officers arrived and read him his rights. They spoke of 'possession of illegal drugs' and he swore he knew nothing about such a thing. He became genuinely frightened when they made him strip and carried out a body search. Finally, after they had him put an all-in-one white suit on, forms were signed and strong hands forced his arms behind his back for handcuffs to be ratcheted on to his wrists. He remembered the sound they made.

The drive into Fort Myers was numbing. The palms and white buildings seemed sinister this time and all that had been wonderfully different now signified a culture that had suddenly become threatening.

They drove into what looked like a large garage and the sunlight gradually disappeared as a roller shutter door descended. He was led along more corridors to find himself in front of a high counter. Still he said 'no' over and over, apart from answering the many questions requiring his personal details. He was charged, photographed and his prints taken before being told to sit in a large seating area, filled with rows of dark green plastic seating, a little like an over-sized hospital waiting room. There were several others in there but he didn't notice them. His mind was a shambles unable to achieve any semblance of cogency.

* * *

Jimmy had only ever been this frightened once in his life but at least this time he had someone to hold him. Nancy had pleaded for some sort of explanation and watched in horrified confusion as they and their luggage was inspected and swabbed. They were left in a room for some time before another uniformed officer strode in, one she hadn't seen before. He set a file down on the desk and opened it before addressing her. "Ma'am, your husband has been charged with possession of illegal drugs and has been taken into custody. You and the boy are free to go."

Nancy shook her head in disbelief, "That's ridiculous. Graham hasn't got any such thing, I swear. Can I see him?"

"No ma'am, as I said, he's been taken into custody downtown at the holding center."

She gasped, unable to find enough air, "This is some sort of nightmare, we should be going home today."

"Do you have somewhere to go, someone you can contact?"

She shook her head, trying to grasp the enormity of it all and realising she didn't even have the Harvey's address. That thought kicked her into gear; she had to get hold of Harvey, he'd know what to do and at least she knew where they were, if only by sight.

She was relieved to find the leather document wallet with their cases though as she checked to see if the cash was still there she noticed that a passport was missing. Two officers escorted them out to taxi rank at the front of the building and an hour later, as they rolled down the sandy drive she caught a glimpse of a figure standing up by the pool to see who was calling.

Minutes later, once the front door had closed on the world outside Nancy crashed. Audrey held on tightly, rocking her to and fro as phrases were thrust out between sobs. Soon though, she realised that Graham needed help soon and she forced herself to calm down.

The Calder's had been to Captiva many times and had come to know a number of the locals. He had wasted no time in contacting them and within half an hour had telephoned the lawyer whose name had come up several times.

Richard Zinc wasted no time with niceties. The situation was set out and he promised to be with Graham within the hour and to telephone them later.

Meanwhile, at the holding centre Graham tried to understand what had happened. Time passed as did a mix of drunks, addicts and thugs. He became aware of a presence and turned to find a female guard staring down at him. He was about to embark on one of the strangest experiences of his life.

"Hi, how are you." She smiled. Her dark green uniform was so spotless and the creases so perfect it might have been new.

"Not very good actually. I should be going home now."

"Oh, and where is that?"

"Leicester, in England."

"Right, I thought your accent was different. So why are you here?"

"They *shay* I had drugs in my bag, which was newsh to me."

"So I guess you're here waiting for your arraignment and bond hearing."

Graham shook his head, "I don't know what'sh happening."

"Oh I'm sure you'll get bail. You'll be out of here by lunch tomorrow, but I guess you'll be heading back to England straight off."

"Humph! Too blooming right."

"You sound put out sir. You do realise that possession of cocaine is an offence in this country?"

"But it washn't mine."

"Well that's not my concern. We can only deal with facts as we see them. Do *you* see how dangerous drugs are."

"Of courshe I do."

"Then why do you use them; what sort of an example do you think you are setting for your young boy."

"I beg your pardon?"

"Well how do you feel about him taking drugs."

"What?"

"After all, you are his role model. Don't you feel a little ashamed?"

"No, I *feel* extremely innocent. I told you they weren't mine."

"I have to ask you to keep your voice down sir. Just explain to me, in a civilised manner why you should use drugs in a family environment. They were in your bag."

"I don't use drugs and I don't know how they came to be in my bag."

"You know, the most positive thing you could do right now is stop denying the obvious. I'm here to help you realise what you're doing to your life and family. There are rehab schemes in England as well as here I'm sure."

"Are you deaf."

"Sir, I must tell you that we do not tolerate disrespectful acts of any sort here, including speech. I am talking to you very reasonably and that was very offensive."

"I didn't mean to be rude, but you won't listen."

"Now please stop accusing me of neglect in that way."

Graham's jaw dropped, "I beg your pardon?"

"Sir, you heard what I said and stop looking at me in that way."

"I'm not sure I can believe thish."

"What do you mean by that sir?"

"I think I've woken up in a madhoushe. This ish like having a conversation with the *White Rabbit*."

"Listen sir, I'm here to help you acknowledge some stuff and calling me a rabbit is disrespectful, I will not warn you again."

"Then why don't you leave me alone?"

"Sir, I am here to be of assistance."

He couldn't deal with this and snapped at her, "The most helpful thing you could do is to GO AWAY."

"You have already been warned sir, why did you continue being disrespectful?"

"Go away!"

"Sir, you have ignored my warnings and your manner has become aggressive. Please reconsider what you are doing. I do not want to take remedial measures."

"Remedial *what*! Pleashe, go away, pleashe!"

"I expect you to be able to discuss your issues with me. For the sake of your family if nothing else."

Graham shook his head, "And I expected you to know what the words 'go away' meant. Shilly me."

"That's enough!"

Graham snapped back, "What are you going to do tie me up?"

He hadn't noticed the signal she had given to a team waiting near the desk was startled to see them running his way with what looked like a black plastic beach chair with two small wheels beneath the seat. He was gasping in shock a many hands grabbed him out of his seat into the chair. It was useless fighting them but as the straps were secured and he was towed backwards from the scene the ignominy was complete when he looked up and saw a man with a camera recording the whole thing. Moments later someone pushed a white hood over his head. They put him in a quiet locked holding room alone and told him to take some time to settle himself down and begin behaving properly.

He wept then.

An hour later they returned with a slightly rushed air. The same vixen appeared, smiling. "There you go honey, you just needed a time to settle yourself. Arms held him as he was paced up and down the cell until he could support himself without pain. Still hand-cuffed, he was led down more corridors to a small room where a dark haired stocky man with a full moustache was waiting. The door slammed shut and the man extended his hand, "Hello Graham, my name is Richard Zinc, Mr Calder has appointed me to act for you. Graham began to weep once more.

Zinc waited patiently for Graham to stabilize. "They told me you've been in the restraint chair. I've heard it called many things, the 'strap-o-lounger', 'we care chair', 'be sweet chair' the 'devil's chair'. I'm sorry, maybe if I'd gotten here sooner." He withdrew a large yellow pad from his case, "OK guy, let's start putting things to rights."

After an hour of Graham's company he'd been as affected as anyone who had met him.

Lawyers were generally despised in the holding centre, one and all, but Zinc did have a reputation for a certain even-handedness, which made it all the more surprising when he kicked the supervisor's door open. The man didn't get an opportunity to speak. As Zinc raged, "I have just spoken with a very gentle man who your people have tried to turn into a beast. From now on that man gets treated as an honoured guest or as God is my judge I will make it my life's mission to bring you to justice you sorry son of a bitch!"

He strode out without waiting for a reply from the wide-mouthed frog sitting on the opposite side of the desk.

The following morning Harvey arrived at the lawyer's office a little early but was shown straight in. With an apology Zinc began by establishing terms and costs, and requesting an advance that Harvey dealt with immediately.

He didn't waste time with platitudes. "Mr Calder, I am not a betting man but if I was I would put money on Graham's innocence. I can only think of one, maybe two occasions in my career when I've been so concerned and I am not going to leave you in any doubt. Right now the state has a solid case against him. All cases of law have a primary requisite, evidence. Due process is founded upon it and the *only* evidence we have so far is the discovery of cocaine in Graham's bag."

Harvey shook his head, "But surely the drugs could have been planted."

"By whom and why? Evidence; evidence is the key, without it Graham's case is lost unless I can find a procedural gaff, and I haven't found anything yet."

"So what does that mean, a fine, probation?"

Zinc shook his head, "In this state, for the amount they found, a three year minimum sentence."

Harvey sat back in his chair aghast, "You're joking!"

The lawyer shook his head sadly, "I'm sorry. Do you know *any* reason why someone should want to plant drugs in Graham's bag?"

Harvey gazed out of the window, struggling with his choices. Finally, he looked up and Zinc was startled to see moisture in the man's eyes. As a matter of due diligence he had checked him out and learned that this man was a hard-nosed entrepreneur who'd created a chain of stores from nothing and sold them for several million pounds sterling.

Harvey spoke, "I need your oath of secrecy and then I need you to understand this man. To do that I need to go back to the beginning."

Twice in the next hour and a half as Harvey struggled to recall the contents of Graham's journal Zinc held up a hand to call through and have his secretary cancel appointments. It was a fairy tale, surely, yet any doubts the lawyer had were quelled when he watched Harvey describe Graham's part in saving his grand daughter's life. Finally he listened to the story of Graham's encounter at the airport.

It was done, Harvey had broken his oath of secrecy and sat now in the sudden, profound silence of the office. Zinc looked down at his empty pad for several minutes before speaking, "Law school, or fifteen years practice didn't prepare me for this one. I'm out of balance here and for once I don't know what to say. Part of me feels like you're telling me to keep one of God's gifts out of jail and the other part can't believe it." He shook his head, "I need more." Harvey gave him three numbers and they agreed a strategy.

They would make the calls with the telephone set at 'hands free' to ensure that Harvey stayed within the guidelines they'd agreed. First was Sarah, "Hello Sarah, it's Harvey, Yeah I'm OK thanks, but listen, we'll have enough time to speak together later, in the meantime I'm going to pass you on to a chap named Richard Zinc. Please trust me now, Graham needs our help and that means telling him everything." He cut her short as she tried to ask something, "No Sarah, we can speak later but now, please, speak to Richard first.

Richard introduced himself and explained the situation. Harvey was sure the receptionist in the next office would have heard the horrified shriek and listened as the lawyer tried to talk her down. In time he was able to establish some sort of dialogue and began questioning her about Graham. What startled him was that she admitted to being the government appointed child protection officer involved in many of the episodes he'd listened to.

His next call followed the same pattern though without shrieks and tears. Doctor Williams was just angry. "You bloody colonials can't be trusted with anything. Get that man out of there and do humanity a favour. You cannot begin to imagine the goodness you are crucifying, and I use that phrase deliberately." Zinc patiently explained that he was acting *for* Graham rather against him and began his questioning. Once again he was confronted with a professional person who had witnessed Graham's gift at work. When he'd finished with questions Williams said, "So you're going to get Graham out of there?"

"That's my aim sir, yes."

"Then remember this, if you fail, and believe me I have never been more sincere in my life, many children will suffer terribly and some will die."

The third call was to a number Harvey selected deliberately, rather than Harding's mobile. The call was answered, "Leicestershire Police, may I help you?" Zinc was even more impressed and after the agreed preliminaries completed his questioning of Detective Sergeant Harding. His answers had been tense but succinct until the interrogation was over and it became Harding's turn. Zinc found himself answering questions at a level of criminal law he hadn't bargained for. Finally, Harding called through, "Harvey, you there?"

"Yes, I am and I'm out of my depth."

"Want me to come over."

"More than you could imagine, and bring a copy of the journal with you, we may need it. Give me half an hour then telephone Arnold at *Distant Worlds Travel*. He'll get you out here tomorrow, and Adam, thanks."

He sat back in his chair, thankful for the opportunity to do something positive.

Zinc was less certain, "Let's suppose all this is true, what does it mean?"

Harvey already thought through the options, all of them ridiculous so that still, only one remained, "The drug was planted."

Zinc nodded, "Which brings us to "Grant Haddon's brother."

"Do you know him?"

"I know of Grant Haddon, he owns a house on Captiva and is a very big cheese. He hails from North Carolina."

"At this stage I'm not sure, but supposing all this was true it's not something you can go to the Police with because one, you have no evidence and two, they're not going to believe a word of your story."

"So we need some intelligence on Haddon."

"That would be a start. For that you need a decent PI, Private Investigator." He opened a desk drawer and removed a card, this guy is as good as they get, we use him. Used to be a cop in Miami but got tired of the politics." He glanced at his watch, "I must go, Graham's arraignment is set for eleven thirty. The bond should be reasonable though. We'll have him back with you for a late lunch."

* * *

The courtroom was geometrically furnished in dark wood, all straight lines and precise angles and to Graham it looked foreboding.

He thought a few gentle curves here and there would be easier on the eye. Even the light grey carpet failed to lighten the atmosphere. The only comfort he had was in knowing that the man next to him would be fighting for him, a man he had only known for sixteen hours.

The prosecution began by reading out the charge; the possession of one hundred and fifty grammes of cocaine. Zinc was asked how the defendant pleaded. He replied, "Not Guilty" and asked for a bond to be set. The magistrate nodded and was about to speak when the prosecution cut in, "We must object to the release of this prisoner on bail your honour." He waved a piece of paper in the air, "This man is a foreign national here on vacation and I have a sworn affidavit from one of the officers in the detention wing who heard him state an unequivocal intention to leave the country as soon as he got out on bail. We would be left with two choices your honour, an expensive and drawn out call for extradition or to suffer the ignominy of having this States' hospitality abused and its laws flouted."

Zinc looked down at the desk with staring eyes and mouthed the word, "What!" He looked as though he'd been sucker-punched but recovered quickly and stood, "Your honour, that's nonsense, the police hold his passport."

The prosecution were ready, "Your honour we all know how easy it is to leave this country. We guard our borders against illegal entry far more diligently than we do for the travel in the opposite direction. A charter boat from the keys or a drive over the panhandle into Mexico would be a relatively straight forward affair. Furthermore, we are considering the addition of another charge.

Possession of unlabelled prescription drugs without supporting documentation. A category three Federal offence."

The magistrate turned to Zinc, "Does your client have a prescription for those drugs?"

Graham shook his head and whispered, "I brought enough to lasht me."

Zinc looked up, "No your honour, but we can have confirmation sent out from England."

The magistrate nodded, "Then please do so. Bail denied, the defendent will be held at the county jail until trial."

Zinc felt like a bystander, viewing a rigged game and there was nothing he could do. As an afterthought he remembered Harvey mentioning Nancy and tried to salvage something. Your honour, my client's partner will be returning to England very shortly. May he be granted immediate visiting rights please.

The magistrate gave it a moments' thought and shook his head, "Denied, she'll have to follow procedures like everyone else."

That meant waiting for Graham to post a request form from the jail for her to complete and return. If completed perfectly she would receive a written notice of the time and day allocated for her visit. If the form was completed incorrectly, in any way, the process would have to begin again.

Zinc collapsed back in his chair, shaking his head, "Something very strange has happened here today." He turned to Graham, "We need to speak, now."

They sat at the small table in the small room they'd been allocated. Graham began to shake as the implications of what had just happened sank in. "They're going to send me to jail."

Zinc tried to catch his client's eye, "Graham, listen to me, we have a lot of work to do." He grasped a trembling hand firmly, "Come on guy, focus now. Tell me about the group."

Mention of the group startled him, "Who told you about the group?"

"Harvey told me everything and I've also spoken to," he glanced down at the list he'd made before leaving the office, "Doctor Williams, Sarah Whiting and Detective Sergeant Harding. Now

I want to hear it from you." He listened then to a repeat of the chronicle Calder had related but this time it was different. Once again Graham's special character came through with a simple and utterly credible honesty. At the end he looked at Zinc and pleaded, "Pleashe, this is shomething we want to keep secret. No-one elshe must know."

Zinc was unnerved and later, in the car he would admit, at least to himself, that in spite of every logical reason for not doing so, he'd become a believer.

For the moment though, he still had work to do. "OK, let's go back to the airport. I need you to tell me exactly what happened, start to finish."

Half an hour later they were done, "OK, on a final note, there are a few things you can do to stay safe in jail. Keep to yourself, do *not* be persuaded to join a group or gang and avoid eye contact. Just keep your head down. If a guard starts to pick on you submit to everything, he's looking for some sport. Trust me, we'll do everything we can to get you out of there."

Harvey and Nancy were waiting for him when he got back to his office, expecting Graham to be with him. He took them into his office and tried to explain the impossible. Harvey waited for him to finish before saying, "You think someone has brought some sort of influence to bear."

Zinc wasn't prepared to go there just yet, "I really don't know what happened but it is certainly most irregular. They also plan to hit him with a charge of carrying drugs without a prescription, another federal offence."

Nancy had hardly slept; somehow she knew it wouldn't be as easy as they all thought. Poor old Graham had taken a tiger by the tail and this morning she'd become angry. No more than angry, she wanted to bite back at that slimy bastard with the white hair, with all the black hatred she could.

They discussed what would happen next and in particular how what arrangements were necessary for Nancy to visit. Zinc asked her to run through the defensive measures he'd need in Jail saying, "These are important things for him to remember Nancy.

It wouldn't do for me to let him go in there unprepared. Jail can be especially bad for people like Graham. It's a pity there's no one in there he could hook up with for protection."

Nancy asked, "Would there be any Hell's Angels in there."

The lawyer chuckled, "Almost certainly."

She searched the leather bag she had brought and removed a slip of paper, "May I use your telephone please?"

She had no idea where she was calling but in the club house at Daytona someone answered, "Yeah."

"Is Bob there please?"

"Who's askin'?"

"My name is Nancy, but I'm calling for Graham, she choked slightly as the words came to her, "He needs help." She gave him Harvey's mobile number and the line went dead.

Harvey stood and shook Zinc's hand, "We'll be going, thank you for what you're doing."

The lawyer shook his head, "Please don't thank me. I need to do some digging and a whole lot more before I earn that."

Ten minutes later Harvey's telephone rang and the caller didn't wait for a greeting, "Let me speak to Nancy." She took it and said, "Hello?" Bob replied, "What's happened."

She gave him a thumbnail summary but the main concern was how Graham would cope with the county Jail. "'Kay, I'll deal with that. Give me your address, I'll be there tonight and you can tell me the whole story."

She did, and the call was ended. Since they were staying with the Calder's she thought to forewarn Harvey.

The private investigator had been appointed but Harvey wanted Harding to deal with him since they would have so much more in common. He was due to land at Fort Myers at teatime the next day and an appointment had been made for the following morning. There was nothing more they could do and little more they could say, so the journey back to Captiva was a quiet one.

The kids had finished their meal and were watching television in the next room. Any conversation was short-lived and none of the adults had eaten much. Audrey had been brought up to speed and now they could only wait. She summed it up well when she said, "Sitting here, unable to do anything but wait makes minutes feel like hours."

At seven o clock they heard the roar of a motor cycle and Nancy said to Harvey, "I think you should open the door before he gets to it." He was too late. The door seemed to jump on its hinges when the crashing blow hit it.

Bob lowered his head as he entered the doorway and nodded at the Calder's before his gaze fell on Nancy and he nodded, "Ma'am."

He was ushered into the kitchen and everyone, children included, followed. Whilst he spoke to Nancy he was obviously addressing them all, "We need to talk in private."

Audrey said, "I'll er, take the kids into the lounge," and hurried them out of the room as Nancy asked, "Can Harvey stay please, he's one of the group."

Bob looked surprised, "One of Graham's group?"

Harvey nodded, "Yes."

A huge and scabby hand was extended, "Then I'm pleased to meet you."

They heard the television come on in the next room and Bob said, "First, I fixed things for Graham, he'll be looked after."

Nancy collapsed into a chair with a small cry. She looked up and said, "Oh thank you Bob."

"S'nuthin'. Now I want you to start at the get go an' tell me everythin'. Is there a beer around here anywhere?"

She told him everything, even describing twelve year old Chrissy and her mother. She guessed, correctly, that the drug had been planted when Haddon's brother and his minder took Graham off for a chat.

By the time she had finished a small forest of beer bottles stood on the table in front of the big man. He said, "I came here 'cos I owe Graham, but now you've given me an edge."

Harvey asked, "What's that?"

"I gotta a twelve year old daughter an' she's still a little kid at heart. I'd like it to stay that way for as long as possible an' I don't like to imagine what you're telling me."

He stood and said, "Now I know what's gotta happen but I ain't gonna say until you guys do. Meanwhile I gotta a lot to do. We'll stay in touch." He strode through the lounge nodding once at Audrey and let himself out of the front door. Moments later the roar of an engine signalled his departure.

Jimmy grinned at Audrey, "Graham calls him Grizzly."

Earlier that evening Graham's spirits fell to a new low when they shackled his ankles, wrists, and finally his arms, to a waist belt. He felt like an animal. People were shouting and he found himself in a line of other prisoners, in a wide corridor that ended at a barred door. More officers appeared and the door rolled open. The line was told to 'move it' and the prisoners shuffled awkwardly out of the door and down a short slope into a large garage. A bus waited for them and as soon as they had embarked the doors were slammed shut and locked. In the sudden silence that followed Graham looked around and realised they were in a totally enclosed wire mesh cage that separated them from the driver and a guard.

More shouts then, followed by a klaxon as a large door rolled back allowing the bus to exit onto a street. Small high windows permitted a restricted view of the night outside, though no one seemed interested, perhaps because they couldn't bear to glimpse the freedom they had lost.

Forty minutes later they slowed to a stop and the interior of the bus was lit up by the forest of floodlights around them. A large sign, set on posts declared their destination to be THE TREBI-TON CORRECTIONAL FACILITY. Ahead a large mesh gate began to roll back and they moved forward into the space beyond. There they waited for the for the first gate to close before two huge double doors at the front of the building in front of them rolled open. Once inside they waited once again for the barrier to close and then the shouting began again.

The process of institutionalising a prisoner began immediately. A lengthy lecture from a short, bespectacled man with a pronounced drawl reminded them all of their transgressions and his intention to administer the punishments prescribed by the decent, law-abiding section of the community. His drawl was so pronounced Graham failed to understand much of it though he did recall a promise to offer them a new path as well, if they chose to take the hand of Jesus.

Either way, he promised that with God's help he would show them a better way, though he closed on one thought. "Make no mistake gentleman, there *may* be a will to make good and there *will* be a rod. One may fail but the rod will always prevail. Heed that."

The next half an hour passed in a blur of noise, buffeting and humiliation until they were dressed in their bright orange outfits and ushered through more gates that were obviously controlled from elsewhere. A roar met them as they stepped into a huge dormitory. The door slammed shut behind them and Graham was startled to see the guards walking away.

The noise assaulted the senses and they were subjected to a barrage of abuse, physical and verbal, as they worked their way down the side of a sea of two-tier bunk beds. There were no guards in sight. Gradually the line ahead dwindled as new arrivals were recognised and taken by friends or fellow gang members, already in the population.

Graham had kept his head down throughout until his path was blocked by three dark-skinned men; he would later discover they were Mexicans. His heart pounded as he looked up and the man in the middle asked, "Who you with chicken?"

Graham had no idea what he should say and settled for "No one."

The man clapped his hands and snickered, "Oh baby, baby . . ."

He was suddenly propelled to one side and three men took over. Two were huge and whilst the third was smaller he looked extremely dangerous. One of the two giants spoke, "He's with us."

The displaced Mexican came back, "Hey man, yo jivin' me, he ain't no Angel."

The giant leaned into the Mexican's personal space, "Since when do I need to explain *anything* to you motherfucker!"

Seconds passed before the Mexican eased away and then strutted off, "Man you're welcome to that one, I can wait for fresher meat than that."

As Graham was ushered away the smaller man spoke, "Bob said Lucy sends her love."

Privately, the Angels were as startled as the Mexican had been but in this State if Big Bob asked you to do something you did it. They all had bits of advice to give Graham but it was soon time for lights out and Graham clambered onto the upper bunk allocated to him. The constant noise, clanging of doors and shouting should have kept him awake but his last contact with a mattress had been two days ago; two of the most harrowing days of his life. He was utterly exhausted and fell asleep immediately.

It was so early, but then the drinking had started earlier than usual as had the tears and recriminations. They were sent to bed just as they expected. There was no work again and they'd watched the depression return. The sky was still fairly light yet the television had gone quiet and one by one the light switches clicked off like a sickening countdown. The same cramping fear returned as the door at the bottom of the stairs creaked. Please Daddy, go to bed, please. The slow stumbling climb up the stairs and paused next to his bedroom door, please, please, let me hear the door open. Another little piece of childhood died as the floorboard on the landing creaked. The handle squeaked and he sensed his presence before his cloying body odour swept over him.

As the weight eases carefully on to the bed he knows he must act, must fight. He has leapt up from the prone position and sits with his legs beneath him and his back pressed tightly against the headboard. No Dad, please. Go to bed and sleep. Please dad, NO! The back handed blow to his face sends his head crashing into the headboard. The shock and pain are overwhelming. This time it is much worse. There is much more force, he feels smothered by a great weight and then awful pain. Time becomes stretched and surreal but eventually there is a realization that the soiling corruption has ended and he is alone again, except for the sleeping form in the bed on the other side of the room. The one that pretends to be asleep each time rather than bear witness and console him. How he has grown to hate her, his older sister.

Things blur, though he knows he's in bed. There is comfort now, yet there is still someone beside him; gradually the scene draws into focus and . . .

* * *

Graham's scream woke the surrounding sleepers who called back with a range of threats. The Angel beneath him pushed at his mattress and said, "Don't worry, you'll get used to it."

Graham rolled onto his other side, trembling. The scene replayed in his mind over and over again.

The bedroom, linen and pillows had all come into focus and the face on the next pillow, sleeping soundly, was his.

That night his heart plumbed new depths as he realized whose memories he'd been sharing all these months. He looked up at the ceiling at murmured, "Dear God Nancy, why didn't you tell me?"

Chapter 22

Harding travelled fairly lightly for the simple reason he didn't actually own that many clothes, let alone those suitable for a sub-tropical climate. The last time even one knee had seen sunlight had been when a crack dealer had set a Doberman on him and the damned thing had taken half his trouser leg off.

Harvey watched from the arrivals lounge as the detective waited for his case and in spite of the circumstances couldn't help grinning. Both the man and his clothes looked dishevelled. When he drew near Harding he raised a hand, "I know, but whatever you put me in I'll still look like a sack of potatoes."

This time Calder burst out laughing and as they shook hands he drew the man forward and hugged him, "Adam, I am so glad to see you. We're in the shit."

It was almost dark when they climbed into the van and Harvey cranked the air conditioning up as he saw his friend suffering the effects of such high humidity. Within moments the chilled air swept over them and Harding's face creased in a grin, "Can I sleep in here?"

Harvey briefed him on the hour-long journey from the airport though the last ten minutes were spent in quiet thought. As they entered the house Jimmy called out "Hello Uncle Adam," and Nancy ran forward and hugged him, "Thank you, thank you so much."

Harvey handed him a beer and Audrey returned to her wine and the salad she was preparing to accompany the marinated chicken.

Over dinner they spoke of the crisis on a couple of occasions but the time was better spent listening to Jimmy describe his adventures. The time to discuss Graham would be after the children had gone to bed.

Before long the two women took the children off to bed and Harding's eyes drooped. Calder realised that he must have been up for at least seventeen hours, given the time zones and said, "Adam, why don't you go to bed, we'll talk about things tomorrow. The detective stirred and shook himself back to life, "No, I'd rather get started tonight. I'll be fine. I'll go and get my notepad."

Very soon, the grown-ups gathered around the table and another meeting of *the group* was convened.

Harvey began with a cautionary note for Nancy, "Some of the things we will discuss may be a bit upsetting you know. If it begins to get too much tell us."

Nancy smiled gratefully, "Right now I see nothing but bad news, the very worst of everything, but just having you all here means a lot." She sat upright and added, "We're not going to achieve anything if we start ducking issues."

Audrey turned to Harding, "Adam, what's your take on this, as a police officer?"

Harding said, "Obviously I am reasonably expert at British law rather than American, but this is still the western world and basic rules of society are the same, though they are enforced and punished very differently, I must admit. That said, we have to take the court's view, which is based solely on evidence. On that basis Graham *will* be convicted. His lawyer can only hope to pick holes in the Police procedures."

Harvey nodded, "That's exactly what Richard Zinc said." He was about to say something else when the telephone rang.

A little while later he rushed into the room, "Audrey love, would you boot the laptop up please?" While they waited he explained, "Richard was doing a little research at home and googled Grant Haddon's name. What he came up with certainly provides us with a motive."

They waited until Audrey nodded, "Go ahead"

Harvey referred to his notes and read out the address of a local television news channel in Raleigh, North Carolina. She turned the screen towards then as a page the station's main page appeared. There on the list of headlines sat 'Governor appoints Grant Haddon as replacement senator'. She double clicked on the heading and a news clip began. It showed the Governor on the lawn of his residence shaking hands with the newly appointed senator and Nancy cried out, "That's him! That's the bastard who tricked Graham!"

As she spoke the telephone rang again. It was Zinc again but this time he sounded subdued. Harvey listened as he explained, "His people have produced a no doubt sanitised bio on the web, but here's the rub, he was an only child. So the guy at the airport who claimed to be the girl's uncle was in fact her father; uncles are brothers."

Harvey thought for while before saying, "So it's about as sinister as we might have feared?"

"I'm afraid so. We'll speak tomorrow."

"OK, and thanks for calling."

They sat in stunned silence as the enormity of Haddon's crime sank in and that he was capable of doing it.

Harding looked around the table, tapping his pen on the writing pad, "First of all, because of our special knowledge, we know that there is truth to this story about Haddon's sexual abuse of his daughter, and now we have a very real motive for wanting it kept secret. A normal citizen would have brazened it out, after all who would believe a diffident psychic looking like Graham? But a politician couldn't afford to risk it. The mere suggestion of incest would be enough for the bloggers to have a field day and ultimately public interest might drag the truth into the open. Finally, whilst we cannot be certain, I am happy to *assume* that Graham doesn't snort cocaine."

Nancy interrupted, "He wouldn't know what to do with the stuff and anyway, do you know what we have to live on each month?"

He nodded, "Good point. So where do we go from here?"

Harvey said, "Well it's no good going to the Police with what we have, as you say much of it wouldn't be believed let alone admissible. And there's another thing, if Haddon is capable of doing this he could be dangerous."

Harding nodded his agreement, "He's certainly going to be slippery *and* very well resourced. I think we need to look at two scenarios. The worst one would be if Graham is convicted. Result; he's going to serve a two plus year jail term and be sent back to the UK in disgrace.

The best one is for Haddon to be found out and convicted. But he won't go down without a fight and over here, with the best lawyers money can buy, that could take a long time. Even then the incest charge wouldn't directly help Graham who needs Haddon or his goon to admit to planting the cocaine. I'm not saying give up but I think we should prepare for the worst."

Nancy spoke, "So what you *are* saying is that whatever happens Graham is going to be imprisoned?"

He nodded, "I'm so sorry Nancy, unless we can come up with something it looks that way."

Harvey said, "But we're not going to give in surely."

Harding shook his head, "No, I have a couple of threads I want to follow and this private detective can help with those. Remember though, I have no authority here."

Nancy felt her anger rising again; the hatred she felt for Haddon defied measure. "OK, I can't thank you enough and I know you'll all do everything you can." She picked up Harvey's telephone and stood, "Now I have to do all *I* can too."

She left the house and dialled the number Bob had given her. He answered on the second ring, "What?"

She took a deep breath, "I'm ready to say it."

Bob interrupted her firmly, "No! Not here on this line you're not. I'll see you tomorrow night." The line went dead yet for the first time in this whole mess Nancy felt a germ of confidence.

* * *

The following morning Harvey persuaded Harding to join him in a visit to *JC Penney's* where they were able to buy some appropriate clothing for the climate. In truth, the portly detective was delighted to find trousers and shirts designated as a 'comfort fit' which were just that.

Suitably attired, *sans* labels he went with Harvey to see the private detective. The office was above a hair salon and the door to the street bore a sign that said,

JOHN MITCHELL
PRIVATE INVESTIGATOR

Of course, they'd prepared themselves for an overweight, cynical, world weary and unmannerly slob of the Hollywood genre. Instead, they were greeted by a slim and quietly-spoken fifty something year old, with cropped grey hair and understated casual dress.

Beyond a small outer office where a middle-aged lady sat typing on a computer lay his office; quite large and like the man, comfortably furnished in an understated way.

Introductions were made and coffees organised via Lynn before they got down to business. Harvey had already agreed the terms but was asked to sign a client agreement. That done John wasted no time with niceties, "I've spoken to Richard Zinc several times and I trust him. I say that because he telephoned this morning to say I should accept what you are going to tell me no matter how fanciful it sounds. Apparently he believes it." He rolled his hands palm upward and added, "Go ahead."

Harvey and Adam glanced at each other and began. It took a long time and when they finally finished Harding held up a sheaf of papers, "This is a copy of Graham's own journal," and passed it over. More coffee was ordered and John read several random episodes in silence." Finally, he dropped the sheaf on his desk and asked, "Can any of that be verified?"

Harding nodded, "Since many of those cases ended up involving either the Police or Social Services they are a matter of official record but so far we have managed to keep Graham's name out of things. It's not as difficult as it may seem, after all, the truth is pretty unbelievable."

John pursed his lips, "Yes, Richard said it would be." He gestured towards the papers, "May I take a copy of that?"

Harvey hesitated and looked to Adam who nodded. "It is a secret we need to protect."

"I understand that, and my clients' confidentiality is too, I assure you." He leaned forward and asked, "So, where do we go from here?"

Adam replied, "The way I see it, we have two aims. First of all we have to establish that the drugs were planted. Secondly, it would be nice to see this man answer to charges of incest though make no mistake our first aim takes priority."

"And you say the mother was at the airport?"

"Yes, but with a large clear drink at breakfast time. My guess would be Vodka."

"So those two, mother and daughter are the weak links."

"That's exactly what I thought."

Mitchell nodded, "The abortion clinic would be a key find but it's my guess Haddon would have had it done in another country and probably under an alias. I'm going to have to go up to their neck of the woods to gather intel; I still have contacts. It's best I go up alone, two of us would look suspicious though I take it you want me to report back to you before taking any action?"

"Yes please. I sense that when the time comes to make contact my being British might help."

"I'll start tomorrow, though I'll copy the journal now if I may, and take it with me."

On the drive home Harvey was buoyed by the thought of something positive being done but Harding was less sure, "We have a long way to go yet chum and very little to work on." Nancy shared that view and spent most of the afternoon walking along the beach, alone with her thoughts. Audrey kept the children amused as much as she could but even they fell prey to the atmosphere in the house. Jimmy had wet his bed the previous night; the first time for months.

Dinner that night was a subdued affair and by ten o clock everyone started preparing for bed. This time Harvey's response was far more timely when the motor cycle roared down the drive and he made it to the door before Bob did. The Angel didn't acknowledge Harvey and strode straight through to the kitchen. Audrey, Adam and Nancy were there and Bob repeated the sentence he'd used in his last visit, "We need to talk in private."

The others made an obedient exit while Nancy pulled a beer from the fridge and they both sat at the table, opposite each other.

"'Kay, what is it you want to say?"

"I think jail could kill Graham, in fact something tells me it definitely would." She took a deep breath, barely able to believe she was going to say it. "Could you get him out, out of jail that is *and* out of the country. We've got a house that we could sell to pay for it, if that would be enough."

"You figured it quicker than I thought you would. They could give him three years but by the time they'd finished messing with him it could be another fifteen. This is the only way. Do you have any small photographs of him?"

"Yes." She dug into the travel bag and extracted the three spare ones from the photo booth they had used for his passport application. He took one and gave the other two back to her, "You'll need those. Now go get some paper there's a bunch of things you need to do."

Twenty minutes later he finished and stood to leave, "Don't go selling your house, this is settling a debt."

He strode back through the lounge and out of the front door without acknowledging any of the adults sitting there and who waited until the roar of the Harley engine faded before joining Nancy in the kitchen. They sat down and waited expectantly.

Nancy looked at them all apologetically, he wouldn't tell me anything except that Graham is being looked after and I've got to go back to England immediately. He's given me a list of jobs to do, but he said it could be dangerous for me stay here."

Harvey said, "I think that's a sound idea and you should go too Audrey."

"No, let's get Nancy and Jimmy back first, I can go back with Esther on Saturday with the original tickets, and that's another thing, you need to organise accommodation for Saturday onwards."

They all saw the sense in that. The last minute tickets for two would be expensive enough.

Harding said, "Before you go can we find a quiet corner. I need you to tell me every detail Graham told you about the airport 'hit'.

She waited for an hour before making the call from the telephone in her room. "Sarah answered with a cautious, "Hello?" It was five am in the UK. "It's Nancy."

Sarah sat bolt upright in bed, "Oh Nancy, I've been worried sick, what's happening?"

Nancy brought her up to date and found herself trying to console her friend. Soon though, she moved onto the reason for her call, swearing her to secrecy, for Graham's sake and in particular, that none of the group should know. Sarah wrote down an address and promised to see to things that morning. They shared a few tears then, before Nancy closed the call.

Chapter 23

At twelve noon the next day Harvey and Audrey hugged them tightly before watching Nancy and Jimmy walk through security. All being well, they would be arriving at Birmingham the next morning where a car would be waiting to take them back to Leicester.

That afternoon they arranged for an open rental of a holiday cottage at Fort Myers Beach from the following Saturday. By moving back on to the mainland they would save over an hour every time they visited either Richard or John.

It was simply a waiting game then. Time did pass a little easier when the men took a cool box of beers down to the dock and fished but as dusk fell the mosquitoes hit them, no matter how much repellent they used. In the evenings none of them wanted to play cards and there was little else to discuss so they ended up like Zombies in front of the television.

Thursday was no better.

Part of Friday was spent packing but by tea time a general lethargy returned, nudged occasionally by Esther, demanding attention. At five o clock the telephone rang. It was John Mitchell, just back and willing to see them within the hour.

His secretary had gone home and when they knocked he ran down to let them in. Once again, he didn't waste time on niceties.

"Mr Haddon is a very wealthy man as we know. It's difficult to pin down how wealthy but certainly topping two billion, it could be more, a lot more. He owns a number of homes, one here at Captiva, but his main residence is a nine million dollar mansion at Chapel Hill, around thirty miles northwest of Raleigh. You were right, Mrs Haddon is a lush, currently being served and serviced by the butler I understand.

She used to be a model, quite famous by all accounts, until a caesarean section put paid to things. Just the one child, Christine, though known as Chrissy now aged 12 years and attending the Sherwood Academy. Mom doesn't venture far but she does go to the Southpoint Shopping Mall, just south of Durham once a week to meet up with an old friend for lunch at an Italian restaurant. Same one each time I understand and always on a Wednesday. I spoke with one of the waiters who reckoned that both women didn't think much of Mr Haddon. They have a television on behind the counter at lunchtimes and they were giving him the finger when his appointment as senator was featured on the news.

The butler drives her, presumably because she's never sober enough to do it herself. From what I could see and learn she hardly leaves the house otherwise. I don't know whether it's normal practice but he seemed to stay in the car the whole time she was in the mall.

Same goes for Chrissy. The same guy drives her to and from school and she seems to spend the rest of her time at home.

'Home' is run by three more staff, a cook, housekeeper and a gardener plus a part-time cleaner who works four mornings a week.

There's more but that's the meat of it. I'll let you have a written report in a day or so."

Harvey thanked him and said they would collect the report rather than have it posted.

Harding had listened to the report with his eyes closed. He always found it helpful to exclude as many distractions as possible when he was trying to absorb information. He asked, "Is there any chance finding out the friend's name, the one she does lunch with?"

"Ah yes, it's here, the table is always booked in her name." He flicked through his notes and read it out, "A Mrs Cindy Laver."

"Could you find an address for her?"

"Sure, that shouldn't be a problem."

"Finally, for now, would you be able to accompany me up there next Tuesday for two or three days please?"

John quickly checked his screen diary and took a few moments to square away the logistics before saying, "Yes I can do that. Do you want me to book the flights?"

"That would be good thanks."

He wrote down Harding's full name and date of birth before raising an item of his own. "That journal makes for remarkable reading and I still don't know where I stand on it. But by God, if it is true you need to get him back to England as soon as you can. Secrets like that don't last long over here."

On the way back to the house Harvey asked, "Do you have a plan then."

Adam shook his head slowly, "No, just the beginnings of one but I'm better off nibbling around an idea on my own. Sorry, just my way." What he didn't want to tell Harvey, who had so far stumped up a significant sum of money, was that he had very little to work with and even that would be a punt.

The following morning they all had to pack and load the van before heading for the airport. There, both Audrey and Esther gave tearful farewells and while Harvey was giving Esther a cuddle Audrey moved across and hugged Adam, whispering in his ear, "Take care of him for me."

The drive back was in silence but as soon as they reached the house Harding telephoned the station in Leicester and spoke to Patricia Geary. They exchanged a few pleasantries and he learned that his mysterious departure to distant shores had attracted all sorts of speculation. Soon though, he got back to business by giving her a list of things he needed scanning and emailing to John Mitchell. He gave her the address but refused to provide any further information other than a promise to get back to Leicester soon.

Geary put the receiver back in its cradle and gazed ahead thoughtfully. The *Mercury* had been following the case of a local man, caught and in jail awaiting trial for possession of cocaine. Graham Parsons, that name again, but lo and behold DS Harding ups and flies to Florida like a bat out of hell. It was the secrecy that intrigued her and she looked forward to seeing him back. If he didn't *give* this time she'd find out for herself.

On Tuesday morning Harvey drove Adam to the airport where John Mitchell was waiting. They arrived at the time he'd given but the relaxed American practice of treating air travel like a bus service meant that they had to hurry through procedures. Harding didn't particularly like flying and mitigated his anxiety by making sure he got to the airport in ample time. Their race to reach the gate on time alarmed him in every sense.

Once airborne Mitchell pulled a clip of A4 sheets from his case and passed them over. On the top was a covering header from Pat Geary of the Leicestershire Constabulary. Mitchell said, I read them, and identified each one in the journal; interesting.

By chance and the direction of air traffic control they were almost directly overhead of the Trebiton Correctional Facility.

Someone had told Graham that there were six million people under 'Correctional Supervision' in the US and he could see for himself that more than half were black. The different gangs had been pointed out to him, with their tell-tale tattoos and markings.

He sat on his bunk and scanned the massive space holding over twelve hundred people, chequered with precisely positioned bunks that made the base of the hall look like a giant punch card of the sort they used to use with computers. There were no guards in the hall; they strolled around the balconies in crisply laundered uniforms and from certain positions it was possible to see the watch-towers in the distance, manned by gunmen. Somehow he could no longer think of them as just prison officers. The system was too brutal for euphemisms.

The routines were rigid and soon learned, though Graham realised how fortunate he was to be under the 'Angel's wings. He smiled at the irony of that thought since they had been proud to point out that the authorities officially designated them as 'organised crime'. He didn't try to rationalise right from wrong or how he should feel about it, he simply knew that without the protection of such a hardened element of the prison population anything might have happened, and that *meant* anything.

There was a terrible anxiety in the place, where an untimely glance might be construed as 'dissing' someone,- showing disrespect. That would earn the certainty of a knife wound, soon, and the victim would know that and live in fear of it.

Twice in the dead of night he had heard struggling and the sound of blows, marking the passage of a group to the toilets. The first time, a young man by the sound of his pleas to be left alone was the victim and soon his muffled cries of pain marked the beginning of his multiple rape just as half an hour later his sobbing marked the end of it.

Another night, there was a sudden and palpable tension in the air as a shadow slipped into the toilets behind another inmate. There was a struggle with a noise that sounded like wet slaps. Soon, a shadow re-appeared and was lost in the mass of beds. Moments later another figure staggered out of the toilets, grunting in pain. It was difficult to tell in the half light exactly what had happened but the glistening wetness pouring from the dark lines that criss-crossed his torso were eloquent enough.

Here, men were brutalised to such an extent that no-one could afford to relax or show weakness. It was a vicious and fearful world where penalties were paid in a terrible currency that included life itself.

Even so, the incidents were intermittent. Graham acknowledged that much and wondered how much the system would tolerate before calling it something out of the ordinary. A riot perhaps.

The worst thing by far was time. Inmates watched the agonisingly slow passage of each minute in a state of boredom that surpassed anything he had known.

Some people spoke of work programmes outside of the prison but places were hard to get and often expensive. He also learned that all manner of things counted as currency from drugs to chocolate and including cigarettes, sexual favours, hooch and even deodorant. Anything someone might have a need for had a tradeable value.

Graham had noticed an elderly black inmate with a head of light grey curly hair and doleful yet kindly looking eyes. The man face was remarkably wrinkle-free except for the deep creases that marked the lower edge of the bags under his eyes. He spent most of the daylight hours sweeping the passage that bordered the area of bunks with a large broom and humming to himself. Surreptitious glances developed into polite nods which in time were accompanied by smiles until one day Graham said, "Hello." He received a bonus nod and smile on that pass but next time, when Graham sat dozing, a gravelly voice said, "Howdy."

Graham came to quickly, prepared to make a run for it, but he found himself facing the sweeper who nodded once more and said, "Mah name is Mule, 'least that's what they call me here an' that's been long enough fer nuthin' else to matter."

Graham responded, "Graham, I'm English. I haven't been here long." They shook hands and Mule chuckled, "Yeah, I seen you arrive. That was somethin', seeing those Mex's get pushed to one side. You did well to find company so quick. There's three mo' o' you English folk in here only one didn't have it so good las' year. Hear tell he lost a kidney."

With a mental shudder Graham sought to change the subject, "How long have you been here?"

Mule turned his mouth down and gave a small shake of the head, "I don't count anymo'. Life is life. One years' no different to anotha."

"There seems to be a lot of black people in here, more than half."

"Weeell, some things never will change."

"How do you mean?"

"Son, some 'olgist of some sort came here a couple a years ago an' I was one o' the ones he spoke to. He tol' me that the number of blacks in the correctional system now is more than there was slaves back in the old days. See, the way I see it, the system couldn't work if ev'ryone had a nice car an' a big house. There's always gotta be some folk at the bottom an' when they get too big for their boots an' want more there ain't any way of gettin' it, 'leastwise not by gettin' fancy jobs, 'cos there ain't none left. So they get that stuff in other ways, then get slung in here."

Again Graham nodded and said, "Well they sheem to have given you a full time job."

Mule grinned and nudged Graham conspiratorily, "Hell, no one gave me this job, but as long as I push this thing folks leave me alone. The prisoners see I'm doin' some good an' the warders figure one o' them gave me the job an' let me get on with it."

From then on Mule would stop by on one of his passes each day and spend a few minutes chatting. Eventually from scraps he let slip Graham guessed that Mule had been in prison for over thirty years. He couldn't bring himself to ask how many years the old man had been sweeping the dormitory at Trebiton, or wonder how many there were left to do before Mother Nature granted him his freedom.

During one of their chats Graham mentioned how upsetting it was to see men chained up like animals, or even slaves and particularly in such a developed society.

Mule grinned, "Son, you just showing off your naivety again, ain't yer? You know what our *Amendments* are, in this *deeveloped* society?"

"You mean like the firsht amendment and shtuff?"

"Yeah, an' stuff. Well, when you get chance read the thirteenth my man, it'll explain a lot."

"Like what."

"Ha, that's fer you to find out."

That morning his thoughts wandered from one thing to another and a rustling of paper from the next bunk reminded him of the folded document that was thrust in front of him to sign earlier that day. When he asked what it was he was told to mind his own business. In that place it was sound advice but he did wonder what he had signed and would have been startled to learn that it was the form Sarah had couriered out to an address in Daytona, requesting a replacement for a lost passport.

* * *

Thousands of feet overhead Harding explained what he planned to do and who he wanted to see. Chrissy was out of the question, since she was either at school, chauffeured by a goon or in the house. In any event, he couldn't see how he could approach a twelve year old girl to discuss her sexual abuse.

"That leaves Mrs Haddon and the only opportunity open to us, or me, seems to be during her regular luncheon date. The trouble is

I'll have a lot of ground to cover in a short space of time, not least of all the time it might take to simply introduce myself and gain her trust, let alone make my pitch. She's more likely going to call the management and have me thrown out of the restaurant. That's where her friend comes in. If we can persuade her to be an ally and let me accompany her to lunch I'll have an introduction and have a head start."

Mitchell asked, "And how do you plan to persuade her?"

"There's only one way, I'm going to have to tell the whole story."

"You know, for something that is so secret, it sure is getting around."

Harding grimaced, "I know and don't think I'm not worried, but my only priority right now is to get Graham out of that place. After that, let's hope the Atlantic is enough of a buffer."

Two hours later they checked into the Sandalwood Inn, on the 501 highway, on the northern edge of Chapel Hill. It was set out in the classic motel style with two storeys of rooms in two wings facing in onto the car parking area. They were four rooms apart and agreed to freshen up and have lunch. Mitchell had telephoned Cindy Laver the previous day and made an appointment for three that afternoon, identifying himself but saying only that he needed to ask her a few questions about a mutual friend.

They stopped at a diner and Harding took the opportunity to order a hot dog and fries with a beer. Mitchell ordered a club sandwich *without* fries and with a diet coke. When the food arrived Harding tucked in with every relish in the English dictionary. Sweet, sour, piquant and of course delight.

The private detective watched in amusement, "I guess you don't get to chase many crooks on foot these days."

Harding wore a hurt look, "You people make the best junk food in the world and I'm just taking this opportunity to indulge in some. Soon, I'll be heading back to the land of gruel and hardship."

"Well do me a favour when you get back and have a cholesterol check."

"You're really set on ruining this gastronomic adventure aren't you?"

Mitchell held his hands up in surrender, "Sorry. That was wrong of me," adding as an afterthought, "It's your body after all."

It took a little over half an hour to drive over to Durham and find the address, in a pleasant part of suburbia. Large lawns with colourful borders and single storey houses set back from the road. By the time they reached the small Toyota parked in the drive the white 'scottie' that lay on the windowsill sprang into action, barking furiously and bouncing up and down on its front legs. Once they reached the door it sprang into the room and reached the front door at the same time as his mistress.

She'd been expecting them but John offered his ID for inspection and tried to make himself heard over the barking. Cindy stooped and picked the dog up, clamping a hand over his snout and stepping back, "Please, come in." As soon as the door was closed she put the dog back on the floor and his defence of the place changed to an ingratiating quest for fuss.

Mitchell started, "I was saying that this is Adam Harding, a British visitor I'm working with."

"Sure, hi." They all shook hands and she asked, "You said you wanted to speak to me about a friend, oh I'm sorry, let's go through and sit down."

They made themselves comfortable in the lounge and Cindy waited expectantly.

Mitchell said, "Mrs Laver, how long have you known Mrs Haddon?"

"April, oh I guess nine or ten years, why, is she in some sort of trouble."

"No, at least in that sense but we need your help in a very delicate matter and Mr Harding would like to explain things to you." He nodded to Harding who began, "Do you have any children Mrs Laver?"

"Yes, three."

He nodded, "Then this is going to be a little easier." He withdrew the copy of Graham's journal and clip of newspaper cuttings from Mitchell's case and began, "I have a friend who has a remarkable gift."

An hour later Cindy stared at the papers in front of her with the correlating newspaper reports, "This is scary stuff, and you're sure it's all true?"

Harding nodded, "Every word and if it was up to date it would include a case study that sits here in Chapel Hill. So far as Graham is concerned it started at Fort Myers airport and this sets out everything we know at the moment." He passed another two sheets of paper to her that contained a summary of all that he'd learned.

She read it in silence save for a small gasp when she covered her mouth with a hand to try and hide her disgust as she learned of Chrissy's nightmare. Things began to make sense.

During the school holidays she loved to accompany her mother to their lunches and have a girly afternoon in the mall. She'd been such a bubbly sort of character and looked certain to be as beautiful as her mother had been. Then, a little less than a year ago she had stopped coming and when Cindy saw Chrissy at their house, a few months ago, she'd been shocked by the unkempt, grunge look of the girl. Cindy remembered saying to her husband that her sparkle had gone. These men had told her something that sounded more like a fairy tale yet it made sense out of the terrible change there had been in the child.

She glanced down at the journal, all of it written in the same hand and including many more stories than there were clippings, though she had checked and the chronology was correct with the stories covered by the newspaper embedded in the whole. It looked so authentic and so frightful.

There was something they didn't know which explained her hatred of Grant Haddon and leant a dreadful credence to this story. Once, April had gotten too drunk and almost became hysterical as she told the story of the Taiwanese businessman. The next day, she'd telephoned Cindy in a fearful panic, making her swear never to tell the story, to anyone. Today she wasn't going to break that oath but these guys had come to ask for help.

She looked up, decisively, "What is it you want gentlemen?"

* * *

"Hey kiddo, sorry I'm late." Harding stayed back and allowed the two friends to exchange greetings but April Haddon had seen their approach and quickly asked, "Who is this?"

"Oh this is Adam, he's visiting from England, I hope you don't mind but I thought you'd like to meet and I can treat you both to lunch."

They exchanged smiles and handshakes, each discreetly assessing the other. She was still beautiful though he could see that now the effects of age and alcohol were being hidden by expensive cosmetics, just as her clothes were a testament to wealth.

There was a lot of ground to cover and Harding couldn't see how an opportunity would crop up in the course of normal conversation so he began immediately, "Mrs Haddon, I need you to listen to me for just a few minutes and when I've finished, if you wish it, I'll leave immediately."

April looked at Cindy and asked, "What is this?"

Cindy reached across the table and held her friend's hand, "Listen to what he has to say hon', please, I beg you."

April removed her hand and placed it on her lap. "This feels like some sort of trap."

Harding said, "Then I'm very sorry Mrs Haddon, but this is a very private matter and I couldn't think of any other way of meeting you, discreetly."

April looked at one and then the other, considering her options. Finally she addressed Harding, "Get it over with, and then on principle, I would like you to leave."

He nodded, "Then I'll get on with it. I have a friend who has a remarkable gift. He can sense, simply from a touch, when a child is suffering abuse. I can't understand it but I can tell you he's saved kids from appalling abuse, with injuries you wouldn't believe a civilised person could inflict. I've actually witnessed it several times. As a Police Detective I've arrested some of the abusive adults concerned.

His name is Graham and last week his contact with a twelve year old girl made him aware of repeated sexual abuse by her father. He even made her pregnant and she suffered an abortion. Graham also sensed some of the abuse was filmed." He glanced at both women, "I know how you two would feel about being *forced* into making a sex film with a stranger, but please imagine what it must be like for a twelve year old girl to be forced into doing that with her own father. The twelve year old girl was Chrissy and because Graham threatened to make it public someone planted cocaine in his bag and he is in jail."

April looked angry and began to speak but he held up a hand and said, "Please! Just ten seconds more. I believe that unless we find proof of what your husband has been doing to Chrissy, Graham will die in there instead of saving countless more kids from misery, *and* your daughter will continue to live her nightmare, until she runs away or commits suicide." He allowed a tiny pause and closed with, "If he's allowed to continue now, it's with your blessing."

April glared at him but kept her voice low, "Get out now and take your filthy accusations with you."

Hardin nodded sadly, and placed a note bearing his hotel and room number on the centre of the table, "I'll stay until Thursday, if you do accept the truth and know anything please contact me. I'll do the rest." He stood and as he turned to leave added, "And please don't blame your friend for this, she really thinks a great deal of you."

As he walked out of the restaurant John Mitchell dropped some notes onto his table and followed. He had been posted as back-up in case the driver had appeared.

A few minutes later, in the car, Mitchell asked, "How did it go? She looked good and mad at the end of it."

Harding sighed, "I made a balls of it, though I didn't have many options. She gave me a few minutes to make my pitch and any hope I'd had for continued dialogue disappeared when she told me to get out. I left her a note with my hotel number and told her I'd wait until tomorrow night."

Mitchell asked, "Want me to stay?"

"I think so, though I'm also aware that Harvey is paying for all this. But if things do develop I'd like someone else with me. Look what's happened to Graham."

They called at a *Wallmart* for soft drinks, nibbles and a book each before going back to their rooms to wait.

* * *

Back in Leicester Sarah sat at the kitchen table opposite Nancy, seeing the drawn features and loss of weight. The press had hounded her for a couple of days but a few ounces of cocaine wasn't enough news to waste much effort on. Thankfully, they'd lost interest.

Paradoxically, that made Nancy feel even more alone. Now, just her tiny group of friends cared about Graham. They waited for news and prayed that it would be good. Time was becoming an enemy of them all.

Today had a particular poignancy in that it was Jimmy's seventh birthday. He was due home from school and Sarah had brought a present. A pile of cards lay on the table waiting for him and a candle-laden cake lay in the fridge. He'd already unpacked the digital camera Nancy had bought and had spent the day waiting to get home and try it. Whatever happened, they had to keep up appearances for his sake, but in those quiet times, like the afternoons it was tough.

* * *

April Haddon couldn't find the oblivion she sought. For some reason the vodka wouldn't take her there tonight. Damned fat Brit, what good was he trying to achieve, sticking his nose into their privacy. God what was happening, she shouldn't have been thinking *anything* much by now. She heard a small movement upstairs. Chrissy moving about. She only stayed in her room when Grant was at home.

She smothered the thought quickly but others came. The smell of other women, his open disdain these days and his employment of a servant to satisfy her when she had an itch. Aiden had admitted as much the last time he performed the act. A crawling disgust swept over her.

But not Chrissy, even he couldn't do that, surely. The imagery of an abortion flickered through her mind and she reached for the bottle, desperate now for the protection it would give her. It was empty and Aiden was in his quarters. Her lip curled back in shame and anger as she resolved not to call him. She would find another bottle herself.

Of course, Haddon kept a few bottles in his study. She struggled clumsily to her feet and made her way there.

It was always his room and his alone. His father's furniture, his books, his smells. She opened the drinks cabinet and in the absence of any vodka selected a bottle of his favourite and very expensive brandy. She held the bottle up and said, "Hurt, you bastard."

As she turned to leave she looked at the desk and decided on a short detour towards the leather bound chair behind it. After collapsing into the chair she began opening drawers. The three on the left held nothing but paperwork and the wide centre drawer was locked but she spent a long time staring into the top right-hand drawer, at the pair of white panties. She was still slim, but she wouldn't have gotten into them. They belonged to a child.

Later, she would have difficulty in remembering the next half an hour but an observer would have seen her unsteady trek down to the garage where tools were neatly hung on the wall or placed in racks. They would have watched as she made her way back to the study with a crowbar and clumsily gouge the front of the drawer as she tried to gain purchase.

Eventually she did, and little by little she splintered the wood surrounding the lock away. She sat down again and rifled through the contents of the drawer, there were surprisingly few, some papers, a couple of golfing medals and a compact disk. But no pictures. She tried to concentrate and finally, saw the disk in that context. The computer lay to one side and she gazed vacantly at the screen as it came to life and asked for a password. She hadn't used a computer for a long time but typed Chrissy in the box and was slightly surprised to see that it still worked.

She remembered what happened next, in fact she would never forget it. After the disk had loaded the screen flickered and she watched Haddon walk quickly away from the camera and through the door

There was a startled scream and she heard Haddon say "Leave it, Mary will clean it up, I need a word."

He extended an arm to direct someone into the room and who said something the microphone didn't catch.

He spoke again, forcibly, "No, it's OK, I said leave it. Just step in for a moment please."

As the figure appeared April heart sank. This time she was close enough to be recorded, "But Daddy, I'm hungry, please, can I eat my sandwich. Please."

April began to share the child's dread as she listened to the next plea.

Pleeease Daddy, I'm hungry and I'm tired. Please Daddy, I don't want to."

She watched her daughter curl up defensively and cringed as he undid his belt and sat behind her, pawing, and clawing, *rutting*.

She knew then that she was also responsible for the atrocity. There had been signs but they were easily passed off as adolescence and in her denial her child had been left to suffer on her own.

She reached into her pocket and as she dialled the number knew she would never forget the look of hatred as Chrissy stared at the camera, it was as though she knew her mother was on the other side.

Harding ran to Mitchell's door and continued knocking until the door was opened. "Come on, she wants to see me, now!"

Fifteen minutes later they pulled up outside the house. It was huge, and the motor housings on the gates confirmed they were electric just as the keypad on the brick pillar told them they would be locked. Seventy yards on stood a large turreted mansion. Harding couldn't see too much detail in the darkness but he thought it looked very new and utterly tasteless

Mitchell pointed to the keypad and said, "Go press the intercom."

Harding had noticed a small wicket gate to one side and shook his head, "I'll try that first, and it's best if it's just me, I don't want to frighten her off by having two of us arrive."

It was unlocked and clearly hadn't been used for a while but as he walked towards the house he did wonder whether he'd been wise in going alone. Intruders were routinely shot by householders in this country. For that reason he tapped the front door timidly instead of using the doorbell. It was enough, and he gave an inward sigh of relief when he recognised April as she walked towards the door, without a single gun in sight.

She let him in and walked away without a word. Cautiously he followed her around a corner to the left into a wide passage. Half-way along she turned left again into a lit doorway and this time, on his own, in the dim secondary lighting, he felt like a trespasser and terribly exposed. He crept to the doorway and peered cautiously into a very expensively furnished study. She was standing to one side, next to some cabinets, looking at him and gestured towards the desk. "Help yourself."

He moved forward and as he walked around the desk noticed that the computer screen was on, showing a blank rectangle with an arrow enclosed in a circle inviting a viewer to click on it for 'start'. He did and while he watched the clink of glass on glass told him where April was heading.

When it finished he said, "May I take this please?"

She took a moment to think of a reply and said, "Bury the bastard."

He nodded and reached for the eject button, but thought about copies. Something told him he should get out of there soon and he certainly didn't want to waste time looking for spare disks. Quickly, he went into the internet explorer and googled his own mail server. He typed as quickly as he could and waited for the file to copy over. Finally, after pressing the 'send' button he went into 'tools' and deleted the record of past activity.

Just as he pressed the eject button he looked up and almost screamed as he saw the figure in the doorway staring at him impassively. He was quite young and dressed in light grey cord trousers and a white open-necked shirt.

April spoke, "Aiden, go back to your quarters." He didn't move and continued to stare at Harding until, as if venting a dreadful fury she drew in a breath and screamed "NOW!" He looked at her calmly and nodded his head before walking away, to make a telephone call.

Harding pocketed the disk but still felt like an intruder, so much so he decided to play safe and behave like one. He withdrew a handkerchief from his pocket and pressed the power switch on the computer. As soon as it had shut down he scrubbed the keys and mentally replayed his movements in the house. The only other thing he had touched was the handle on the inside of the front door when he had closed it. He walked out of the room, pausing beside April to murmur "Thank you" but responding then to an overwhelming urge to get out of there. He almost ran to the front door, polished the handle with his handkerchief and hurried down the drive.

* * *

"Let's get out of here!"

Mitchell nodded and remained silent, he'd seen that desperate relief before and knew Adam would need time to settle down.

Five minutes later Harding said, with feeling, "I couldn't be a villain. Too bloody stressful."

* * *

It took thirty minutes to fly from Washington DC to the smaller Horace Williams Airport and just fifteen minutes drive to the house. Two minutes later he looked at the damage caused to his desk and saw what had been taken. He strode back to the hall and removed a pair of leather gloves from a table drawer. Thus prepared he walked into the lounge. April was startled to see him so unexpectedly and stood up unsteadily. Without pausing he punched her, splitting her lip, snapping a tooth off and sending her cart wheeling over the side of her chair. He stepped around and grabbed her by the hair, pulling upwards as hard as he could. The agony prompted her to push herself up off the floor until they were facing each other again. This time he punched her twice in the stomach forcing the air out of her lungs. She collapsed to the floor and vomited. The need for air and conflicting passage of vomit caused her to choke violently as he watched her. He hadn't spoken a word so far and waited until her breathing returned to a semblance normal before he asked quietly, "Where is it?"

He allowed her a few moments and grabbed at her dress, snatching upwards with enough force to tear the material and throwing her into the chair. He spoke to one of the two goons but continued to stare at her, "Karl, go and get Chrissy." He leaned in to April and said, "You're going to watch this time and these two will have her as well."

"Nooooooo." He stepped back as she struggled to her feet, her face a stricken mess of tears, mascara, blood and snot. She was crying hysterically and the trembling told him she would go into shock before long but he saw the slip of paper appear out of her pocket and took it. This will be the man you had lunch with yesterday presumably. He held out the note, "Karl, find out whose number this is."

He stepped forward again and spoke quietly, "If you ever try to do something like this again I won't pay an employee to run up between your legs, I'll have him strap concrete there and then drop you into Jordan Lake." He turned to move away but still needed more. With every ounce of strength he pivoted back towards her and delivered a back handed blow to her face. She went down without a sound as Karl came back, "It's the Sandalwood Inn."

* * *

Harding had packed his few belongings ready for the morning flight they had managed to book and lay on the bed, thinking about strategy. What they had got wouldn't free Graham and wouldn't even convict Haddon because the disk might not be admissible evidence. Issues like 'chain of custody' and the manner it was obtained would compromise it, but he knew the authorities couldn't ignore it either. Chrissy would be given care and once that process was in hand he felt sure Mrs Haddon would be persuaded to testify. There were staff too. The goons were tough but in America deals were made with the District Attorney's office all the time and that would be where Graham's salvation lay. Last but not least, there was blogging. That would cause enough of a bush fire to wreck Haddon's political aims.

All in all, a good start.

He must have dosed off and wasn't sure what he'd heard but there it was again, a light tapping on the door. It had to be John. The detective must have thought of something and was cautiously checking to see if he was awake. He twisted the handle and realised he hadn't put the chain on as the door smashed into his face and threw him against the wall. Stunned, he tried to regain his balance as three men walked in. Two he recognised as heavies and Haddon was the man they'd seen on television. He began to speak but Haddon held up his hand, "You burglarised my house this evening and stole property of mine."

"I don't think Mrs Haddon would agree with that."

"Oh but I think she would. She's a different woman now, you wouldn't recognise her and of course my butler saw you rifling my desk." As he spoke one of the goons put the laptop he was holding down by the television and emptied Harding's holdall onto the bed, flicking through the pile of clothes before checking the jacket that had been hung on the back of a chair. He held a disk up and Haddon nodded, "Karl, boot up the computer."

Haddon took the disk and signalled the goon to join his colleague next to Harding before loading it in to the computer.

Harding said, "This is a little public to watch that sort of thing isn't it? Shall we turn the other way while you do whatever you need to do when you watch it."

Haddon showed no sign of having heard him but once he'd completed his check and removed the disk he held it up, "And the copies?"

Harding could think of nothing better to say, "Sod off, there's a good chap."

The roundhouse that buried itself in his midriff drove the air from his lungs. It had come from nowhere and without any warning. Gasping, he tried to straighten up as his assailant walked away and removed his jacket. He hung it in the back of the chair and casually made his way back.

Guns were appearing on the streets back home but they were still relatively rare and the Police response was immediate and extreme. Not here. The casual way the goon moved with the gun holstered under his arm was unnerving and for Harding, the black polished metal might just as easily have been a spitting cobra.

Haddon held the disk up again but said nothing. Harding held on to his stomach with one arm and pointed around the room with the other, "Do you see a computer?"

Haddon thought for a moment and then nodded, "Good. Then all that remains is for me to spell out a few truths for you. Your friend will be out of jail in just over two years, provided his friends on the outside behave. Alternatively, solitary is a bad experience and if, or rather *when* he starts breaking rules his punishment will become much worse for a lot longer. Remember, you are now responsible for his wellbeing." He turned and walked towards the door and addressing the goons on the way, "I'll see you in the car."

The blow to his head with a leather blackjack served to split his ear and sent his senses reeling. What followed was a professional and systematic beating.

Satisfied that things were back under control Haddon made one more call before his return to Washington, the thought of going back to his house and wife disgusted him.

At the house Aiden had finished tidying the study up and casually walked back to his quarters without a glance at the figure curled up on the lounge floor. That mess would wait until the morning.

She waited until his footsteps had faded before struggling into a sitting position. Her jaw hurt terribly and one eye was already closing, but what was so much worse was what lay ahead. She knew now that there would be no escape. He would do whatever he wished and there was nothing anyone could do. She began to cry as she realised the enormity of it all. His threat to kill her was genuine and a milestone from which there could be no going back.

In the small hours she managed to get to her feet and climb the stairs. She couldn't bear the thought of sleeping in the marital bed and staggered on to Chrissy's door. Using just her fingernails she tapped on the door and almost immediately heard a small voice, "What is it?"

April leant her head on the door and said, "It's me Chrissy, he's not here." The door opened and they stood looking at each other, both hurting, then Chrissy stepped forward and wrapped her arms around her mother. Time passed until the girl stepped back and took hold of her mother's hand, easing her into the room and locking the door once more. Silently they moved to the bed and climbed in. There Chrissy pulled the quilt up and they held each other until finally, sleep came.

* * *

The room was in darkness when he came to and his whole body throbbed, so much that he could only lie there and try to carry out an audit on his injuries. He knew from the specific ache and the stickiness his face lay in that his nose was broken and his searching tongue established the absence of some teeth. His torso just ached terribly but then he felt the cold wetness of his trousers and began shaking. They had paused, just once and one drew the gun, flicking the safety catch off as he pointed it at Harding's head. He emptied his bladder then and heard them laugh.

Somehow, after a long and agonising series of tiny steps he managed to get to his feet and shuffled to the telephone. With shaking hands he finally managed to key Mitchell's number and when it was answered muttered, "'Elp."

Thankfully, they had left the door off the latch and Mitchell was able to walk straight in, "Oh shit, what happened?"

"'Addon."

Mitchell did a quick visual check and said, "We need to get you to hospital and call the cops."

Adam reacted instantly, "No! No cops. Fer Gwaham's sake."

Details would have to come later but the meaning was clear. With his jacket draped over his shoulders Harding allowed his colleague to half carry him to the car and soon he was in the care of an emergency room. After another age, in which they carried out their own audit of his injuries he enjoyed the blessed relief of a painkilling injection.

The final list was not as bad as he had feared. A split ear, now stitched. A broken nose, now strapped and two blackening eyes. Two teeth, permanently lost and gum now stitched. Massive bruising to the torso but thankfully, no broken ribs. Bowel control perfect but leaving an open fissure in the memory that would never properly heal.

Armed with painkillers he made it on to the evening flight and three hours later allowed a distraught Harvey help him into bed.

Mitchell had dropped him off and since little had been said on the journey promised to call in the next morning for a debrief.

* * *

At six am Florida time Nancy had just returned home from her cleaning job. Having something to do for a few hours each day helped use some of the time up and to some extent took her mind off the nightmare they were living through. The doorbell rang and her heart skipped a beat when she saw the courier van. The envelope contained one item, the signed passport application form. There was no covering letter but with her pulse racing she reached for the telephone. She knew exactly what had to be done. Sarah was there within thirty minutes and an hour later, after Doctor Williams had endorsed Graham's photograph with his verification, she delivered the payment and documentation to the main post office in Leicester for the 'Fast Track' service that promised to provide a new passport within seven days. This one, at least, was a better day.

* * *

That same morning Patricia Geary opened her mailbox. She'd been in court for all of the previous day and anticipated a pile of electronic mail. She was startled to see a message from Harding and opened it first. It read,

Pat, please make three copies of the attached file and find safe places for them. On no account discuss or share. Will be in touch. AH

Intrigued, she glanced around to check that she would remain alone and opened the attachment. "Christ," she muttered, "What's he up to now."

When Mitchell arrived Harvey let him in, "Thank heavens you're here, Adam's frantic about something." As they entered the living room come diner Harding didn't wait for greetings, "John! We forgot about Cindy. She needs to be warned."

John's eyes widened as he made the connections, "Shit." He ran from the house and returned a few moments later with his case. In a trice he dialled her number.

"Hello Mrs Laver, this is John Mitchell . . . ,"

She didn't let him say another word, "I don't want to speak to you. Leave me alone, *please, I beg you*, I can't help you anymore." The line was cut.

He looked at Harding, "They've already got to her, she's terrified."

Harding sagged in his seat, "I hope to God they didn't hurt her."

The debrief was extended because of the need to bring Harvey up to date. Mitchell had contributed some of it up to Harding's visit to the house but after that Harding was the sole speaker. When he closed with a catalogue of injuries Harvey carried out a visual audit of his own. Both eyes were black, in stark contrast to the white dressing on his nose and there was bruising around the jaw. Apart from the dressing on his ear the remaining injuries lay out of sight. Adam was clearly still in pain but showed signs of recovery.

Harvey tried to be optimistic, "Look this isn't the end. We can still beat this thing, I'm certain."

Harding shook his head, "I think Haddon's influence will ensure that doesn't happen." He didn't mention the copies of the film he had sent to Geary because he was ashamed of what he had to say, "He made it clear that if we do anything else he will make sure that Graham suffers and that he'll have enough pinned on him to extend his sentence." He shook his head sadly, "That night, when they did their number on me I realised how far out of our depth we are. My warrant card is meaningless here and certainly doesn't afford any of us the protection it would back home." He looked at Harvey, "I'm sorry, truly, but I think it's time to go home."

Mitchell said, "In that case, unless anyone has any ideas, we have to hope that the defence can find some holes in the procedures. It still happens, often."

Harvey buried his head in his hands, "Christ, I feel responsible for this mess, if we hadn't brought them over here he'd be safe."

"You can't think like that Harv, it's just because of Graham's special sense."

Harvey looked up a spoke with dread, "That's exactly what I should have thought about."

They saw Zinc later that day but as hard as he tried, visiting rights would not be granted.

Two days later, with leaden hearts, they boarded their flight home.

Chapter 24

Their return to Leicester was painful for everyone and so low-key it felt furtive. Both men called on Nancy, though separately and with the awkwardness normally associated with visits to the bereaved.

She was having to be strong for Jimmy who was clearly concerned but often distracted by Susie's demands for play. His bed wetting was becoming more frequent though and occasionally he would voice concerns as they came to mind. One, that took Nancy to the very edge of control, was when he asked if Graham would be back for Christmas. For the most part though, she put up a brave front. At night, in the quiet loneliness of their kitchen she would let go and weep.

When the men called she found she had to be strong for them too. She sensed their underlying shame, and sought to reassure them. In the end her advice was the same for both. Don't give up hope.

Richard Zinc had contacted her with news that the court date had been set for January the twenty third.

On the fifteenth of December Sarah waited for Nancy to call and by lunchtime was frantic. At three o clock her mobile rang and she recognised the caller ID. "Nancy! Has it arrived."

"Yes, the courier people collected it a short while ago."

"So what now?"

Nancy sighed, "I have no idea." There was little else to say and the call soon over but as she replaced the receiver Nancy felt another pang of anxiety. The courier service had cost a hundred and twenty pounds each time and without Graham's wage their savings were disappearing quickly.

* * *

Three days later, in Daytona the envelope was opened and final instructions issued. Nancy had no idea what was happening in Florida and certainly didn't realise that the two hundred and forty pounds courier charges were nickels and dimes compared to the sums changing hands over there.

* * *

On the morning of the twenty first three regular members of *The Community Work Programme* went down with stomach disorders which were thought to be food poisoning. For the sake of authenticity, they had been required to take an emetic which proved to be so powerful that two of them failed to make it to the toilets in time. They were quickly quarantined in case it was contagious and for all that they had received a sum of money that no one would have refused. In fact a lot more money had changed hands to ensure that they would be replaced by three specific individuals.

Graham was startled to find himself trying to keep up with two huge Angels as they made their way to the hall exit. More passageways, doors, shouts, and bangs but eventually they found themselves in an assembly area. He tried to ask what was going on but received a terse, "Wait" in response. Others joined them and before long a line of twelve orange suited prisoners waited.

The governor was a stickler for rules and one required that all members of the work party should be read General Statute 198-44. Thus, they all stood in line as a guard read from a laminated card for the benefit of the three new men.

* * *

"All able-bodied prison inmates will be required to perform all work assignments they are given under the Community Works Programme. The failure of any inmate to perform such work to the best of their ability may result in disciplinary action. These work assignments are for the public good and will help to mitigate the costs of incarceration while enabling inmates to acquire skills and work habits that will help them to secure honest employment when they are released." He looked at Graham and his two companions, "Any questions?" They all shook their heads and a roller shutter door behind him began to rise.

Warm air wafted in and as they were marched out towards a truck Graham realised how different the air was. He could smell grass, diesel oil, the warmed tarmac and so many more, all of them better by far than the stink of humanity he'd become used to. It was intoxicating.

A man in a beige cotton shirt and dark blue trousers held a clipboard and counted them on. He wore a reflective tabard over his shirt that bore the same logo on the front and back; *Dept of Transportation.*

The State deemed 'Minimum Custody Inmates' such as these to be tame enough to do without armed guards. Instead they trained staff from the Department of Transport to do it for them. Most of the DOT staff hated this part of the job and avoided the training that resulted in being a *Designated Correctional Agent*. Those unfortunate enough to be so designated were expected to take their turn in supervising a road crew like this.

Tom Fitch was the exception. Not overly bright and certainly lacking any imagination he was avoided by his peers wherever possible and more often than not sat alone in the canteen at lunch times. Everything about him seemed slightly under par and that manifested itself in many ways. He had a low work ethic, no ambition and took boring discourse to new depths. His single saving grace was that he would always stand in for people who could think of a plausible enough excuse to duck the duty. He was a perfect candidate for the job. Perfectly happy to sit watching twelve men work all day or button-hole some of them for an hour or so. Prisoners tolerated the boredom of his monologues in exchange for a long rest in the sunshine.

Once on board the truck they were required to sit on the benches that ran along each side. Crude lap straps that the prisoners called hip-poppers served as safety belts. Tom climbed on last and strapped himself in before signalling the driver to head out.

Graham would never forget that twenty minute journey, his head raised, and senses heightened, a little like a dog with his head out of a car window. He isolated and relished each experience. The movement of air in the trees, shrill birdsong, smells, even the calming sight of cattle grazing. His eyes filled and an observer would assume it was the result of facing the passage of air but in truth, it was emotion. He swore he would never, ever, take those things for granted again.

Twenty minutes later they pulled off on to the side of the road, eight miles north of Labelle on the 27. The men were allocated reflective tabards and a long handled shovel each before they spread out down the road behind the truck. Fitch paced out a ten yard stretch for each man so that they were spaced out over a distance of a hundred and twenty yards. They then set about the vegetation that had encroached onto the highway, re-establishing the edge that was defined by the metalled surface. Once each man had cleared his ten yard stretch they would move on to repeat the exercise. Sound working practices required a guard to patrol that line but Tom knew better, after all he did this more than anyone else in the department and he just knew that from his vantage point on the back of the truck, next to the cool box, he could see them all so much better. Hell, if he was down there marching up and down he'd have his back to them half the time. Of course, had he rousted the driver out of the cab to fulfil his role as support guard they could have done the job properly.

By ten o clock they had finished the first stretch and were moving on when an Angel closed to where he could whisper, "Graham, you hear me?"

"Yeh."

"Just keep lookin' forward dammit! In a short while things are going to happen. You are not to think. I'm gonna say that again. You are not to think. Just do exactly what you're told an' we'll have you out of here." There was a pause before the man said something that chilled Graham to the core, "Word is that bad things are gonna happen to you if you stay inside." But it helped him to prepare for what was about to happen.

* * *

Five, six, even ten bikes fail to stir much interest, especially when they are observing the speed limit and that is why no-one else knew that over fifty Hell's Angels approached the road crew at eleven o clock that morning.

There are four routes into Labelle, at staggered intervals rather than at a central crossroads, with the last Junction away from the built up areas so that the hoard didn't become significant until after they had crossed the Caloosahatchee river just north of the town. A little further on they were joined by a fifth contingent from route 78 westbound.

When Tom Fitch saw them approach the whole road was filled with a single mass of machinery. As they drew closer he was fascinated more than anxious and slipped off the back of the truck to watch them go by, though he knew that he'd be relieved when they had done.

They didn't though. At one point it looked as though they weren't paying the prisoners any attention then suddenly, the lead bike was thrown into a ninety degree turn and somehow, stopped just a foot away from Fitch who began fumbling for his telephone. The driver looked in his mirror and threw himself onto the floor of his cab.

The noise and smell of exhaust fumes were overwhelming though Tom just about heard the leader call out, "You have any or our brethren we need to pay our respects to?" He was terrified and struggled for an appropriate reply. He certainly didn't notice the bundle that fell from a bike next to the three most distant prisoners.

"Nnooo I don't believe so." He was desperately trying to open his telephone without being seen but had got it the wrong way round. The spokesman held his gaze as he revolved it but the girl riding pillion spoke into the man's ear. Suddenly the engine revved and the bike lurched forward until it touched Tom's leg. The man pointed at the telephone, "We're here in an act of peaceful kinship. If you want to change that status, say into aggression, we can oblige,—with enough force to wreck your outing and career long before any law enforcement officer arrives. You hear me?" Tom gave a mute nod. The man continued, "Now I believe that you would prefer to take this opportunity to say 'Hi, have a nice day and farewell fellas. Am I right?" Tom nodded again as the leader glanced behind, a number of Angels had propped their bikes on stands and were urinating at the roadside. He turned back and said, "Then that is exactly what we'll do as soon as they've relieved themselves." Tom began to take whole breaths again as he looked down and waited for the comfort stop to end.

Graham had been as impressed as anyone by the spectacle but as soon as the leader began speaking to Fitch a bundle of denim rolled towards him and a voice said, "Get down!" As he dropped down on the ground hands from both sides wrenched his clothes off and shouted at him to help them push him into a denim jacket and shorts. One pair of hands pushed a pair of boots onto his feet and the other pushed a red skull cap onto his head. It had taken less than a minute and as they pulled him to his feet, one put a pair or wrap-around shades on his face before pushing him towards the nearest bike. The rider was staring ahead but he was pointing a gloved finger at the footrest Graham should use. He climbed on and sat perfectly still, unable to find a cogent thought as other bikers began to climb back onto their machines. Suddenly the leader looked back and scanned the hoard before giving Fitch a wave. Engines were gunned in a mind-numbing cacophony of sound as the lead bike turned back in the direction they had come from, through the corridor that had appeared in the mass and which gradually filled as bikes poured into it.

If Fitch had known anything about Hell's Angel lore he would have been surprised by the number riding 'Bitch Style', with an Angel riding pillion and otherwise known as 'Packing Double'. Normally, a rare occurrence. But then he also didn't notice that one more pillion rider left than arrived. He was too concerned with dialling his duty manager. It took four attempts, his hands were shaking so badly.

When his call was answered, he began with a shaky laugh, "Hey, Frank, you will *never* guess what just happened here. It took Tom almost twenty minutes to tell his tale, without realising that the receiver at the other end had been placed gently on the desk while Frank got on with next weeks' work schedules. When it was over the driver stood at his side to share his recollections and the road gang also gathered around to add their comments, so that it was forty minutes before Fitch finally took a proper look at the road gang.

By then Graham was airborne.

* * *

They had ridden back to the junction with route 78 where a rusting red pick-up truck waited, as though letting them pass by before joining the road they were on. They all slowed as Graham was taken to the front of the truck and told to swap over. Independent thought had long gone and Graham did as he was told, just as he did when the driver handed him a bundle of clothes and told him to change. Apart from being given a red baseball cap and being told to keep it on at all times no other word was spoken. The driver was old, in his sixties certainly, with the weathered look of a farmer and from the way they kept so far within the speed limits, Graham thought he drove like one too. He'd have been startled to learn that his driver was Vic 'Venom' Cantor who at sixty two was Florida's oldest Angel and as his name implied, was as mean as a rattlesnake.

Ahead the bikers had disappeared, having reverted to type and stormed through the Labelle without regard for speed limits, stop signs or red lights and particularly law enforcement officers. What they did want though, was to be noticed. In town they turned right on to route 80 and twenty five minutes later were heading north on the I 75.

Graham's was dressed in jeans and a check shirt by the time they reached town and his driver turned left, still on the 80 but in the opposite direction. Thirty three minutes later they pulled up alongside a hangar at the Airglades Airport and the driver told him to get out and go around the corner.

There a red and white Cessna waited, pointing in the opposite direction with the door open. As soon as the pilot saw him the engine roared into life and he was beckoned forward urgently. Graham clambered inside and strapped in as directed. He then watched, fascinated as the pilot pushed a rod in towards the dashboard and the engine noise filled the cockpit. The pilot looked to be in his fifties with long grey hair tied back into a ponytail and a great walrus moustache. He spoke into the microphone that was attached to a set of headphones and as they turned onto the runway gave a small nod when given clearance to take off, as though he could see who he was speaking to. The engine noise became deafening as he pushed the throttle all the way forward and they began to pick up speed. In no time, the ground fell away and soon they began a gentle turn to the north.

Once they reached the cruising height and speed, tabs were set and the aircraft settled into straight and level flight. The pilot reached behind Graham and unhooked a set of headphones, directing him to put them on. Immediately the engine noise became muted and the pilot spoke to him, "Hey man, welcome to Happy Valley Airways, mind if we have some music?"

Graham shook his head and said, "No, that'sh fine."

His headphones filled with a medley of seventies and eighties music while Graham peered out and watched Florida pass by. Apart from the occasional interruption of short dialogues with air traffic controllers, nothing more was said.

* * *

"Oh sweet Jesus, who's missing?" No one said anything until one of the Angels scratched his head as if mystified. "Hell, Graham ain't here." He pointed into the trees, "I saw him trotting into there when them bikers were here. I thought he was just going for a shit."

His hands were shaking just as much as when he tried to make the earlier call, but this time he managed it in just two attempts. Ten minutes later the first patrol car arrived and once the facts were established procedures slipped into place. It was all fairly relaxed. They were in the middle of nowhere, so the runaway Brit wasn't going to get far. As road blocks were being set up around a ten mile radius a call went out for the dog teams. Thirty minutes later they arrived and within five more minutes they found a prison uniform buried under the debris the road gang had shovelled off the road.

Fitch pointed at the Angel and raged "You said you saw him running into the trees."

The Angel shrugged his shoulders, "I was sure it was him; certainly looked like a man." He looked thoughtful before adding, "Could've been a monkjack I suppose."

"So you didn't see him just change out of tho ... " His mouth formed a wide hole of horror as the true dawned, "Oh Shit, it was them Hell's Angels."

At that moment the Hell's Angels were abeam Tampa still heading north on the I75 and Graham was crossing the state line into Georgia at an altitude of two thousand feet.

Things had become a lot less relaxed at Graham's point of departure. Soon major assets were mobilised and a call went out for the pack of bikers. Within minutes three Highway Patrols had called in with sightings that indicated a sustained journey north. Calculations were made and a helicopter was directed to the Tampa area to locate them. Unfortunately, the calculations failed to take into account the Hell's Angels disregard for speed limits and it took another Highway Patrol report and the re-positioning of the helicopter before they were found forty miles further north, passing Bayhead Landings.

Then it became a question of logistics, taking another hour to assemble the minimum number of officers deemed necessary to deal this many Hell's Angels, who by then had almost reached Gainesville. Throughout the journey gang members had peeled off at junctions to refuel before gradually catching up with the main pack, but afterwards it would serve to waste more time and reserves to stop those who were behind when the roadblock was finally established. Over two hundred law enforcement officers were involved, with enough firepower to start a war.

All southbound traffic had been stopped and as soon as the pack passed the junction with route 121, just south west of Gainesville they stopped all northbound traffic there as well. Shortly after, at the junction with route 24 a sea of blue flashing lights marked the roadblock and the gang drew to a gentle stop. The officers remained nervous but couldn't help but wonder at the ease of it, particularly in the silence that followed the switching off of their engines. Teams of officers combed the mass of bikes and everyone feigned surprise as they learned the reason for the block. The officer in charge called in with the negative result and asked if they should pull them all in for questioning but whoever was in charge had the wisdom to know how futile that would be.

The leader's reaction was enough to plant a seed of doubt when he asked who the escapee was. Someone finally told him and he gave out a roar of outrage, "Are you tellin' me that you think we sprung a fuckin' rabbit? Be fuckin' real man!"

Any possible connection a British white civilian could have with the Hell's Angels was an issue the authorities would question in the days that followed.

A little earlier, at one thirty, the Cessna landed on runway two three at County Cook Airport, Lenox, in Georgia. They taxied up to a light beige hangar and as soon as the engine was shut down a slim blond woman with pronounced red lips and chunky looking spectacles came and stood at Graham's door. The pilot removed Graham's head set and popped his seat belt, indicating with a smile and hand gesture that he should get out. Graham opened his door and slid out onto the ground but before he moved away turned and smiled at the pilot, "Thank you. Loved the music." He pointed to each other, "We're from the shame era."

The pilot grinned, "Glad to hear that dude. Happy travels."

Graham waved and turned to the woman who said, "Come on," as she walked towards a gate in the chain-link fence. Moments later he was strapping himself into the front passenger seat of a grey Ford Taurus. She had just one instruction, "You're to keep that hat on, at all times."

The pilot strolled into the hangars where two technicians were working on a Piper. They had seen him fly out for a fishing trip two days earlier with that guy, who they noticed was still dressed in the clothes he went out in. As the pilot drew near one of them asked, "So where are the fish man? I've already bought the charcoal."

"The pilot grinned, "Sorry, too big, I wouldn't 've got off the ground with it. Gave it to some nuns instead."

The original travelling companion had most certainly changed his clothes and flown back into nearby Albany the previous day on a commercial flight.

* * *

It was late in the afternoon and growing dark, his backside was aching dreadfully. Mile after mile they had trekked through Georgia into South Carolina, stopping once for fuel when he was told to stay where he was. Any changes in the scenery were lost to the drudgery of the highway. She saw him shiver once and said, "There's a jacket on the back seat. In a short while you can get in the back and sleep some."

The short while turned out to be another two hours and he was desperate to use the restroom. He was barely able to walk when he first got out of the car and attempted a few clumsy calisthenics to try and encourage the desired blood flow. He had asked twice how long the journey would be and received the same answer both times, "Be a while." Her unwillingness to divulge anything irritated him, though he was grateful for the hotdog she brought back. They left immediately and she ate hers whilst driving.

He'd climbed into the back seat at the filling station and settled down across the back seat even though he wasn't tired. He reasoned that if he stopped looking outside and simply closed his eyes to day-dream a chunk of the journey would pass by unnoticed. Minutes later he was watching Jimmy play with Susie, who kept taking the toe of his slipper in her mouth and shaking her head violently. He heard her small growls and then he heard Jimmy's laughter.

It was after one when he stirred. Not wishing to ask the same question for the third time he tried to think of another way asking. He tried, "Where are we?" and was delighted to receive a definitive reply, "Maryland."

He sat back in his seat and tried to picture his schoolboy maps of America. He shook his head, it was no use, he still had no idea where they were, until shortly after, when they passed into Pennsylvania. He spoke it out aloud and asked, "Isn't that where New York is?"

She nodded, "That's where we're headed."

He slumped with relief, it was like arriving in the right county back home.

It wasn't though, they still had another two hundred and fifty miles to go. Outside, there was frost on the ground and in places patches of snow. By the time they drove over the toll bridge into Brooklyn he was set to go stir crazy. Fifteen minutes later, at ten thirty am, they pulled up outside a low red brick building and she told him to follow her as she got out and walked towards the door. He almost fell out of the car before struggling after her like a drunkard.

Inside he recognised some of the insignias immediately. He was in a Hell's Angel clubhouse. The lobby was empty but he followed the sound of voices and opened another door into a large clubroom. His driver was talking to a tall, shaven-headed man and they both glanced at him as he entered. She said something he didn't catch and walked out of another door on the opposite side of the room as the man approached, holding out his hand and saying, "Good morning Graham, welcome to New York. My name is Dan."

He had a slight rasp to his voice and though Graham wouldn't have known it, had a broad New York accent. He had a goatee beard with a moustache and wore a heavy sweater under a leather waistcoat that bore the usual insignia and the name of this club, though in his fatigue he forgot it almost immediately.

They shook hands and Dan pointed at a canteen style counter with a kitchen beyond, accessed via the door on one side, "Coffee's in there, help yourself."

Graham looked around, and asked, "Where is, "and realised he didn't even know her name, "The lady, that drove me here?"

"She's gone." He chuckled, "Reckons she's eaten so many *Pro Plus* tablets it'll be the New Year before she gets to sleep."

Graham soon made a coffee and joined Dan at a table where he had been reading a newspaper over his own coffee. Nothing was said for a few minutes until an article had been finished and then Dan folded the paper and looked at Graham. "Take your hat off." He looked at the cleft and said, "Hmm, I see what they meant. We've been a shade tense over the last twenty four hours." He pointed at Graham's forehead, "With that and your Brit accent phoney ID would have been a waste of time. Still we've got it pretty well covered from here on in." With a gesture at the coffee, "When you've finished that, there are a few rooms with cots in them, feel free to use one. You'll be leaving here tonight but in the meantime stay inside and do not go near any uncovered windows, savvy?"

Graham nodded and asked, "Where will I be going?"

"Best you don't know 'til you get there."

* * *

That morning John Mitchell telephoned Leicestershire Constabulary and asked for Detective Sergeant Harding.

The same detective who had returned from America looking as though a truck had hit him and who had savaged Patricia Geary when she sought to discuss the film he had sent her. For the last ten days he had been morose and downright rude at times. As for Christmas, it was a relief all round when he failed to show at the Christmas party.

"Harding."

"Hey Adam, have you heard the news?"

"What news?"

"About Graham's escape?"

Harding stood up abruptly, "Tell me!"

"It happened yesterday morning and for reasons that haven't yet been made clear the Police went off on a wild goose chase after a bunch of Hell's Angels. Finally stopped them at Gainesville and drew a blank. Right now they're the laughing stock and a spokesman has admitted they haven't a clue where he might be. It's over twenty four hours now, he could be anywhere, though they reckon he's still in the State."

Harding knew the authorities had been right to go after the Angels *and* that somehow they had been hoodwinked. He whispered "Bob."

"Hello? Adam, are you there?"

Harding shook himself and began to shout excitably into the telephone, "John, I'm going to send you an email. Once you've watched the attachment call me back please."

He put the telephoned down and paused for just a moment before raising his arm and yelling, "Yes, you bastard, it's our turn now!" He looked across the office at Patricia Geary! "Pat, get over here we've got work to do."

Ten minutes later, after the email had gone, Harding began to tell her the story of his American visit and had virtually finished by the time the call came back.

"Sweet Jesus Adam, it's sickening."

"So, it's your legal system, what do we do now?"

"Yeah well, I've had time to think about Haddon since you left. I think his influence here and in North Carolina is too strong, we've seen that. I know someone in Washington, got a transfer up there from my old squad in Miami. Haddon's a relatively new kid in that town and also they're used to dealing with politicians. I'd like to let him have it."

"Sounds good, I'll give you my home number, if there is any news please let me know."

"No problem, I hope we can give a young girl some hope this Christmas."

"Ha! As you lot say over there, amen to that. Thanks John."

He was grinning when he put the receiver down and finished off telling his tale to Pat Geary. At the end she said, "OK sir, now what about this chap Parsons, just how has he been fitting in these last months?"

He grimaced and asked meekly, "Can that wait for the moment please?"

"Sure, no problem." She went back to her desk with a lighter step. At least she had been able to confirm one thing. Graham Parsons did have something to do with it all.

Having someone else mention Graham prompted him to think of Nancy. He reached for his telephone and dialled her number, but just as the ringing tone came through a sense of caution made him cut the connection. Graham might have escaped from jail but he was now being hunted by one of the most sophisticated law enforcement systems in the world, who would be desperately keen to make sure he didn't get out of the country. He dare not build Nancy's hopes up before making certain the escape was complete, yet she was entitled to know and would expect him to pass the news on. Suddenly, his new-found optimism was marred by an unwelcome responsibility.

He sat back in his chair and considered the options and finally decided on a compromise. It would be safer to tell Nancy after another forty eight hours. If Graham remained free after then there was a much greater chance of success. He realised the irony of his anxiety for Graham and a profound hope that he should get out of the US, given his own vocation as a policeman.

Four hours later Mitchell called back on Harding's home line and didn't prevaricate, "It's not enough Adam."

"What do you mean?"

"Well we already talked about the chain of custody thing and how that disk wouldn't make it to court."

"Yees." Harding's pulse began to slow.

"Well my pal reckons that with the sort of lawyer this man can afford, pulling him in won't achieve anything. Same goes for his goons."

"What about the wife and daughter."

"It's our guess they will be too frightened, and remember what they did to you. Can you imagine what he might have done to his wife?"

"So what are you saying?"

"My friend in Washington recommends that we keep this film under wraps until we can use it strategically. In the meantime he's going to start digging."

"And in the meantime that kid is going to carry on being raped."

"We'll do the best we can Adam, but we need admissible evidence. I'm sorry."

Harding put the telephone down and walked towards his kitchen. Images came back at him like physical blows; Chrissy's look of hatred, Haddon's arrogance in the motel room, the gun in the shoulder holster and the blows. He didn't lose control normally it wasn't his way but he threw a kick at the pedal bin in absolute rage. The stinking, days old leftovers spread across his kitchen floor and he cried out, "Oh shit." That was another job he'd forgotten to do. That bin should have been emptied days ago.

Fifteen minutes later he struggled to get a new bin liner into the empty bin. He hated the job. The plastic sacks had to be opened and the sides separated or the air locked into the bin on the outside of the sack wouldn't allow it to open and accept rubbish. He thrust his arm into that bag and shook it from side to side without thinking about anything in particular and then it hit him. Dropping the bin he ran to the telephone and dialled Mitchell's mobile.

"John, the bag of cocaine they found on Graham, did they check it for prints?"

"I doubt it, and by now any number of people could have handled it."

"Yes I know that, but just close your eyes for a moment and imagine you're trying to put some powder into a small plastic envelope. What would you do first?"

"Open the bag."

"OK so how would you do that."

"Squeeze it at the sides."

"But this is plastic bag it will just fold on you."

"Then I'd stick my—finger—inside." There was a pause, "We need to get that bag over to Washington. Leave it with me, I'll get back to you."

Graham had spent the day finding things to occupy his mind; a crossword in Dan's newspaper, a couple of Sudoku puzzles in a magazine, but once again a nap in the afternoon helped time pass by unnoticed. Another minder, who didn't bother to introduce himself or for that matter say anything took over from Dan. He did bring a pack of sandwiches though, that Graham devoured hungrily.

At seven o clock Dan came back with a slim, pale woman with cropped brown hair and wearing a thick black hooded coat. She set the carrier bags she had been carrying down on a table and exchanged a few words with the afternoon minder before he picked up his jacket and left.

They had brought more sandwiches, enough to share this time and as they ate Dan explained what they were going to do. "See, we have to do something about that parking slot in your head. Now we've figured that if you'd been the front seat passenger in a car accident that side of your face could have been messed up some and need dressings, so Linda here is going to fix you up. She's a trained nurse so it should look right."

They finished eating and Linda emptied one of the carrier bags on to the table before setting the contents out neatly. There was a range of dressings and bandages some scissors, clips and a small dark bottle of iodine which she used first, with a pad of cotton wool to provide a credible border to the dressing. After that Graham enjoyed the comfort he always had when a professional applied a dressing. It was so often a soothing experience, particularly when there was no painful injury involved. A little like having the fine neck hairs trimmed beneath the collar line after a haircut.

Once finished she called Dan over, "OK, he's all yours."

Dan walked over and had Graham stand so that he could inspect her work. Eventually he nodded and began to gather the front of Graham's shirt in his right hand. He smiled kindly, "Now Graham I want you to do somethin' for me you unnerstand?" Graham nodded uncertainly as Dan continued, "I want you to stand very still for me OK? Graham nodded again and from the look on Dan's face realised he was already in breach of the agreement. Dan did another quick inspection and murmured, "A couple should do it."

The two left jabs hit like missiles.

The first blow from the massive fist struck Graham on the upper cheek and the natural reaction would have been to duck down to avoid any more. Graham was more concerned about the 'why' and did what came naturally to him, by looking up at Dan's face. The next blow was already inbound and the result unavoidable. He felt and heard a tooth snap then almost immediately felt the warm wetness pour down from his upper lip but even in shock he heard Dan howl, "You dumb fuck! Why d'yer look up!

Linda wrenched Graham round and said, "Dan, look what you've gone and done. Fucking hell!"

Dan was shaking his bleeding fist, "Look what he did to my fucking hand, dammit! I told him to hold still!"

Linda was getting a small black case out of her jacket pocket, "Shit, it's a good job I came prepared, I was expected this, though I thought it would have been his eyebrow."

Graham was in such pain he was rocking to and fro, moaning as she sat him down and cleaned the wound. When she sought to begin stitching the split lip she shouted, "This time do as you're told Graham and fucking freeze!" By the time she had finished and sprayed some sort of clear sealant over the wound his eye was beginning to close.

She tidied her things up and before leaving gave him a hug, "Real sorry about that hon', take one of these every four hours." He looked down at the small bottle she had put in his hand and nodded then watched her grab her coat and walk towards the door. Even in the midst of shock and pain he noticed she had a very mobile bottom and thought of Lucy.

Dan re-appeared, with a cloth wrapped around his hand and sat opposite. He looked a little remorseful but explained, "We knew that just the dressing would look too phoney, or at least enough for one of the border guards to maybe run a check on things, the hospital an' such, so if there was something he could see for himself we figured he'd buy it."

Graham nodded and said, "Phank you," but it sounded far more like "Fuck you," which Dan accepted as entirely understandable.

Just before nine o clock a slim dark haired man in a suit walked in and whilst little was said a thick woollen jacket was removed from the other carrier bag and thrust onto Graham. Dan took him to the front door and nodded, "Good luck man." They shook hands and Graham stepped outside.

The man in the suit had opened the passenger door of a dark blue saloon and was hurrying around to the drivers' side. Once inside, Graham slammed his door shut and looked across to wave farewell but Dan had already disappeared. Without a word, the driver moved off and Graham noticed that outside it was snowing, heavily.

The driver introduced himself as Ian Weston, a native of Toronto, Canada and an hour out of New York he passed a dark booklet over. After flicking on the reading light he said, "You are Gerald Stanton and we are related by marriage, i.e. you are my brother-in-law. You've been involved in a traffic accident in Boston and I've had to come down to take you back to Toronto. I'm doing it overnight because I can't afford to take more than half a day off work."

Graham looked at the booklet cover. It was dark blue and embossed with gold lettering. At the top the word 'Canada' headed what looked like a coat of arms. Beneath were the words, 'Passport' and 'Passeport'. Inside he found a photograph of someone with a distinct likeness to him and began to memorise the particulars; name, address and next of kin. At least it helped to pass a little more time.

After three hours they stopped for fuel and the driver came back with two coffees and some snacks. The whole side of Grahams face had settled down to a throbbing ache and as soon as the fluid was cool enough he slurped another painkiller down." The snow had eased slightly and whilst the road remained passable there were banks of swept snow at the roadside.

Graham had tried to sleep but the pain and his aching backside wouldn't permit it. After a further two hours, they slowed for an exit to somewhere named Batavia and as they drew onto the forecourt of the petrol station Graham asked if he could lie down on the back seat for a while. He received a curt "No."

Refuelled, they set off again though this time without refreshments. Finally, once they were back on the I 90 Ian explained, "The border is less than an hour away, you need to be alert."

Graham's heart spiked. Somehow he had managed to avoid thinking about border controls while he was cocooned in the care of his guides and minders. Now as he saw the road signs his anxiety rose as the miles fell.

Finally they pulled on to the huge 'Peace Bridge Plaza' that spread out into a large fan of traffic lanes. Ahead lay a row of booths though at that time of night most were closed and they joined a queue of ten or so cars. Graham sat taking short breaths, his pulse increasing very time they moved forward. He so wished they would speed up yet he didn't want to get there.

In spite of the wait the lurch towards the booth seemed to happen suddenly and it was a shock to find himself under scrutiny by a stern-faced border guard who kept looking at the passport in his hand. "Sir, what happened to you?"

Graham knew then that it was over. He wasn't going home. His eyes watered as he sucked back the saliva that had leaked out of the injured side of his mouth. In the anxiety of the moment he pressed his lips together before speaking and winced in pain. Ian cut in, "He was in the passenger seat of a taxi in Boston, when someone a 'T' boned them. I've had to go get him back."

The officer looked back at Graham and considered the bruising and swollen watering eye, but the glistening beads of blood Graham had just caused to appear clinched it. He handed the passports back and said, "Have a safe trip sir."

They drove over the Peace Bridge into Canada in silence and half an hour later stopped at a petrol station at St Catherines. They each had a warmed pastry, which Graham managed to push inside the dressing and into the uninjured side of his mouth. He had never tasted anything finer. He was still sipping the tepid remains of a coffee an hour later as they approached the outskirts of Toronto. Ian had been far more amiable after the border and the time had passed quickly.

At six fifty five am they pulled on to the drive of Ian's single storey house. The street and drive were clear but snow lay everywhere. It was bitterly cold but inside the house was pleasantly warm. Ian showed him where the bathroom and toilet and pointed to the end of the hall, "Kitchen's down there. Join me when you're done."

Fifteen minutes later he stepped into a large kitchen diner that was filled with the fragrances of fresh coffee and toast and sat at the table where Ian pointed. After buttering his toast he tore a small piece off and eased his dressing to one side. Ian noticed and called out, "Wait," before walking over to a cabinet and removing an envelope. "You can take that thing off now, you're legit."

Graham gingerly removed the British Passport that lay inside and opened it to reveal his own picture and details. He flicked the back cover open and saw her name listed under 'Emergences'; Nancy Arnold, 38 Randall Avenue, Mapton, Leicester, England. His head dropped and he began to weep, quietly, but once he had started he couldn't stop. Ian got up quietly and headed for the bathroom, giving his charge some privacy.

When he returned half an hour later Graham had removed the dressing and now the patches of iodine looked a little incongruous. He had dealt with his emotions, at least for the time being, and was eating 'soldiers' of buttered toast when he thought to ask, "What now?"

Ian smiled, "Now you can grab some rest, my wife won't be back today so we have the house to ouselves and at eight forty tonight you should be taking off on a *British Airways* flight to London.

Graham nodded, "Then I'll start with a bath if I may pleashe."

"Sure, and two doors on you'll find a bedroom you can use, there's a fresh set of clothes on the bed."

Graham said, "Thank you, for everything," and left the room.

It was dark when Graham's aching jaw woke him and the bedside clock advised him that it was four o clock. He dressed carefully in the new clothes welcomed the thick sweater they had provided A small rucksack had also been left for him and inside he found some sweets and a detective novel by an author he hadn't heard of. He packed the stale clothing he had travelled in rather than leave them, they represented so much. In the kitchen Ian gave him a welcoming smile and asked, "Sleep well?"

"Yesh, thank you."

A plate of sandwiches and a bottle of beer were taken out of the fridge and set down on the table, "There you go, we'll head out in about an hours' time." And they did.

At six o clock Graham presented his ticket and passport to the check-in desk at Pearson International Airport and went on through security immediately while Ian watched. He had been ordered to wait until Graham was safely through there before his task was complete.

The next two hours passed as slowly as any he'd lived through since his arrest. As he sat in a quiet corner of the departure lounge the crashing impact of an arrest seemed imminent. Any encouragement he had felt by getting this far was tempered by the knowledge that he was arrested at this very point in another journey. He tried to sleep but it was impossible, even with Linda's painkillers. Security announcements and armed Police all unnerved him so much so that when the jet way desk became manned his anxiety actually heightened rather than waned. The trek down to the aircraft was made without a dog appearing and from then on his nerves eased with each step. The doors closing, the engines running up and the tiny nudge as they were pushed away from the stand. There was a queue of aircraft on the taxi way waiting to take off but finally, at five past nine they left the ground.

* * *

Nancy gradually came to as the telephone rings penetrated her sleep. Panicked, she leapt out of bed and ran for the stairs. No calls at this time of night were good news and her heart was pounding. She snatched the receiver off the hook and said, "Hello?"

"That Nancy?"

She recognised his voice immediately, "Yes, yes it is."

"Your man is safe ma'am. He'll arrive at London Heathrow tomorrow morning, on the British airways flight from Toronto. Tell him we're even."

Her breathing stopped and she fell sideways against the wall, trying to arrest the dry heaves that started in the pit of her stomach. With a supreme effort she gasped, "Thank you" but the line had already gone dead.

Chapter 25

It wasn't over but as the aircraft climbed away from Toronto Graham sat back in his seat, exhausted. There was just one more hurdle.

It came six and a half hours later when his ears told him that the aircraft was descending. They couldn't turn back now, he would be back in England soon.

He smiled and thanked the hostess as he disembarked and she replied "Merry Christmas." It might have been the way she had said it but something made him pull his ticket out of his jacket pocket and check. It was dated for the twenty third of December and with an overnight flight behind him it was now Christmas Eve.

On the trek through a maze of passageways to border control he thought how wonderful the low grey clouds looked in his English sky. Today they felt like a comforting blanket.

The immigration officer took his passport and scanned it before asking, "Been in the wars sir?"

Graham gave an emphatic nod. "A 'Ell's Angel phumped me."

After a short pause he added, "Twyshe."

Author's Note

I do hope you enjoyed this story; one of a trilogy.

Graham continues to be the key character throughout, though each book has a distinctly different storyline.

A Child's Eye View

Graham's Chronicles I

Graham Parsons is a *man ordinaire* whose well-ordered life is changed beyond measure when he witnesses the manslaughter of a 7 year old boy, Christopher. Whilst holding the dying child he experiences a profound out of body experience and minutes later suffers a life threatening attack, leaving him with permanent disabilities.

His recovery brings with it a telepathic connection with children who need help. An affinity which threatens his sanity, marriage and eventually his life.

This tale of discovery begins with a fearful and confused denial which takes him to the edge of reason until eventually, he accepts and employs his remarkable gift with a charming pragmatism that disarms doubters and helps to salvage blighted young lives. His simple, candid honesty wins the support of four friends from very different backgrounds; Christopher's mother, a GP, a Child Protection Officer and a Detective Sergeant.

This story chronicles the shocking, moving and yet sometimes heart-warming episodes in his new life.

Help Out House

Graham's Chronicles III

Graham Parsons is back in England, a fugitive from US law, but his freedom is still threatened by a vengeful US Senator and extradition.

His life goes on hold, in a stasis of anxiety while in America, Chrissy Haddon and her mother confront their own demons of abuse and alcoholism. Is it time for Senator Haddon to answer for his deeds and make amends?

The *'Gang'* rally to Graham's side once more, with support and practical help on both sides of the Atlantic that become quite extraordinary. But like Graham, with his telepathic connection with children needing help, they all know others would think their experiences were no more than fiction.

As things begin to fall apart help comes from an unexpected source and the US State Department are persuaded to join in.

Meanwhile, in Leicester, Lori is a frightened fifteen-year old, trapped in a world of drugs and prostitution. Yet in the darkness shines a tiny glimmer of defiance. Only she knows her real name is Marya, until she sees Graham's advertisements and 'puts her message in a bottle', triggering a dreadful reaction which causes Graham to suffer one of his worst nightmares.